Praise for

Nominated for the Edgar Award for Best First Novel

One of the Best Books of 2016 according to the *New York Times*, the *Washington Post*, the *New York Times Book Review* and Amazon.com

'[*IQ*] kicks off what is apt to be a madly lovable new detective series about this smart guy and the vibrantly drawn criminal culture that surrounds him . . . Ide packs a lot of action and scenery into the book's investigation scenes. But he has also built and bolstered Isaiah as a fine, durable character' *New York Times*

'One of the most original thrillers of the year . . . [A] sometimes scary, often whimsical, off-the-wall delight' *Washington Post*

'Wonderfully quirky . . . Exhilarating language and [an] oddball cast . . . A total laff-riot' *New York Times Book Review*

'A crackling page-turner of a debut' *Entertainment Weekly*

'Joe Ide introduces one of the coolest investigators working the mean streets of Los Angeles' *Chicago Tribune*

'With its street poetics and truer-than-life characters, this beautifully spun first novel is going to blow through the crime fiction world like a fire hose-blast of fresh air'

Gregg Hurwitz, author of *Orphan X*

'I don't know how fast Joe Ide writes, but from now on he'll have to write faster. Everyone who reads *IQ* will be clamoring for the next book, and for the one after that. This is one of the most intriguing – and appealing detective characters to come along in years'

Carl Hiaasen, author of *Scat* and *Chomp*

Joe Ide grew up in South Central Los Angeles. His favourite books were the Conan Doyle Sherlock Holmes stories. The idea that a person could face the world and vanquish his enemies with just his intelligence fascinated him. Joe went on to earn a graduate degree and had several careers before writing *IQ*, his debut novel, inspired by his early experiences and love of Sherlock. Joe lives in Santa Monica, California.

www.joeide.com

IQ

Joe Ide

WEIDENFELD & NICOLSON

First published in Great Britain in 2017
by Weidenfeld & Nicolson
an imprint of the Orion Publishing Group Ltd
Carmelite House, 50 Victoria Embankment
London EC4Y 0DZ

An Hachette UK Company

1 3 5 7 9 10 8 6 4 2

A CIP catalogue record for this book is
available from the British Library.

ISBN (Mass Market Paperback) 978 1 4746 0718 6
ISBN (eBook) 978 1 4746 0719 3

Printed in Great Britain Clays Ltd, St Ives plc

www.orionbooks.co.uk

For Mom, Dad, Bea, and Harry

Saving you is the only thing that will bring me peace for all the wrong I have done. That is my truth.

Jillian Peery, *TigerLily*

IQ

Prologue

B oyd parked his truck across the street from the school and waited for the bell to ring. It was ninety-plus degrees outside, the air in the cab as still and stifling as a closed tomb. Boyd's fishing cap was dark with sweat; streams of it trickling down his face, getting in his eyes, and making his sunburn sting. To get some relief, he flapped the collar of his T-shirt and got a cloud of armpit steam so foul it made him laugh.

Boyd had spent hours in the bathtub, half submerged in the gray, lukewarm water, seeing himself do it one way and then another. *Jesus Christ, that's so STUPID, think of something else, Boyd, come on, come ONNN, Jesus Christ, don't be so STUPID.*

When he broke a front tooth he almost called the whole thing off. It happened in the kitchen while he was trying to make chloroform. You couldn't buy the stuff unless you were a doctor or a laboratory but he'd found a recipe online: acetone and swimming pool chemicals. Putting it together was easy enough but he inhaled too much vapor and passed out, smashing his tooth on the sink as he slid to the floor.

Later, when he stopped being dizzy, he ate some Chunky Monkey to soothe his bloody gums and wondered what he'd do if the girl wasn't scared or laughed at him or thought it was a joke. He thought about going to the dentist but the need was a giant

3

tapeworm twisting in his gut, frustrated, hungry, and blind. He was halfway through his second pint of Chunky when he started to get angry. So what if he was missing a tooth? He was already weird-looking. His mouth was a wavy line on his big round face, his other teeth jagged and coffee-stained, his black button eyes set too far apart. The rest of him was shaped like an egg.

When he was eleven years old a wild girl named Yolanda called him Humpty Fucking Dumpty while she and her friends from the soccer team kicked him with their cleats until his legs were covered with green and purple bruises. Yolanda had warned him not to say *hellooo, Yolanda* but he did it anyway. It was sort of a trademark, something he did even though he knew it annoyed people. *Hellooo, Ernesto. Hellooo, Laquisha. Hellooo, Mr. Bleakerman.*

Boyd still annoyed people. On league night he'd stand at the line staring at the pins like he was trying to remember what they were while the whole team groaned and said *Boyd,* Nick telling him to hurry up, asshole. When he finally rolled the ball, he held on to it too long so it flew up in the air and bounced down the lane, dropping into the gutter or taking out the six pin. Then he'd yell *FUUUCK* and stomp back to his seat with his fists clenched at his side, muttering *Come on, Boyd, COME ONNN* like all he had to do was bear down, Nick saying What were you aiming at, numb nuts, the fucking sky? That always got a laugh.

The bell rang. Boyd played the bongos on the steering wheel and watched the kids pour out of the building, pulling on their backpacks, poking at their phones, messing with each other, screeching like monkeys. *Akeem! Over here, dude! Oh my God, that's like crazy! Text me, okay? Don't forget!* The energy coming off them was thrilling at first but then it made him angry and sad. None of the girls fit the bill. They were too old or too big or too grown-up looking.

Come on, come ONNN, there's got to be SOMEBODY. And then he saw her. Pretty and skinny, her hair in a long braid that went down below her waist, her laugh like the wind chime on his grandmother's front porch, the boys punching each other to get her attention.

Somebody called her. "Carmela! Carmela! We're going now, okay?"

Her name was Carmela.

Boyd went back to his shitty apartment and took a bath. He floated in the water like a corpse and imagined the panic in her eyes when she woke up in the dark and felt the duct tape stretched over her mouth and heard his hot breath whistling through the space where his tooth used to be and saw the black button eyes, vicious and glittering.

Hellooo, Carmela.

CHAPTER ONE

Unlicensed and Underground

July 2013

I saiah's crib looked like every other house on the block except the lawn was cut even, the paint was fresh, and the entrance was a little unusual. The security screen was made from the same heavy-duty mesh they used to cage in crackheads and bank robbers at the Long Beach police station. The front door was covered with a thin walnut veneer but underneath was a twenty-gauge steel core set in a cold steel frame with a pick-proof, bump-proof, drill-proof Medeco Double Cylinder High Security Maxum Deadbolt. You'd need some serious power tools to get past all that and even if you did there was no telling what you'd be into. Word was, the place was booby-trapped. A cherry eight-year-old Audi S4 was parked in the driveway. It was a small, plain car in dark gray with a big V8 and sports suspension. The neighborhood kids were always yelling at Isaiah to put some rims on that whip.

Isaiah was in the living room, reading emails off his MacBook and drinking his second espresso, when he heard the car alarm go off. He snatched the collapsible baton off the coffee table, went to the front door, and opened it. Deronda was leaning her world-class badonk against the hood, smothering a headlight and part of the grill. She wasn't quite a Big Girl but damn close in her boy shorts and pink tube top two sizes too small. She was pretending to sulk, sighing and sighing again while she frowned at the sparkly things on her ice-blue nails. Isaiah chirped off the alarm, one hand shading his eyes from the afternoon glare.

"No, I didn't forget your number," he said, "and I wasn't going to call you."

"Ever?" Deronda said.

"You're looking for a baby daddy and you know that's not me."

"You don't know what I'm looking for and even if you did it wouldn't be you." Except she *was* shopping around for somebody who could pay a few bills, and Isaiah would do just fine. Yeah, okay, he did make her uneasy, he made everybody uneasy, checking you out like he knew you were fronting and wanting to know why. He looked okay, not ugly, but you'd hardly notice him at a club or a party. Six feet tall, rail thin, no chain, no studs in his ears, a watch the color of an aluminum pan, and if he was inked up it was nowhere she could see. The last time she'd run into him he was wearing what he wore now: a light-blue, short-sleeve shirt, jeans, and Timberlands. She liked his eyes. They were almond shaped and had long lashes like a girl's. "You not gonna invite me in?" she said. "I walked all the way over here from my mama's house."

"Stop lying," he said. "Wherever you came from you didn't walk."

"How do you know?"

"Your mama lives on the other side of Magnolia. Are you telling me you walked seven miles in the heat of the day in flip-flops with all those bunions growing out of your feet? Teesha dropped you off."

"You think you know so much. Could have been anybody dropped me off."

"Your mama's at work, Nona's at work, Ira still has that cast on his leg, and DeShawn lost his license behind that DUI. I saw his car in the impound yard, the white Nissan with the front stoved in. There's nobody left in your world but Teesha."

"Just because Ira got a cast on his leg don't mean he can't drive."

Isaiah leaned against the doorway. "I thought you said you walked."

"I *did* walk," Deronda said, "just, you know, like part of the way and then somebody else came and I—" Deronda slid off the hood and stamped her foot. "Dang, Isaiah!" she said. "Why you always gotta fuck with people? I came over here to be sociable, aight? What's the damn difference how I got here?"

It made no difference at all but he couldn't help seeing what he saw. Things different or things not right or out of place or *in* place when they shouldn't be or not in sync with the words that came with them.

"Well?" Deronda said. "You gonna make me stand out here and get heatstroke or invite me in and pour me a cocktail? You never know, something good might happen."

Deronda looked down at her ankle, turning it to one side like something was stuck to it, probably wondering where Isaiah's eyes were. On her dark chocolate thigh gleaming in the California sunshine or her dark chocolate titties trying their best to escape over that tube top. Isaiah looked away, uncomfortable deciding for the both of them what would happen next. She wasn't his type, not that he had one. Most of his love life was curiosity sex. A girl intrigued by the low-key brother who was so smart people said he was scary. That hadn't happened in a while. He opened the screen.

"Well, come on then," he said.

Isaiah sat in his easy chair rereading his emails. He was hoping he'd missed something. He needed a payday case but nothing here was coming close.

Hola Senor Quintabe

I am a frend of Benito. He tell me you are trusted. A man from my work is saying blackmail to me. He say if I dont give him money he will tell INS I no have green card. My son cannot stay for his school. Can you do something to help me?

Dear Mr. Quintabe.

Late at night while I am asleep in my bed, a man comes in and fondles my private areas. I know this for a fact because in the morning my nightgown is all bunched up and I have a funny feeling down there. Please don't tell anyone as I have been ridiculed about my suspicions before. Can you come over Sunday after church?

Isaiah didn't have a website, a Facebook page, or a Twitter account but people found him anyway. His priority was local cases where the police could not or would not get involved. He had more work than he could handle but many of his clients paid for his services with a sweet potato pie or cleaning his yard or one brand-new radial tire if they paid him at all. A client that could pay his per diem gave him enough income to support himself and helped him pay Flaco's expenses.

"Dang," Deronda said, looking into the fridge at the FIJI Water and cranberry juice. "You ain' got nothing to drink?"

"Just what's there," Isaiah said from the living room.

There was nothing to snack on either. Deronda might have thrown something together if she knew a recipe for plain yogurt, some plums, a bag of trail mix with no M&M's, I Can't Believe It's Not Butter!, bread with birdseed stuck to the outside, and Cage Free Eggs, whatever the fuck those were. There was a complicated machine on the counter. Stainless steel, big as a big microwave with handles and buttons and a double spigot over a grill like a soda machine. A tiny coffee cup and a little metal pitcher were set on the grill. "Is this your coffee machine?" she said.

"Espresso."

"You need a bigger cup."

Isaiah kept reading the emails and tried not to think about Deronda, ripe and juicy as one of those plums. Reluctantly, he kept his Diesels zipped up. Not an easy decision. If he'd had sex with her he'd come home one night to find her three-year-old son tearing up the place while she watched *Idol* and ate the last few pieces of Alejandro fried to a crispy golden brown. When he told her to keep her clothes on she wasn't so much put out as she was surprised.

"You don't know what you missing," Deronda said, "I be doing some crazy shit."

Dear Mr. Quintabe.

My daughter dint come home for two weeks. I think she is gone with a man named Olen Waters who is to old for her. She need to be took away from him before its too late. Could you get her plese? I can pay not much.

Dear Mr. Quintabe

Two months ago my beautiful son Jerome was shot to death in his own bed. The police said they don't have enough evidence to make an arrest even though everybody knows his wife Claudia was the one that pulled the trigger. I want to hire you, Mr. Quintabe. I want you to bring that bitch to justice.

The living room was cool and dim, soft bands of sunlight and shadow coming through the burglar bars, the place so clean there weren't even dust motes in the air. Isaiah didn't look up as Deronda padded barefoot out of the open kitchen and across the polished cement floor. It had come out differently than he'd anticipated but he liked it. Amorphous shapes of gray and green like a satellite map of the rain forest. Deronda plunked down on the sofa across from him and put her feet on the coffee table. Strewn across the glass were car keys, a cell phone, a Harvard cap, and the collapsible baton.

Deronda spotted a black box under the table. "What's that thing?" she said, like she suspected a booby trap.

"Subwoofer and get your feet off of my coffee table."

"Who went to Harvard?"

"Nobody."

"Can I watch TV?"

"Do you *see* a TV?"

"You ain't got no PlayStation?"

"No, I don't have a PlayStation."

"You need some more furniture."

Aside from the burgundy leather sofa and armchair, there was the chrome and glass coffee table, a lacquered wicker ottoman, a cherry wood end table, and an antique-looking, long-necked reading lamp. That was it unless you counted the floor-to-ceiling bookcase that took up an entire wall. There was a huge collection of LPs and CDs lined up neat as bar codes and an elaborate stereo; Coltrane's sax braying from the speakers, angry and hoarse.

"Can I put another record on?" Deronda said, wincing like she was listening to the garbage disposal.

"No."

Isaiah kept his head down and read another email. Deronda was going to ask him something. He'd sensed it as soon as he let her in, looking at him like a baby daddy wasn't all she needed. Passing on the sex had taken away her opening and now he could hear her cheeks squeaking on the sofa as she squirmed around trying to pick a moment. Maybe if he ignored her long enough she'd give up.

"Can I ask you something?" she said.

"No."

"Could you maybe like, you know, hook me up?"

"Hook you up with who?"

"Blasé. You all tight with him and everything." She waited a moment before saying, *"IQ."*

An article had appeared in *The Scene* magazine titled:

IQ

Isaiah Quintabe is Unlicensed and Undaground.

The article recounted a number of neighborhood cases but the one that made the tabloids was the simplest to solve. It involved the R&B singer Blasé. During a party someone had stolen his camera, which contained a video of him bent over an ironing board getting pounded from behind by his live-in keyboard player. If the tape got out there'd be more than a scandal. Blasé promoted himself as a heterosexual sex symbol. The cover art on his last album, *Can I Witness to Your Thickness,* showed Blasé in a thong and priest's collar leading a choir composed of three women in crazy blond wigs and shorty choir robes, their backsides bulging like babies were in there. Blasé received a note that said: *My demands will soon follow. Obey them or your transgressions will be revealed and your career will be over.*

"The language," Isaiah said. "Your transgressions will be revealed. It's biblical. Were any of your guests religious?"

"Heavens no," Blasé said. He took a deep breath. "But my mother is."

Blasé's mother was a fundamentalist Baptist from a small town in Georgia. When Isaiah confronted her, she told him she was going to use Blasé's camera to take video of the rose garden and got the surprise of her life. After resting and drinking tea made from Valerian root she decided to blackmail her son into abandoning his life of sin and iniquity.

"I am who I am, Mother," Blasé said. "But if I can't accept myself, there's no reason you should."

Blasé was grateful to Isaiah for bringing him to that moment but Isaiah didn't know what he'd done besides read a note. Blasé came out on *The Shonda Simmons Show*. His record sales suffered but the people who bought them also bought the sex tape available online for $39.95, half the profits going to his mother's church.

"I need Blasé to help me with my career," Deronda said. "He might be gay but he's a celebrity and all I need is a leg up. I mean like, once I'm circulatin' in that uppa level and the shot callers can check out my style up close and personal? I'm off to the big time."

Isaiah could feel Deronda looking at him, waiting for him to say it's only a matter of time or don't give up or some other such nonsense, but he kept his eyes glued to the MacBook. Deronda sulked, this time not pretending. "I shoulda been gone from here a long time ago, much star quality as I got," she said. "I'm an up-and-comer, you know what I'm sayin'? I was *born* to be a celebrity. I should have the spotlight all over me."

"Spotlight all over you — for what?" Isaiah said.

"What do you mean for what? That Kardashian girl's booty could fit *inside* my booty and you talking about for what. You know she made thirty million last year?"

Isaiah knew other girls who felt that way. Somehow believing a big booty was like owning real estate or having a college degree, something you could put on a job application.

Alejandro came bobbing and pecking his way out of the hall making little buck-buck sounds and giving Deronda the beady red eye. Alarmed, Deronda lifted her feet off the floor. "You let that thing just walk around in here?" she said.

"You leave him alone he'll leave you alone," Isaiah said.

Isaiah got Alejandro and a recipe for arroz con pollo as payment from Mrs. Marquez. Isaiah didn't like cleaning up the chicken shit but the floor didn't hold a stain and he felt bad about leaving the bird in the garage all day. The other morning he forgot to close the bedroom door and Alejandro roosted on the closet bar and crapped all over his clothes.

"Come on, Isaiah, help me out," Deronda said. "All I need is a leg up."

"A leg up is not what I do."

"You wrong, Isaiah."

"I'm wrong every day," Isaiah said. He closed his laptop, grabbed the car keys and collapsible baton, put on the Harvard cap, and stood up.

"You taking me somewhere?" Deronda said.

"Uh-huh. I'm taking you home."

Boyd parked his truck in the same place as yesterday. He was really nervous but felt ready. Everything he needed was in the lizard-green bowling bag on the seat beside him. Duct tape, rubber gloves, and a boning knife sharp enough to cut see-through slices off a mushy tomato. Also in the bag, a big blue sponge and a water bottle filled with his homemade chloroform.

Boyd worked at F&S Marine, a distributor of Chinese-made

marine supplies. The cement-block building was in a bleak industrial zone next to a storage yard for propane tanks and a no-name warehouse with razor wire coiled on top of the fence. The LA River flowed past, the wide green watershed cutting through East Long Beach and emptying into Long Beach Harbor.

Nick Bangkowski, Boyd's manager at F&S, had spiky hair and wore Hawaiian shirts stretched tight across his expanding bulk. Five years ago, Nick was drafted in the second round by the San Diego Chargers. He had a great training camp and was in the running for starting linebacker but a week before the first preseason game he blew out an ACL getting off the team bus.

"I was there," Nick would say after his first six-pack. "I was right fucking there. I had my own locker. I had a jersey with my name on it. I was on the fucking team. *I was on the fucking team.*"

Nick gave Boyd all the shit work. Unplugging the filthy toilets, greasing the forklift chains, picking up the beer cans and used condoms in the parking lot, and inventorying the thousands of interlock switches, hex cap screws, piston pins, and crankshaft bearings. Boyd whined but never got mad, even when Nick kicked him off the bowling team. "I've got to cut you, Boyd," Nick said. "Ron's back from vacation and he averages what, one seventy-five? On a good night you barely break a hundred."

"What about Maxine?" Boyd said. "She bowls worse than me."

"Well, yeah, score-wise but she's got tits out to here. She's good for morale."

"But I want to bowl too."

Nick clapped Boyd on the shoulder, something he'd never done before. "I know you do but there's a tournament coming up and you don't want us to lose, do you? How about it, Boyd? Take one for the team? Everybody'll love you for it, what do you say?"

The night of the league tournament Nick stayed at the office and had a few Budweisers before heading to the bowling alley. He was in the parking lot getting into his Altima when Boyd tiptoed up behind him like a cartoon cat and hit him with a six-and-a-half-pound boat anchor wrapped in a burlap bag.

"How about it, Nick, take one for the team?" Boyd said, whomping on him again and again.

Everybody at F&S thought it was a mistaken identity thing or a pissed-off husband. Nick was known to screw around with the housewives at the bowling alley. Nobody suspected Boyd. He was weird and semiretarded but he wouldn't hurt anybody. Maxine went to visit Nick in the hospital. She said he looked like a bag of raw hamburger and didn't remember who she was. Boyd signed the get-well card.

The bell rang. Boyd nearly jumped out of his skin, stretching his neck looking for the girl. *Where are you, Carmela? Where ARE you? You better be here, you better be here. Come on, Carmela, BE HERE.*

Carmela was with a group of her friends. She was wearing a short denim skirt and a white top, her hair in the long braid. Boyd was relieved, afraid she might have changed it. She took her time, sending a text, laughing as she read a text, laughing as she showed it to her friends, and laughing as she sent another text.

"Hurry up hurry UP!" Boyd shouted. "What are you DOING? Go home already. Jesus Christ, GO HOME." Carmela finally broke away from the group, waved goodbye, and walked toward the street. "Okay," Boyd said, "this is it."

Isaiah lived in Hurston, a small neighborhood on the western edge of East Long Beach, two minutes from the LA River and two and a half from the 710 Freeway. He took Anaheim, driving through the area Snoop had rapped about in *The Chronic,* his rhymes the most notable thing about the area. Block after block of strip malls, liquor stores, auto body shops, beauty salons, discount dentists, and weedy empty lots.

"For real, Isaiah," Deronda said. "I need to change my social standing. I need to change my cultural environment. I need to change my address."

Deronda was eighteen when she was crowned Miss Big Meaty Burger at a BMB restaurant in Culver City. A TV reporter from Channel 5 was there and Deronda got seven seconds of screen time on the morning show. Her name and picture appeared in the *Long Beach Press-Telegram* and people came over to see the plastic tiara and the red-and-gold Big Meaty Burger sash.

She was interviewed on KHOP. The DJ asked her if she did anything special to keep her donk fresh and was she naturally thick or did she have to work at it and when was the last time she had some icing on that cake. The highlight of the whole experience was an actual photo shoot and getting her picture featured on the BMB advertisements. The ads showed a giant triple-decker burger dripping burger juice. Deronda was looking over her shoulder, her smile wide and inviting, her cheeks gleaming like polished mahogany and split down the middle by a DayGlo-pink bikini. The caption said:

THE BIG MEATY BURGER

LA's Juiciest

You Know You Want Some

At the time, Deronda thought this was it, her launching pad. Somebody must have noticed her and seen her charisma and potential but nobody called, there were no more interviews or newspaper articles, and after a few months BMB changed the girl on their advertisements. Deronda stayed hopeful. Something was bound to happen, how could it not? Celebrity was her dream, her destiny, and somehow that made it okay, even sensible to do just what she'd been doing. Getting her hair and nails done, partying with Nona and them, and watching *Jersey Shore* and the *Housewives of Atlanta* and *Bad Girls* and *Keeping Up with the Kardashians* and the *Housewives of Orange County* and *The Bachelorette*. She made ends meet stripping at the Kandy Kane wearing nothing but the sash and tiara. Deronda's father, a supervisor at Metro Transit for twenty years, urged her to find a new direction and stop frittering her life away but Deronda only got more stubborn and determined to wait for that white-hot bolt of lightning to come ripping out of the sky and blow her up large.

"Don't you want to get out of the hood?" Deronda said.

"I don't know," Isaiah said. "Maybe."

"Maybe? Shit, that's crazy. I mean like, if I had your profile I'd be a brand by now."

Isaiah turned off Anaheim onto Kimball.

"This ain't the way to my house," Deronda said.

"I've got to stop off at Beaumont's," Isaiah said. Beaumont's was a corner store called Six to Ten Thirty. It sold everything from cold beer and microwave burritos to piñatas and *Scarface* posters.

"You know how they say nothing stays the same but change?" Deronda said. "Where is it? I don't see no change."

"Things can change and still be the same," Isaiah said.

They were coming up on the Capri, a Section 8 apartment complex. According to HUD regulations you could only live there if the value of your bank accounts, stock portfolio, and real estate holdings didn't exceed fifty percent of the median income for the area, which was around forty thousand give or take. There was a long waiting list.

A group of East Side Sureños Locos 13 were hanging on a strip of grass near the entrance, a spot chosen with care. There was a low cinder block wall for cover and banana palms to hide their straps in. A lot of the homies were in county lockup for gun possession. Most of the Locos were in their teens but hard-core killas for real, everybody in uniform today. Baggy shorts, oversize white T-shirts or football jerseys, and a splash of red. A wristband, a cap, a flag hanging out of a pocket. Red was their color.

"Check that out," Deronda said, pointing with her chin at a Loco drinking from a forty-ounce bottle of Miller that looked like pee. "How's he ever gonna be anything but a damn criminal with Locos 4 Life stamped all on his forehead?"

The Locos knew who Isaiah was but threw up signs and talked shit just as a matter of principle. One vato with a hairnet over his bald head was nodding all exaggerated. "This ain't your hood no more, esé," he said. "Drive your fucking ass on." Isaiah looked at him neither afraid nor disrespectful. He'd grown up with some of the OGs but these youngsters didn't care about anything. If you weren't a Loco you were a victim.

Isaiah's cell buzzed. He checked the number and hesitated. Some people were like the oldies you hear on the radio, evoking another time, another place, and who you were back then. The sound of Dodson's voice and the rhythm of his speech stirred up a stew of memories burned black at the bottom of his heart. The last time they'd spoken was at Mozique's funeral but it took a day or two before the burnt taste was out of his mouth.

"Who is it?" Deronda said. "It's a girl, ain't it?"

Isaiah thought about sending the call straight to voice mail but if Dodson wanted something he'd keep calling and maybe show up at the crib. He put the call on speaker. "Hey," he said.

"Whassup, Isaiah?" Dodson said. "It's been a long damn time. I ain't laid eyes on you since we put Mozique to rest. That was a sad sad day, wasn't it? Bad a nigga as he was I always thought he'd die by the sword and what happens? The boy wins the Trifecta at Santa Anita, drives over to Raphael's to buy some weed, and gets hit by an Amtrak train. Just goes to show you, luck beats money any day of the week. You got some luck the money will come looking for you."

Deronda rolled her eyes and said: "Oh no, is that Dodson?"

"Yes, this is Juanell Dodson and judging from the ho-ish quality of your voice you must be Deronda."

"How come you ain't in the joint?"

"I got no reason to be in the joint. My criminal activities are a thing of the past. I'm a legitimate businessman now, not that it's any of your never-mind. Maybe if you focused more on your own sorry-ass situation you might be doing something more productive than booty clappin' at the Kandy Kane."

"You still selling them tired-ass counterfeit Gucci handbags out the trunk of your car?"

"No, I give 'em away free just like your tired-ass counterfeit pussy."

Not in the mood for a ten-minute snap exchange, Isaiah said: "What's going on, Dodson?"

"What's going on is a case," Dodson said. "An opportunity to help someone in need and possibly save a life."

"Oh yeah?" Isaiah said. He regretted the words as soon as they left his mouth. He sounded condescending but couldn't help himself. He could feel Dodson holding back, wanting to call him an uppity motherfucker with a freakishly large brain.

"The client wants to talk to you," Dodson said. "He's got money, unlike most of your people. I heard Vatrice Coleman paid you with some blueberry muffins she bought at the store."

"I don't have time for another case," Isaiah said.

"Let's meet somewhere, chop this up."

"I said I don't have time."

"I ain't asking you for your time, I'm asking for five mutha-fuckin' minutes to hear me out."

"I've got to go."

"Go? Go where?"

"Away from you," Deronda said. "He's kicking you to the curb, moron."

"I'll see you later," Isaiah said. As he ended the call he heard Dodson say fuck you, Isaiah.

A white pickup truck was parked in the red zone across from the school. Officer Martinez stopped his cruiser behind it, wondering if the guy didn't see the sign that said NO PARKING IN RED ZONE. He hoped the guy was making a phone call and not high or drunk or jerking off. He'd be off shift in twenty minutes and didn't want to stand around for an hour writing the guy up and waiting for a tow truck. Today was his thirty-first birthday. The kids were at his mother's house and Graciella was waiting at home with a medium-rare rib eye, garlic mashed potatoes, and a see-through nightie no bigger than a Ziploc sandwich bag.

Martinez was hopeful until he saw the driver. The guy was ner-vous, sweating like a pig and looking at the school like it was a gallon of lemonade and he was dying of thirst. *Nothing suspicious going on here,* Martinez thought. *Jesus Christ, is that BO?*

"Hellooo, Officer," the guy said.

"What are you doing here, sir?" Martinez said. The guy didn't move his big Charlie Brown cabeza and stared straight ahead like the answer was over there in the azalea bushes. "Sir, I asked you what you were doing here," Martinez said.

"I'm not *doing* anything," he said. "I'm just sitting here. I'm not breaking any laws." New beads of sweat were appearing on the guy's face like time-lapse photography of morning dew.

"Do your kids go to school here?" Martinez said.

"Ohhh no, no kids for me," the guy said, like he'd narrowly dodged that bullet.

Martinez bent down and looked in the window, his eyes darting around the interior of the truck, holding on the bowling bag a moment before coming back to the guy. "License, insurance card, and registration, please," he said. The guy dug the stuff out and gave it to him. "Any outstanding warrants?" Martinez said.

"What was I doing, Officer? I wasn't *doing* anything."

"Any outstanding warrants?"

"No, no warrants."

"Put your keys on the dash and stay in your car."

"I wasn't *doing* anything. Jesus Christ, I'm just *sitting* here."

Martinez kept Boyd's license and headed back to his patrol car. If this asshole made him late he'd charge him with everything he could think of.

Boyd grabbed the steering wheel with both hands and shook it like a pissed-off chimpanzee in a cage, yelling: "FUUUCK!" Everything was going so good too, not like the other times when he'd done everything on impulse.

Boyd was living in Portland the first time he assaulted a girl. He was fishing off the boat docks at the Hayden Island Marina when he saw a tiny thing in a polka-dot bathing suit and lime-green sunglasses go into the women's bathroom. She was a screamer and wouldn't shut up even when he hit her. The second time was on a Halloween night. Boyd wanted to look friendly and wore a bunny mask with big ears. The girl he chose was carrying a wand and wearing a long black robe like a judge. Boyd grabbed her off the street and dragged her into a hedge. She fought like a tiger, bit him twice, and he had to hit her too. The third time he followed a girl home from school and bulled his way through her front door. He chased her into a bedroom and woke up her brother, who worked nights as security at Wild Bill's Hotel and Casino. The brother got Boyd in a wrist lock, forcing him to his knees so the girl could hit him over and over again with a trophy she'd won in a spelling bee. Boyd was on his way to the prison hospital when he thought the next time he should have a plan.

Boyd got forty-one months for attempted rape at the Snake River Correctional Institution and he had to register as a sex offender. He was supposed to ask his parole officer for permission to leave the state and reregister when he got to California but he hadn't done either. Now his name would come up on the computer and the cop would look in the bowling bag and that would be it, game over. They'd lock him up with the black guys and the Mexicans and he'd have to sweat it out, hoping nobody would find out about his record. Somehow, murderers were okay but normal guys like him got beat up or raped, usually at the same time. He wasn't going to let that happen. Not again.

In the side mirror, Boyd could see the cop standing next to the patrol car talking on his radio. You could tell from his expression he was hearing something bad. Boyd tried not to move his upper body as he reached over and unzipped the bowling bag just enough to slip his hand inside and close his fist around the warm slim handle of the boning knife.

Beaumont came out of the storeroom with Margaret Cho tucked under his arm. The Korean comedian was wearing a red miniskirt and black fishnets, her hands defiantly on her hips, back arched, her lips pooched out like she'd just shouted fuck you at somebody who'd picked on her back when she was an overweight nobody. When Beaumont got to the front of the store he saw Isaiah at the magazine display reading the *LA Times*. He was so still he reminded Beaumont of the egrets that stood in the tide pools waiting for a meal to swim by. A hoochie-looking girl with a backside like two hams in an Easter basket was looking into the cooler.

"Can I get a soda, Isaiah?" Deronda said.

"Get what you want," Isaiah said.

Beaumont stood with his arm around Margaret like she was his adopted daughter. "Here she is," he said. "Put her together myself."

"Who's that supposed to be?" Deronda said.

"I didn't realize you was into Asian women," Beaumont said, hoping Isaiah would say why he wanted the thing but he didn't.

Deronda and Margaret squinted at each other. "I know who that is," Deronda said. "That's the waitress at the Mandarin Palace."

Isaiah found the cutout on eBay, the seller saying he could make one of anybody or anything. People, pets, plants, landscapes, body parts. Margaret Cho was no problem. It cost eighteen dollars plus four-fifty more for the Dr Pepper, Red Vines, and peanut butter cheese crackers Deronda had put on the counter.

Isaiah fished a wad of cash out of his front pocket and separated some bills. He could have ordered the cutout himself but if UPS had left it on his doorstep somebody would have stolen it. Isaiah knew people who didn't do anything *but* steal packages left by the UPS trucks.

"I appreciate your trouble," Isaiah said.

"Wasn't no trouble," Beaumont said, "I was happy to do it."

Isaiah was self-conscious around Beaumont. He was there when Isaiah was the wonder boy and when his brother Marcus was killed and the war terrorized the neighborhood and he'd seen Isaiah rebuild his life and become a man everybody but the hoodlums admired. Beaumont was among his fans but Isaiah didn't like that he knew about his past and things he was ashamed of.

"You're looking good, Isaiah," Beaumont said. "Glad to see it."

"Thanks, Beaumont. I'll see you later."

Isaiah picked up Margaret and headed for the door. Beaumont couldn't let it go. "What does somebody do with a thing like that?" he said.

"It's a present," Isaiah said.

Boyd was driving back to his apartment when he saw her walking down Kimball. She was a little older than he liked but she was skinnier than Carmela and her hair went halfway down her back. No one was around, the heat driving everyone indoors. Back at the school, Boyd thought he was done for but the cop got a call on his radio about shots fired and an officer down at an address in Cambodia Town. Boyd was pissed about leaving Carmela but if something happened to her the cop would know who did it.

The skinny girl was yakking on her phone now. Boyd unzipped the bowling bag all the way and it opened like a mouth.

Isaiah came out of the store and started toward the Audi parked at the curb. He stopped to let a girl walk by. She was probably in middle school, a twig of a thing in her pipe-stem jeans, down vest, and Ugg boots, never mind the heat. You wore your best clothes until you wore them out. She was talking on her pink cell, laughing as she said: "I mean like seriously, right? Ramón isn't even into her."

Without a moment's break in her conversation the girl smiled at Margaret and continued on her way. Isaiah chirped open the Audi just as a pickup truck crept by at walking speed. It was a white Silverado, ten years old, blue racing stripes on the side that were peeling off, a big dent in the quarter panel. The engine was stuttering. Fuel injectors, Isaiah thought. The man at the wheel was wearing a cap with a logo on it. He was missing a front tooth and his face was shiny with sunburn. He was staring at something. Isaiah should have guessed what was going on. Why was the man driving so slow and if he wasn't looking at Isaiah or Deronda who was he looking at? But in the moment, Isaiah missed all that. He was distracted, thinking about how he needed a payday case and trying to fit Margaret into the backseat while Deronda talked at him wanting to know if he was getting some from the waitress at the Mandarin Palace and if mu shu meant dog in Chinese.

As Isaiah stood up from the car and Deronda got in he caught a whiff of something that made him freeze in place. He'd read somewhere that chloroform doesn't have a smell but it does. A little like acetone with a trace of sweetness to it. The sound of the stuttering engine at full throttle drew his eyes to the right. The pickup was speeding away, turning the corner so sharply a rear wheel bumped over the curb, something round and reflective on the back bumper. The girl was gone but her pink cell was on the sidewalk.

"Oh no," Isaiah said.

Thirty seconds later the Audi slid around that same corner, Michelins squealing and smoking, the tail end drifting. Isaiah straightened the car out and dropped the hammer, three hundred and forty horsepower WAHHing like a hive of mega-wasps, pinning Deronda to the seat, the ice-blue nails gripping the doorsill and digging into the dash. "The hell you doing, Isaiah?"

Boyd drove on autopilot, not really believing he'd pulled it off. Adrenaline was sluicing through his veins, the missing tooth whistling like an out-of-breath bird, his heart thumping so loud he didn't notice the suspension bottoming out as the truck bounced through a big pothole. The girl was behind him in the extra cab, sprawled on the seat, unconscious, drool pooling on the upholstery. That chloroform really worked. She was too busy yakking on her phone to notice him coming up behind her. He clamped the sponge over her face with one hand, his other arm around her waist. She kicked and swung her little arms but her body went limp by the time he put her in the extra cab. Nobody saw him. Down the block there was a black guy with his head stuck in a car and a girl standing there talking but they didn't notice him. Gleeful now, Boyd bounced up and down in the seat, banging his fists on the steering wheel and laughing. "I've got her," he shouted. "Jesus Christ, I've GOT her!"

The Audi shot down the street, the neighborhood going by in a blur. Isaiah's jaw was hard-set but he was otherwise expressionless. He knew the man had thought about this, coming to a sketchy neighborhood with his chloroform, looking for the right girl. He got her in the pickup fast too, had his moves figured out in advance, and you don't do all that just to go somewhere random. The man had plans.

Deronda put her hands in front of her face. "Isaiah!"

Isaiah slammed on the brakes, the Audi screeching to a halt at a stop sign. The man could have gone left, right, or straight ahead.

"Could you please tell me what's going on?" Deronda said.

Isaiah looked left. Houses on either side, a dozen driveways to duck into. Kids were playing hockey in the street. They wouldn't have had time to move the nets, let the truck go by, and set them up again.

"I know you after somebody," Deronda said. "I don't know who or how you got onto it but—"

"Be quiet," Isaiah said, so much weight in his voice she immediately shut up, and when he looked right she did too. More houses, more driveways. A group of men were hanging on the corner a block away. Isaiah could ask them if they'd seen the pickup but he'd have to drive down there to find out and the truck's lead was getting longer by the second. Straight ahead the street continued on but curved away so you couldn't see all the way to the end. Isaiah's eyes snap-zoomed on a pothole, a bloom of muddy splash marks around it. He slammed the Audi into gear and took off down the narrow street, whipping by parked cars so close you could reach out and touch them.

"Please, God, *please*," Deronda said with her eyes closed.

Isaiah came to a hard stop at Pacific, a big street, traffic swishing by in front of him. He got out and hopped up on the hood of the car. A one-eighty scan took in a KFC, a parking lot, Five Star Auto Parts, a Chevron station, Del Taco, Top Notch Appliances, and

Reliable Public Storage. It wasn't likely the man had stopped to pick up some spark plugs, have a bite to eat, or buy a refrigerator, and his pickup wasn't at the gas station. But he might have gone into Reliable. Isaiah knew the place. Row after row of identical storage lockers with roll-down doors. The girl could be in one now, just waking up, dizzy from the chloroform, the man a looming silhouette as the door came down and blacked out the sky.

Deronda stuck her head out of the window. "What are you doing, Isaiah?" she said.

Isaiah's shirt was stuck to his back, his scalp tingling. The man was getting away, the girl having no idea what she was in for. *What did you see, Isaiah, what did you* see? When Isaiah came out of Beaumont's he saw the skinny girl walking by, the pickup creeping after her, the man staring hard, his face shiny with sunburn. His cap had a logo embroidered on it. A fish with a lure stuck in its lip, and there was something reflective on the back bumper. A trailer hitch.

The man had a boat.

Isaiah got back in the car and floored it, running the red light, cars honking. If the man was heading to the marina he would have been driving south. Instead, he was headed west toward the LA River. Maybe his intention was to assault the girl in a warehouse or an empty building but a boat was better. Be alone with her out on the ocean, do what he wanted, and throw her body overboard.

"Call 911," Isaiah said. Deronda dialed her cell, put it on speaker, and held it up to Isaiah's ear.

"911," the dispatcher said. "What is your emergency?"

Isaiah had to shout over the roaring V8. "A kidnapping," he said, "a little girl."

"When did this happen, sir?"

"A few minutes ago. I'm chasing the guy, he's getting away. Going west on Dover, just passed Pacific."

"Did you see the kidnapping?"

"No, I didn't see it. He chloroformed her, put her in his truck."

"Sir, you said you didn't see it."

"I smelled the chloroform, they're probably in his boat by now."

"Chloroform doesn't have a smell—what boat?"

"Isaiah!" Deronda said, dropping the phone.

The river was coming at them fast, filling up the windshield. Isaiah downshifted, jerked the wheel right and then cranked it hard left, the car sliding sideways onto the bike path, Isaiah stomping on the gas, dust and gravel shooting out from behind the car as it raced off downriver.

"Why didn't I get out of the car?" Deronda said. *"Why?"*

The Mercury outboard chugged along, the *Hannah M* moving at wake speed down the wide green LA River. Upstream the water was too shallow but here near the harbor there was just enough draft. Boyd stood tall on the bridge of his twenty-one-foot cuddy cruiser. The air was a warm wet blanket on his face but it felt good anyway.

Boyd was living in his grandmother's second bedroom when she died of old age. The house went back to the bank but she'd left him some money in a safe-deposit box. Not a lot but enough to buy a secondhand boat with Bondo patches on the hull, a cracked windshield, and rust flaking off the gunwales. He loved the boat, by far the best thing he'd ever owned. Nick let him park the boat trailer inside the chain link enclosure with the forklift providing he could use the boat whenever he wanted. Backing the trailer into the water took no time at all.

The skinny girl was stashed in the cabin below. Boyd had laid her down on the mildewed mattress and put duct tape around her wrists and ankles and over her mouth. She'd moaned a couple of times, her shirt pulled up over her incredibly small waist. Boyd kneeled next to her, listening to her breathe and feeling the tapeworm in his gut growing and twisting, filling him with rage. He'd almost attacked her right then and there but decided to stick with the plan.

Hannah was veering to starboard. Boyd snapped back to the present and saw a black guy in a gray car driving on the bicycle path. *Is that the same guy? No, it can't be.* Boyd steered back to the center of the river and pushed the throttle lever forward, the Merc blatting louder, the boat surging ahead. But the car caught up and stayed even. *Who is this guy?* Now he had his arm out of the window and he was pointing—no, not pointing, he was wagging his finger like a windshield wiper and saying something over and over again, you could read his lips: *Don't you do it. Don't you do it.* Boyd pushed the throttle to the max, the boat lunging, building speed, the car staying even, bouncing over dips and swerving around the bicyclers and joggers. "Who *is* this guy?" Boyd said.

Boyd knew the black guy would run out of road soon. The bicycle path ended a half mile downriver at the Seaside Freeway overpass. He'd get stuck there and Boyd would be home free. A few more minutes to the Queensway Bridge, where the river widened and went past the fancy marinas, the lighthouse, and the *Queen Mary* and on into Long Beach Harbor and then through the buoy line and into the open ocean where the loudest scream in the world wouldn't be heard by anything but the jellyfish. Boyd wasn't worried when the black guy sped up and drove away. What could the guy do? Nothing. "Fuck you!" Boyd shouted, cupping his hands around his mouth. "Fuck you, asshole!"

Boyd went down and took a look in the cabin. The girl was still out of it. Good. He didn't want to chloroform her again. He wanted her awake. Wide awake. He grinned and rubbed his palms together. He imagined himself ripping the duct tape off her face and saying *Wake up, you little bitch. You belong to me now.*

Isaiah parked the Audi near the overpass abutment. He got out quickly, went around to the trunk, and opened it. The floor panel and spare tire had been removed making the compartment extra deep. Plastic storage boxes of various sizes were neatly arranged and labeled. HAND TOOLS, SOLDER/WELDER, RESTRAINTS, DRILL/CIRC SAW, PRY TOOLS. The WEAPONS boxes held, among other things, a stun gun, a taser, a rubber bullet gun, bear strength Mace, a fighting stick, and a sap cap. It looked like an ordinary cap except it had a secret compartment loaded with lead pellets. Smack somebody and you'd break every bone in their face. The Determinator was in its own yellow hard plastic case.

"What's a Determinator?" Deronda said.

Boyd was bouncing on the balls of his feet when the Seaside overpass came into view. He threw up his hands like Rocky. "Yahooooo!" he yodeled. He started jiggling and shaking like he had to take a pee. "You did it, Boyd, you did it!!" And then his voice wound down and his face went dark. "What now?" he said. The black guy and a girl were climbing down the riprap to the shore, the girl holding her flip-flops and complaining. The black guy was carrying something. It was too short to be a rifle and too fat to be a pistol. It looked like a caulking gun. Boyd laughed. *Good luck with that, you stupid idiot.* He waved like he was meeting the black guy at the airport. "Shoot me! Shoot me, asshole! Shoot me!"

* * *

The Determinator HX Grenade Launcher was hard to aim. It weighed six pounds, had a pistol grip, and was two feet long with the stock extended. The barrel was as big around as a can of tennis balls. Isaiah loaded a grenade into the breech and snapped it shut. The flash-bang type was for law enforcement only but you could buy a fireworks grenade online. Isaiah calculated angles. The boat would pass right in front of him but it was going fast, bow up, pushing a wake to either shore. If he fired point-blank, the grenade would explode on the wraparound windshield. It would scare the man but that would be all. He'd have to let the boat go by just far enough to shoot the grenade into the *back* of the windshield.

The boat was getting closer, the engine screaming. The man was half turned around and had his pants down to his knees. He was wiggling his butt and yelling *Shoot me, shoot me*. Isaiah raised the launcher.

"Why aren't you shooting me?" the man laughed as the boat sped by.

Isaiah fired. The grenade went over the man's left shoulder and slammed into the back of the windshield. There was a huge explosion of red-and-white sparks. The guy let go of the wheel and staggered backward, hands over his eyes, his T-shirt on fire, his pants twisted around his ankles. He fell to the deck, hitting his face against a rod holder on the way down. The boat was going in a circle at full speed, sparks whirling out of it.

"It's the Fourth of damn July," Deronda said.

The man got to his feet and was immediately slung overboard. He splashed and floundered, choking on water poisoned by a million storm drains, submerging and coming up again until he found his footing and plodded toward shore, wiping the slime out of his eyes.

Isaiah went out to meet him with the collapsible baton. "The girl better be all right," he said, thinking how much she must have suffered already. He hit the guy across the head with the baton hard enough to make Deronda wince. The guy fell over and went under. Isaiah thought about letting him drown but grabbed him by the collar and lifted his head out of the water. "She better be all right, do you hear me?" he said. "She better be just fine."

Twenty minutes later, patrol cars and an ambulance were parked around the overpass, a helicopter whap-whapping overhead. Cops were standing around pointing at things and talking, Boyd's boat tied up and webbed with yellow tape. The girl was on a stretcher, conscious but shaken and nauseous, a paramedic attending her.

"What's your name, sweetheart?" the paramedic said.

"Teresa," the girl said.

"You're gonna be all right, Teresa. Now I'm going to put this oxygen mask over your face and I want you to breathe deep for me, okay?"

Teresa pushed the mask aside. "Where's my phone?" she said.

An officer was taking Boyd to a patrol car. Boyd was cuffed, wet like a wet dog, no pants, his T-shirt in charred rags, burn marks on his face; he'd lost his other front tooth, his mouth a bloody hole. "I sidn't soo anysing," he said.

"You didn't do anything to who?" the officer said. "The little girl you kidnapped and had tied up in your boat?"

Boyd thought about saying he was just showing her around but that sounded stupid even to him. "Whas abou suh guy who sot suh bomb ass me?" he said.

"You mean the guy that shot the bomb at you and saved the little girl you had kidnapped in your boat? Shut the fuck up and get in the car."

*   *   *

Teresa's dad, Néstor, arrived. Teresa told him she was walking near the store and somebody put something wet over her face and when she woke up she was in the boat and this black guy was asking her if she was okay.

"Did he do anything, you know," Néstor said.

"No, Dad, you don't understand. He wasn't the guy that kidnapped me, he was like rescuing me. He was nice, I could tell." Teresa told Néstor how the black guy carried her to shore, set her down, and told her to breathe deeply. After she could sit upright without holding on to him he said the police would be there soon. Then he got in his car with a girl and left.

"He just left?"

"That's what I said, Dad."

Néstor wondered why the guy didn't stay and be a hero, get his picture in the paper, and be on TV. Néstor would have to find him and thank him personally. A black guy who shot grenades at people couldn't be too hard to find. Néstor decided to let Teresa recover for a day or two before he asked her why she was near the store, which wasn't on her way home, and if she was going to see that pendejo Ramón he'd take away her phone.

Isaiah carried Margaret across the lobby to the elevators, a group of people already waiting there. Nobody smiled or said anything. Too many crazies around these days, she might be his girlfriend.

Flaco was in physical therapy now. On the ride up, Isaiah decided to put Deronda together with Blasé. Maybe he could put her in a video and who knew, maybe she'd get discovered and be on TV. It was all luck anyway. Like the skinny girl walking past Beaumont's as he was coming out. If he'd stayed inside another minute she would have suffered in ways he didn't want to think about. She got lucky and maybe he did too. When you owed as much as he did you didn't expect the coins to be put in your hand.

Isaiah had been to the hospital hundreds of times but always had a moment when he thought about coming back later or not at all but what would be the point? There was nowhere he could go, no road that went far enough or jet that flew fast enough to free him from his past. He wished he could be like Dodson, just go about his business like nothing had ever happened.

Isaiah had seen Dodson twice since the war. The first time was at Mozique's funeral. The second time he was coming home late and saw a patrol car with its lights flashing and Dodson sitting on the curb with his fingers laced on top of his head. One officer was searching the car, the other talking on his radio. Dodson was outraged. "We got terrorists and serial killers running around everywhere and you muthafuckas ain't got shit else to do but profile a law-abiding brutha on his way to a job interview? Yes, I know it's one in the morning, you think a nigga ain't got a watch? I what? I smell like marijuana? Oh you know that for a fact? You one of them drug-sniffing dogs disguised as a big-ass white man? Yes, I recently completed a sentence at a state correctional facility but what's that got to do with anything? I'm out now. I don't deserve this kind of harassment. I *paid* my debt to society."

Isaiah drove on, thinking that was what angered him most about Dodson. The way he could hustle himself out of his own conscience and his simple-minded equation for all the wrong they had done. Do some time, see your probation officer once a month, and it was over, it was done. Your debt was paid.

When Flaco saw Margaret his eyes lit up and he grinned his lopsided grin. Jermaine, the physical therapist, put the boy in his chair and he wheeled over, trying to put words together. His brain knew what they were but his lips would forget how to say them. *Oh my God, that's so cool!* came out *Oh...ny...gone...nats...tso coo.*

Isaiah made the cutout stand up by itself, Flaco gaping at it, steam on the inside of his glasses. "I tweet her every day," he said. "She invited me to her concert at the Greek." Which probably meant he got a group email.

"We'll try to get some tickets," Isaiah said. Flaco had always accepted Isaiah's explanation that he was a volunteer and Isaiah was content to let it stay that way. Flaco was seventeen now but he looked twelve. He had a narrow, undernourished face and searching eyes, his shiny blue tracksuit draped over a body made of pickup sticks, his hair like somebody chopped at it with a meat cleaver. Isaiah used to pay Ira to come in and cut it but it didn't make any difference.

A girl on crutches arrived. "Is that Margaret Cho?" she said.

"Isn't she cool? She invited me to her concert at the Greek!"

Isaiah sat on the leg press machine with Jermaine. "What's he going to do when he turns eighteen, stay with you?" Jermaine said.

"I offered but he wants to have his own place," Isaiah said. "He wants to be independent, be his own man."

"Does he know how much it costs to be his own man?"

"His social worker talked to him about it but I don't think he understood her. He told me he wants a cool place by the beach."

Flaco would have to leave the group home after his next birthday. He'd get an SSI check and food stamps and Isaiah had arranged a part-time job for him packaging dog biscuits for a pet boutique. Add all that up and even with a housing voucher he wouldn't be able to afford more than a Section 8 apartment. Maybe get one at the Capri next door to that Loco with the hairnet. Isaiah considered renting him a place but that was money down the drain. Then he found a condo that would work. One bedroom, ramps, flowers in the flower garden, close to shopping. It needed repairs but nothing he couldn't handle. A short sale, a hundred thirty thousand. But Isaiah already had a mortgage and would need a second. Tudor, his mortgage broker, said if he came up with a thirty percent down payment he'd consider it. Two or three payday cases and Isaiah might make it if he stopped eating and paying his utility bills.

"What's with Flaco and Margaret Cho?" Isaiah said.

"Do you know about her?" Jermaine said.

Jermaine grew up in San Francisco like Margaret and he knew a lot about her. She was raised in the Castro District, a haven for misfits. Hippies, bikers, hookers, drug addicts, drag queens, and artists of all kinds. Margaret was a misfit too. Not white and she didn't feel Asian and she was bullied and ostracized at school.

"She wanted to be a comedian," Jermaine said. "You wonder where that idea came from. Asian girls weren't exactly known for their sense of humor but Margaret didn't care. She was going to do her thing no matter what and she went ahead and did it. Broke the stereotype and blazed her own trail in her own way."

"I thought Flaco would go for one of those teenage pop stars," Isaiah said. "Somebody closer to his age."

"No, it's more than a crush," Jermaine said. "Look at it this way. If you were going to be in a wheelchair for the rest of your life and you wanted to be independent, be your own man? Margaret Cho isn't a bad person to idolize."

As he rode back down in the elevator, Isaiah checked his emails hoping to find a new payday case, but there was none. He checked them again when he got home, hoping something had come in during the fifteen-minute drive from the hospital. He ran through his list of options but nothing was viable the first two times he'd gone through it and surprise, surprise, nothing was viable this time either. He stalled, eating some soup even though he wasn't hungry. Writing checks for bills that weren't due. Mixing up a solution to clean some LPs that didn't need cleaning. He thought he'd almost rather go back to thievery than do what he had to do.

Call Dodson.

CHAPTER TWO

Everything

May 2005

saiah's cell buzzed. It was probably Dante, wondering why he wasn't at the practice for the academic decathlon team. They had a meet tomorrow against Crenshaw High but Isaiah couldn't have cared less. He'd been lying facedown on the sofa since last night, the tweedy fabric imprinted on his cheek, his mouth dry as burnt toast. He was waiting. Hardly breathing. The kitchen faucet plinking slow. Any second now, Marcus would come out of the bathroom in a cloud of steam, smelling like ocean-fresh deodorant and singing some old Motown song. "Let's Get It On" or "I Wish It Would Rain" or "Sugar Pie Honey Bunch."

"I like a melody," Marcus said whenever Isaiah looked at him funny. "I like a *song*." And Marcus didn't hedge when he sang. None of that humming with a few lyrics thrown in. He sang out, full-throated and he did the moves too. Rolling his hands like a hamster wheel or throwing his arms out because he couldn't keep himself from loving you and nobody else. When he sang "My Girl" he wanted Isaiah to join in on the my-girl-my-girl-my-girl part but Isaiah refused, saying it was too corny. But he wished he could be that way. Act a fool and not be embarrassed. Not caring what anybody thought.

The faucet was plinking faster now. Isaiah could sense the anguish and horror crackling toward him, curling his edges, burning away his denial. Marcus wasn't coming out of the bathroom and he never would again and Isaiah felt himself turning to ashes and crumbling into nothing.

They were on Baldwin walking home from McClarin Park. They'd just played two-on-two with Carlos and Corey and got their butts kicked, Isaiah hardly getting off a shot.

"Corey's too big," Isaiah said, "he's a grown man."

"So why were you trying to muscle him?" Marcus said. "You've got to stay aware of yourself, keep your emotions in check, see the big picture, see the situation. Instead, you got all macho and played Corey's game instead of your own. You're quicker than he is, you should have made him chase you. And your defense, if you could call it that. Corey was scoring like you weren't even there."

"He kept taking me down low."

"You should have picked him up higher, made him put the ball on the floor, kept him off his spot. He was catching the entry pass too easy."

"You couldn't tell me this during the game?"

"I was waiting for you to tell yourself."

Isaiah didn't much care for basketball but Marcus did. That was reason enough to play.

"You gotta get off first," Marcus said. "Take the initiative, dictate the action. You can't just react. That's letting the other guy call the shots. You see the difference?"

A lot of kids would have rolled their eyes at all the advice and admonitions but Isaiah didn't mind. He liked to watch Marcus talk; flashing that big sunny smile or frowning with urgency, one hand judo-chopping the other.

"You won't be a basketball star," Marcus said, "but you *will* be a star — at what is up to you. Most of us have to play the hand we're dealt but you and that mind of yours? You can deal your own hand, play whatever game you want to play, and there's nothing out there can stop you but yourself."

Isaiah felt bad when Marcus talked like that, like his life was cast in stone, like nothing new could happen for him. He was only twenty-five and the smartest person Isaiah knew. Smarter than Sarita, who was in law school. Smarter than Mr. Galindo, who coached the academic decathlon team, and smarter than Dante's parents, who were both psychiatrists.

"You go where God calls you," Marcus said. "Teacher, doctor, scientist, book writer. I don't really care as long as you do some good out there. You could make a difference, Isaiah. A big difference. I'm talking about raising people up, easing their suffering, bringing some justice to the world. Money don't enter into it, you understand what I'm telling you? God didn't give you a gift so you could be a hedge fund manager. You take that road, disappoint me like that, buy a Bentley or put a golf course in your backyard? I will kick — your — ass."

"Yeah, you told me that before," Isaiah said.

"I know I'm on you a lot but you're my little brother, my blood, my pride and joy. I want everything for you. Everything."

"You told me that too."

They stayed on Baldwin all the way to Anaheim and waited for the light to change. It was rush hour, heavy traffic in both directions.

It was hard to believe there could be so many cars. They just kept coming like they were on a loop; like in a hundred years they'd still be going by if climate change hadn't put the city underwater.

"What do you want for dinner?" Marcus said.

"I don't care," Isaiah said.

The number nine bus went by, gusting hot air and stopping at the bus stop, people lined up there ready to board.

"I'm going to the store. You go on home, get that homework done. You only got a ninety-six on that calculus test."

"Only?"

"Those Korean kids get a ninety-six with one hand and play the violin with the other. You want to get into Harvard you're gonna have to do better than that."

"Oh I'm going to Harvard now?"

"You will if I have anything to do with it. You feel like meat loaf?"

"Yeah, meat loaf is good."

"What about stew? We've got that top round in the fridge."

"Whatever's easiest."

The light turned green and Marcus backed into the crosswalk. "I don't care about easy," he said, "just tell me what you want."

It happened so fast. The growl of the engine, the flash of chrome, the awful moment of impact, metal and velocity crushing flesh and bone; Marcus bent in half, cartwheeling through the air and slamming down on the pavement so hard he bounced, a swirling wake of exhaust and dust as the car sped away. There were screams and shouts but Isaiah didn't hear them. He was stumbling toward his brother, falling on his knees beside him, and screaming help, help, somebody help.

Marcus looked like a marionette thrown out of a car window, too still to be a living thing, his arms and legs splayed at unnatural angles. The paramedics were hovering over him, getting things from orange equipment boxes, and talking to each other. One of them cut Marcus's backpack off with a scissor. There was blood on it and blood on the paramedic's gloves. Isaiah couldn't watch anymore and turned his head. He wanted to ask if Marcus was okay but was afraid of what the answer might be.

The paramedics wouldn't let Isaiah ride in the ambulance so a cop took him to Long Beach Memorial. In the waiting room he couldn't sit down, pestering anyone who went in or out of the authorized personnel doors. *Is Marcus okay? He's still in surgery? When's the doctor coming out? Could I go talk to him?* Isaiah called Marcus's friend Carlos, who was there in ten minutes. "Marcus is gonna be all right, he's a tough guy," Carlos said. "He's going to be fine, wait and see."

After a three-hour wait, a doctor came out. He had a Jamaican accent and looked young even with the receding hairline and rimless glasses. He said they'd done everything they could but Marcus had suffered massive internal injuries and had passed.

Isaiah shook his head and smiled like he knew the doctor was messing with him. "No, forget it," he said. "Marcus is in there, I know he is, just let me talk to him—just let me—" A sound erupted out of him; raw, searing, and so sorrowful he could have been a conduit for a prisoner in hell. Carlos tried to hug him but Isaiah pushed him away and sobbed into his hands.

Carlos said Isaiah could stay at his house. His daughters could double up and Isaiah'd have a bedroom to himself. Lucy had dinner waiting for them. Isaiah told Carlos his grandmother was coming in from El Segundo and that she'd meet him at the apartment. Carlos didn't know there was no grandmother and Isaiah's only other relatives, whom he'd never met or talked to, were in North Carolina.

*   *   *

Isaiah got up from the sofa, went to the bathroom, and threw up in the toilet. He stayed there a long time, his head resting on the cool edge of the bowl, freeze-frames blinking behind his eyes. *Blink*. The car coming. *Blink*. Marcus hit. *Blink*. Marcus folded in half. *Blink*. Marcus tumbling through the air. *Blink*. Marcus on the pavement, crushed and broken, his head pressed against the curb.

How could you do that, Marcus? Why didn't you look? You're so stupid, man, why didn't you look?

Marcus's girlfriend, Sarita, showed up. She banged on the door and called Isaiah's name but he didn't answer. What were they going to do, hug each other and cry and say how much they missed Marcus? He couldn't deal with that.

The afternoon sun was blazing through the windows. Isaiah shut the drapes, unplugged the phone, turned off his cell, and sat in the corner under the spider plant. He kept still, hugging his knees, trying to make himself small but the pain found him anyway, hitting him as hard as that car hit Marcus, demolishing thought, reason, spirit, everything. He rocked back and forth and said Marcus Marcus until it was dark outside and his throat was sore. He'd almost nodded off when he heard that impact sound, sickening and final. He lurched and threw up again but nothing came out. He was empty. A birdcage without a bird.

Marcus had a policy from the Neptune Society. A nonprofit organization that provided low-cost cremations. Isaiah got Carlos to call the Society's 800 number and make the arrangements. They moved the body from the morgue and took it to the crematorium. They handled the death certificate, the disposition permit, and the rest of the paperwork. A few days later, Carlos came by and slipped Marcus's last paycheck and a note under the door. The note said UPS would deliver the ashes.

Isaiah stayed in the corner under the spider plant, his world reduced to sounds: TV chatter, doors opening and closing, sirens, crows squabbling, somebody yelling at their kids. At some point he began to tremble. The last thing he'd eaten was a Snickers bar just before the game with Carlos and Corey. He ate a can of tuna, got a bottle of water, and went back to his corner. He lost track of time. Dozing, waking up with a start, wondering where he was, where Marcus was. He'd stand up like an arthritic old man, crying and cursing, trudging to the bathroom or the kitchen, and back again. He ran out of food, nothing left in the kitchen but condiments. He forced himself to go to the store, the wheels of his brain turning in sludge as thick as his heartache.

School. He'd been absent eight days and the maximum number of excused absences permitted in a school year was ten. After that, a note wouldn't be acceptable. The school would want to talk to Marcus and if they found out he'd died they'd send a social worker and Isaiah would get shipped off to a foster home. Isaiah wrote himself a note and went back to school but it was impossible to act normal, his friends coming up to him. *Where you been, Isaiah? What happened to you? You got stuff all in your hair. Are you high? You look high.* He told them he was getting over the flu.

Some things were impossible. Eating lunch in the noisy cafeteria or hanging with Dante and his friends or working in the computer lab with the other kids who had great futures. The note said he had laryngitis. That got him out of PE and speaking in class. He sent Dante a text saying he was quitting the academic decathlon team and told the kids he tutored to find somebody else.

The prospect of leaving the apartment terrified him. Sharing a room with kids he didn't know, strange adults telling him what to do. Out there in the world without Marcus backing him up. Without Marcus. The apartment was all he had left of him. His brother was in the air and embedded in the walls, his smell in the bedsheets, his sneakers on the floor, blue blobs of his shaving gel still on the sink. Whatever happened, Isaiah wasn't leaving.

Money. Marcus worked for Carlos exterminating termites when he couldn't find other work. The check Carlos slipped under the door was for fifteen hundred dollars, more than Carlos cleared in a week and he owned the business. That plus the eight hundred dollars in the checking account wouldn't last long. There was rent to pay. He remembered what Marcus said, to take the initiative, dictate the action, not let his emotions call the shots. If he wanted to stay in the apartment he had to get a job.

Marcus was a jack-of-all-trades, master of everything. Plumbing, electrical, tile, drywall, masonry, cabinetmaking, and fine carpentry; he could do it all as well as any professional. He'd crafted a cherry wood rocking chair for Harley Barnes, assistant director at the Long Beach Public Library. The rocking chair was a present for Harley's mother who was turning eighty. She said it was too beautiful to sit on and kept it in her living room like a Christmas tree. Harley got Isaiah a part-time job checking out books and reshelving the returns. It paid minimum wage and that wouldn't be enough. Marcus had also worked at Manny's Deli. He installed new plumbing in the men's room, replaced the locking mechanism on the walk-in freezer, reglazed the windows, stopped the leaks under the steam table, and basically kept the place from falling apart.

"Marcus was a good guy," Manny said. "He had a good heart. The best." Isaiah bowed his head and cried. "You need help?" Manny said, putting his hands on Isaiah's shoulders. "I'll help you, but working, right? No charity. Your brother would kill me." Manny put Isaiah to work on weekends, busing tables, mopping floors, and washing the mountains of dishes.

IQ

Isaiah calculated his take-home pay from both jobs would be about seven hundred and eighty dollars after taxes. Six hundred and seventy for the rent left thirty dollars a week for groceries, cell phone, DSL, bus fare, and everything else. Dictating the action was easier said than done.

It was luck how he met Dodson. Both of them were waiting in the admin office, Isaiah for the guidance counselor, Dodson for the vice principal. Dodson had worn his gold chain to school and bling wasn't allowed. When he was told to remove it he refused, saying the two Jewish kids wore those beanies and it was the same thing. Dodson sat in an orange plastic chair with his feet stuck straight out and talking on his cell. He was wearing jeans, Pumas, and a white T-shirt but somehow looked slick. You could tell he was short, even sitting down.

"My Auntie May kicked me out, you believe that shit?" Dodson said. "Talkin' 'bout she knew I was selling drugs and didn't want the devil's minion in her house. Shit. I ain't no minion, I'm her goddamn nephew."

The receptionist, Mrs. Sakamoto, was glaring at him. She had short gray hair, a dark blue dress with yellow trapezoids on it, and a bunch of gold hoop bracelets that sounded tinny when they clinked. "Put the phone away, please, or you'll get detention," she said.

Dodson ignored her and dialed another call. "It's me," he said. "What? I *was* at Omari's but not in his house. I was sleeping in that shed, yeah, in the backyard, one of them plastic things you get at Home Depot, couldn't even stand up inside, in there with the flowerpots and fertili—hey, that shit ain't funny."

"Young man," Mrs. Sakamoto said, "put that phone away."

Dodson ended the call and dialed another. "Well?" he said.

"Yeah, I can pay some rent. Where do I sleep? In the same room with who? Your grandmother? Fuck you, Freddie, and fuck your grandmother too."

"Did you hear me?" Mrs. Sakamoto said as Dodson dialed another call. "Put the phone down immediately or you'll get detention!"

Isaiah felt sorry for her. No leverage except something the guy didn't care about. Like threatening a stone with water.

"Your daddy don't want a gangsta in the house?" Dodson said, his voice going up an octave. "*You* a gangsta!"

"I'm going to get Mr. Johnson," Mrs. Sakamoto said, her bracelets clinking as she walked away.

"Tell him I'm not giving up my chain," Dodson said.

Isaiah talked to Mr. Avery, the guidance counselor. Avery wore black socks and sandals and wanted Isaiah to call him Seth. Isaiah told him he was quitting the team because Marcus was out of work and he had to get a job.

"Yeah, it's a tough economy," Mr. Avery said. "Tell Marcus it'll be okay. When one door closes another one opens."

What a bunch of bullshit, Isaiah thought. *There are no doors without Marcus.*

"You're one of my favorite people," Mr. Avery said, "and I have to be honest with you. We need you on the team. We're not going to win the sectionals without your help. Now don't take this the wrong way, but when I write recommendations for your college apps, well—just sayin'."

He's threatening me? This prick is holding college over my head if I don't stay on the team? Like college means anything without Marcus?

"I don't give a shit about college, the team, or you," Isaiah said as he got up and walked out. "Just sayin'."

*   *   *

Dodson was at his locker when Isaiah caught up with him. The inside of the locker door was plastered with pictures of Tupac and oiled-up naked women. Isaiah wondered if he was making a mistake but his brain was sizzling with static and he was in a near panic about losing the apartment.

"I've got a place," Isaiah said.

"A place? What place?" Dodson said.

"A place to stay. A room to rent."

"You got an apartment?"

"Yeah."

"Who else is living there?"

"Nobody."

"You got your own apartment? You ain't no older than me."

"You need a place or don't you?"

"You fuckin' with me you'll be one sorry nigga."

"Forget it," Isaiah said. He was too tired for this. He started walking away.

"Where you going, nigga?" Dodson said. "Wait a goddamn minute." Isaiah stopped but didn't turn around. "How much is the rent?" Dodson said.

Isaiah thought a moment. When Dodson was on the phone he said he sold drugs. His gold chain looked real and he was wearing new Pumas. "Two-fifty," Isaiah said.

"Two-fifty? Kinda steep, ain't it? You smoke weed? Let's make a little trade. I got some Sour Diesel that'll make you forget who your mama is — where you going, nigga?"

Isaiah could hardly stand it, watching Dodson snoop around like a health inspector, turning up his nose at the kitchen, pinching the drapes like they were a suit he was about to buy, touching things he didn't know the value of, things Marcus had touched. Dodson looked in the bathroom and said uh-*huh,* like he expected the worst and wasn't disappointed. Isaiah was exhausted but he'd be damned before he'd let Dodson take advantage of him. Marcus said when somebody's trying to screw you on a deal don't argue, just hold the line.

"How'd you get this place?" Dodson said.

"None of your business," Isaiah said.

"Your TV ain't but twenty-seven inches."

"Buy your own TV."

"You got air-conditioning?"

"Do you *see* an air conditioner?"

"What's all this?" Dodson said, looking at Isaiah's awards displayed on their own wall. Honor Roll, AP scholar, Academic Mathematics Award, Honorable Mention in the Lipton Science Essay Competition, Academic Decathlon District Champion, a letter from the McClarin Park Community Center thanking him for teaching seniors how to use computers.

"Don't worry about it," Isaiah said.

"Is that the bedroom?" Dodson said, nodding at the door.

"You're sleeping on the sofa, turns into a bed."

"I thought you said you had a room."

"This *is* a room. You got the kitchen and the bathroom too."

"That's bullshit. I ain't payin' that kinda dough for sleeping on no sofa."

"Then don't."

"Let me explain something to you, son. I can't have nobody peepin' up on me. I'm a businessman. I need my privacy."

"I don't care about your business and if you need that much privacy stay someplace else."

"Who you talking to, nigga?" Dodson said, getting chesty. "Disrespect me and I'll fuck your shit up right now."

"Your call," Isaiah said. He bristled at the threat but knew Dodson was bluffing. If they had a fight he'd have no place to stay. Dodson pivoted.

"For two-fifty I should get the bedroom," he said.

The idea of Dodson sleeping in Marcus's room was sacrilege. "Not gonna happen," Isaiah said. "Don't even think about it."

Dodson was a member in good standing of the H-Town Deuce Trey Crip Violators. He was jumped in at the age of fifteen. A dozen or so of his future colleagues beat the shit out of him in the parking lot behind Vons. Afterward, as they were peeling him off the asphalt, it was nothing but love. *You one of us, nigga. You in for life, nigga. It's real now, son, you rolling with the VIPs. You in the uppa level, dog, you bangin' with the big ballas now.* Yeah, uh-huh, and now that he was homeless all the VIP big ballas had a damn excuse and he was sleeping in Keenya's ten-year-old Ford Escort with the Saran wrap windows and cat hair embedded in the dusty seats. He did his washing up in the men's room at the Econo gas station and ate microwave burritos from 7-Eleven and Value Meals at Mickey D's. He'd seen Isaiah around, hanging with some unaffiliated kids, the kind that wore backpacks and had carrot sticks in their lunch bags. At first, he thought Isaiah was running some kind of game; all hunched over like his Auntie May, his eyes red, lint in his hair, clothes like he'd just rolled out of bed. No way in the world a fucked-up seventeen-year-old kid could have a place that wasn't fucked up too. Except it wasn't. The apartment reminded Dodson of his parents' house. Everything clean, put away, and done up nice like somebody cared. He absolutely wanted to stay here but he'd never paid full retail in his life.

"You short on the rent or I wouldn't be here," Dodson said. "Without me you out on the street."

"Without you I'll go find somebody else and you can go back to living in that plastic shed."

"Straight up? I need some slack here, brutha."

"Don't call me brother."

"Two-fifty's out my tax bracket. How 'bout we make it one-fifty?"

"How about we make it three hundred?"

"How 'bout one seventy-five?"

"How about five hundred?"

"You a hardheaded li'l nigga, ain't you?"

"You in or you out? Make up your mind."

Dodson knew he had to give in, at least for now. He needed to take a shower, put on some clean clothes. He'd find a way to recoup later on. "I'm in, aight? I'm in."

"Where is it?" Isaiah said.

"Where's what?"

"The money."

"I'm a little short this week. How 'bout I give you a hundred now and the rest next week?"

"How about you come back when you got the two-fifty?"

Dodson felt a wave of humiliation, bested by this chump. He stood there looking at the ground, head slightly tilted, one fist clenched. He wanted to pop the boy a few times, let him know who he was messing with. Instead, he sneezed. Fucking cat hair. Dodson turned and walked away, thinking, *This ain't but the first round, muthafucka.*

CHAPTER THREE
Where's My Samitch, Bitch?

July 2013

Dodson was sitting in a metal folding chair on the auditorium stage at Carver Middle School. He vaguely remembered being a student here, although calling him a student was a stretch. His attendance was so bad his history teacher said he should wear a visitor's badge. Homework was like a strange ritual they did in some foreign country where everybody was blond and wore wooden shoes.

Dodson was sharing the dais with a firefighter in a big canvas coat, a Filipina nurse in green scrubs, a bulky-looking woman in a gray uniform who worked as a prison guard, and an old man in oil-stained coveralls and an STP cap who owned a wrecking yard. Above them hung a banner in blue and green tempera that said: CAREER DAY. Dodson saw Isaiah slip into the back of the auditorium and he smiled to himself. This could only mean one thing. Isaiah needed money and he needed it bad.

The old man was up first. He started his presentation with a joke. "All right," he said, "so this black man walks into a bar, you see, and he's got a parrot on his shoulder. Big beautiful bird, all kinds of colors in it and everything, and the bartender says, man, that thing is beautiful. Where'd y'all get it? And the parrot says, Africa."

It was all downhill from there. The nurse had an accent and that was the end of her and the firefighter put everybody to sleep talking about good grades and character. The woman prison guard said her job was tough but it was union and they couldn't fire you unless you smuggled in dope or had sex with an inmate.

The vice principal, Mr. Ingram, came to the podium. He was wearing khaki Dockers and a baby-blue polo shirt, a weariness about him like he should have followed his dad into the carpet cleaning business. "All right, everybody, let's settle down," he said, looking at a clipboard. "Our next speaker is a prominent entrepreneur and well-known local businessman, Mr. Juanell Dodson. Mr. Dodson?"

Dodson stood up. He was wearing a chalk-striped charcoal double-breasted suit with a canary-yellow tie and matching pocket hankie. He could have passed for an ordinary businessman if it weren't for the diamond studs in his ears and the Stacy Adams black-and-white spectators. He strolled across the stage, a hitch in his stride like a pimp on his birthday, snapping his cuffs and glancing at his sundial-size watch, so many dials and buttons on it you could hardly tell the time. The kids hooted and whistled but they might have been birds chirping for all Dodson cared.

A table and a projector were set up at center stage, a mike on a mike stand next to the table. Dodson squared up to the mike, took a slow, deep, charitable breath and surveyed his audience, a look on his face like he smelled something past its sell-by date. The kids continued to snicker and whisper but Dodson waited...and waited...and waited...until there was absolute silence. A circumstance so unusual the kids were looking at each other.

"Losers," Dodson said, "I don't see nothin' but losers. Bad hair, ashy elbows, prepaid cell phones you ain't even allowed to use unless you get kidnapped, and sneakers with logos on them nobody's ever seen outside of Hong Kong and Vietnam. Don't you wish there was one thing about you that was stylish? That was now? Something your mama didn't buy at the Kmart after-Christmas sale? Something you could be proud of and flaunt in front of your friends? Well of course you do, you know you do." Dodson raised a hand like he was fending off a reporter's question. "Oh I know what you thinkin'. What could my raggedy self ever possess that would give me the status and attention I may or may not deserve? What vestige of the good life could somebody from my pitiful demographic ever hope to acquire? Well, pay attention, young people, Juanell Dodson is about to make your dreams come true."

Dodson got out his cell and swiped the screen and music came through the PA system, Tupac's "California Love"; the kids bobbing their heads and smiling at each other. Dodson swiped the cell again and a PowerPoint slide show commenced on the onstage screen. The first slide was of Jay-Z, smoking a cigar and wearing a gold curb chain fat as a boa constrictor. Nelly wore an all-diamond chain with matching studs. Flo Rida's chain was relatively modest but the diamond-encrusted Jesus pendant was the size of a chicken pot pie. "Check out them joints," Dodson said, beaming like he'd crafted the chains in his own workshop. "Makes you feel like a playa just looking at 'em."

As the music flowed and the kids danced in their seats, there were more slides of rappers, singers, actors, record producers, and pro athletes, all of them wearing outrageous gold chains. "Oh I know what you thinking," Dodson said, that hand coming up again. "How could somebody as financially challenged as me afford bling like that? Get a job? Doing what? Who's gonna hire my illiterate ass? Maybe my parents could help? Please. Ain't no extra income on their monetary horizon. You not gonna get a raise if you pushing a hot dog cart or working the cash register at Shop 'n Save." Some of the kids laughed but most of them didn't. "But Juanell," Dodson said, "why are you even showing me these treasures when you know I'm broke and even if my whole family died at the same time the only thing they'd leave behind is some lottery tickets and a car note? Well, don't despair, young people, Juanell Dodson's rent-to-own financing plan can put you in a genuine fourteen-karat rope big enough to put a crick in Kanye's neck for only pennies a day."

As Dodson was doing the riff about Kanye, Mr. Ingram put his hands on his knees and pushed himself out of his chair. This was all he needed, as if five classes of health ed with kids who had mustaches and got more sex in a weekend than he did in an entire year weren't enough to ruin his day. He walked over to Dodson and put his hand on the mike. He tried to sound outraged but it came out like a plea. "Okay, Mr. Dodson, I need you to stop now," he said. "This is a school assembly, isn't that obvious? We're here to educate, not provide you with an opportunity to hustle up business."

Dodson looked saddened, as if Mr. Ingram had been stricken with some rare disease. "It's a hustler's world, son," Dodson said, "and if you ain't doing the hustlin'? Somebody's hustlin' you."

The assembly was over. Dodson came off the stage and handed out his business cards to the kids filing by. "W W W dot Juanell Dodson Rent to Own," he said. "That's all one word. Just fill out the application form and we'll be in touch." Isaiah was still standing at the back of the auditorium, waiting to be noticed. Dodson kept passing out cards until there were no more kids and the auditorium was deserted. He went up onstage, got his briefcase, and fussed with it for effect.

"You know I'm here," Isaiah said, coming toward him. "You saw me when I came in the door."

"Isaiah!" Dodson said, like Isaiah was an old girlfriend he'd run into at a party. "What a surprise. Did you enjoy the presentations? I thought it went well, didn't you?"

"I need to talk," Isaiah said.

"Oh I'm sorry but I'm in a bit of a rush. Can we do it next week?" Dodson came down off the stage and walked right past him.

"Come on, Dodson, quit messing around," Isaiah said, trailing him.

"I'm afraid I don't know what you mean," Dodson said. He quickened his pace. Make Isaiah hurry up, reduce him to a kid chasing after his mom.

"I want to talk about that case," Isaiah said.

"Case?" Dodson said. "I have a lot of cases at the moment. Could you be more specific?" You had to be careful with Isaiah. Push him too far and he'd walk away from the table no matter what it cost him.

"The case you told me about," Isaiah said. "The one with the client who can pay."

"That could be any one of my clients. They're a very exclusive group." Dodson knew he was reaching Isaiah's limit but couldn't resist. It wasn't like this uppity, condescending muthafucka didn't deserve it. "Oh wait, I remember now," he said. "Yes, yes, it's a very complicated situation. It'll take me at least five minutes to explain and I'm afraid I don't have the time."

*　　*　　*

There wasn't much to look at on the drive over to the client's house. Ivy-covered berms and concrete walls blocked the view on either side of the freeway. Not that you were missing much. Come in on an airplane and all you'd see is borderless urban sprawl clear to the horizon. Long Beach, Compton, Carson, Torrance, Westwood, Studio City — just names on a map.

Isaiah drove, resisting the urge to speak. Dodson was messing with him. After the assembly he didn't say anything about the case, making Isaiah ask and giving him a vague answer. Then he'd made a call and said they had to go meet the client right away, not telling him who the client was. Then he wouldn't let Isaiah crack open a window, saying it would mess up his hair, his cologne stinking up the car. It smelled to Isaiah like somebody'd put fruit-flavored chewing gum, a new leather glove, and a man's sweaty balls into a blender and put it on pulverize. Now Dodson was picking his teeth with a toothpick and bobbing his head to Tupac, music he insisted would clear his mind for the case.

In one of his previous incarnations, Dodson was a record producer. His most promising protégé was a Charles Barkley–looking kid who called himself Da Chunk. Chunk had a song that went to number one hundred and ninety-eight on the rap singles chart. It was titled "Where's My Samitch, Bitch?" Dodson wrote the lyrics:

I be at the strip club, gettin' me some hot rub,
tokin' on a big dub, hungry for some big grub.
Split to the crib, nuttin' in the fridge,
ho was doin' sack time, woke her up double time.
(chorus)
Where's my samitch, bitch? I said!

Where's my samitch, bitch? I said!
Where's my samitch, bitch? I'm hongreee!
Where's my samitch, bitch?

"Could we listen to something else besides Tupac?" Isaiah said.

"Yes, we could, but this is who I want to hear right now," Dodson said. "Tupac's my boy. Did you know he went to art school in Baltimore? Studied jazz, acting, poetry. Moved to Oakland when I was comin' up. Pac was an icon in my hood. I played his records every day."

"I remember. Drove me out of my mind."

"This album right here, *Don Killuminati*? It's a classic, didn't come out 'til after Tupac was dead and gone. The music world lost a giant that day."

"He was just one more thug to me."

"Now you showing your ignorance."

"You mean he wasn't a thug?"

"Not like I used to be if that's what you mean. When Tupac said thug he meant a brutha that had nothing but still held his head up, didn't take shit from nobody, and did what he had to do. Tupac was all about positivity and he cared about his people too. Rapped about poverty, injustice, getting beat down by the system. Suge Knight said Tupac is still alive and living on an island."

Isaiah had some rap in his collection, even a couple of Tupac albums, but he'd stopped listening to that music a long time ago. All those word images about a life he'd never aspired to. Nowadays he listened to all kinds of music: Coltrane, Beethoven, Segovia, Yusef Lateef, Yo-Yo Ma. But no singers. Music without words let him fill his head with images of his own making or no images at all. He still had Marcus's Motown records but he never played them. If he heard a song in a store or on somebody's radio he walked away.

Dodson's toothpick flicked a tiny speck onto the dashboard.

"Hey, don't get stuff on my car," Isaiah said.

Dodson looked for the speck, his face an inch from the dashboard. "Do you have a magnifying glass? Because I can't—oh, there it is, I see it, I thought it was a flea."

"Whatever, just don't get stuff on my car."

"Still a touchy li'l nigga, ain't you? It's like the apartment all over again."

"Could you please tell me about the case before we get there?"

Victorious, Dodson smiled. "The client is Black the Knife," he said, expecting Isaiah to be impressed.

"Who?" Isaiah said.

"Black the Knife, the rapper? Are you that behind the times? He was in that Nelly, Ludacris, Mystikal, Busta Rhymes generation. He got the houses, the cars, clothing line, his own brand of tequila, his own cologne. I got it on now. Why you making that face? I'm trying to give you the background." Dodson knew Isaiah would do his impatient, condescending thing. Hard not to react but there was serious money on the line. "Black the Knife's real name is Calvin Wright," Dodson said. "Grew up in Inglewood over by Hollywood Park. Ran with the Damu Bloods before he got into the game. Anthony said somebody tried to cap him at his crib, almost got him too."

"Who's Anthony?"

"My second cousin, you never met him? A year ahead of us. Got a scholarship to college somewhere, worked for Bobby Grimes. I think that's how he met Cal."

Isaiah didn't know who Bobby Grimes was but he wasn't going to ask.

"Anthony said he couldn't talk about it over the phone but it was urgent," Dodson said. "Cal won't leave the house and he's supposed to be recording an album."

"His crew can't protect him?"

"That's the part I don't understand. His security is the Moody brothers, Bug and Charles. I don't know 'em but I heard about 'em. They some bad muthafuckas. You had them along you could walk down the middle of Afghanistan Boulevard and not worry about a thing."

"Why didn't they go to the police?"

"Anthony said this was under wraps and he said it twice. Made me swear I wouldn't tell nobody but you."

"What about the fee?"

"This is where it gets good. You get your per diem plus a fifty-thousand-dollar bonus if we solve the case."

"*Fifty* thousand? That can't be right. It's too much money."

"You can thank me for that. I told Anthony we were starting another case and the client was giving up a serious stack of paper. Anthony said how much and I said twenty-five thousand. He said he'd match it and I said why would we cancel a case if all we get is the same money? He said thirty-five and I said fifty. Twenty-five for the work and twenty-five for the lost client. He asked Cal and Cal said okay."

"That makes no sense," Isaiah said. "For fifty grand they could hire one of those high-tech security firms. They've got databases, law enforcement connections, and investigators that are ex-FBI."

"Cal and them is some real niggas," Dodson said. "You know they ain't hiring no ex-FBI and they got that mentality. You don't pay big money, it ain't worth big money."

"You know I'm going to work the case myself."

"Not gonna happen. I told Anthony we was partners, part of my sales presentation. And this is an opportunity to expand my network and form new business relationships and I'm not giving that up just 'cause you got an attitude problem."

"I work alone so I can do things my own way and don't have to worry about anybody but myself."

"You work alone 'cause you don't respect nobody but yourself and in this particular situation that's too damn bad. And just out of curiosity, why are you so broke? You spend too much on the car?"

"I'm not broke and I *built* the car."

"Nigga, please. Nobody can build a damn Audi, not even you. And while we're on the subject of money, my cut is half. Don't look at me like that. The money wouldn't be on the table if it wasn't for me and I don't mind telling you it took my ceaseless energy, business acumen, and no small measure of people skills to make this deal happen and I expect to be compensated accordingly."

"You know that's not true," Isaiah said. "Anthony read that article in *The Scene,* didn't he? He remembered you and me were in the same class and called you."

"Yes, but I *did* negotiate the fifty thousand dollars and I *do* deserve fifty percent."

"The hell you do."

By the time they got to Calvin's crib, Isaiah had argued Dodson's cut down to twenty-five percent and neither of them was happy. Calvin lived in Vista Del Valle, an exclusive hilltop development in Woodland Hills. A security guard at a kiosk checked them out and made a call before he let them through. The houses were massive, the lawns smooth as pool tables, luxury cars in the driveways. No one parked on the street. The only pedestrians were nannies pushing thousand-dollar carbon-fiber baby strollers.

"Look, when we get there let me handle things, okay?" Isaiah said. "This is what I do."

"I know you got the detective part down," Dodson said, "but customer relations at this level ain't the same as finding somebody's lost dog. You need diplomacy, finesse, and salesmanship. Qualities your surly unpleasant ass is sadly lacking. You lucky you got skills, son, 'cause if you had to survive on your personality you'd be working at the morgue with dead people."

Cal's house was a gigantic salmon-pink Mediterranean-style villa with palm trees and exotic ferns and a fountain with leaping dolphins spitting out streams of water. An equally gigantic Cape Cod shared the same cul-de-sac, the two houses like twins wearing different outfits. Isaiah parked the Audi in the circular driveway behind a Ferrari F1 convertible, a '64 Chevy lowrider, an Escalade, and a Lexus IS 350.

Dodson checked out the Ferrari, running his fingers over the pearlescent black paint and the buttery leather upholstery. "You know what this reminds me of? Cherise after she puts moisturizer on her ass cheeks." Dodson kept talking about the Ferrari while Isaiah's eyes swept over the house. The ground-floor windows were leaded, the massive oak front door shielded by a heavy wrought iron security gate. A bullet cam was set under an eave and aimed at the cul-de-sac. Another covered the driveway and a dome camera was mounted over the entry. Small red-and-white signs were posted in the shrubbery that said ADVANCED SECURITY, a high-end company. Isaiah knew their work. If somebody broke into this house he knew what he was doing.

The rapper's house was on the next hill over. The man with the dog had his hunting binoculars trained on the two guys in the driveway.

The taller one was clearly in charge. The way he was standing there, not so much looking around as he was *studying;* taking his time, nodding when he made a mental note, turning from the house to the cul-de-sac and back again to see what was where. He had focus. Hadn't said a word since he'd gotten out of his car. The little guy climbing around the Ferrari couldn't stop blabbing.

The tall guy definitely wasn't another rapper. He might have been a friend but that didn't fit either. He was nothing like the people who went in and out of that house. None of that swaggering bullshit. He was probably IQ, the guy he'd been warned about. What a stupid fucking thing to call yourself. The man thought about getting his sniper rifle out of the truck but there was no need for anything extreme at this point. The rapper would only get more reclusive, maybe even leave town. Anyway, what could this so-called IQ do? There were no clues to find, no evidence to follow. *IQ.* What a fucking joke.

The dog growled and surged against the spiked collar. Some asshole with a German Shepherd was walking on the other side of the street. *What's with the look? Oh you think that mutt would stand a chance? You're lucky I don't turn my dog loose. Two minutes and he'd kill and eat you both. Wait, I don't believe it. Did that asshole just smile at me?* "Hold still, Goliath," the man said. "I want to take off your leash."

Dodson rang the bell, Isaiah still looking around. Something was wrong, something in the air, something in those hills on the other side of Ventura Boulevard. He got the same feeling when he drove through Loco territory. That eyes were on him he couldn't see, that bullets were coming ahead of their gunshots.

"Welcome," Anthony said as he swung open the door. "It's good to see you, Dodson." He sounded almost relieved, like he was being rescued. He shook hands in the traditional way, confusing Dodson for a moment, but he finally got the hang of it.

"Good to see you too, cuz," Dodson said, meaning it. "It's been a long damn time." There was no family resemblance Isaiah could see. Anthony was good-looking in a collegiate, white boy kind of way. Soft features, nerd glasses, a close-fitting sweater with different-colored triangles on it, and peg-leg pants.

"You must be Isaiah," Anthony said. "I've heard a lot about you."

"Good to meet you, Anthony," Isaiah said.

"Please, come inside."

The foyer would have been a good-size room in anybody else's house. An ornate gilded mirror and a white travertine floor reflected light from a huge chandelier, a dramatic marble staircase sweeping up to the second floor.

"You always keep an AK in the umbrella stand?" Isaiah said, looking at it.

"Remind me not to come over here when it's raining," Dodson said.

"It's a long story," Anthony said. "Part of the reason you're here. Cal's going to meet us in the game room." Isaiah saw anger and exasperation in Anthony's eyes like he'd been forced to work overtime too many nights in a row. Anthony led them through the house, walking fast like he was late for something, more chandeliers lighting the way. "In case you're wondering, I'm Cal's majordomo," he said. "I deal with the lawyers, publicists, and promoters. I organize his schedule and run interference with his record label and whoever else wants a piece of him."

Isaiah knew houses like this existed but he'd never been inside one. The sheer quantity of overstuffed furniture, marble flooring, life-size paintings, exotic statuary, burnished woods, heavy drapery, and gilded mirrors made the house feel like a furniture store after everyone had gone home.

"I don't know what Dodson told you," Anthony said, "but the situation here is at the breaking point. Cal hasn't been out of the house for three weeks and then this craziness happens over the weekend. Now the place is an armed camp. He wanted me to carry a gun but I refused. To be honest, I'm sorry I called you but Cal insisted. The whole thing is so ridiculous."

As they entered the game room, Dodson said, "What game do you play in here, polo?" The sprawling space looked sparse even with the pool table, foosball table, card table, craps table, pinball machine, three TVs, fireplace, two wet bars, and islands of white leather furniture expansive enough to seat the Lakers' front line. A glass wall with a sliding glass door looked onto a brick patio and a gas barbecue the size of a buffalo. The pool was postcard blue, the lawn almost too lush and green to be real; a full-size basketball court off to one side.

"I know," Anthony said.

The Moody brothers came in together. Junebug, aka the Bug, was one of those people who could make a room look smaller. He was bald, purple-black like an eggplant, and wide as a Sub-Zero refrigerator. Most of the weight was around his middle but he looked more fearsome than fat, a .357 Magnum in a shoulder holster adding to the effect.

"You must be the Bug," Dodson said. "It's a pleasure to meet your notorious ass."

Bug ignored him and walked up to Isaiah, heat coming off him like a hot stove with some Kush in the oven. "You him, huh?" he said. "The great IQ?"

"My name is Isaiah," Isaiah said.

Bug held his meaty paw in the shape of a handgun, shooting it for emphasis. "Well, I'm gonna tell you straight up," he said. "You might be something in Long Beach but you ain't shit up in here. Get disrespectful and your shit is over, you feel me? Cal's my nigga. You fuck this up and oh my GOD I'll put a hurtin' on you."

Isaiah looked at him like he'd come to the door selling five-dollar candy bars you could buy at the store for a dollar. He hated threats. Some asshole like Bug demanding respect as if bullying was a quality to admire like wisdom or kindness.

"What? What?" Bug said, metronoming his head. "You got nothin' to say? You a muthafuckin' mute? Don't just stand there, nigga, say something."

Dodson stepped between them with his palms out. "Ease up, Bug, everything's cool." There wasn't much Dodson was afraid of and he could handle himself better than most. He was featherweight boxing champ at Chino State Prison, beating a whole string of wiry little tattooed Mexicans. "Ain't no need to get hostile," he said. "We here on business."

"Was I talking to your pip-squeak ass?" Bug said. "Get the fuck out my way."

"Charles," Anthony said, "could you call your brother off?"

Charles looked at Bug, who huffed through his nose and went to the bar. "We handle our shit in-house, you feel me?" Charles said. "We don't need two outside niggas meddlin' in our shit." Charles was long and lanky, a sloucher whether he was standing up or sitting down. He had a triangular face, mean eyes, and a goatee that came to a point. When the females saw him coming they said here comes the devil.

"Nobody's meddling," Dodson said, "we got an invitation from your boy."

"Don't mean shit to us," Charles said.

"You work for him, don't you?"

"More or less."

Calvin Wright, aka Black the Knife, came in, a little unsteady on his feet. "More or less?" he said. "Is that what you do, Charles, more or less? You ask me you do less." Cal was bloated, unshaven, his cornrows undone. He was wearing mirrored aviators, a black bathrobe plush as a fur coat, and velvet slippers with gold tassels on them. A big marmalade cat was lounging in his arms. The cologne smell was like a force field.

"Cal," Anthony said, "this is Isaiah Quintabe and Juanell Dodson."

"It's about damn time," Cal said. "Which one is Mr. Q?"

"My name is Isaiah," Isaiah said.

"Oh it is, is it?" Cal said. "Well, I don't give a fuck, Mr. Q. I'll call you whatever I feel like calling you and if you don't like it you and your name can get the fuck up outta my house."

Isaiah's eyes flared and he started to reply but Dodson cut him off. "It's a genuine pleasure to meet you, Cal," Dodson said. "I been following your music ever since *Up from Nothin'*, got every record you ever made. Did you know *The Scene* got a list of the top one hundred rap records of all time and they had you in there second? What kind of bullshit is that? How they gonna say Biggie's album is better than yours? I canceled my subscription right on the spot. Biggie *wishes* he could spit good as you."

"Well, I don't know about all that," Cal said. "I mean like Biggie's an OG, a forefather, I got much respect for the man."

"I do too but second? You know that ain't right."

"Yeah, I know, but what can I do? People feel sorry for the dead. Y'all want something to drink?"

"Thank you, Cal, but we're good," Dodson said, smiling at Isaiah.

"All right, everybody," Anthony said, like he was herding old people into the community room. "Let's get seated, shall we?"

Cal stood nuzzling the cat while the fellas arranged themselves on a U-shaped sofa that curled around a Sharp ninety-inch HD smart TV. The brothers sat on one end, Isaiah and Dodson on the other, Anthony in the middle with the remote. The TV screen was divided into a grid of six smaller screens, each showing a different part of the house, the images crisp, clear, and in color.

"This is Friday night," Anthony said.

The time code said 10:47. Cal came out of a bedroom and moved down the hall. He walked slowly with his feet close to the floor, almost gliding. In the hooded robe and aviators he looked like the Fly turned monk on his way to evening prayers. The house felt deserted, like people had escaped.

"I can speed this up," Anthony said, "nothing happens for a while."

"No, let it play," Isaiah said.

Anthony toggled the remote, the screens following Cal down the sweeping staircase through the foyer and into the living room, where he stopped to stare at some paintings before moving on.

"Please don't be offended," Dodson said, "these questions are just routine. Charles, where were you that night?"

"Clubbin' with Kartel and them," Charles said.

"I see. Would Kartel and them be available for an interview?"

"Fuck no."

Isaiah was cringing inside. Dodson was doing *CSI*.

"Bug was supposed to be here all night," Anthony said, "but he left early."

"Cal was asleep," Bug said. "What am I supposed to do here by myself?"

"Where did you go, Bug?" Dodson said.

"To see that PAWG," Charles said, smirking.

"What's a PAWG?" Anthony said.

"Phat Ass White Girl."

"Sorry I asked."

"We might want to contact the PAWG for further questioning," Dodson said. "Can I have her name?"

"Uh-huh," Bug said. "Her name is bitch."

Cal massaged the cat, feeling it purr through his fingertips. He recalled that night in some detail. Funny, because what he'd done since this morning was a blur. He remembered how glad he was when Bug left early and he was alone and how he'd dropped some pills and smoked a joint and how he'd gone through the house not believing all the shit he'd bought. What was he thinking, paying real money for a fourteenth-century Scottish battle-ax or the monogrammed platinum candlesticks or the chandeliers that looked like the spaceship from *Close Encounters* or the massive teak throne he'd never sat in or the seven-piece Mistral sectional that was still wrapped in plastic, and where did those paintings come from? His portrait didn't look anything like him. Since when did he have shoulders round as cannonballs and a stomach like six bricks were stuck under his skin? And what was so important about Michael Corleone sitting in an armchair that he had to be taking up space on the living room wall? Cal recognized Malcolm X in the third painting but couldn't remember anything about him except that Denzel played him in the movie.

Cal watched Anthony's cousin trying to play cop and not really pulling it off. It was hard to act official when you looked like Katt Williams.

"What time did you leave the house, Bug?" Dodson said.

"Ten-thirty," Bug said. "I locked up, turned the alarm on, checked the windows and doors, everything. I was gonna come back like I always do, two three in the morning."

"Anthony?" Dodson said. "What about you?"

"I went to see a friend," Anthony said, "and her name is none of your business."

"The mystery girl," Charles said, "if it *is* a girl. Where you get that sweater, man?"

Cal saw himself on the kitchen screen getting some takeout boxes out of the fridge. Strange, seeing yourself when you're high. Moving in slow motion, so out of it you had to think hard to remember what you were doing; no clue what was coming next. The other screens showed the hallway, the game room, and the backyard. The outside cams had night vision, everything in a green haze except the pool, the glow from the underwater lights wobbling on the patio and an ivy-covered wall, the second story of the Cape Cod just above it. The lawn separated the pool from a line of trees at the back of the property. Mr. Q was watching the tape like he was sucking in every pixel through his eyeballs. Charles was smiling, fucking with him like he did to everybody.

"What's up, Mr. Q?" Charles said. "Y'all figure it out yet? Got all your clues and shit, ready to make the bust?"

"You ain't gonna believe this," Bug said. "This shit is crazy."

"Could you be quiet, please?" Anthony said.

"Fuck you, Anthony," Charles said.

Except for Cal in the kitchen everything was still. The brothers leaned forward, smiling, nodding. "Watch this, watch this," Charles said.

On the backyard cam, a dog came out of the trees, its nose surfing the grass, its eyes gleaming in the green darkness. Cal shuddered under his bathrobe and felt like he had to pee.

Dodson looked at the dog like it was a twenty-foot crocodile. "Where'd he come from?" he said.

"The question of the hour," Anthony said.

The dog crossed the lawn and into the glow of the pool lights. You could tell right away it was a pit bull. The sledgehammer head, cropped ears, powerful chest, the wide belligerent stance. Dodson pulled his feet off the floor and turned his knees sideways. "That's a goddamn pit," he said. "I hate them muthafuckas."

The dog had no collar and no markings on its shiny black coat. And it was big. Really big. You could almost mistake it for a Great Dane. Cal had seen a lot of pits but never one that size.

"Watch this, watch this," Charles said.

Suddenly, the dog's ears shot up like someone was shouting its name—and then it started moving, uncertain at first, coming around the pool and stopping. Again, its ears shot up. Still hesitant, it crossed the patio, circled the gas barbecue, and went toward the house, its ears going up and down. It went under the portico and up to the back door.

"I hope that dog don't have a key," Dodson said.

"The shit gonna get crazy now," Bug said.

Cal remembered standing at the center island, eating takeout from a restaurant called the Natural. Barbecued tempeh with steamed kale and Jessica's Vegan Quinoa with Edamame. He hadn't quite figured out chopsticks yet, most of the food spilling onto the countertop and getting on his bathrobe. The book said this kind of diet would draw the toxins out of his body but it didn't say it would taste nasty or have no taste at all. He was about to get the Krispy Kremes out of the fridge when a dog came through the doggie door. At first, Cal was overjoyed, thinking Hella had escaped from Kwaylud and run all the way back from Atlanta to be with his master. But Hella was a Rottweiler and this was a pit bull. A big black muthafucka. Fear trickled into Cal's stomach, curdling the tempeh and shriveling the edamame. He didn't move, didn't make a sound. The dog remained by the doggie door, its eyes adjusting to the rows of recessed lights and the reflections off the stainless steel appliances and the white marble floor. It looked more like a movie monster than somebody's pet. Massive T. rex head, Iron Man chest, fangs like ivory daggers, its blacked-out pig eyes wide apart and ruthless. And it was panting slow. *Heh...heh...heh...heh.* The dog went still for a moment. Then it snarled, hunched down to get its legs underneath it, and launched itself across the kitchen like it was flung from a catapult.

"Oh SHIT!" Cal said. He turned for the door and caught a glimpse of the dog slipping on the travertine as it came around the island, sliding into the stove, a copper pot crashing to the floor. Cal ran into the hallway, his robe flapping open, the dog streaking after him with its ears pinned back, its nails scrabbling and clicking on the slippery floor. Cal got to the game room and juked between the chairs and tables, the dog right behind him. He saw his reflection in the sliding glass door, the dog about to pull him down like a lion on a wildebeest, but he one-hopped it from the sofa to the pool table and back down to the floor without breaking stride.

The dog went wide around the pool table giving Cal just enough time to reach the sliding door. He yanked it open, got outside and tried to close it but the dog was right on his heels, the heavy door slamming on its neck and holding it there like a hunting trophy. If the dog felt anything you couldn't tell. It squirmed, twisted, and snarled, slinging drool off its fangs. Cal leaned into the door handle with both hands, his legs out behind him like he was pushing a car, the dog berserk with blood lust. Cal started screaming like he was already being ripped apart. His legs were giving out, he was losing leverage, his slippers slipping on the bricks.

The dog got its shoulders through the door and was wriggling the rest of its body through. Cal let go of the door and ran across the patio, the dog on him in three strides, grabbing the back of the robe, jerking him to a halt. Cal leaned forward like a plow horse, grunting and straining, but the dog was strong, yanking on the robe with its legs splayed out in front of it. Cal was crying and slowly sinking to his knees. He hoped he'd die quick and not get disfigured, be like one of those burn victims you could hardly stand to look at. He couldn't hold out any longer, his knees were almost touching the ground—and then the robe ripped. Cal twisted free, stumbled forward, and went face-first into the pool. There was the shock of the temperature change and then it was peaceful, nothing but the sound of bubbles coming out of his nose. He thought he'd like to stay down here, away from the dog, away from the world—until he realized he couldn't breathe. Panic seized his lungs. He kicked and pawed his way upward, breaking the surface, taking huge choking breaths.

The dog was at the edge of the pool, barking relentlessly, leaning out over the water. Cal couldn't believe it when the beast dived in and started swimming right at him. This muthafucka was like the bad guy in *Terminator 2*. Cal tried to swim backward, flapping his arms and kicking, making more commotion than sharks in a feeding frenzy but staying in the same place. He was exhausted and every breath he took was mostly water. If he didn't drown on his own, the dog would drag him under. He couldn't go on anymore, too tired to dive or do anything else. The dog was approaching fast, only the blacked-out pig eyes above the surface.

The woman next door came out on her balcony. A rich bitch with nothing to do, always complaining about the music and the smell of weed. "The police are coming! The police are coming!" she shouted. Cal thought her next words were *you fucking nigger* but he might have imagined that. The dog didn't seem to care and kept coming. Five feet away, four, three . . . Cal could see down its throat, smell its sour breath—and then its ears shot up like they had on the patio and it veered away. Cal had never been so happy in his whole life. With a new burst of energy, he flapped his way to the edge of the pool. And then he heard what the dog had heard. *Sirens,* and they were getting louder. He shouted at them: "I'm in the swimming pool! Help my ass!"

Isaiah watched the tape, trying to wrap his head around what he was seeing. Someone sent a *dog* to kill Cal? Someone used a dog like an *assassin*. Who would do that?

On the tape, Cal had made it to the edge of the pool, the woman next door yelling nonstop. The dog was in a panic, paddling furiously to get out of the pool.

"What's the dog gonna do now?" Dodson said. "How's he gonna get out?"

Isaiah focused on the trees at the back of the property. The man would come from there, nowhere else he could be. And then he appeared. He was wearing a ski mask, cargo shorts, a T-shirt that said THE WHITE STRIPES, and big rubber shoes like clogs.

"Who's that?" Dodson said.

"Exactly," Anthony said.

The man jogged across the lawn. Isaiah had him in his late twenties, five-ten or eleven, a hundred and sixty-five pounds, in good shape. He had an awkward up-and-down gait, his arms going back and forth like a speed-walker. The woman leaned over the railing to yell, as if she wasn't being loud enough. He ignored her and drew a handgun with a long barrel. She screamed and fled inside. The man got to the pool and saw Cal way down at the end just as the flashing lights of a police car flickered red against the house next door. The cops were in the cul-de-sac. The man thought a moment, put the gun away, and said something to the dog. Then he walked alongside the pool, leading the dog to the shallow end. He jumped into the waist-deep water, grabbed the dog under its hindquarters, and lifted-shoved it over the edge of the pool and onto the cement. The man got out and the two of them trotted back into the trees.

Moments later, the police came around the side of the house with their guns drawn. Cal shouted at them, waved—and sank. The action was over but Charles and Bug were still watching the tape like this was the good part, chuckling and nudging each other.

"How a nigga gonna have a pool and can't swim?" Charles said.

"I bet he don't leave dry land for the rest of his life," Bug said.

"You two niggas see something funny?" Cal said, freezing their shit. The cat was looking at them as if to say *You unemployable muthafuckas are in trouble now.* "'Cause what I see is your meal ticket almost drowned to death," Cal said. "Oh there's gonna be some housecleanin' around here, y'all can believe that."

The fellas got up and started moving around. Isaiah kept staring at the screen, trying to process what he'd seen.

"Cal, do you want to tell Isaiah about the situation?" Anthony said, nodding instead of saying can we get on with it.

"Situation?" Cal said. "What situa—oh yeah, right, right, yeah, Mr. Q is here."

Dodson bit Isaiah's tongue off with a look. "How can we help you, Cal?" he said.

"You can help me by putting that evil bitch Noelle in jail," Cal said. "Get some video or some fingerprints or some DNA. You know, police-type shit, get her locked up where she belongs. Let her do her diva thing with them women got the short hair, no makeup, and mop handles."

"Cal thinks his ex-wife is behind the dog attack," Anthony said, giving Isaiah a look.

"I don't *think* she's behind the attack," Cal said. "She *is* behind it, ain't no doubt about it. Who else would want to kill me with a goddamn dog? Only an evil bitch would think that shit up. I might wake up tomorrow morning with a dinosaur after my ass."

"I'd like to talk to you privately, Cal," Isaiah said.

"You need to know something, ask Anthony," Cal said, moving for the door. "That's what I pay him for. I'm gonna take a nap, y'all niggas leave me be."

"What about the album?" Charles said.

"Fuck the album and fuck you for bringing it up, Charles."

"Aw, come on, Cal, we got work to do," Bug said.

"You mean *I* got work to do. You muthafuckas ain't got shit to do. Nail her ass to the wall for me, Mr. Q. Did Anthony tell you about the bonus?" Cal shuffled out of the room, the tension easing like someone had turned off a smoke detector.

"Really, Isaiah," Anthony said, "I know this must seem ridiculous to you. If you don't want to take the case it's okay. We'll pay you for your time."

"Don't let him off the hook," Charles said. "Nigga's supposed to know something."

"Yeah, *IQ*," Bug said, "what you got to say?"

"How did the man on the video direct the dog to the doggie door?" Isaiah said, talking to himself.

"He told it to," Charles said.

"You mean he was shouting all that time? He'd have to when the dog was on the other side of the pool and for all he knew Cal might have heard him. No, he did something else."

"Like what?" Charles said. "Send it a text?"

Isaiah meandered over to the pool table, picked up the nine ball, and let it slow-roll out of his hand.

"I told you this wasn't gonna be shit," Charles said.

"This will go a lot faster if you let the man think," Anthony said.

"Thank you, Anthony," Dodson said. "Isaiah cogitates best when there are no distractions."

"What's he need to cogitate for?" Charles said. "He saw what we saw."

The nine ball bounced gently off the far cushion and came back, Isaiah cupping his hand over it. "Whistles," he said.

"Did you say whistles?" Dodson said.

"The man was using whistles, giving the dog directions like those sheepherders do with their dogs. Like a high-low for going left and low-high for going right. The dog's ears went up every time he made a turn."

"But why use a dog at all?" Anthony said. "It makes no sense."

"Yeah," Charles said, "it's stupid."

"If you're the hit man, you're on a deadline," Isaiah said, drifting toward the glass door. "You'd have to be. Nobody would hire you to kill somebody without a time frame, but the hit man didn't plan on Cal staying in the house for three weeks. The alternative was shooting him through a window but the drapes were always closed. The hit man's only option at that point was to get *inside* the house but he couldn't because there's an alarm and cameras and people with guns. So now what does he do?" Isaiah reached the glass door and looked out at the pool. "He sends in his killer dog."

Anthony was nodding. Charles was rubbing his goatee. Bug's face was screwed up like it was too much information.

"Any questions?" Dodson said.

CHAPTER FOUR
The Hatchet Man

June 2013

Three weeks before the dog attack on the rapper, Kurt walked along the Santa Monica Pier, unconsciously massaging his arm and reminding himself that that was his name today. The weather matched his shitty mood. The air was damp, the sky a washed-out gray, the ocean dark and sluggish. There was a breeze but it wasn't strong enough to blow away the smell of grease, stale popcorn, French fries, and hot dog water. The only decent thing out here was the old-fashioned merry-go-round. The rest was a bunch of stupid rides, fast-food stands, kiosks selling hats and key chains, and a restaurant called Bubba Gump's from that boring movie about the retarded guy. Some old gook asked him if he wanted his name painted on a grain of rice. "What for?" Kurt said. "Who's gonna read it?" He joined a family of foreign tourists watching the most interesting thing out here, a Mexican guy reeling in a spiny brown fish. "You eat that and you'll be shitting mercury," Kurt said.

They called him the Hatchet Man, a ground-and-pound heavy-weight with an eighteen-and-eight record. His last fight was against a Korean fireplug nicknamed Seoul Man. With a minute to go in the second round, Seoul Man locked Hatchet Man up in a vicious arm bar. The pain was unbearable but his face was smushed into Seoul Man's right calf and his arm was pinned under the Korean's left leg. He couldn't speak and he couldn't tap out. The ref called it when he heard Hatchet Man's ligaments pop and his humerus splintering like a green twig. Everybody in the arena groaned. A guy in the front row threw up.

Three surgeries and months of rehab later, Hatchet Man regained some arm strength but nothing like before. Some of the nerves were permanently damaged and it was more comfortable carrying the arm at an angle. He could unbend it if he wanted to but his range of motion was limited. Still, he was dangerous. Some guy in Dona-hue's made a wisecrack about the arm and Hatchet wrapped it around his neck like a python and choked him into unconscious-ness. But bar fights weren't cage fights and he had to retire. Now he was doing security for one of DStar's clients.

Kurt took the wide wooden stairs leading down from the pier to the parking lot and the beach. The lot was almost empty. He walked along the second aisle from the right, trying to look nonchalant. Just a regular two-hundred-and-forty-three-pound guy in a lime-green muscle shirt and beaded dreadlocks, jagged scars under both cheekbones, his right ear shredded to nothing and an arm bent like he was escorting a date to the prom. It made him nervous, knowing he was being watched. All this cloak-and-dagger stuff was bullshit. He'd refused to do the job himself so the boss had him call DStar for a reference. That man knew people.

"You want somebody dead, my guy won't let you down," DStar said. "He's a real lunatic. I mean they're *all* lunatics but this guy is—" DStar hesitated like he couldn't find the words. "Let me put it this way. He *always* gets it done."

What's a real lunatic that always gets it done? Kurt thought. Would the guy come cartwheeling across the sand dressed like a ninja or pop up out of the ocean wearing a headband and firing an M16?

A homeless guy was sitting on a parking block holding a cardboard sign that said HUNGRY. He was filthy like he'd been living with wolves, bundled up in an old gray blanket, rags wrapped around his feet.

"Sir, can you spare some change?" he said.

"Get a job, you fuck," Kurt said.

There was a business-type guy sitting in a convertible Benz and thumbing a text. Kurt slowed as he walked past but the guy didn't look up. Now a knock-kneed Asian girl wearing complicated high heels tottered toward him like a baby giraffe, Kurt wondering if the girl, the rice-painting guy, and Seoul Man all knew each other. The girl smiled and made eye contact, Kurt thinking no, it couldn't be.

"This is way to pier?" she said.

Kurt looked at the pier big as life and looked at her. She couldn't be the hitter, she was too stupid. "Yeah," he said, "this is the way to the pier." He kept going and reached the end of the lot. The beach was empty except for a bunch of seagulls camping on the sand. He waited, getting pissed off, not knowing if he should stand around like a dummy or blow the whole thing off.

"Kurt? I'm Fluke." It was the kid with the HUNGRY sign, Kurt wondering why anybody would choose Fluke as a code name.

It was hard to tell what he looked like underneath the dirt and the wig. You'd have a tough time picking him out of a lineup, which was no doubt the point. Even so, you knew right away something was off about him. It was the eyes—twinkling and vicious. They reminded Kurt of that serial killer who dressed up like a clown to entertain the kiddies.

"You mind telling me why we had to meet out here?" Kurt said.

"Right, right," Fluke said, frowning. "We should have done a Deep Throat. You know, met in an underground parking garage at midnight and be the only two people down there." He snapped his fingers. "Or the art museum! Yeah, sit in front of the *Mona Lisa* and pretend like we don't know each other!" Kurt didn't crack a smile. "No, seriously," Fluke said, "I can see the whole deal from here." He wiped a hand across the length of the pier. "Who's coming, who's going, who's walking in a loop, who's standing at the rail doing nothing. Basically it's a tradecraft thing."

Kurt was self-conscious talking to someone who looked like a bum. He didn't talk to bums, hippies, or college types. He was afraid someone might think they were friends or mistake him for one of those assholes that marched around with signs when a black guy got shot.

"Hope you don't mind but I need to search you," Fluke said. They stepped behind his F-150 with a camper on the back. "Wow, you're like solid muscle," he said. "It's like patting down a tree. Say, could you turn your phone off? I'd like to watch you do it."

They sat in the truck with the stereo on. A bunch of dickheads screaming and banging on guitars.

"You're really DStar's guy?" Kurt said, turning down the volume.

"Yup, I'm him," Fluke said, turning it back up. "Whose guy are you?"

"Funny. How come you picked *Fluke?*"

"That's what everything is, right?"

The guy had a point. Fluke looked out at the ocean. "There's supposed to be five-foot swells at First Point. I should have brought my board. You surf?"

"Surfing? You want to talk about surfing?"

"Oh I guess you can't, huh? The arm?"

Kurt could do most everything with the arm except jerk off and reach the top shelf in the supermarket. He wanted to use it now. Grab this asshole by his hair and slam him into the dashboard.

"I've got a disability too," Fluke said. "Four toes on my left foot. Can you believe it? Were you born that way or was it an accident?"

"You know, you don't really seem like a hit man," Kurt said.

"Oh yeah? What do I seem like?"

"A kid playing dress-up."

Fluke smiled like he was glad Kurt had said that. "You've got to see this," he said, already getting out of the truck.

Kurt watched Fluke set a backpack on the hood and dig out a Nikon 8X monocular. Fluke scanned the pier like a pirate. "Bear with me," he said. "Gotta find the right one . . . okay." He gave Kurt the monocular. "There's a girl right next to Bubba Gump's."

A pasty-faced Goth girl was straddling the rail and eating a corn dog, a guy with a hooded army jacket talking to her. "Yeah, I see her," Kurt said. "What about her?" He heard Fluke rustling in the backpack.

"Just stay on her," Fluke said. "Don't let her out of your sight."

Thirty long seconds went by, Fluke saying hang in there, hang in there, stay on her, stay on 'errrr. Kurt was about to tell this asshole to fuck off when he heard a coughing sound and the Goth girl's corn dog blew up, cornmeal and wienie shrapnel splattering all over her, the army jacket guy saying oh fuck oh fuck.

Kurt lowered the monocular. Fluke had his elbows resting on the hood, hands gripping a handgun with a long barrel, not even a scope on it, a wisp of smoke pirouetting out of the suppressor.

"Not bad, huh?" Fluke said. "For a kid that plays dress-up?"

DStar was right, Kurt thought. This guy really *was* a lunatic.

They got the hell out of there and drove to Palisades Park, a green strip overlooking Pacific Coast Highway. Fluke insisted they use his truck. For all he knew, Kurt had a recording device in the Vette he'd parked two blocks away from the pier. Every time you see a woman talking to an undercover cop she thinks is a hit man, where are they? In a car.

Fluke hopped over the balustrade and stood on the edge of the bluff yelling what's up, bitches at the cars a hundred feet below.

"Could you get off of there?" Kurt said. "You're making me nervous."

"What's the deal?" Fluke said.

"A rapper. He needs to not be here anymore."

Fluke never asked the reason for killing somebody. Not knowing made it more like a job. Like he was a dentist and a tooth needed pulling. "A rapper, huh? Is he black?"

"Why? You only do white guys?"

"No, I'll do your parakeet if you want me to. Remember that scene in *Dumb and Dumber* when Jim Carrey sold the dead parakeet to the blind kid?"

"It has to be a drive-by."

Fluke was disappointed. Drive-bys were boring. He liked to be creative, do new things, surprise his clients; get that *holy shit* reaction. You did *what?* Then they'd laugh or shake their heads or look like Kurt did when the corn dog blew up. Fluke used a tactical

87

crossbow on a whistle-blowing bureaucrat. Put a titanium hunting bolt through the guy's neck while he was washing his minivan. He set a bear trap for a gourmet lawyer who liked to go mushroom hunting in the woods. When the jaws of the trap snapped shut on the lawyer's leg he went into shock, blacked out, and bled to death. Another one of Fluke's targets was an elderly Japanese woman. Her son was into the yakuza loan sharks and he needed his inheritance a little early. Fluke backed her into her koi pond with a samurai sword and she drowned.

Fluke picked up a rock and flung it down at the cars.

"What are you doing? You could hurt somebody," Kurt said.

"When do you want this done?"

"The sooner the better." Kurt gave him the details and paid him the deposit. "What if you can't pull it off?" he said.

"Basically?" Fluke said. "That's never happened."

CHAPTER FIVE

That's Where the Best Dreams Are

May 2005

Everything Dodson owned was in three garbage bags and a cardboard box. "You need to travel light when you homeless," he said. "I almost got me a shopping cart." Isaiah gave him some bedding and space in the closet and Dodson was officially a tenant. He lay out on the sofa, his hands behind his head like he was at the beach getting a tan. "Home sweet muthafuckin' home," he said.

The money issue resolved, Isaiah got his first decent night's sleep since the accident, but when he woke up the next morning he couldn't believe he'd done something so stupid. Let Dodson, a bona fide gangsta, stay in the apartment Isaiah had shared with Marcus since forever. And it was Saturday. Isaiah had to work at Manny's until six and Dodson would be here alone. Isaiah sat on the edge of the bed with his head in his hands. "What did you do?" he said. "What did you *do?*"

All day long Isaiah scraped gravy and potato salad off the plates and racked them in the dishwasher, imagining Dodson and his gangsta friends turning the apartment into a shambles. After he got off work he ran all the way home and bounded up the fire stairs. The hallway smelled like fried meat but he didn't hear rap music or the TV when he got to the door. He made extra noise with the keys, afraid he might surprise somebody and get shot. "Hey," he said.

Everything was the same as when he left this morning. Neat as a pin. Nothing missing, nothing broken. He could smell fabric softener, Dodson's T-shirts and underwear were folded neatly on the sofa. A frying pan and some dishes were in the drying rack but the kitchen was spotless. So was the bathroom but it was disturbing, smelling a different shampoo, the air humid from a stranger taking a shower. Isaiah checked the drain, not a hair in it. "Well I'll be," he said.

Isaiah had gone to work by the time Dodson got up. He felt good, his life settled for the time being. He took a shower and put his dirty clothes in the machines downstairs. He decided to make breakfast and went to Vons for groceries.

Dodson grated some potatoes, melted butter in a pan, and got the hash browns going. Then he fried some ham and scrambled three eggs the way Lupita taught him. He remembered her in those panties that said CASH ONLY on the back, whipping the eggs so hard she jiggled under her T-shirt.

"You have to get air in them," she said. "That's what keeps them light. Stop looking at my ass, pendejo."

Dodson's eggs came out moist and fluffy. By then the hash browns had a crust on them, the ham was still warm, the sourdough toast slathered with butter. He took a moment to admire the plate. "Like the cover of a Denny's menu," he said.

Dodson ate slowly, shaking his head with pleasure, timing it so there was just enough toast left to wipe up the last bit of egg. After, he watched some classic Mike Tyson fights on TV, clipped his toenails into a wastebasket, and thought about calling Kinkee and them. Get them to come over, see the new place, smoke some weed, play *GTA*. But Kinkee and them would raid the fridge, spill their drinks, drop their joints between the sofa cushions, miss the toilet, and piss on the wall. Better to leave the fellas out of it, tell them he was staying with a girl somewhere.

Dodson and the fellas dealt drugs out of an apartment on the backside of an old commercial building. The landlord had cut the building up into individual units, eight or ten people living in a tiny room, two bathrooms per floor. They called the apartment the House. They moved it every few weeks for security reasons but no matter what the location it was always the same. Cavelike and musty, windows too milky to see through, the drapes in shreds, black patches on the floor where the linoleum was torn off, the walls covered with gang signs and pictures of big dicks. The bathrooms were always terrifying. The rent was shared by Dodson, Kinkee, Sedrick, and Freddie G. Everybody strapped. Get bold enough to try a robbery and you'd be hard-pressed to get out alive.

Dodson got his dope from Kinkee, who got his dope from Junior, top of the food chain. Nobody knew if Junior was the name on his birth certificate or if there was a Senior Junior running around somewhere. Junior didn't come to the House much and seemed to spend most of his time getting chauffeured around in a massive white Navigator with blacked-out windows, gold BBS rims, and a sound system you felt through the sidewalk before you heard it. Junior liked to use big words to make himself sound smart but it usually had the opposite effect. Once Dodson heard him say: "This female had the most magnanimous titties I have ever substantiated." Michael Stokely was his wheelman, Booze Lewis rode shotgun, both of them looking like their mug shots and armed like SEAL Team 6.

Junior bought kilos of raw cocaine from a cartel connection in Boyle Heights. He added his cut and sold it in halves, quarters, and eighths to block captains like Kinkee. Kinkee added his cut, cooked the cocaine into crack, and sold it rocked up to low-level dealers like Dodson, everybody doubling their money. On most days Dodson made more than his colleagues. He never hyped his product, didn't make fun of his customers or demand a blow job, and he put a little extra in the bag when the quality was low.

The worst thing about the job was the working conditions. Serving it up to a sad parade of glassy-eyed dope fiends; twitching, scabs on their faces, brown teeth gapped as gravestones, rambling on about a situation with their associates or the government drone that was following them around night and day. Some of the customers lit up right in front of you, the crack fumes smelling like burnt rubber, clouds of it swirling into an atmosphere already thick with weed smoke, Thunderbird, and body funk. It was a wonder you didn't get cancer just being there. Most of the fiends came and went as fast as they could but there were always a few more discriminating shoppers who held the rock up to the light and said is this the good shit?

Dodson was bored and restless. The House was more suffocating than usual and business was slow. Kinkee was down to kibbles and bits, the crackheads finding better product elsewhere. Dodson went outside to get a breath of fresh air that smelled like dirt, weeds, and dogshit. There wouldn't be any new product until Junior did his reup run to Boyle Heights. Until then, it was a lot of waiting around. Dodson knew he needed a new hustle, something more worthy of his talents; something that wouldn't get him arrested, shot, or killed by asphyxiation. What exactly that hustle would be he hadn't figured out.

An hour went by and no more customers came in so Dodson went back to the apartment. He took a long shower, scrubbing himself with a loofah to get the stink off. Isaiah was almost never home. On the rare occasions when they were in the apartment together they were self-conscious and careful, like there were hidden rules and neither of them knew what they were. It wasn't hard for Dodson to figure out who the apartment belonged to. There was an older guy in the photos on the bookshelf who was probably Isaiah's brother, who was most likely dead and that was no doubt the reason Isaiah was so messed up. His face was either blank as Dodson's math assignment or his eyes were tight and his jaw hard-set like he was about to smack somebody. He stayed out on the balcony for hours, holding his head in his hands or staring into the dark. Late at night, Dodson could hear him pacing around the bedroom talking to himself; low and fierce with some crying mixed in. Dodson was afraid the boy was cracking up.

When Dodson got out of the shower, he changed and went to the kitchen to get something to eat. Isaiah was on the floor messing with the back compartment of the refrigerator. There were tools, wires, and electrical parts scattered around him and his hands were black with grime. "What're you doing?" Dodson said.

"Fridge had a leak on the low side," Isaiah said. "Condenser's shot."

"I got food in there."

"Everything's in the sink."

Dodson was impressed. The refrigerator was a scary appliance, that cage on the back holding in a nest of killer bees, the ones that kept buzzing on and off.

Isaiah grunted, struggling to remove what looked like a midget kettle barbecue.

"What's that?" Dodson said.

"Condenser," Isaiah said. He put it aside and maneuvered another one into the vacated space. "This one might be in worse shape than the one I took out."

"Where'd it come from?" Dodson said.

"One-oh-four. Got it out of that fridge."

"The door was open?"

"No."

"What, you picked the lock? Used a bump key?"

Isaiah didn't answer, focusing a little too hard on what he was doing. Dodson smiled. "Damn, Isaiah," he said, "if I'd have known you was into thievery we could have robbed the whole building."

"I'm not into thievery."

"You are now."

Isaiah could be an asset, Dodson thought. Someone to be used and profited from. All those awards on the wall and now he was repairing the fridge. No telling what else the boy could do.

When the fridge was humming again, Isaiah went to clean up and when he came back, Dodson was cutting up some defrosted chicken. He was stripped to the waist, his body thin like a cell phone and hard as a railroad spike, illegible tats on his chest. A swarm of scars covered his left arm and back. They were shiny and welted, some circular like bullet holes, others ragged blotches. Isaiah wanted to ask about them but didn't.

"Stir that for me," Dodson said. A soup kettle had something that looked like mud bubbling in it.

"What is this?" Isaiah said.

"A roux—stir the muthafucka 'fore it burns—stir faster and scrape the bottom—yeah, like that."

Isaiah stirred the mystery mud while Dodson chopped some vegetables and smashed a few garlic cloves with the back of a knife. "I'm a bad muthafucka in the kitchen," Dodson said. "Don't even have to be soul food. My lasagna is off the planet. You ever seen that show *Iron Chef*? It's like a contest, got these dudes called Iron Chefs. They like the Michael Jordans of the kitchen. They go up against these other chefs from all around the world and they some bad muthafuckas too. So then they give 'em a secret ingredient like ham hocks or corn on the cob and they gotta make four or five dishes with it. Cats is bad ass too. Them dudes make all kinds of crazy shit. Bobby Flay? That motherfucker can turn a soup bone into a birthday cake. I need to get on that show. I believe I could give Bobby a run for his money."

Dodson poured hot chicken broth into the roux, added the chicken, some cut-up chorizo, the vegetables, the garlic, a few spices, and what looked to be a dried leaf. Then he put on some rice, measuring the water by eye. He did all this with a kid's enthusiasm. Stirring, tasting, adding salt and pepper. "Lupita Tello, you know her?" Dodson said. "I was hittin' that 'til she moved to the Valley. Girl wanted to be a chef, taught me how to cook, said I had a knack for it. You know, different techniques, what tastes good with what. Even my old man liked my cooking. I had something going on the stove he be looking over my shoulder talking 'bout, what you got happening there, Private? You make enough for the troops? Muthafucka was in the marines. Didn't know how to talk to you unless he was giving you an order. You *will* make your rack every morning rain or shine. You *will* be back in this house by oh five hundred. Muthafucka liked to *you will* me to death." Dodson checked the rice and trimmed the stems off some okra. "Yeah, he did a few tours in Iraq," he said. "They be banging for real over there. Make our shit look like kindergarten. Messed him up too. He was drinking that vodka like strawberry Kool-Aid, went to work drunk every day. He was an inventory manager at Best Buy 'til they fired his ass for sleeping in his car. He took the whole family back to Oakland, that's where I'm from." Dodson threw up some gang signs. "Northern Cali, baby, West Coast on the Bay." He woot-wooted like a train. "You got any hot sauce?"

"Cupboard on the left."

The mystery mud was a gumbo. Thick and rich, served over rice with okra fried crisp, the color of maple syrup. Isaiah ate like food was new to him, taking cautious bites and nodding his head. "Good," he said, "real good." But he couldn't taste a thing. He felt self-conscious, Dodson watching him, looking for more of a reaction.

"That okra's good, ain't it?" he said. "Soak it in vinegar first, get the slime off."

"Yeah, that's good too."

After he'd eaten all he could stand, he pushed the rest of the food into a pile so it would look like he'd eaten more. He thanked Dodson and went to his room to do his homework. All his classes were Advanced Placement. Environmental science, calculus, computer science, human geography.

"I know your classes are hard," Marcus said, "but they're the pathway to your dreams. Lots of folks can't stay on their pathway or their dreams don't make sense. Look at those kids on *American Idol,* the ones that don't make the cut. Can't sing worth a damn and what do they always say after they've been humiliated? But it's my dream and Mariah Carey said I shouldn't give up! Yeah, well, you don't have Mariah Carey's voice so get that dumb-ass dream out of your head. What Mariah Carey *should* be telling them is to follow their abilities and *make* a dream out of what God gave them." Marcus smiled that big sunny smile and saw the future in Isaiah's eyes. "God gave you wings so you could fly up that pathway to the very top," he said. "That's where the best dreams are."

Isaiah always thought Marcus should have been an engineer or an architect but he'd only just graduated high school when their mother died during an operation and their father fell into a deep depression and killed himself. Marcus was left caring for a ten-year-old boy and ended up a jack-of-all-trades. Isaiah had watched for signs of disappointment but never saw any or heard anything in Marcus's voice. He always sounded like things had turned out exactly the way he'd planned them.

Isaiah couldn't finish his homework. He slung his books into the wall and stormed around the bedroom spitting out words like cobra strikes. *Fucking Marcus. How could you do that? Why didn't you look? Are you stupid? Fucking Marcus. What am I supposed to do now?* It was happening all the time now, the rage boiling up inside his chest, threatening to explode and kill everyone around him. He stopped and stood there with his fists clenched and nothing to punch. It was luck how things turned out so why even try if you were going to get hit by a car? Why not coast if your fate wasn't in your hands? Why do anything at all if Marcus wasn't there?

Isaiah's anger was consuming him. It had nowhere to go,

nothing to focus on. He knew if he went on this way he'd end up in a mental ward. He was out on the balcony at dawn when the idea came to him, lifting and warming like the morning sun on his face. He'd go after Marcus's killer. Find him. Hunt him down, tell him he didn't kill just anyone, he killed Marcus, the best person in the world—*and then make that murdering piece of shit pay.*

CHAPTER SIX

Burnout

July 2013

Isaiah and Dodson went around the pool and headed toward the stand of ficus trees at the back of Cal's property. The dog and the man had come from there.

"You talk too much," Isaiah said. "All that stuff about do you have any reason to believe—"

"I'm trying to give you the appearance of professionalism," Dodson said.

"Didn't I tell you about this? Didn't I tell you I do things my own way?"

"You ask me, your way needs a serious overhaul, you hope to make it in times like these. You can't be standing there talking to yourself and staring off into space like some kinda damn psychic. You need to communicate with your clients, be optimistic, make them feel like they getting something for their money."

"They'll feel like they're getting something for their money when they get something for their money."

They arrived at the trees and saw a cluster of footprints on the damp ground. The dog prints were big, like the clawed feet on

Auntie May's antique chifforobe. Isaiah kneeled and took a closer look. Dodson knew the crew was watching from the house so he kneeled next to Isaiah and pointed at a nonexistent clue.

"What you looking for?" Dodson said. "We already know the dog and the dog man was here."

"The dog man was wearing Crocs," Isaiah said. "Those big goofy rubber things with holes in them? The brand name is imprinted on the sole, see it there?"

"What are all those?" Dodson said. There were dozens of cylindrical impressions about eighteen inches long, all of them facing the same way.

"One of those low beach chairs," Isaiah said. "The dog man sat here watching the house."

"Why didn't he watch from out front?"

"Private security would have been on him. Nobody parks in the street."

It was just like old times, Dodson thought, trying to trip Isaiah up or make him say I don't know. "If the dog man was back here how could he tell when to send in the dog?"

"He was here for weeks," Isaiah said. "He knew what the cars sounded like. When they all left he knew Cal was alone."

Behind the trees, a tall wooden fence separated Cal's property from an alley where the trash bins were picked up. A hole had been cut in the fence just big enough for a man and his dog to get through.

"Well, guess we know how he got in," Dodson said. "I think that's Bobby Grimes."

Bobby Grimes was hustling across the lawn, the crew hurrying to catch up. "You must be Mr. Quintabe," he said. "I'm Bobby Grimes. I've heard a lot about you."

"Pleasure to meet you," Dodson said. "I'm Isaiah's senior associate, Juanell Dodson. My card."

Bobby pinched the card like it was a live grasshopper. He was sharp in his cobalt-blue Savile Row suit and white shirt open at the neck, the wink of a platinum Piaget just under his cuff. "I'm afraid I'm short on time so I'll get right to the point," he said. "Now I'm sorry to have to say this but from my perspective this investigation of yours is a complete waste of time. Yes, I've seen the video and I realize the murder attempt was real and that we should all be concerned but there's nothing we can do about it right now except take precautions and go about our business."

"Bobby's right," Charles said. "I mean like, we got to get the show on the road, do what we do."

"Was I talking to you?" Bobby said. "No, I wasn't. And until I do, why don't you keep your trap shut?"

"Damn, Bobby," Bug said. "Why you gotta be like that?"

"When I need to hear from you, big boy, I'll wave a ham sandwich," Bobby said.

"Cal says Noelle set up the dog attack," Isaiah said.

"Oh please," Anthony said. "Noelle hates Cal but even she wouldn't do something that ridiculous."

"Who else would want to kill Cal?" Isaiah said.

"Who doesn't?" Charles said. "Cal fucked over all kinds of people. There's niggas back in Inglewood still want to shoot his ass."

"Kwaylud," Bug said. "They been beefin' since the old days."

"What's important right now," Bobby said, glaring at the brothers, "is getting Cal back into the studio. The rest of this mess is a distraction."

"How long were Cal and Noelle married?" Isaiah said.

"Three years," Anthony said.

"Kids?"

"No. Why?"

"No kids and a short marriage, the judge probably gave her alimony for half that time. She might be out of money. Did Cal have life insurance?"

"Oh please, are we really going there?" Anthony said.

"Will you listen to this Columbo muthafucka?" Charles said.

"Yes, Mr. Quintabe," Bobby said, "Cal has life insurance. I wouldn't want you finding out for yourself and thinking you've accomplished something. There's a five-million-dollar policy on Cal's life and a condition of the divorce was that he continue to pay the premiums. Does that answer your question?"

Isaiah just looked at him.

"All right, let's approach this from a different direction, shall we?" Bobby said. "Suppose it *is* Noelle who tried to kill Cal for the life insurance."

"It isn't," Anthony said.

"It could take weeks or even months to resolve this, if it can be resolved at all. And Calvin doesn't have weeks or months. He's contractually obliged to make my record by Monday after next and the longer this so-called investigation goes on, the longer he has an excuse to hide in his house."

"What do you want from me?" Isaiah said.

"Cal doesn't listen to his friends anymore, but he might listen to you," Bobby said. "I want you to tell him that what he wants isn't possible and that it's perfectly safe for him to go back to work and make my record."

"I don't know it isn't possible and I don't know that he's safe. Whoever wants Cal dead was serious enough about it to hire a hit man."

"Oh now we're assuming it was a professional? Why couldn't it be somebody from his past?"

"That's what I said," Charles said.

"Shut up, Charles."

"You mean that white man on the video is somebody from Inglewood or one of Kwaylud's crew?" Isaiah said.

"He could be one of those rapper-hating rednecks," Bobby said. "Cal gets threats from those kinds of people all the time. You're jumping to conclusions, Mr. Quintabe."

"The man wasn't in a panic when he came out of the trees," Isaiah said. "And when the police lights started flashing, did you see what he did? He hesitated, he was thinking. Cal was at the far end of the pool. If the man went down there and shot him he might not have had enough time to come back, save his dog, and get away, the police were in front of the house. And he knew he wasn't going to drag that big wet dog out of the water, it weighed almost as much as he did. So he led it to the shallow end and got in the pool himself where he had leverage. Could you have been that calm in that situation? And did you see that gun? It had an extra-long barrel. The Glock the cops carry has a seven-inch barrel. The one on the man's gun was at least nine, had to be custom-made. And it was shaped like a tube, what they call a bull barrel. You see them on target guns made for accuracy. But even with a gun like that, hitting somebody through a window who might be moving is not an easy shot from what, thirty-five, forty yards away, especially without a scope. If you've got that kind of confidence, you know how to shoot. And remember now, this guy had been sitting in these trees for three weeks, maybe more. No unpaid redneck would do that because he hated rap music. This man had patience. This man was used to pressure. This man was a pro."

"Any questions?" Dodson said.

There was a moment of quiet, Isaiah and Bobby looking at each other. "All right, Mr. Quintabe," Bobby said, "I can see you won't be persuaded otherwise, so let me put this another way. Assuming we take all the necessary precautions, will you reassure Calvin as a personal favor to me? I'll owe you one, and Bobby Grimes owing you one is no small thing."

"Can't do it," Isaiah said. "I work for my client, not you."

"Be realistic," Anthony said. "You guys have got nothing to go on except a videotape of a dog attack. Where would you even start?"

"An excellent point, Anthony," Bobby said. "The fact of the matter is, you're starting from less than zero, Mr. Quintabe. As far as I know you have no police connections and I'm more than certain Noelle won't talk to you voluntarily. Where in fact *would* you start?"

"The hit man is the only link to whoever hired him," Isaiah said, "and the only link to the hit man is the dog."

Everybody waited for him to go on but he didn't.

"What are you saying, Mr. Quintabe?" Bobby said. "That you're going to *find* that dog? That *particular* dog?"

"That's stupid," Charles said.

Dodson looked like he was about to say it too.

"I'm sorry," Anthony said, "but for once, I agree with Charles. How is it possible to find one pit bull in a city full of pit bulls?"

"I'll call if I come up with something," Isaiah said, turning to go.

"You're on a fool's journey, Mr. Quintabe," Bobby said.

"That's okay. I've been a fool before."

As soon as they got in the car Dodson said: "How're you gonna find that dog? There's a million of 'em out there and it could be from anywhere. Long Beach, Compton, Carson, Lawndale. Shit. East LA got more pit bulls than people."

"The hit man isn't from the hood," Isaiah said.

"How do you know?"

"He wears Crocs, for one thing. And you saw the security footage. Remember his T-shirt? Do you know anybody from the hood that listens to the White Stripes?"

"What if the hit man ain't from around here? What if he's from Mexico or Miami? For all you know he could be back there right now."

"You mean when the hit man found out Cal wasn't leaving his house and he went back to Miami or Mexico to get his dog? No, he's local."

"What does local mean? His house is driving distance from Woodland Hills. *Mexico* is driving distance from Woodland Hills. You arguing just to argue now. Ain't no way in hell to find that dog."

It was eleven o'clock in the morning. Noelle was in bed wrapped in a silk kimono with pink and black birds on it and talking on the phone. "Say that again?" she said. "Cal hired a detective? When did this happen? Well, why didn't you tell me sooner? Oh yes, it *is* a problem. I swear to God, that damn Calvin will plague me until the bitter end."

Before she married Cal, Noelle was a singer in the Mary J. Blige mold. Bobby Grimes had her under contract but her career stalled out because she had the voice but not the soul. She met Cal singing backup on one of his albums. He was drawn to her elegant beauty and sophisticated style, way different from the Lil' Kims he was used to. Noelle knew all the stories about rappers' girlfriends but was seduced all the same. Calvin was sweet and charming when he wanted to be and he had that street swagger she'd vowed to stay away from but couldn't. But what put her over the top was the lifestyle.

"Think of somethin' and you can have it," Cal said.

It was true. If she thought of something she wanted she bought it without even glancing at the price tag. The attention was mind-blowing. All she had to do was walk to her car wearing short-shorts and she'd be on the E! channel and TMZ the same night. But there were downsides. After she married Cal her mental development got put on hold. There was no need to read anything but tabloids and fashion magazines and no reason to challenge herself or create anything more worthwhile than a line of handbags to sell on HSN. There were six thousand of them in a warehouse somewhere. She thought about getting a job but Calvin was against it unless she found something hip to do. Nothing to sully up the brand. Their home life was nonexistent. If Calvin wasn't recording, he was clubbing, hanging with the fellas or on tour for weeks at a time.

And Noelle discovered that even unlimited excess loses its charm, the thrill of getting anything she wanted wearing thinner and thinner. Wasn't that the whole point? Wanting, waiting, struggling, and *then* getting it. Not wanting and getting in the same damn breath. She found herself thinking about the ordinary issues everybody else thought about. How can I feel good about myself? What am I passionate about? Can I succeed on my own? How do I get Charles and Bug out of my fucking house?

Calvin was unhappy with the marriage too. His blue-ribbon trophy wife who looked like a billion bucks on his arm and who told him she'd take a bullet for him and shaved his balls for him and wore thongs and stilettos to cook breakfast for him was bitchy and moped around and complained about everything from the size of her closet to their seats at the Image Awards. Not a word about the house in Coconut Grove right across the bay from LeBron's place or her six hundred pairs of shoes or hanging with her friends at the Pasha Club drinking thousand-dollar bottles of Cristal or her personal hair and makeup artists or that beast of a bodyguard that followed her around, like she needed one to watch her eat lunch at the Ivy. And Noelle wasn't interested in kids. Not that Calvin wanted them but having kids was *in,* a fashion statement. You didn't have a baby and name it Zippy or Apple Pie you were off the blade.

In the beginning, Noelle went on tour with Cal to shoo away the hos and chicken heads but he cheated anyway. Her girlfriends said that was the price of being married to a rap star. Noelle lived with it for a while but the reports became so numerous and persistent it got to be humiliating. The straw that broke the camel's self-respect was a tabloid photo of Cal with his tongue down Tierra's throat. She was another singer at Bobby's label and they'd never gotten along. Noelle retaliated. She locked Cal out of the house, slashed his suits with a box cutter, threw his Montecristos in the swimming pool, and had his Mercedes Black Series SL65 towed away. Cal retaliated for the retaliation by bringing Tierra back to the crib and doing her in the marriage bed. When Noelle found five used condoms on the bedroom floor she said: "Oh, the shit is on now."

Even in the rap world their fights were legendary. Cal was performing at the Nokia to a sold-out house. He was doing the finale, "Up from Nothin'," putting a little extra into it because Snoop and his entourage were supposed to be in the greenroom watching. He was midway through the second verse when Noelle came out of the wings and hit him with what people said was Bishop Don Juan's pimp cup. He grabbed her by her weave and slung her into the audience. At a Thanksgiving dinner, Cal cooked Noelle's Stella McCartney shoulder bag in the microwave and she slapped him with a turkey leg. She nearly bit his finger off when he pointed at the door and told her to get out and he mashed his waffles into her face at Roscoe's. Noelle air-freighted Hella to Kwaylud, a rival rapper who lived in Atlanta, and Cal threw her hairdresser out of a second-floor window. On her Facebook page, she posted a picture of him masturbating. He hired a cement mixer to fossilize her shoe collection in concrete. After the divorce it didn't stop. He cut a diss track, rhyming about her cottage-cheese ass and different-size titties, the nipples big as cupcakes. Noelle responded with a radio interview and described in graphic detail how Cal liked baby talk and how his dick was shaped like a knitting needle with an army helmet stuck on the end. Bobby Grimes said the tabloids should have gotten together and given them an award.

"We've got to do something about this," Noelle said to her caller. "I don't know but I know I don't want somebody they call IQ sniffing around my business and in case you've forgotten, we're in this together. I realize that but the story's not over until it's over. All right, call me later."

Noelle went into her cathedral-like closet, more clothes in there than the Prada store on Rodeo Drive. She was making an appearance on *The Shonda Simmons Show* and wanted to look fresh, make a statement. Let the world know she was doing just fine without her scalawag husband. All she had to do now was decide what to wear when she went out shopping for something to wear.

Consuelo, the housekeeper, was dusting in the bedroom. "Consuelo?" Noelle said. "Could you tell Rodion I want to go shopping?"

"¿Quieres decir que el monstruo feo?" Consuelo said. "I don't want to."

Cal was curled up on the double-king Duxiana like a cooked shrimp. Above him was a poster-size black-and-white photo taken in an underground club somewhere in South Central. Cinder block walls, low ceiling, klieg lights reflecting off a field of captivated faces and holding clouds of weed smoke in the air. Cal was part of a trio back then and that was his debut as front man. He was stripped to the waist, his body like bundles of fibers jeweled with sweat, holding the mike like he was drinking the last drops of nectar from a golden goblet. Cal knew the song well. It was the one that put him on the map. He lay there mouthing the words:

I'm up from nothin', I come from nowhere
goin' solo on the road to everywhere
Don't need the hard sellin', feelin' the ground swellin'
The blade of my saber sickle-cellin' the haters
flossin' traitors to vapors while I be makin' that paper
if I want ya I'll take ya, circumvent your equator
There's nobody can save ya, my shit is greater and greater
I've become the Creator

"Up from Nothin'" went multiplatinum and stayed on the *Billboard* charts for six weeks. Life as a rap star had begun. Luxed-out tour buses, sold-out concerts, signing autographs and riding in limos, smoking spliffs big as ice cream cones, and staying in hotel suites the size of his mama's backyard. He hung out in the VIP section with the celebs, did a commercial for a tequila company, performed at the BET Awards, and got a Grammy nomination. He shot a pilot called *No Diggity* and got the part of a demented drug dealer in a movie about street racing. He'd always been popular with the females but this was a whole different level, bitches lined up like job applicants arguing over who got to give him a blow job first.

Cal made thirteen more albums. Four multiplatinum, four platinum, and the rest gold. He was a full-on star, king of the block, an MVP in the game everybody wanted to play. Along the way he married Noelle. Yeah, the shit went bad but they had some good times, he had to give her that. When exactly he began to fall apart he couldn't remember. It snuck up on him gradually, nobody noticing at first. How he got more and more reluctant to go out, spending most of his time at the crib incommunicado. If you asked him what he'd been up to he'd shrug or act like he didn't hear you. When the fellas talked him into playing *Madden* he'd fumble on purpose or punt the ball sideways into the stands. He slept twelve, fourteen hours a day or had insomnia and wandered around the house until five in the morning. He got paranoid. Said some of his jewelry was missing and somebody was tampering with his food. He stopped showering and shaving. He lived on Krispy Kremes and Spicy V8. He complained about allergies, headaches, and backaches but Dr. Macklin couldn't find anything wrong. He adopted a stray cat.

Bobby Grimes didn't know about Cal's condition until they were recording new tracks for the first of Cal's new three-album, fifty-five-million-dollar deal. It had happened a week earlier at the Rock Steady Studio in Santa Monica. Bobby arrived late.

Charles and Bug were on their phones texting. Anthony was staring at a photograph of a seagull like it was flying away with his youth.

"How's he doing?" Bobby said.

"See for yourself," Anthony said.

Cal was in the booth, supposedly working on a hook for the single. He stood at the mike, haggard and hopeless, his stomach like a soccer ball underneath his nine-hundred-and-ninety-five-dollar cashmere bathrobe. He rapped in a monotone:

My brain is in pain with none of the gain
what's happening in my mind I can't quantify or justify
my lifestyle eatin' me alive like Bug on a chicken thigh,
my sex drive in a nose dive
off the high board, don't need the awards
I'm prerecorded, exploited, I need to be Sigmund Freuded

Bobby watched, horror and disbelief billowing up inside him like a mushroom cloud. "Why is he in a bathrobe?" he said.

"He says they're more comfortable," Anthony said.

"More comfortable than what, clothes?"

"He says he's tired."

"He doesn't look tired, he looks mentally ill. My God, he's big as a house."

Cal droned on:

I got to stop roamin', be a pigeon goin' homin'
back to Mississippi, make some homemade chili
while I be chillin' with my kinfolk

I ain't seen since I was an egg yolk
in my daddy's egg sack,
I can't see, I can't feel, my world is going black.

Bobby sat down at the mixing board with Big Terry, Cal's long-time producer. "Why are you letting him go on like this?" Bobby said.

"Cal does what Cal wants," Big Terry said, "you know how he is."

"Well, could you get him back to work, please?"

Big Terry turned on the intercom. "The fuck you doing, Cal?" he said. "Your kinfolk are in Inglewood and you couldn't find Mississippi on a got-damn map. You better get serious in there." Cal didn't seem to hear him, staring at a horizon only he could see.

"This is unbelievable," Bobby said. "I knew he had problems but I had no idea it was this bad. How long has he been like this?"

"He's been going downhill since the divorce," Anthony said. "I could hardly get him to the studio."

"And you didn't think to tell me this before I signed him to a three-album, fifty-five-million-dollar deal?"

"Really, Bobby, I thought he'd have snapped out of it by now."

"What about you?" Bobby said to Bug and Charles. "You didn't think to give me a heads-up?"

"We figured he was sick or somethin'," Bug said. "Like he had the flu."

"The flu? You thought he had the flu? All that blubber and not a single brain cell."

Cal was unintelligible now, murmuring into the pop filter like it was an ear and he was telling it a secret.

"What's he on?" Bobby said.

"Weed, prescription pills," Anthony said.

"Look at him. There's no more chance he'll make a decent record than Bug turning down a Family Meal at Popeye's."

Cal came out of the booth and zombie-walked through the control room.

"Cal, are you all right?" Bobby said.

Cal staggered into the men's room and locked the door behind him. He was sweating and breathing hard. A humming he thought was the fluorescent lighting was inside his head, a swelling pressure behind his eyes. And then, for the first time since he was five years old, he wept like a five-year-old. "I'm messed up, I'm messed up," he said, "I'm losing my muthafuckin' mind." When he finally stopped crying he felt as empty as the box of Krispy Kremes he ate in the car, nothing left but the crumbs. He was blowing his nose in a paper towel when he heard the Voice.

"I don't know who I am anymore," the Voice said, "and I have no idea what's wrong with me."

At first, Cal thought the words were coming from him but he looked in the mirror and his mouth wasn't moving.

"I'm isolated," the Voice said. "I have no one to confide in, no one who understands. My friends and family are useless."

Cal hated being with the crew. Anthony always impatient, Charles and his attitude, Bug doing his tough love thing. *Come on, son, show me your man bones and get the fuck up out that bathrobe.*

"I've lost interest in everything but sleeping," the Voice said. "The activities I used to enjoy seem ridiculous now."

These days, Cal would no more go to a club than he would a rodeo. The deafening music, the blinding strobes, the drunk rowdy crowd waving their arms and woo-hooing like it was enjoyable being squeezed into a dance floor like Pringles and paying sixteen dollars for a cocktail. And a rap star couldn't relax in public. You had to be cool every damn minute in case somebody took a video of you picking your nose that would be on YouTube until the end of time; standing there talking shit with a bitter-ass cigar in your mouth and holding a bottle of Gran Patrón by the neck like it wasn't no thang or laughing with the fellas like only an insider would get the joke, turning smooth for the ladies, every line said a thousand times before.

"I've forgotten how to enjoy myself," the Voice said, "how to have fun."

The last time Cal could remember having real fun was when he was a kid and his dad drove him around the Forum floor on his forklift or when Angie and her friends came over and they did stupid dances in the living room. The Running Man, the Soulja Boy, the Chicken Wing.

"My eating is out of control," the Voice said. "I'm drinking too much or doing a lot of drugs."

Cal had gained twenty-five pounds. The only thing he felt comfortable in was a bathrobe and he was eating pills like a food group. If Snoop knew how much weed he was smoking he'd organize an intervention.

The Voice went on: "My job is so pointless and soul-depleting I don't even want to think about it."

Cal was supposed to be writing songs for the new album but he didn't know what to write about. More bitches, blow jobs, and bling? More Rémy, Dom, and Courvoisier? More whips and straps and world domination? All the rhymes had been used up. Cal had thought about taking Kanye's route, do some songs about his mom, Jesus, materialism, and whatever else. He gave it a try, laying down a couple of tracks in his home studio. The first track was twenty-three seconds long and titled "The Fuck Am I Doing on This Earth?" The second was thirty-five minutes long, didn't have a title but the first line was: *They changed the recipe at In-N-Out, the meat don't feel right in my mouth.* When Cal heard the tracks played back he ordered Charles and Bug to take all the recording equipment out of the house and throw it in the ocean.

"Frankly," the Voice said, "I wouldn't bother getting up in the morning but I have no choice. I have bills to pay, people that depend on me, and obligations to fulfill."

There was alimony for that evil bitch Noelle, tuition for his nieces and nephews, mortgages on the houses and the condo he bought for his parents. He was supposed to be a presenter at the Soul Train awards show and he'd promised interviews to *XXL* and WBL. He was supposed to audition for a buddy movie with Ashton Kutcher. He owed back taxes and he'd canceled appointments with his business manager ten times. Then there was Bobby Grimes. Cal felt like a Winnebago on a one-lane road, Bobby a Porsche Turbo, weaving around behind him blasting the horn.

The Voice continued: "I don't know how long I can keep this up or if I can keep it up at all. I'm at the edge, the end of my rope, I have to keep going but I can't keep going. I'm burned out."

"Burned out?" Cal said. That sounded about right. Wristing the tears off his face, he turned around to see this Mr. Voice but no one was there. He thought he'd lost his mind for real but a janitor's cart was parked against the far wall, a portable radio on the top shelf.

The radio host said, "For those of you who have just joined us, we're talking with professional life coach Dr. Russell Freeman. He's the author of the new book *Stuck in a Lifetime, or How to Cure Burnout and Stop Spinning Your Wheels.*"

"I appreciate your having me, Dan," Dr. Freeman said.

Cal couldn't believe it. Somebody named Dr. Freeman was the Voice.

"That was a very powerful passage you read, Dr. Freeman," the radio host said, "but let me play devil's advocate here. Isn't burnout just another one of those Oprah diseases like shoe addiction and mother-in-law phobia?"

"Burnout is very real. I see it in my practice on a daily basis. Men and women from every age and walk of life are so overwhelmed they can hardly function."

"Maybe they're just working too hard."

"A common misconception. A person can suffer from burnout even if they're a couch potato. You can burn out from being idle just like you can burn out from success. The common denominator is prolonged frustration."

"Spinning your wheels."

"Exactly. The feeling that no matter what you do you're in the same place as you were yesterday. That there's simply no reason to continue because you'd still be sunk in the same mire, running on the same treadmill, dancing the same tired dance. The housewife, the cop, the slacker, or the business tycoon can all suffer from burnout."

Cal nodded. If there was ever anybody who was spinning their wheels it was him. The monotony of fame, the rapper's cookie-cutter life.

"So if burnout is the disease, what's the cure?" the radio host said.

"The most effective treatment is group therapy," Dr. Freeman said. "A burnout can be with other people who have the same problems and talk about their shared experiences under the guidance of a therapist."

Cal tried to imagine himself sitting in a circle with a bunch of white people. What shared experiences could he talk about? How his diamond-and-emerald-encrusted grill gave him cold sores and how he couldn't stay awake because DStar had run out of Adderall and how sex wasn't worth the trouble? A hit off his last album was titled "Bonin' 'Til the Break of Dawn." The last time he was in bed with a girl he nutted in three minutes and rolled over to sleep. The girl thought about it a moment, shook him and said: "It ain't dawn yet."

"But a lot of people don't have the time or the resources for group therapy and that's why I wrote the book," Dr. Freeman said. "I've developed a series of lifestyle changes and exercises that are designed to, and I'm going to get technical here, get you unstuck. Give you a fresh perspective, reenergize you, alleviate your symptoms, and put you back in control."

Anthony was knocking on the men's room door. "Cal, are you okay?" he said. "We've got to get back to work. Everybody's waiting."

"And burnout doesn't go away," Dr. Freeman said. "If left untreated, the symptoms can be severe. Body aches, stomach distress, addiction, obesity, panic attacks, and increasing isolation. The effects can be devastating and sometimes irreparable. Some of my patients come to me too late, after they've lost friends, family, home, career, bank accounts. Everything."

"Everything?" Cal said. He knew he was fucking up but he didn't know it was about *everything*. Shit. The crib, the cars, the clothes, the bitches, the primo weed. No way he was going to lose all that.

"Well, this has really been informative, Dr. Freeman," the radio host said. "And I think this was a wake-up call for a lot of our listeners. Thanks for coming in."

"Thank you for having me."

Cal breathed in hope like a hit off a bong. There was a light at the end of the tunnel, a chance to get his swagger back and be his old self again, and he wasn't fucked up in some general way, he had a specific condition — burnout — and burnout had a treatment and maybe he couldn't go to group therapy but he could sure in the hell buy that book.

Anthony was still knocking on the door. "Cal, we've got to get going. Cal? Everybody's waiting."

CHAPTER SEVEN
Kill on Sight

July 2013

When Isaiah was in his teens, he worked for Harry Haldeman and wondered even then how the man could stay in a state of perpetual indignation; his fierce dark eyes glaring through the Coke-bottle bifocals resting on his great beak of a nose, his snow-white hair sticking up like a toilet brush. Isaiah thought he looked like an orchestra conductor. Harry's wife, Louise, said he looked like an eagle wearing glasses.

"Pit bulls," Harry said, "my favorite subject. Here you've got a high-energy, high-maintenance dog and pound for pound one of the most powerful creatures on the face of the earth and some god-damn teenager buys one because he thinks it makes his dick bigger. Some cities have banned pits altogether but what they ought to do is ban the goddamn teenagers. Did you know pit bulls are abandoned by their owners more than any other dog? We've got five or six right now and we'll get another one before the day is over."

Harry, Isaiah, and Dodson were walking through the canine cell block at the Hurston Animal Shelter, past one howling, mewling, sulking, dejected, pissed-off dog after another, the cacophony of barking louder than Dodson could turn up his car speakers. Dodson was walking against the wall as far away from the dogs as he could get without becoming part of the paint.

"It's a goddamn shame," Harry said. "People get a dog, can't take care of it or they're too stupid to shut the damn gate and the dog has to be put down. People are idiots. I'd rather be with dogs any day of the week. Ask Louise." Harry had an encyclopedic knowledge of dogs. He'd written a book about dog body language and bred grand champion bloodhounds. He judged at dog shows all over the state and had been supervisor at the shelter for sixteen years. He'd seen thousands of dogs of every size, type, breed, and crossbreed.

"Take this fella here," Harry said. A fawn-colored pit bull had its paws up on the chain link of its kennel and was barking relentlessly like it wouldn't stop until it was let out, fed, yelled at, played with, talked to. Anything. Dodson looked a little panicky, hurrying ahead to get past the dog. "Fella brought her in yesterday," Harry said. "Tells me he got the dog to protect his sports car while he was at work, it was some sort of classic. He left the dog in the garage all day. Well, I guess the dog got fed up because the fella comes home and the car's convertible top was torn off, the seats were ripped up, and the running boards were chewed right off the car and you know what this idiot said? I didn't expect the dog to do something like that. *I didn't expect the dog to do something like that.* I said how would you feel if I locked *you* in a garage all day? Wouldn't you want to destroy my car? Go buy a burglar alarm, you cheap bastard. Time to feed the birds."

"I like birds," Dodson said.

Harry peered into a wire cage at five baby crows in a salad bowl lined with paper towels. They had no feathers yet, just patchy fur with gray skin showing through. They were waiting to be fed, squalling with their beaks wide open. Harry fed them cat food on an ice cream stick. "You know," he said, "you may find this hard to believe but there was a time when the pit bull was the dog least likely to bite you. It's true."

"None of them live around me," Dodson said. "I know pits that'll dress up like Santa Claus and come down your chimney to bite you."

Harry looked at him. "This goes back to England in the 1800s," he said. "Dogfighting was as popular as cage fighting is today. Now you'd think fighting dogs would be high-strung and dangerous around people but they weren't. They couldn't be. Before the fight started you had to let your opponent wash your dog just in case you put something on the dog's coat that was slippery or tasted bad. So you couldn't have a dog that would bite a stranger even if the man was pouring water on its head. And the dogs were valuable. If your dog got hurt during a fight you took a break and patched him up. Well, if you're going to get bit that's the likeliest time, when the dog's all hyped up and in pain. So even if the dog had a tendency to bite you culled him. Put him down. In other words, human aggressiveness was bred *out* of the breed."

"Yeah, well, it's back in again," Dodson said.

"You can blame your teenagers for that," Harry said. "It's Murphy's *other* law. Anything that involves a teenager will be a goddamn horror show. Little brain-dead creeps breed aggressive dogs to aggressive dogs and then train them to be vicious. Sick, if you ask me. You treat a pit like a member of the family, socialize it, train it, and you'll never get a better pet. But most people are stupid and lazy and when they find out how much work that is they throw up their hands and chain the dog to a tree like it's the dog's fault."

Isaiah had a copy of the surveillance tape on his tablet. "Take a look at this, Harry," he said.

Harry watched the tape, tipping his head back to find the sweet spot on his bifocals. "Just when you think you've seen everything," he said. "Your average pit weighs around sixty pounds. This dog must be a hundred and thirty. That's as big as a bull mastiff. Unheard of. Go back to the beginning where the dog is in the kitchen." Harry watched the dog come through the doggie door, hold there for a few moments, and then go after Cal. "I don't like this," Harry said, "I don't like this one bit. The dog saw that fella and attacked. No warning, no posturing, no hesitation—and dogs, unlike your goddamn teenagers, need a reason to attack. It might be a dog reason but it's still a reason and I don't see one. This fella wasn't on the dog's territory. He wasn't being threatening and there was nothing to fight over like food or a female and he didn't run until the dog went after him." Harry seemed to shrink a little, the fierce eyes weary now. "Dogs," he said. "Devoted, courageous, love you even if you're an asshole. They'll do anything we ask of them and you know what this breeder did? He trained the dog to attack on sight."

Harry closed the cage and moved on to another. Three baby hummingbirds huddled together in a ball of cotton, each no bigger than a bumblebee. Harry fed them sugar water with a syringe. "I told my neighbor Peterman not to cut back his boxwood until nesting season was over but he went and did it anyway. Lucky I found these little guys. Their metabolism is so high you've got to feed them every twenty minutes. *Peterman*. Ought to be sterilized."

"Harry, how did that dog get so big?" Isaiah said.

"Well, it might be a one-off, like a kid that grows up to be seven feet tall and all his brothers and sisters are normal heights. But

one-offs are rarer than hens' teeth. You could breed a hundred litters and not get one and with a dog this big you'd expect the conformation to be out of whack. You know, his proportions would be
way off and there'd be a deformity or two. But this dog looks like
any other pit. Definitely not show quality but good enough for most
people. If I was to guess I'd say the dog was bred this way. Bred for
size. Not an easy thing to do."

"What do you mean?"

"Okay, let's say you *do* have a big dog. Well, you could mate it
to a regular-size dog and you might get big pups and you might
not. The surest way is to go out and find another big dog. Now it's
no guarantee but you're more likely to get big pups that way and if
you're lucky one of them will grow up to be bigger than its parents.
Then you take that dog, breed it to another big dog, get an even
bigger pup, and then it's wash, rinse, and repeat, each generation
getting bigger and bigger until you've got the giant on your video.
It's like my brother, Barry. He wasn't too bright to begin with and
he goes and marries a woman who's thirty-four years old and
flunked her GED twice. Then they have a son that's dumber than
a box of hair, *he* gets married and has kids that play hide-and-seek
in the rosebushes. Can I see that kitchen shot again?" Harry held
the tablet this way and that. "Yeah, that's what I thought," he said.
"This dog has been crossbred. Somewhere in his pedigree, a pit bull
parent was bred to something else. Happens all the time. People
breed pits to Dobermans, Rottweilers, Catahoula Leopard dogs, all
kinds of things. Now it's hard to make out here but your dog has
some dewlap, wrinkling on the forehead, the legs are a little long
and the tail's got a curve in it. Could be Great Dane or mastiff but
I'm thinking Presa Canario, which would explain a lot of things."

"Presa what?" Dodson said.

"Presa Canario. It's originally from the Spanish Canary Islands. Big strong dog, weighs over a hundred pounds. Ranchers bred them to kill predators and for dogfighting. They call it a pit bull on steroids. It's got an unpredictable temperament and it's human aggressive. Mix that together with a pit's fearlessness and determination and train it to attack on sight and I don't know what you've got." Harry closed the cage and wiped his hands on his shirt. "And I'll tell you something else," he said. "Whoever the fella is that bred this dog is one crazy son of a bitch."

CHAPTER EIGHT

Jiffy Lube

May 2005

Hunting down Marcus's killer gave Isaiah focus; something to occupy his mind besides his grief. A reason to get up in the morning. He called the East Long Beach police station and spoke to Detective Purcell who was in charge of the investigation. Isaiah told the detective he was calling on behalf of his mother. She was too upset to talk and wanted to know if there was any progress tracking down the driver.

"I'm afraid I don't have much to tell her," Purcell said. "In a hit-and-run people tend to look at the victim first and only see the vehicle as it's leaving the scene."

"Nobody saw anything?" Isaiah said. He could hear Purcell thinking *Why didn't you?*

"There was a witness at the bus stop," Purcell said. "He stated the vehicle was a late-model Honda Accord, silver, the up model. He couldn't describe the driver, everything happened too fast." Purcell said there were stories about the accident on the local news and an article had appeared in the newspaper but nobody called the hotline.

"Anything else you can tell my mom?" Isaiah said.

"It's an ongoing investigation and we're doing everything we can," Purcell said. "If there are any developments we'll contact you."

For the first time since the accident, Isaiah went back to the intersection of Anaheim and Baldwin. Not much traffic this time of day. A woman filling up at the Shell station. An old man sweeping the sidewalk in front of a liquor store. A homeless kid with two dogs walking by. Normal, like Marcus was never here. Like Marcus had never died. Isaiah tried not to look at the patch of asphalt where his brother lost his life but couldn't help it. He saw Marcus lying there, a bag of broken bones and smashed arteries, the luminous smile snuffed out forever. Isaiah felt a surge of heat coming from his insides, pushing sweat out of his pores, his face burning up. Light-headed and nauseous, he sat down on the bus bench. Somebody asked him if he was all right and he waved them away.

On the SB5 Stanford-Binet intelligence test Isaiah's reasoning scores were near genius levels. His abilities came naturally but were honed in his math classes. He was formally introduced to inductive reasoning in geometry, a tenth-grade subject he took in the eighth. His teacher, Mrs. Washington, was a severe woman who looked to be all gristle underneath her brightly colored pantsuits. Lavender, Kelly green, peach. She talked to the class like somebody had tricked her into it.

"All right," she said. "Inductive reasoning. It's what those so-called detectives on *CSI, SVU, LMNOP* and all the rest of them call *de*ductive reasoning, which is wrong and they should know better. It's *in*ductive reasoning, a tool you will use frequently in geometry as well as calculus and trigonometry, assuming you get that far and that certainly won't be you, Jacquon. Stop messing with that girl's hair and pay attention. Your grade on that last test was so low I had to write it on the bottom of my shoe." Mrs. Washington glared at Jacquon until his face melted. She began again: "Inductive reasoning is reasoning to the most likely explanation. It begins with one or more observations, and from those observations we come to a conclusion that seems to make sense. All right. An example: Jacquon was walking home from school and somebody hit him on the head with a brick twenty-five times. Mrs. Washington and her husband, Wendell, are the suspects. Mrs. Washington is five feet three, a hundred and ten pounds, and teaches school. Wendell is six-two, two-fifty, and works at a warehouse. So who would you say is the more likely culprit?"

Isaiah and the rest of the class said Wendell.

"Why?" Mrs. Washington said. "Because Mrs. Washington may have *wanted* to hit Jacquon with a brick twenty-five times but she isn't big or strong enough. Seems reasonable given the facts at hand, but here's where inductive reasoning can lead you astray. You might not *have* all the facts. Such as Wendell is an accountant at the warehouse who exercises by getting out of bed in the morning, and before Mrs. Washington was a schoolteacher she was on the wrestling team at San Diego State in the hundred-and-five-to-hundred-and-sixteen-pound weight class and would have won her division if that blond girl from Cal Northridge hadn't stuck a thumb in her eye. Jacquon, I know your mother and if I tell her about your behavior she will beat you 'til your name is Jesus."

The driver who killed Marcus was going east on Anaheim, ran a red light at Baldwin, and went past the witness, who was standing at the bus stop thirty feet away. According to the bus schedule, the number nine stopped at 6:05. Rush hour. The witness, Isaiah thought, was probably on his way home from work and if that was the case he took the same bus every day.

Isaiah waited. Three Latina women showed up a little before six. Probably domestics with their steadfast faces and oversize handbags. Then a chubby black man with merry eyes and a bow tie arrived, smiling at everyone like he was ever so pleased to make their acquaintance. Seven Latino men came next in ones and twos. They wore rough clothes and rugged shoes, a few of them carrying lunch pails. Any of these people could have recognized an Accord but the witness told Detective Purcell it was the *up* model and if you could distinguish between the models you were into cars. The witness came last. He was stocky, short hair, a square face, and powerful hands that would never be clean. A red-and-white logo on his shirt said JIFFY LUBE. If he was changing oil all day he knew his cars.

Isaiah followed the Jiffy Lube man onto the bus. He'd be cornered on there, a captive audience. Jiffy sat down on a bench seat near the back, folded his arms across his chest, and closed his eyes. Isaiah stood near him and held the pole. He didn't know what to say. If he came on too strong or used the wrong words the guy might get pissed or scared and not talk at all. "You saw the accident," Isaiah said. "The hit-and-run." Jiffy didn't react, didn't even open his eyes. "You were standing at the bus stop and you saw it," Isaiah said. Jiffy was staring hard at the floor now, the people around him tensing up and looking out the windows. "My brother was the one who got hit," Isaiah said. "I want to find the guy who did it. Can you help me out?"

Jiffy glanced quickly at Isaiah and shook his head. "It's bad to see it like that," he said. "I wish I don't see it. It's bad."

IQ

"The cop said the car was an Accord," Isaiah said.

Jiffy cringed, leaning back a little, like the memory was too brutal to remember. "Yes, it's an Accord, like the silver color?" he said. "The fancy one, I seen the dual exhausts. The other ones only got one."

"Did you see the driver?"

"It's going too fast, I don't see him," Jiffy said. His shoulders drooped, his eyes misted over. "It's like my friend César," he said. "He die from his heart. He's like young too, like only forty-one. It takes you down, man, messes you up."

"Anything else? I've got no place to start."

"I not sure, okay? But I think I seen a sticker, like a Lakers one." Jiffy nodded, telling Isaiah he *was* sure.

"A Lakers decal?" Isaiah said. "Where was it?"

"On the window, like on the back? The car was like driving away, you know? But I think I seen it."

"How do you know it was the Lakers?"

"It's gold with purple writing, that's like their colors. My stop is coming," Jiffy said, sounding relieved. He stood up and moved for the door. "I'm sorry for your brother," he said. "It takes you down, man, like all the way."

Isaiah went home and got online. The up-model Accord was called the EX and it listed for twenty-seven thousand dollars and change. Add in tax and license, call it thirty. Not a blue-collar or a young man's car; the average age of an Accord driver was fifty. Middle-aged black men and Latinos no doubt bought Accords but in Isaiah's experience they tended toward big American cars, SUVs and pickup trucks. And the driver was heading east into East Long Beach. Sixty percent white according to the census figures. Playing the odds, the driver was white.

Okay, so where was this guy going? If his destination was Signal Hill, he would have been on Willow or PCH. If he was heading to the harbor area, he would have been going south. Maybe he was taking Anaheim *through* East Long Beach to Blair Field or Colorado Lagoon but somehow that felt wrong and that had to do with where the driver was coming *from*—the west. Head that way on Anaheim and you'd go under the 710 Freeway, passing a bleak industrial zone, and then on into Wilmington, neither area known for white guys driving new Accords. Either that or the driver was on the 710 and got off on Anaheim but if he was going to Blair Field or Colorado Lagoon there were easier ways to get there. No, the guy lived in East Long Beach.

The Laker decal Jiffy Lube said was in the back window was a gold basketball with *Lakers* written over it in purple script. In Isaiah's eyes it was ugly and decals weren't easy to get off once they were on. You'd have to love the Lakers to stick a thing like that on your thirty-thousand-dollar car. And on the same day Marcus was killed, the Lakers were playing Allen Iverson and the Philadelphia 76ers. No real fan would miss that game and it was on at six-thirty because of the time difference. The accident happened around six, so maybe the driver was in a hurry to get home to see the game and just happened to murder Marcus on the way.

The driver was white, mature, had a good job, lived in East Long Beach, and was a Lakers fan.

After running over Marcus, the driver probably avoided the whole area. He'd be a fool not to but time had passed. Maybe he was back to his usual routine. If he didn't get off the 710 at Anaheim he'd have to keep going, get off on 7th, and double back. Marcus always said habits were hard to break. Didn't matter if they were good or bad.

*　　*　　*

At five-thirty the next day, Isaiah seated himself on the retaining wall next to the Anaheim off-ramp. He watched cars go by, dozens and dozens. He used his phone to take pictures of the Accords. Three were late-model but none were silver or had a Lakers decal. The pictures came out fine if the car stopped at the light. You could see the license plate number and the driver's face. But if the light was green and the cars were moving, the photos were blurred and useless.

At home again, Isaiah microwaved a burrito and went out on the balcony. It was twilight. The crows were gathering, arguing over whose sky it was; smells of onions, garlic, and cilantro drifting up from below. He was mad at himself. Furious, in fact. Marcus was killed right in front of him and he couldn't give Detective Purcell a single clue. And it worried him, the prospect of seeing the Accord and not being able to remember the license plate or what the driver looked like. He'd be as useless as he was now.

Next day, he sat on the retaining wall and played a game with himself. He'd look at a car for three seconds. A thousand one, a thousand two, a thousand three. Then close his eyes and say what he remembered. He figured three seconds was about as long as the Jiffy Lube man had to see the Accord. What Isaiah found out was that three seconds is not a lot of time.

Homegirl, something on her head like a scarf, different colors, the car was a—shit, I don't know. License plate number B R—shit.

Latino guy, pickup truck, twenties? Wearing a brown shirt, writing on the door, ARGO Construction? AGRA? AFCO? License number 2 U—shit.

Hundreds of cars later, he was getting the hang of it. He had to block out the engine noise, the exhaust fumes, the glare of the sun, the stares from the drivers, and the kids yelling hey, mister, are you a bum? And see. Not think about seeing or telling himself to see, just *see*, cutting everything out of the frame except the car and taking a snapshot with his eyes.

American car, big, green like pea soup, white guy, glasses, thirties or forties. What was he wearing? Shit. License plate X R 7 G U — shit.

Buick Regal, gold color, black guy, fifties, bald, double chin — what else? Dammit, there was something else. License plate R 7 5 3 B — 9 — C9? C8? Shit.

New Prius, blue, Latina woman, twenties, wearing scrubs, oval sunglasses, parking pass on the mirror, license plate 5 6 7 M 8 9 — shit, almost had it.

Acura TSX, black, late-model, blacked-out windows, rims, white kid, twenties, white T, red-and-gold cap, Trojan logo, X R 7 0 9 4 D.

He stayed out late every night and walked. It was better than not sleeping or standing on the balcony staring at nothing. Take Henderson all the way to Shoreline Drive and look across the LA River at the *Queen Mary,* all lit up, people partying over there. Or take PCH to Martin Luther King and eat greasy Chinese food at the Mandarin Palace. Snoop, Nate Dogg, and Warren G did their demo right across the street at VIP Records. It was closed now but it used to have a full-time DJ who knew your beats and played them as you walked in the door. Every night a different route: Cambodia Town, East Village, Rose Park, MacArthur Park, Downtown. Along the way he memorized gang graffiti. Barrio Viejo, Crip Violators, Headhunter Crips, Boulevard Mafia, Latin Time Playboyz, Mid City Stoners, Sons of Samoa, Asian Boyz, Sureños Locos 13. A coded street map growing in his head like tree roots. He quit school. He only came home to shower and sleep. He ate when he remembered to. He quit his jobs and forgot about money. He was obsessed.

When he wasn't on the retaining wall, he walked up and down Anaheim asking anybody who'd talk to him if they'd seen a late-model silver Accord with a Lakers decal in the back window and maybe some damage on the right front bumper. Nobody knew anything. He began to observe and memorize randomly. See, hear, smell. Watch for changes.

Different ad on the bus bench. OutFast Bail Bonds. The plants in Louella's window are wilted. Wonder if she's okay? Liquor store put up another Bud Light sign. Mr. Singleton's having fish tonight. Price of regular at the Shell station went up a half cent. The neighbor's TV sounds better, got a new one. Another scratch on Aldo's lowrider, he must be pissed. The homeless kid's little dog has a different collar.

Weeks went by but Isaiah learned nothing new about the Accord or the driver. He was worn down and exhausted, his feet so swollen his shoes didn't fit. He felt like a Styrofoam cup bobbing around in the harbor, moving but not going anywhere. The investigation was over and he knew it. To do any more was futile. Marcus's killer would get away scot-free.

It was a blistering day. Isaiah had walked for hours in a self-induced trance. He could do that now. See without seeing, hear without hearing. There was no point being observant anymore. It only reminded him that he'd failed. He didn't stop because he had nothing else to do. When he got home he went straight to the fridge and grabbed one of Dodson's Dr Peppers. He popped the top and guzzled it, the bottom of the can aimed at the ceiling. Dodson came in. Isaiah choked and spit up some soda. "I'll pay you back," he said.

"Ain't nothing to worry about, drink up," Dodson said.

"I'll go to the store right now," Isaiah said.

"Don't nobody give a shit about a damn Dr Pepper. You got bigger problems you need to think about."

"Problems like what?"

"Like being broke. You think I didn't notice when you was short on the rent? Don't worry, I covered it."

"It's temporary. I'll get another job."

"Be real. You know you ain't going back to washing dishes," Dodson said. He got himself a Dr Pepper and poured it in a glass. He'd been thinking a lot about how to use Isaiah in some kind of hustle. It didn't occur to him until right this minute to let Isaiah figure that out for himself. "I can't carry you," Dodson said. "You don't make some money we'll both be out on the street. You need to think about options."

Isaiah shrugged. "I have," he said.

"No, you been thinking about regular options, nine-to-five options, minimum-wage options. I'm talking about criminal options." Dodson drank some soda and belched. "Boy with your brain gotta have a few ideas."

CHAPTER NINE

Game Bred

July 2013

D og breeders of any particular breed are like a club. They share the same love for the Dalmatian, the malamute, or the pit bull, or whatever their chosen breed. They compete against each other at dog shows. They socialize, sell dogs back and forth, and read about each other in the blogs and trade magazines. There are rivalries, jealousies, controversies, and more gossip than you'd see on the E! channel. Ask any breeder about another breeder's dogs and you'll get a long list of conformation faults, health problems, and poor bloodlines. Everybody knows everybody else's business.

Harry called his pit bull breeder friends and every one of them said he must be talking about a bully pit or some other kind of dog because there's no such thing as a hundred-and-thirty-pound pit bull. Harry asked about big dogs. George Aguilar at American Pride Pit Bulls in Denver had an eighty-five-pound female but he gave it to his niece who rode it in the Cinco de Mayo parade like a horse. George said Derek Austin at All American Pit Bulls in Flagstaff had an oversize dog. Derek said yes, he used to have an eighty-two-pound stud he never bred because the judges didn't like them that big but a guy drove all the way from California to buy the dog. The guy didn't haggle and paid cash. When Derek asked him why he wanted a pit that wouldn't show he grinned and said he liked big dogs. No, Derek didn't remember the guy's name. It was a cash deal and he didn't record it. Why pay the tax man any more than you had to?

Mary Settler, a professional handler, said she arrived at a show in Redlands and people told her some crazy guy had entered a giant pit bull that was so aggressive it was disqualified before it got in the ring. Nobody knew the guy's name. Bob Walters at Champion Pit Bulls in Victorville said he ran into a guy at the vet that had a new litter. Good-looking pups. The dam was a WindFlyer dog, the sire was from Minnesota. Dauntless something. One of the pups was huge. The guy said it was eight weeks old but it looked twice that. Said his name was Skip something.

Harry called John Cisco, president of the USA Presa Canario Club. John sent out a group email asking if any of the members had sold a dog to somebody named Skip. Ben Mason of Invincible Presa Canario in Temecula said a guy named Skip bought a one-hundred-and-twenty-eight-pound stud named War Monger. It was a beautiful dog but Ben said he was going to put it down because it went after anything that moved. Ben said he warned Skip about the dog but Skip said he trained dogs for the military and it wouldn't be a problem. Skip's last name was Hanson. He was from Blue Hill Pit Bulls in Fergus, a desert truck stop on Highway 58 between Barstow and Boron.

"Fergus is a block long and that's one too many," Ben said. "No reason to stop there unless you like shitty coffee."

A dirt road began behind the Drop In Diner where a sign said MUNICIPAL WASTE MANAGEMENT LANDFILL 6 MILES. Blue Hill Pit Bulls was somewhere along the way. The road was bumpy, nothing but bleak scrubby desert in every direction. The Audi was already covered with dust, gravel clattering against the catalytic converter.

"Looking for a dog," Dodson said, disgusted. "What if you *find* the dog? Then what? Call the police and say, see that dog in the video? It's the same one we saw at Blue Hill. What's that, Officer? How do we know? Well, they both big and black. That's how y'all identify niggas, ain't it? I don't think my phone works out here."

"What's wrong with you?" Isaiah said. "Are you really that afraid of dogs?"

"I ever tell you about this? I was seven, eight years old, had a Kool-Aid stand in front of my Auntie May's house. A nickel a glass and I tripled my money even after I paid for the sugar."

"Yeah, okay—"

"So there I am selling my Kool-Aid and minding my business and I see Javier's dog, Biscuit, one of the raggedy junkyard pits. You know, white with red around the mouth like he ate a cat for breakfast and that muthafucka's coming right at me. Shit. I dropped the pitcher, ran into my auntie's yard trying to get to the porch, but that muthafuckin' dog had me 'fore I got to the steps. Bit the shit out of me too. Would have killed my ass if my uncle hadn't come out and shot it with his deer rifle. Dog fucked me up. Lost so much blood I had to get a transfusion. Took a couple of hundred stitches to sew my ass up." Isaiah remembered Dodson in the old apartment, at the stove cooking gumbo. All those scars on his arm and back. "I couldn't stand to look at a goddamn dog for five or six years," Dodson said, "not even a puppy. You see why I don't want to be out here?"

The odometer read two miles when they got to a plywood sign nailed to a eucalyptus tree that said BLUE HILL PIT BULLS in dripping white letters.

"What blue hill?" Dodson said.

The one-story Spanish looked strange all by itself in the vast empty desert, like the owner thought other houses would be built around it. The screen door was missing, shriveled bushes under the windows. A shovel and a ceiling fan with wires coming out of it were lying on the dirt lawn. A bright blue F-150 sat under the carport.

Isaiah and Dodson got out of the car. "I don't hear no dogs," Dodson said, relieved. "Shit it's hot."

A young guy came out of the house talking on his cell. "Don't worry, Bonnie, I got this. Sooner than you think." The guy ended the call and smiled like he knew something. "What can I do for you?"

"You could tell me where the air-conditioning is," Dodson said.

"I'm looking for a dog," Isaiah said.

"Basically, I don't sell to the general public," the guy said. "I sell to some gangster with three dogs and a website my bloodlines get corrupted, no offense."

"Don't matter to us," Dodson said, "we ain't gangsters."

"I'm Skip."

"Isaiah."

"Juanell Dodson. Pleasure to meet you."

Skip was the same height and weight as the man on the video. He moved the same way too. That awkward up-and-down gait. He looked ordinary; scruffy, dirty blond hair, a soul patch so sparse you wondered why he bothered. He wore baggy shorts and a T-shirt that said THE BLACK CROWES. He wore Crocs. He could have been a guy on the Venice boardwalk selling puka shell necklaces and hash pipes.

"Bob Walters said you've got a new litter," Isaiah said. "Bred your WindFlyer bitch to a Minnesota dog."

"Dauntless Road Master Castaway," Skip said. "AKC champion, best of breed at four nationals."

"That's the dog's name?" Dodson said. "How do you call him? Here, Dauntless Road Master Castaway?"

"Isn't Dauntless out of Amy Sullivan's dog?" Isaiah said.

"Sin City Castaway," Skip said. "I tried to buy her but Amy wouldn't sell. Have you seen Amy? She looks exactly like my mom's Pekingese. I hated that fucking thing."

"How are the pups looking?"

"Great, really great. Want to take a look? They're in the barn."

They followed Skip along the side of the house, a graveyard for the miscellaneous. A scarred surfboard with the fin broken off. A trash bin full of crushed Red Bull cans. Two screen doors, the screens busted out. A mountain bike with a bent fork. A golf club broken in half. *Skip's got a temper,* Isaiah thought. An archery target was stapled to a piece of plywood, arrows stuck in it. Some of them all the way through.

"You into archery?" Dodson said.

"Yeah, I'm pretty good too," Skip said. "I was going to try out for the Olympic team but I got shingles. Ever had those? They're the worst."

"You don't mind my asking, why do you live out here?"

"Taxes are cheap and no neighbors, right? The dogs make a lot of noise. The bad part, there's nothing to do. Takes me an hour to get to Redlands, two hours to get to LA. What'd it take you? More like three, right? I surf at First Point in Malibu, takes me just as long. Do you guys surf? Oh right, not a lot of surfing in the hood."

Skip saw the moving cloud of dust when it was over by the diner. He went up to the hayloft, opened the bay door and pulled the beach towel off the Minox 15X56 hunting binoculars. They were set on a tripod and prefocused on the crossroads. A car came to a stop, two black guys in it arguing. This had to be about the rapper. Skip got Goliath out of his kennel and made him lie down in the living room. He would stay there not making a sound until he was whistled for. Skip went to the front window and watched the black guys drive up and get out of the car. It was an Audi, weird for a black guy and a big engine by the sound of it. They didn't look threatening, out there yawning and stretching and no guns Skip could see. He got the subcompact Beretta out of the wastebasket and stuck it in his back holster. That's when Bonnie called.

"You used a fucking dog?" Bonnie said. "What's wrong with you?"

"I didn't have a choice."

"Well, the guy's pissed at me for referring you."

"Tell him I'll get it done. Don't I always?"

"Look, just shoot the guy," Bonnie said. "No dogs, cats, blow-guns, boomerangs, or any other fucking thing, just shoot him."

Skip went outside and watched the black guys come up the walkway. "Don't worry, Bonnie, I got this."

"When?"

"Sooner than you think."

The back of Skip's house was as derelict as the front. The kitchen door was open, the smell of fast food and stale laundry drifting out. Isaiah was grateful Skip hadn't invited them in. A cement square with weeds in the cracks served as a patio, a rusty hibachi was set on a cinder block. There was no place to sit down except a low beach chair with frayed yellow webbing. The squalor aside, Isaiah was uncomfortable, the feeling of loneliness like an atmosphere, unseen but all-enveloping.

"You train attack dogs?" Dodson said, looking at the heavily padded jumpsuit puddled near the hose.

"For the military," Skip said. "Yeah, the marines take them all over the place. Europe, Asia, Germany. My dad was in Iraq, did like five or six tours. Got a Purple Heart."

"Oh yeah? My old man too."

The patio looked onto an exercise yard. A garbage can with a rake stuck in it was the only survivor on a battlefield of craters, mounds of dug-up dirt, dried-out palm fronds, a couple of old tires, crushed plastic soda bottles, and coils of dogshit. A ten-foot chain link fence went around the perimeter. Two wires threaded through ceramic insulators ran along the top. Worn-out palm trees gave up some shade.

"This way," Skip said. They went around the yard. Skip didn't seem to notice the hundreds of shell casings on the ground or the bullet holes in the wheelbarrow, metal storage shed, paint cans, and fence rails. He smiled weakly when they passed some sheets of plywood with people drawn on them, some with big lips and wide-open eyes. "Yeah, my gun club meets here," Skip said, "they get carried away."

In the distance, Isaiah saw a bald hill the color of a cardboard box. Small white circles dotted the hill like thumbtacks on a cork-board. "Hold on a minute," he said, and stooped to tie his shoe.

"Can you make any money in the dog business?" Dodson said.

"Basically, no," Skip said. "To breed my WindFlyer bitch I had to get her cleared for eyes, cardiac, thyroid, hip dysplasia, and I had to get a progesterone test to target the best conception date. Yeah, no kidding, right? And Road Master's stud fee was two thousand bucks and get this: the semen had to be fresh-chilled and FedExed in a special box with semen extender and ice."

"Semen extender?" Dodson said.

"I haven't made a nickel off the dogs. It's one of those passion things. God, I hate that word. But wait 'til you see the pups, they'll blow your mind."

"*Semen* extender?"

The barn had a big sliding door and a regular door, Isaiah noticing there was no lock on either. The dogs had sensed the visitors and were barking wildly. Isaiah thought if Dodson wasn't black he'd be pale.

"Damn," Dodson said, "how many dogs you got in there?"

Skip opened the regular door a few inches. A slate-gray pit bull with laser-green eyes jammed its head in the opening and snarled at the newcomers. "Oh shit!" Dodson yelled, jumping back. Isaiah was waiting for it. No other reason to have unlocked doors unless there was some other kind of security.

"Can't you just see somebody trying to break in here?" Skip said, grinning. "Back up, Attila. Sit."

Attila backed up and sat. Skip swung the door open and a swath of sunlight cut through the cool, dark barn. Isaiah smelled wet cement, wet dog, sawdust, gun oil, cordite, some sort of disinfectant, and the faintest whiff of dogshit. Chain link kennels were lined up against one wall. They'd been recently hosed down. There were sleeping pallets to keep the dogs off the cement and water bowls with clean water in them. Two of the kennels were empty, one of them twice as big as the others. The dogs were all pits, different colors, most of them normal-size. Except for Attila, who hadn't moved, all the dogs were barking savagely, the volume almost unbearable.

"Okay, shut up," Skip said like he was talking to his little sister. The quiet was immediate and shocking, the only sound the dogs' panting. *Heh-heh-heh-heh-heh.*

"Damn, Skip," Dodson said. "They know who they daddy is, don't they?"

*   *   *

Dodson had heard dogs could smell fear and if that was the case he was stinking up the barn. He could smell it himself. Like spoiled milk with a little BO mixed in. The dogs were watching him. Only him. Their long tongues hanging over their toothy grins. It reminded Dodson of his first day at Wayside, walking along the cell block carrying his bedding, the inmates making kissing noises, calling him lean meat and asking him if he liked to toss salads.

"Those two look really big," Isaiah said, pointing with his chin at two black dogs. "What are they, ninety pounds?"

"I like big dogs," Skip said. "Cool, huh? They freak people out. Go ahead, the litter's in the back." Dodson led the way, past neatly stacked bags of kibble and cases of canned dog food. He thought it was strange how Skip took better care of the dogs than he did of himself. Shiny metal food bowls were stacked on shiny metal shelves. Igloo coolers were marked GROOMING, FIRST AID, EARS, EYES. Spiked collars and muzzles that looked like flowerpots hung on nails. What looked like a long two-pronged barbecue fork with a thick yellow handle was hung separately like a clock or scroll.

"Is this them?" Dodson said, like he was looking at a nest of tarantulas.

"Yup," Skip said, beaming. The litter was in a pen made from temporary fencing. The cement floor was covered with wood shavings, a child's swimming pool full of shredded paper in the middle. Next to the pen, a lightbulb on a wire hung over an old couch bowed in the middle, a slumping pile of magazines on the floor.

"Want to get in there with them?" Skip said.

"No thank you," Dodson said. "A baby shark is still a shark. He'll just eat you in smaller chunks."

*　　*　　*

Isaiah and Skip sat in the pen, the puppies bumbling over their laps, yipping, tugging on Isaiah's shoestrings, and chewing on Skip's Crocs. Each pup had a different-colored spot of nail polish on the top of its head. The green pup was twice the size of the others.

"How old are they?" Isaiah said.

"Ten weeks," Skip said.

"What about this one?" Isaiah said, scratching the green pup. "Can't be ten weeks. Is it from the same litter?"

"Looks good, right? His eyes are set right, full dentition, good tail set, topline, bone structure. Could be a winner."

"Are you going to show him?"

"No, but I'm gonna take him to dog shows." Skip batted the red puppy around with his hands. "Come on, red, be tough," he said. "That's it, there you go, mix it up, mix it up. My dogs have great bloodlines. Redboy, Carver, Bourdaux. Every one of them game bred."

"What's game bred?" Dodson said.

"Game bred means the dog's parents fought in the ring," Skip said. "It's like your mom and dad are Mike Tyson and Ronda Rousey. A game dog has like a really high pain tolerance and won't back down no matter what. Like it'll keep fighting even if it's losing, even if it's getting torn apart and dying. You should see my dogs. They won't quit even if they're *winning*. Seriously? If the other dog was dead and buried my dog would dig it up and kill it all over again."

Like that's something to be proud of, Isaiah thought. Training a dog to be good for nothing but killing. Not thinking twice about letting it tear somebody apart. Skip was a sociopath, which only confirmed what Isaiah knew the moment he came out of the house. This was the hit man.

"Oh listen to this," Skip said. "There's this Mexican guy lives out near the landfill? He's got a herd of goats, rents them out for brush clearing. Seriously, those fucking goats will eat anything. So one of my dogs escapes and get this: he kills the whole herd. I'm not kidding, like twenty of them." Skip grinned. "They were running around, climbing over each other. BAAAH BAAAHH. I got blood all over me."

Isaiah looked at this creature that murdered people for a living, his eyes impish and depraved, delighted at the carnage he'd caused. Probably thinks he's a professional like a race car driver or an opera singer. Thinks it's cool because he saw Tom Cruise play a hit man in a movie. Doesn't cross his mind that he's a sick, twisted sociopath, his dogs more human than he is.

"Okay, blue, it's your turn," Skip said. "Step up, step up, come on, be tough."

"How did the dog escape?" Isaiah said. "Did he break out of the barn?"

"He was in the yard. Come on, blue, keep coming, keep coming."

"The dog climbed over that fence?"

"He's a pit bull, what can I say?"

"It's two miles from the diner to your place and the landfill is six. That dog went down the road another four miles to the Mexican guy's place and found the goats by accident?"

"Seriously? A dog's sense of smell is two hundred times better than humans'. It can smell a goat if it's in San Bernardino. I used to live there, what a shithole."

Isaiah thought, *Skip has killed people. Somebody's mother, father, sister, brother taken away forever just like Marcus.* "I don't understand something," Isaiah said. "If the dog escaped, how could you be there to watch it kill the goats?"

"Who said I was?" Skip said. He looked puzzled, like the question had come out of the blue.

"You said the goats were climbing over each other and you got blood all over you. How did that happen if you weren't there?"

"What's with all the questions?"

"Your dog didn't escape over a ten-foot electrified fence. *You* couldn't escape over a ten-foot electrified fence. You drove the dog over to the Mexican guy's place and let it loose on those goats. Part of the dog's training, let it taste blood, get into killing things. Was that the special dog, Skip? The giant one you sent to kill Cal?"

"Cal? Who's Cal?" Skip said. The twinkling eyes had gone dark, the grin lacquered on. He was holding the blue puppy like he was protecting it from the rain.

Dodson slipped behind Skip, his look saying *you're pushing him too hard,* but Isaiah was too angry to care. "Where is he, Skip?" he said. "Where's the special one?"

"I don't know what you're talking about."

"You've got thirteen dogs and fifteen kennels. One of them is Attila's, who's the big kennel for? He's in the house now, isn't he? That's why you left the door open so you could whistle if you needed him. Trained him good too, just like the others, that little be-quiet trick was pretty cool. Use that cattle prod a lot?" Isaiah said, nodding at the barbecue fork. "Hung it up there where they could see it, remind them who's boss. By the way, what happened to the Presa Canario? Served its purpose and you put it down? Matter of fact, what happened to all the other litters? You'd need a lot of them to get size like that. You buried them out there in the desert, didn't you? Dug a hole and threw dirt on them because they weren't big enough or game enough or didn't kill something when you told them to."

"I gave them away," Skip said, barely audible.

"Gave them away?" Isaiah said. "Bullshit. You've been bullshitting since we got here. The arrows in that target are eighteen inches long. They're bolts for a crossbow and the crossbow isn't an Olympic event. What unit, Skip?"

"What?" Skip said.

"What unit? Your father was in the marines. What unit?"

"I forgot," Skip said.

"Your father wasn't in the marines any more than you were," Isaiah said, "and what was all that nonsense about a gun club?"

"You're lucky they're not here," Skip said, his voice in a wringer, his eyes like knife wounds. "They're not too keen on the brothers."

"Do all the members of your gun club sit in that one chair? Do they all drink Red Bull? Do all their burgers fit on that one hibachi? Where do they eat them? On the picnic table you don't have? It's just you, Skip. Lying on that couch at night reading to the puppies."

The blue puppy squealed. Skip was squeezing it too hard. "Seriously?" he said. "It's time for you to go."

They stopped at McDonald's and ate inside. Isaiah didn't want the smell in his car. "I think it's true these fries got crack in 'em," Dodson said. "I wonder if you can rock 'em up and smoke 'em? I know some niggas that would try."

Isaiah was pushing lettuce around with a fork trying to find the premium part of his Premium Southwest Salad. A mess of wilted greens, dried-out chicken cubes, a few black beans, and corn kernels in a plastic box. The dressing looked like snot. "I don't know what this is," he said.

At the next table, a woman wearing three cardigans was gurgling Sprite vapor through a straw.

"You want this?" Isaiah said, offering her the salad.

"Sure," the woman said.

"Well, I guess we found our man," Dodson said. "That was some cold shit you put on that boy. Do all their burgers fit on that one hibachi. I thought he was going to cry."

"We've got no way to link Skip with whoever hired him," Isaiah said. "I shook his tree."

"Is that what you were doing? Looked to me like you was humiliating the man. Taking his fucked-up life and sticking it in his face, especially that part about reading to the puppies. You know he's gonna come after you, don't you?"

"I hope he does. He's too pissed off, he'll make a mistake."

"*You* the one got pissed off and you the one made a mistake. Now he knows we're onto him."

"Doesn't matter, he already knew. It took us about three hours to get from Long Beach to Fergus. Remember what Skip said when we were walking around the side of the house? He said, how long did it take you to get here, three hours? We could have been coming from anywhere. San Bernardino is an hour away. So is Riverside. LA is two."

"So who told him?" Dodson said. "Only people who know anything are Bobby Grimes, Anthony, and the Moody brothers."

"And one of them is Skip's employer or works for Skip's employer."

"I ain't buying it. They all want Cal to finish the album and he can't do that unless he's alive."

"If Cal finishes the album he'll have to go to the studio."

"So?"

"So he'll be out in the open where Skip can put a bullet in his head."

The woman gave the salad back, lettuce spilling out of her mouth. "Are voo kiffling?" she said.

CHAPTER TEN

Pet City

July 2005

No guns. Isaiah wouldn't budge on that. He knew his way around computers but hacking was an FBI crime. Out of his league. There was selling drugs but the gangs had that sewed up. Designer drugs were in his wheelhouse but they were rave drugs, white people drugs, nobody around the neighborhood used them. Isaiah was an excellent poker player but you needed a stake.

"Ain't nothing left but thievery," Dodson said. He was at the stove frying bacon for BLTs. "My boy Duane and his partner Dakor was gonna rob an auto parts store but they had to get high first and that took a while. Coupla niggas in a '72 Cutlass driving around at three in the morning. Got busted before they got to the freeway."

"What for?" Isaiah said.

"For being two niggas in a '72 Cutlass driving around at three in the morning. This other time they got into an electronics store over in Carson. They was heisting TVs but forgot to measure the car. Fools was trying to stuff a sixty-inch plasma into the backseat of that Cutlass when the cops showed up. Both of 'em had records, did their bids up in Vacaville. Soon as they got out they went right back at it. Hit a drugstore looking for oxy and some people across the street saw 'em and called the police. They went straight back to Vacaville, didn't even have to change the sheets. Duane got his throat cut in the chow line. Dakor's gonna be in there 'til he's on Social Security."

Dodson took the bacon out of the pan and let it drain on a paper towel. "Ain't easy being a bandit these days," he said. "All them cameras everywhere. They put your ass on TV now. Got the whole city looking for you. Roamin wore a Halloween mask but got recognized by his hair. Must be the last brutha on the block with a Jheri curl. Prescott wore a ski mask with just his eyes showing but they ID'd him by his ink. Nigga had his ex-wife's name running up and down his neck. She's the one who turned him in. Prescott's in Vacaville too, in there making jailhouse chili and playing tonk with Dakor."

"Don't you know any successful thieves?" Isaiah said.

"They're all successful 'til they get busted," Dodson said. He put the BLTs on plates and gave one to Isaiah. "Eat up," he said. Dodson's version of the BLT was double-smoked bacon on toasted rye with some kind of spicy lettuce, thick heirloom tomato slices, and Best Foods mayo with herbs in it. Isaiah took a bite. It was the first thing he'd actually tasted in a long time and he couldn't believe how good it was. He had to stop and look at it.

"But you know what gets niggas busted more than anything else?" Dodson said. "They partners. Shit. You got a brutha looking at a ten-year charge he'll roll over on your ass before he gets to the police station—where're you going?"

Isaiah went out on the balcony with his BLT and his laptop and stayed out there for a long time. When he came back in Dodson was playing *GTA*. "Damn, this game got some lame-ass dialogue. They couldn't get a real Mexican to play Chico?"

"Let's go for a ride," Isaiah said.

They took Marcus's five-year-old Explorer. Marcus didn't care about cars and usually drove a clunker. He'd buy something on the cheap, run it into the ground, and buy something else. He bought the Explorer so Isaiah wouldn't be embarrassed when he got his license.

"The cops get thousands of burglar alarm calls a year," Isaiah said, "and over ninety percent of them turn out to be false."

"*Ninety* percent?" Dodson said.

"That's why they came up with this rule. Your business gets two false alarms but on the third one you have to pay a fine and if there are more false alarms the fines go up. That's why the alarm companies try to verify if it's really a burglary and not somebody working late."

"How do they verify a burglary if there's nobody there but the burglars?"

"When the alarm goes off the system sends a distress signal to the alarm company. The alarm company calls the owner and there's a conversation. Name, are you the responsible party for the property at such and such an address. Were you aware your alarm has gone off, is there anyone on the premises with your permission and whatever else. Okay, so once the alarm is verified, the alarm company calls the police burglary line and there's another conversation with that dispatcher. Which company is this, what is your registration number, has the alarm been verified, what are the points of activation, and *then* the call goes out to the cop on the street and he's still got to get to the location. All that takes time."

"What if the call ain't verified?"

"Unverified calls are most of the calls and they're low-priority.

The cops will respond if they're in the area and have nothing better to do. Like give out a traffic ticket, break up a bar fight—"

"Eat a donut, bust a nigga upside the head."

"One way or the other, we have time to do the job."

"How *much* time?"

"I saw burglar alarm response times that were all over the map. Seven minutes, ten minutes, twelve minutes, forty-five minutes. No way to tell. But the fastest response times are for 911 calls, emergencies. No verifying, no conversations, and these are for things like armed robberies, shootings, hit-and-runs. Average response times nationwide are in the six-minute range. I think to be on the safe side we stick to that."

"Six minutes? What can we steal in six minutes that's worth anything? Unless you're talking about jewelry stores. Shit. If it ain't smash-and-grab it'll take you more than six minutes just to get *in* the damn place."

They were somewhere in El Segundo. Isaiah pulled the car over and parked. "Over there, across the street," he said. "That's the place."

"What place?" Dodson said. "Ain't nothin' over there but a pet store."

A girl with frizzy red hair and a purple vest greeted them as they came in the door. "Hi," she said. "Welcome to Pet City. How can I help you today?" Pet City was a chain store, big and well stocked, smelling of cat litter, kibble, wood shavings, alfalfa, and medicine. Aquarium pumps were buzzing and birds were tweeting. Other young people in purple vests were helping customers with gluten-free dog biscuits and smart toys for their hamster.

Isaiah told the redheaded girl they wanted to look around. They took a tour, Dodson not believing what people bought for their pets. "Keep your dog's breath fresh?" he said. "You can smell your dog's breath you standing too close—rat food? Is that what that says? Somebody needs to tell these people you don't need no special food for a goddamn rat—oh Lord have mercy, that can't be right. Monkey diapers? *Monkey* diapers? You got a monkey wearing diapers you went to the wrong delivery room."

They went to the dog treat aisle. Isaiah took a clear plastic envelope off a display peg. In the envelope were three seven-inch leathery sticks that looked like Slim Jims but more irregular and dried out. "They call them bully sticks," Isaiah said. "They're dog chews. They make them from bull penis."

"Lupita told me there's people that eat the balls," Dodson said. "Now I know what they do with the dick part."

"Look. The package weighs two point six ounces and check the price."

"Twenty-one ninety-five? Shit. I wouldn't pay twenty-one ninety-five for something for *myself* to chew."

"There's what, twenty-five packs there? That's five hundred dollars and you could put them in a paper bag."

In the health aisle, feline epilepsy test strips were forty-six ninety-five. Four tablets of dog dewormer, fifty-five ninety-five. The flea medicines were in a glass case that a clerk had to open with a key. A six-month supply of Frontline came in a flimsy cardboard box no bigger than a paperback book and weighed three ounces. Seventy-two ninety-five. A wireless fence was almost three hundred dollars. There was nothing to it. A plastic transmitter, a collar, and some sensors.

"How's that supposed to be a fence?" Dodson said.

"If the dog tries to go outside the yard the transmitter zaps him through that collar," Isaiah said.

"I know some niggas should have that collar on," Dodson said. He was getting the concept. Isaiah was targeting pricey items that were small and easy to carry. And Pet City had security but nothing like Radio Shack or Zales Jewelry. Who robbed a pet store?

They drove around to the alley side. Isaiah took a casual stroll past the back of the building and came back to the car. "There's a floodlight and a bullet cam over the door," he said. "The knob lock is ordinary but the dead bolt is going to be tough and there might be a sliding bolt on the inside."

On the way home they stopped at a Foster Freeze and ate soft ice cream. "We have to think this through," Isaiah said. "Be methodical. Make a plan."

"I ain't got nothin' against plans," Dodson said.

"No mistakes, nothing stupid that'll get us busted."

"I hope you not calling me stupid."

"That's not what I mean. You're into that gangsta thing. Walk up and stick a gun in somebody's face."

"The gangsta thing ain't a technique, it's an attitude. You either make something your bitch or you gonna *be* the bitch."

"Okay, but no guns. We clear?"

"Yes, nigga, we clear. Will you get on with it?"

They went home and talked some more, Isaiah figuring out detail after detail, making lists in a notebook. Dodson was impatient. Isaiah did all the figuring out and talked over any of his suggestions. They went shopping. Rite Aid, Big 5, the Goodwill store.

"What we gonna do with all this stuff?" Dodson said.

"Eliminate mistakes," Isaiah said.

"Whatever the fuck that means. And what about the door? We gonna pick the lock or use a bump key?"

"The knob lock is easy but the dead bolt is an ASSA High Security model. Can't be picked or bumped and you can't drill it out unless you've got an industrial drill press."

"How come you know so much about locks?"

"My brother. He knew everything."

"So what do we do?"

"I was watching the news last night. Cops raided a crack house in Compton."

"Yeah, so what else is new?"

"I think they're onto something."

They went to an army surplus store. Isaiah told the bald guy sitting behind a case full of knives what he wanted. The guy took them to the back and found it leaning against the wall behind a rack of petrified field jackets.

"Damn, Isaiah," Dodson said. "You ain't playin' around."

It was a little after eleven when they got to Pet City. Traffic was light but enough for cover. Dodson was more hyped than afraid. He was used to high-pressure situations, crack dealing was a high-pressure business. He shot Lil Genius, who was shooting at him. He was robbed at gunpoint twice, got busted twice, did a stretch at YA camp, and had a fight with a Cambodian or a Mexican every day. Some Locos chased him into a marsh near the Dominguez Channel and he hid in the nasty-smelling reeds for an hour and got chewed up by the mosquitos. He glanced at Isaiah. Yeah, uh-huh, Mr. Eliminate Mistakes looked like he was about to jump off a cliff, sweating and taking deep breaths. Yeah, I bet you wish you had some gangsta in you now.

Both of them had on button-down shirts and reading glasses with the lenses taken out. The Explorer was washed, had stolen license plates, and a UCLA decal on the back bumper. Just two nice college boys on their way home from volleyball practice. They drove past Pet City, turned the corner, and made another turn into the alley behind the store. "Remember," Isaiah croaked, "we're methodical, we're following the plan."

"I heard you the first four hundred times," Dodson said. He could see the fear of getting caught in Isaiah's eyes, hear it when he swallowed dry. "I sho' hope we pull this off," Dodson said. He shook his head, his brow crinkled with fake worry. "Last time I was in juvie camp some white boys caught me in the laundry room and tore my ass apart. I couldn't walk for days."

"Could we not talk, please?" Isaiah said.

Isaiah turned off the headlights and crept the car along, gravel crunching under the tires. The dark changed everything. Even Dodson was a little unnerved. The telephone poles were burnt trees, the dumpsters hiding places. It was quiet, peaceful even, but it didn't feel like that. It felt like the SWAT team was inside the store loading their Uzis and talking on their radios. *Pigeon One and Pigeon Two are at the location. Do you copy?* Isaiah parked the Explorer and sat there like he'd forgotten what was next. Dodson started to change clothes. "What you sitting there for, Cap'n?" he said. "Ain't you gonna lead the charge?"

They parked behind the building and got out of the car. They were covered head to toe. Ski masks, sunglasses, long-sleeve shirts, latex gloves, and headband flashlights like coal miners wear. Isaiah stood there and cleared his throat. His mind was a blank. Dodson smirked, strolled up to the back door and a floodlight came on, lighting up half the alley. He drew the gas-powered pellet pistol they'd bought at Big 5, held it sideways, and shot out the light. "Take that, bitch," he said, glass tinkling to the ground.

The battering ram they got from the surplus store was the same kind the cops used on that drug raid in Compton. Three feet long, shaped like a submarine with handles on it like a pommel horse. It weighed fifty-three pounds and needed two people to swing it. When Barry Bonds smashed a home run over the right-field fence into China Basin his bat generated eight thousand pounds of force. The battering ram hit with forty thousand. Isaiah and Dodson practiced at a construction site and bashed through a cinder block wall.

Isaiah couldn't feel his hands and his throat was so dry he couldn't speak above a whisper. "Ready?" he said.

"Shit," Dodson said, "I *been* ready."

They swung the ram like a pendulum. Back and forth, back and forth, getting a rhythm, tensing for the power stroke: Together, they said, *"One — two — THREE!"* The ram slammed into the lock set like a smart bomb, the knob lock and dead bolt ripped right out of their strike plates, the door torn away from the jamb. Isaiah was stupefied. It worked.

"Damn," Dodson said.

They stepped inside. The storeroom was stuffy as a crowded locker room, the cardboard smell like boiled eggs and vomit, the siren so loud it was thick, like something you had to walk through. They turned on their flashlights and swept the beams over the rows of shelves and stacks of cartons that went clear to the ceiling. Isaiah said six minutes but Dodson was already gone.

Isaiah took the right side of the storeroom, going up and down the aisles, looking for items on the shopping list. His ski mask itched, his glasses kept slipping down his nose, and the flashlight beam was going up and down like the needle on a seismograph. In horror movie cuts he saw reptile sand scoopers, grapeseed oil, smoked pig ears, feline toothpaste, wild birdseed, and duck confit dog food but nothing on the list. Some of the boxes were upside down or the back was facing out or only showed a code: LT SN 67J9990 100PC, R997 SMPGTR LG 10PC. Isaiah was slipping into panic mode, breathing like a swimmer swimming in sweat, the adrenaline screaming through his veins, the siren putting fault lines in his skull. The fucking sunglasses were so fogged up he couldn't see. *And the time.* Four minutes gone already. He couldn't think. He didn't know what to do. There was nothing but the siren. *I can't take it. I can't take that fucking siren.* He was about to call it quits when his flashlight found a label: F.C.E. INC FRONTLINE PLUS DOG 4588 LB/3 PACK 20PC. A stack of small cartons were on a top shelf. He'd gone past them twice. "I got the Frontline," he said like he'd discovered a gold seam. He stood on a lower shelf and pawed the cartons to the floor. He shook open a garbage bag and tried to put them in but the bag wouldn't stay open. "What are you *doing?*" he hissed. He got down on his knees and stuffed the cartons into the bag one at a time, stopping again and again to push the glasses back up his nose.

Dodson came hustling down the aisle, all business, holding two full garbage bags. "The fuck you doin' down there?" he said as he went by. "You see the time?"

They drove out of the alley yanking off the ski masks and breathing like they'd come up from a dive. "Oooh shit," Dodson said. "That plan was meticulous, son, I was working it. Hey, slow down, the fuck you doing?"

Isaiah sat ramrod straight, his hands choking the steering wheel, his eardrums reverberating like rung bells. He cracked open a window. The cool air felt lifesaving.

Dodson was talking like he'd scored three touchdowns in the Super Bowl. "You see me in there?" he said. "I was *Ocean's 11, 12,* and *22.* Them bully things? I grabbed a million of them mutha-fuckas. Hard to believe there's that many bulls running around dickless. Wasn't but three of them fences left but I got a whole box of them epilepsy things. What was the price on them?"

"I don't remember," Isaiah said in a sticky whisper.

Dodson smiled. "I seen you running around all crazy," he said. "Shit got real for you, didn't it?"

"I had a couple of problems. No big deal."

"Is that what was happening? I'd hate to see you if you was scared. You wanna pull this off, Isaiah? You need to find your inner gangsta."

They snuck the goods into the apartment and piled the boxes up on the living room floor. Dodson looked at them, his grin as wide as his face. "What do you think?" he said. "Three, four thousand dollars' worth?"

Isaiah shrugged. "Yeah, around in there."

Isaiah sprawled on the bed where Marcus had slept, replaying what happened in the storeroom, feeling what he felt as he ran up and down the aisles, his pulse rising and falling as he saw each part of it, sweating even as he lay there. A tidal change was rolling over him. His heartache, pain, and sorrow were ebbing away and in their place, the roar of adrenaline, the thrilling shock of fear, and the cool clear ecstasy of getting away.

CHAPTER ELEVEN

Lucky

July 2013

Skip clustered his shots on the black guy's crotch, the .22 match-grade long rifle ripping the plywood target to shit. That fucking smart-ass with all his fucking questions. *How did the dog get out? What unit were you in?* Skip slapped another clip into the Buck Mark and blasted away. He liked the gun for work because it had less recoil than a .9 or a .45, and killing somebody was all about placing the bullet and penetration, not stopping power. An added bonus: the small round bounced around in your cranium so it was harder to match it to a gun.

The black man's crotch was kindling and Skip switched to his everyday gun, the .40-caliber Colt Delta. He blasted some more targets. A cop, a zombie, a snarling woman with a knife. That fucking IQ had made him feel small and stupid and ashamed like he had all his life. One way or another he'd get that smart-ass prick.

Back in high school, Skip was a long list of nots. Not an athlete, not an honor student, not in drama club, not a banger, a doper, a techno-geek, a hipster, a surfer, and he was definitely not cool.

What he was, was anonymous. A fringe kid that walked the hallways pretending he had somewhere to go and laughing while he talked on his cell phone to an imaginary homie. He told the other kids he surfed at First Point in Malibu and that his girlfriend was a cheerleader at another school and that his dad, whom he'd never met, got a Purple Heart in Iraq. None of it helped and neither did his name. Magnus Vestergard. What else could his nickname be besides the Maggot? He often thought his life would be completely different if he had a regular name like Jeff, Brian, Bill, or Skip. He liked Skip. It sounded friendly and cheerful. And a different last name. Less foreign and more American. Miller, Parker, Goodman, Hanson.

Everything changed when he saw a video on YouTube. A dork just like him stuck a Roman candle between his butt cheeks and galloped around his driveway with sparks shooting out of him, his friends laughing themselves stupid. It got a quarter of a million hits. *A quarter of a million.*

Magnus began his own YouTube career the very next day when he was cutting through the alley behind Shop 'n Save and found a dead homeless guy sitting in a wrecked Barcalounger. The guy was wearing wino pants with a huge pee stain around the crotch and tuxedo shoes with no laces. He'd spent his last moments inhaling gas duster, his sooty hand still wrapped around the can. Magnus thought the guy looked a lot like Gilligan from that old TV show. Skinny face, stupid haircut, a big honker, and thick lips. Magnus hunched down next to him with his phone and videoed himself doing an interview, putting a pretend mike up to the guy's cocked-over head. "What's up, Gilligan?" he said. "How's everybody on the island? What's that? You guys grew some weed? Gee, that's great. What's that? Mr. Howell got the munchies, ate a whole coconut, and died? Bummer. So what happened to Mary Ann and Ginger? They hooked up and always walk around naked? Shit, man, I'd buy tickets to see that. You know, there's something I always wanted to ask you, Gilligan. What'd you do for sex? Wait, say that again? You were hittin' it with Mrs. Howell? Jesus, what was that like? Fifteen minutes to get her panties off, huh? Wow."

The kids at school were all over him. *Dude, dude, that was crazy! Eeeww, how could you like, do that? You're a fucking psycho, dude. He was like, really dead?* Magnus did more videos. He took a dump on the hood of a cop car and shot a pigeon out of a potato gun. He paid a bag lady to tongue-kiss him and he set fire to an entire lot of Christmas trees. Magnus went from being anonymous to that crazy dude that makes the videos. He got suspended, arrested, was a neighborhood celebrity, but he still didn't make any friends, even at juvie boot camp.

After Magnus didn't graduate, he looked for work but nobody would hire him because of the videos. Then his mother convinced her brother-in-law Hugo to take him on. Hugo Vestergard's Guns America store in San Bernardino was the third-largest gun dealer in California. Magnus was thrilled, like a kid on his birthday and the NRA was throwing him a party. Guns were something he could get into and Guns America was a supermarket of firearms. The store offered the usual selection of Glocks, Smith & Wessons, Berettas, Walthers, Brownings, and Remingtons but Uncle Hugo also carried the S&W .500-caliber handgun, the PS1 pocket shotgun, the Kel-Tec P3AT micropistol, the M110 semiautomatic sniper rifle, and the Chiappa triple-barrel shotgun. Privately, Uncle Hugo liked to say: "If you want to kill somebody with something unusual, come on down."

Uncle Hugo also kept a large inventory of preowned guns. When the recession hit and people were struggling to make their next mortgage payment they brought in their guns to sell. Uncle Hugo scooped them up for pennies on the dollar.

"Why do you buy so many?" Magnus said.

"Because this is America," Uncle Hugo said, "and sooner or later there's going to be another mass shooting and what happens after every mass shooting? The gun control nuts come crawling out of the woodwork talking about banning this and banning that and the next thing you know everybody and their cousin wants a gun. Well, if they can't afford a new one I'll sell them an old one. Something for everybody."

Many of the preowned guns hadn't been inventoried yet so it was easy for Magnus to borrow a few. He'd hike into the desert and try them out. What he discovered was that he had an honest-to-God talent for shooting things. He could pick lizards off a rock at fifty feet, hit a rabbit on the run, and shoot crows right out of the sky with a pistol. The Colt Delta Elite was his favorite. It shot a 10mm FBI load that had a flatter trajectory and longer range than a 9mm. Magnus set up his own shooting range and could have passed the Marine Corps's rifle and pistol tests and been certified by the American Sniper Association.

But what was the point of being good with all those cool guns if nobody knew? He started showing the guns off to the Caltrans workers and truck drivers behind a strip club in Redlands. Sometimes he'd take a bunch of guys out in the desert to shoot watermelons and soda bottles. It was a hoot but afterward nobody wanted to get a beer.

Magnus started selling the guns. His prices were low and he had a lot of customers. He traded a Heckler & Koch submachine for a six-year-old pit bull named Carver's Lucky Seven. The dog had a long pedigree of game-bred fighting dogs. Magnus and Lucky slept in the same bed and took showers together. Magnus ate fast food but Lucky got grass-fed organic beef, free-range chicken, and low-glycemic vegetables. In the evenings they'd go hunting for coyotes, Magnus shooting them and Lucky finishing them off. Magnus stopped going to the movies because he didn't want to leave Lucky alone for three hours, and he only had sex with a hooker if Lucky liked her. Uncle Hugo loved the dog, saying it was the perfect mascot for a gun store.

Things were going good until Debbie Bellweather, the busybody bookkeeper, noticed a mismatch between the number of preowned guns purchased and the number waiting to be put in the system. She told Uncle Hugo, who put two and two together and called the police. Magnus was convicted of grand theft and selling guns without a license. He took a plea deal, got a ten-thousand-dollar fine and an eighteen-month sentence at CSP Solano. First day in, he mouthed off to a guard named Studdard and got the shit beat out of him.

While he was inside, Magnus boarded Lucky with Al Gunderson at Sentinel Pit Bulls in Fergus. He called every chance he got but the old man wouldn't accept the calls because they were collect.

Magnus's cellmate at Solano was Jimmy Bonifant, a drug dealer based in LA. Magnus told Jimmy everybody called him Skip and he explained about getting busted by Uncle Hugo and Debbie Bellweather and how they'd be sorry once he got out. He told Jimmy about the guns and how good he was and how he could have passed all the Marine Corps tests and could shoot crows out of the sky with a Delta Elite that shot 10mm rounds that had a flatter trajectory and longer range than a 9mm. He gave Jimmy his email address: luckysharpshooter@gmail.com. "Easy to remember, right?" Magnus said. He asked Jimmy for an email address but Jimmy said he didn't have one.

When Magnus got out of prison he couldn't pay Lucky's boarding fees so Gunderson let him work it off. He was in poor health and needed some help. Magnus cleaned the kennels, fed and exercised the dogs, helped train them, and prep them for shows. When Lucky died of canine hepatitis, Magnus had him cremated and put some of the ashes in a sniper shell that he carried around his neck.

During his months with Gunderson, Skip got a PhD in pit bulls. The old man had been in the business for thirty-five years and knew everything there was to know about the breed. His dogs had won dozens of titles for conformation, weight pulling, jumping, and agility. Elsa, Gunderson's wife, hated the dogs and said if she had to dust one more trophy she'd kill herself.

When Gunderson died of a brain tumor, Elsa wanted to sell the property and live with her sister in Pasadena. A place that wasn't a hundred degrees every day and you could look out your window and see actual human beings. But the real estate agent told her nobody in their right mind would buy a run-down house in the dead center of nowhere saturated with dogshit, so Elsa quit-claimed the property over to Magnus. With her life insurance money she bought a new Buick and left everything else behind, telling Magnus there wasn't anything she owned that didn't have *dog* on it.

Magnus couldn't believe his luck. What a fluke! He loved the dogs. He already knew them individually from sleeping in the barn, and as Gunderson got sicker and sicker, Magnus became the pack leader. He started calling himself Skip Hanson and changed the name of the kennel to Blue Hill Pit Bulls. He built new kennels and enlarged the exercise yard. He took the dogs hunting in the desert and swimming in Silver Lake. Obedience and attack training every day. The cattle prod for slackers. A little fear went a long way.

Magnus couldn't describe how he felt when he watched the dogs in the yard, jawing and chasing each other, their coats gleaming in the desert sun. Or when he opened the gate and they surrounded him, jumping and barking, wanting his attention and no one else's. Or when he went hunting with them in the desert, his army of pit bulls scouring the brush, Skip the squad leader barking out orders. Or when they were in the house floor-surfing and scarfing up Pop-Tart crusts and lying around on the cool pavers and sleeping with their noses under the bed and putting their paws on the windowsills and barking at the wind. The dogs didn't fight. Skip wouldn't allow it. Goliath stayed close to him, at his feet or next to him on the couch while he watched TV. None of the other dogs came near.

With Blue Hill up and running, Skip went back to San Bernardino and dug up the stash of Uncle Hugo's guns he'd hidden in the desert. He did some target shooting to sharpen up. There was unfinished business to take care of.

Jimmy Bonifant, Skip's former cellmate at Solano, was doing a booming business selling heroin and cocaine to Hollywood's elite. He had a house in the Hills, drove a Maserati Quattroporte, and his girlfriend was second-runner-up Miss San Diego. Jimmy hadn't given a thought to Skip until he saw a story on the news about Hugo Vestergard of Guns America and his bookkeeper, Debbie Bellweather, getting shot at close range with a handgun that shot unusual 10mm FBI rounds. On the same day, Jerry Studdard, the guard at Solano, was shot and killed as he was coming out of Bar None, a hangout for prison personnel. Police said the shooter was nearly a mile away and probably ex-military. Jimmy, who paid a Jamaican psychic two dollars a minute to tell him he wouldn't be killed or busted in the foreseeable future, believed seeing those stories was no accident. The universe was sending him a message, and not coincidentally, one of Jimmy's sales associates had made off with five hundred thousand dollars' worth of black tar heroin and a longtime business rival was threatening Jimmy's life. And Skip was right. Luckysharpshooter@gmail.com was easy to remember.

Over the next few years, Skip did jobs for Bonifant and his circle of criminal associates, making a decent but unspectacular living. Skip was almost happy but even with taking care of the dogs, he still had a lot of hours to kill. Out of curiosity, he went to a dog show and couldn't believe how stupid it was. A judge, who looked like Skip's parole officer, molested everybody's dog, made them trot around in a circle and then picked a winner. How was a fucking mystery. Every dog there, including Skip's, looked exactly the same, and if you won you got a ribbon that didn't even have your name on it. Skip wanted to blow people's minds, freak them out, get that *oh shit* reaction, only this time he wanted to do it with the dogs. Skip got the idea for a big dog watching the new Godzilla movie. The humongous lizard was stomping around, crushing buildings, collapsing bridges, and causing tidal waves, the people scurrying around like ants; screaming, hiding, praying, crying, and calling out for their loved ones.

One of Gunderson's dogs was a seventy-five-pound female named Zelda. Gunderson kept it as a pet but to Skip, Zelda was his ticket-to-ride dog, his breakout dog, his dead-guy-that-looks-like-Gilligan dog. It took a lot of phone calls and emails but Skip found a match. An eighty-two-pound two-year-old stud at All

American Pit Bulls in Flagstaff, Arizona. Skip bought the dog, mated it with Zelda, and a pup from that litter grew up to be bigger than either of its parents. He kept repeating the process, adding in new bloodlines and the Presa Canario, the dogs getting bigger and fiercer until Skip got his masterpiece, Goliath. One hundred and thirty-two pounds of muscle and bloodlust. Goliath killed the goats. He killed a wild donkey. He attacked a mail truck and chased it all the way to the landfill. He killed the Presa Canario in a minute and a half.

Skip entered Goliath in a show and caused an uproar, the other owners calling Goliath a freak of nature and Skip Dr. Frankenstein. Skip laughed in their faces and imagined turning Goliath loose and watching the people scurry around like ants; screaming, hiding, praying, crying, and calling out for their loved ones.

Skip kept shooting until all the targets were obliterated. His gun hand ached and his ears had shut down. He went into the barn to rest and be with the dogs. He called Kurt.

"What?" Kurt said. That was how he answered the phone.

"Q Fuck was here," Skip said.

"Who?"

"IQ, the black guy."

"Shit."

"Basically, he needs to go, the smart-ass prick."

"I'll call you back."

An hour later Kurt called back. "Do what you want about IQ but get the rapper. That's what we paid you for."

"Basically, the rapper's still in his house," Skip said.

"Basically, figure it out."

"I need some intel."

"Intel? *Intel?* What are you, the CIA?"

"Do you want the job done or not?"

"Okay, I'll see what I can do."

Skip ended the call and listened to the palm trees creak and shiver in the wind. All the hits he'd done and the cops didn't know he was alive but that smart-ass prick had found him just like that. Skip had almost shot him while they were sitting with the puppies but somebody else might have known he was at Blue Hill and the other guy would have had to go too. Messy. Especially at his own place. Skip thought about how he'd kill that prick. Kneecap him first and say something cool while he was on the ground, begging for his life, and then shoot him so many times he wouldn't be identifiable with dental records.

It was late. Skip got up from the sofa, the naked lightbulb casting his giant shadow on the wall. He thought he'd go in the house and watch TV with Goliath, maybe have something eat. He could do that now. The puppies were asleep.

CHAPTER TWELVE
Goodbye Goodbye Goodbye

July 2013

Heaped in the laundry basket were three handguns, an assault rifle, a Mac Air, two iPads, a Bose iPod dock, an Xbox, a Blu-ray 3-D disc player, a PlayStation, and a bird's nest of wires. Cal toted the basket out of the house to the patio and the chest-high mound of his belongings already heaped there. He'd been working on it for the last couple of hours, popping Focalins to keep his energy up and Ativan to keep his nervous system from vibrating into dust. He upended the basket onto the pile and said: "Goodbye, goodbye, goodbye."

He'd started with a base layer of furniture and bric-a-brac. A white ash Eames ottoman and the Mistral sectional. A Fiam Italia coffee table, Akua'ba fertility statues, a sculpture of a Rottweiler with his face on it, and the life-size oil paintings of Michael Corleone and Malcolm X. He was getting to like the one of himself. After that came dozens of custom-made suits and shirts, silk underwear, stacks of NBA and NFL jerseys, cashmere sweaters, three-hundred-and-twenty-five-dollar Cucinelli T-shirts, thirty bottles of his cologne, his huge collection of sneakers, copies of his latest contracts, thick as phone books, and a bundle of rolled-up antique Persian prayer rugs from his two weeks as a practicing Muslim.

Also in the pile were tangled clumps of jewelry, most of it made by Teddi the Gleam, jeweler to the stars and CEO of Xtreme Custom Jewelry, his outrageous bling must-haves among the hip and famous. In addition to multiple chains and pendants, Gleam made Cal a grill. The teeth were cast in gold, the two front ones inset with one-carat solitaire diamonds certified for VS1 clarity and achromatic D-grade coloration. The incisors and premolars were etched with gang signs and inlaid with Brazilian emeralds. The bottom teeth were inscribed with the words RAP GOD and adorned with more diamonds and emeralds. The Gleam had also created Cal's favorite piece, a customized watch. Gleam started with an ordinary eighteen-karat-gold Rolex with diamonds on the dial, around the bezel, and embedded in the band. Gleam replaced those ho-hum diamonds with Argyle Pink diamonds, squeezed in some new ones, switched the hands with ones made from a rare mineral extracted from a meteorite that crashed in Siberia, and changed the band to a rolo chain bracelet that was described by one blogger as heavy enough to secure the front gate at the US Embassy in Beirut.

Cal brought out a couple of baskets full of liquor, a nod to Chapter 4 of Dr. Freeman's book, "Avoiding Drugs and Alcohol." Cal used both hands to empty bottles of Bacardi 151, Nouvelle-Orléans absinthe, Glenfiddich Snow Phoenix, thirty-seven-year-old Rémy, and Everclear, a 190-proof grain alcohol, onto the pile. This was largely a symbolic gesture. There were cases of liquor stacked up in the racquetball court. Cal's arms were getting tired and he dumped the rest of the bottles onto the pile unopened. "Goodbye, goodbye, goodbye."

*   *   *

Hegan, Bobby's driver, was sitting in the BMW 750i with the window rolled down. Bobby had called a meeting in Cal's circular driveway. He liked to do that, talk to people in driveways, parking lots, hotel lobbies, and on his way out of restaurants. It made him seem like he only had time for a quick word or two so you better let him say his piece. Bobby liked to say if you control how long you talk you control what's talked about. And the man could talk you into the ground. The best bullshitter Hegan had ever seen and he'd seen more than a few. Like he was doing now with that IQ kid, the one that crazy fuck Cal hired to investigate the dog attack; Bobby doing his busy-man-trying-to-be-patient routine in a sea-green Armani, suede slip-ons, and no socks, talking to the kid like a prosecutor, letting him know who was in charge.

"Let me see if I understand, Mr. Quintabe," Bobby said. "You're telling me the man that orchestrated the attack on Calvin is a dog breeder and a gun collector named *Skip* and he lives in a town called Fergus?"

"That's what I'm telling you," the kid said. He was leaning against his car with his hands in his front pockets.

The kid's buddy, the short guy, was sitting on the edge of the fountain with Anthony, the smart one, who always looked late for something and dressed like Pee-wee Herman. Charles couldn't stay still, walking around in little circles and rubbing the back of his head. Bug was standing with his feet apart and his hands clasped behind his back like one of those black power guys at roll call.

"Well, can you tell us anything else?" Bobby said.

"His real name is Magnus Vestergard," the kid said. "He's got a record going back to high school. The only job he's ever had was working in his uncle's gun store but he got busted for selling the inventory. He did time at Solano, dropped out of sight for a while, and when he reappeared he was raising pit bulls and calling himself Skip Hanson. No more arrests, no social media. His website has pictures of his dogs but he doesn't sell them. He owns his house and drives a new truck."

"And you got all this from—"

"Public Records dot com."

"This is unreal," Anthony said.

Charles looked up at the sky. "This is bullshit," he said. "This muthafucka ain't doin' nothing but eatin' up the clock."

"Yeah," Bug said, "this is bullshit."

"With all due respect," Bobby said, "I don't see how public information moves us forward or helps us to resolve our situation one bit. But let me ask you something else. While you were visiting your alleged hit man, did you happen to see the suspect, a giant killer dog?"

"No, I didn't see the dog, but he was there."

"He was there but you didn't see him," Bobby said flatly. "What do you think of that, Anthony? You're the one who brought Mr. Quintabe on board."

"I know, Bobby, but he's here now," Anthony said. "Can we move on, please?"

Bobby looked at him. "As for the dog breeder having a lot of guns," Bobby said, "I have a lot of guns and I daresay everyone here has a lot of guns but none of us are killers, at least on a professional basis. I'm sorry to say this, Mr. Quintabe, but I'm disappointed with you. Very disappointed."

Hegan liked the kid. He kept his cool, stayed within himself and wasn't intimidated by Bobby, and most people were. It was like the kid was waiting, holding back, letting Bobby punch himself out before he lowered the boom. Hegan wanted to see that.

*　　*　　*

Cal's last basket had an animal theme: a white ermine Cossack hat, a python-skin bomber jacket, eel-skin gloves, sharkskin cowboy boots, ostrich-skin messenger bag, chinchilla pillows, and a full-length overcoat made from six endangered cheetah hides. Cal wondered where his things would be after he was dead and gone. His suits on a rack at the Goodwill, a crackhead bundled up in the overcoat, the jewelry on that show his mother liked to watch about people who hoped their cuckoo clock was worth something. "Goodbye, goodbye, goodbye."

Bobby was still talking and Hegan could sense the kid was getting tired of playing defense. All he needed was an opening.

"Now here's what I need you to do, Mr. Quintabe," Bobby said. "I need you to go in there and tell Calvin that what he's asked you to do is impossible and that he should get back to work before he's permanently damaged his career and that you are apologizing for wasting everyone's time with somebody named *Skip* who can't be verified as anything other than a dog breeder and a gun enthusiast and if there *was* a giant killer dog you didn't see it."

Hegan saw it in the kid's eyes and the way his jaw was set. He was coming off the ropes.

"No, I didn't see a giant killer dog," the kid said, "but I saw a kennel twice the size of the others and a washtub for a water bowl and what kind of dog breeder needs an alias, doesn't sell his dogs, or have a Facebook page? And how does somebody who hasn't drawn a paycheck since he was eighteen years old buy a thirty-five-thousand-dollar truck and pay the upkeep on fifteen dogs? And the man doesn't have a lot of guns, he has an arsenal. I saw shell casings for .38-, .40-, and .45-caliber pistols, 7.62 rounds for assault weapons, and .338 Magnums for a sniper rifle, and he's set up targets on a hill a half mile away and there's no sense putting them up there if he can't hit them.

"I picked this up at Skip's place," the kid said. He showed Bobby a bullet. It looked like a regular .45-caliber round but the bullet was blunter. "This is a multiple-impact round. When you fire the gun, the bullet breaks into three fragments held together with strings of Kevlar. The fragments come at you spinning like a South American bolo and they hit with a fourteen-inch spread. In other words, I could shoot at you, miss by thirteen inches, and still blow your brains out. Now I don't know if that verifies Skip as a hit man but it verifies him as *something*."

Bobby looked like he'd opened his safe and found a head of cabbage. Hegan turned away to hide his smile.

"Any questions?" the short guy said.

The kid lifted his head. "Something's burning."

Earlier that day Cal had skimmed Chapter 9 of Dr. Freeman's book, "Letting Go of *Things*." Dr. Freeman wrote: "If you're suffering from burnout then you know it's a constant struggle keeping up with what's in, what's new, what's hot; always desperate to acquire that next meaningless possession. And the next. And the next. This obsession with things holds us back, keeps us in burnout mode, perpetuating the feeling of futility because going forward only means accumulating more meaningless possessions. My patients invariably experience a great sense of relief when they stop investing their self-worth in what they can buy. One of my patients, who happened to be a very wealthy young woman, said: 'Once I stopped giving a sh-t about what Jennifer Lopez was wearing and if the new iPhone could speak Swahili, I felt free. For the first time in my life, I felt really free.'"

Cal longed for freedom. From what, he wasn't exactly sure, but he knew he had to get away from it or be lost forever. He wadded up a contract, lit it with his platinum Cartier weed lighter, and threw it on the pile. The alcohol in the liquor ignited and the pile began to burn. Cal held his arms out like a crucifix and looked up at the fluffy white clouds floating in the blue, blue sky. "I have said goodbye to all my meaningless possessions," he said. "I am free. I am free."

The contracts, clothes, prayer rugs, and other flammables would have flamed briefly and smoldered if it wasn't for the underlying layer of furniture and bric-a-brac. Like the vent at the bottom of a barbecue, it let oxygen draft upward and keep the fire burning. Cal waited to feel the freedom Dr. Freeman said he'd feel but all he felt was drugged and confused, no different than before. He looked at the fire and watched his two thousand dollar Pierre Corthay patent-leather dress shoes and his three thousand dollar Bottega Veneta Intrecciato messenger bag blister and turn black. A sharp realization pierced the pudding in his brain. "My shit is burning up," he said. "I have burned up my shit."

Bobby came out of the house and double-timed it across the patio, the others trailing behind. He couldn't believe what he was seeing. His star artist was standing in front of a fucking bonfire with his arms out like some kind of high priest in a cashmere bathrobe. "Get away from there," Bobby said, grabbing Cal and pulling him back. "You're going to set yourself on fire."

"It never stops," Anthony said.

The cologne bottles were cracking in the heat. The yard reeked of burnt chemicals, evil spirits of black smoke escaping into the sky. The woman next door came out on her balcony. "What's going on over there?" she said.

"Go back in your house, bitch," Charles said.

"My shit is burning up," Cal said. "I have burned up my shit."

"I'm going to get you some help," Bobby said.

"I already got help. Dr. Freeman is helping me."

"You should have taken that damn book away from him, Anthony."

"He bought out Barnes and Noble," Anthony said. "Forty or fifty copies."

"What about the drugs?"

"Let's see, today it was Focalin, Fentanyl, Klonopin, Wellbutrin—"

"I don't care about the goddamn names. Can't you confiscate them?"

"DStar's people deliver twenty-four seven."

Bobby turned to Isaiah. "Do you see why you have to end this, Mr. Quintabe? He's ruining his—Mr. Quintabe? Are you with us?"

Isaiah was staring into the fire at the unopened liquor bottles. "Run," he said. He took off. Dodson hesitated a moment and then ran after him.

"The fuck's wrong with them?" Charles said.

"Well, that does it," Bobby said. "Our illustrious investigator has gone berserk."

A liquor bottle exploded. Sparks, broken glass, and a cloud of ashes erupting out of the flames, Bobby and the fellas scattering like a flock of scared pigeons. Bobby lay facedown on the patio with his hands over his head. He wished he could stay like this, his cheek on the warm bricks, inhaling the comforting childhood smells of cut grass and chlorine. His nightmare seemed to have no end, every day worse than the last, his hope fading like the sunsets he could see from his office window. "Kill me now," he said. "Put me out of my misery."

*   *   *

More bottles blew up. Isaiah and Dodson were behind a palm tree. "How'd you know them bottles was gonna blow up?" Dodson said.

"The alcohol in the bottles was turning cloudy," Isaiah said. "It was vaporizing and the pressure had nowhere to go."

"I figured you knew something," Dodson said as another bottle exploded. "Look at Bobby all down on the ground. Looks like the Taliban's shooting at his ass. And speaking of Bobby, why'd you go at him so hard? You lost your temper again, didn't you?"

"I don't care about Bobby," Isaiah said. "I care about my client."

"Well, you better get out your water wings. Your client is drowning again."

Despite his earlier experience, Cal had jumped in the pool and was thrashing around, swallowing water. "Help," he gurgled. "Somebody help Calvin." He went under, one hand waving like he was hailing a cab.

Charles and Bug were behind the gas barbecue, too disgusted to laugh. "How'd that fool ever get to be a star?" Charles said.

Anthony was sitting out in the open with his back against the house. He looked like a man who'd lost his dignity and was too tired to go get it. "Maybe we'll get lucky and he'll drown," he said.

Isaiah looked from Anthony to Bobby to Bug and Charles. One of them was keeping Skip in the loop. One of them was the inside man.

The explosions stopped. Cal yelled at Anthony to help him get out of the pool. "Oh there's gonna be some housecleanin' around here, y'all can believe that," Cal said, trying to look like a Rap God in a sopping-wet robe, a lens missing from his sunglasses.

Sirens were coming.

"That's my cue," Bobby said, heading for the house. "You people figure out what you're going to tell the police because Calvin does not go to jail. Do you understand? Calvin does *not* go to jail."

"Why would Calvin go to jail?" Cal said.

"Reckless endangerment, public nuisance, fire regulations," Anthony said, "and I don't know if those guns are registered."

The sirens were getting louder.

"Well, *somebody's* gonna take the charge," Cal said. "Can't be you, Anthony, I need somebody to be my flunky."

Bug and Charles looked like the guilty rapists in a lineup, the victim staring right at them.

"I guess that leaves you two niggas," Cal said, looking from one to the other. "Who's it gonna be? Eenie or meenie? Meenie or eenie?"

"Shit, Cal, you know that ain't right," Charles said.

"It's right if I say it's right and I say it's you."

"Mutha*fuck!*" Charles said, walking in a circle and rubbing the back of his head. "Come on, Cal, don't be like that."

"Don't be like what, Charles? Don't be like what? The shot caller? Well, I can't help that 'cause I *am* the shot caller and I'm calling on you to take the charge and stop whining like a bitch."

"This is bullshit," Bug said. "You should take your own charge."

"I'll take my own charge when you write your own check. How 'bout that, Bug? When you write your own check."

Charles told the cops he drank too much and lost his mind. Isaiah watched him give everything in his pockets to Bug before they cuffed him and took him away, Bug's eyes shooting tracer rounds into Cal's back as he slogged into the house. "One day, muthafucka," Bug said. *"One day."*

Bobby sat in the backseat glaring at Hegan like it was his fault the day had gone to shit. Hegan was probably wondering why Bobby smelled like smoke and wasn't yelling into his cell at his lawyer or one of his acts or Eva, his Amazonian girlfriend who wore high heels when she shopped at Whole Foods.

"Did something happen back there?" Hegan said.

"Yes, something happened back there," Bobby said. "I almost got killed, no thanks to you."

"You okay?"

"No, I'm not okay. I'm not even close to okay."

When Bobby first moved from Sacramento to LA, he lived in Mar Vista and shared a one-room apartment with a voracious tribe of roaches. He drove a clapped-out Lincoln Continental and lived on ramen like a frat boy. Ramen and eggs. Ramen and Spam. Ramen and fried baloney. Once he was so broke he ate Ramen and cat food. Before he started Bobby Grimes Music and Entertainment, he held four different titles in eleven different companies and had taken more than his share of hard knocks. Over the years he'd been cheated, evicted, thrown out, beat up, laughed at, and sued more times than he could remember. Bobby could teach classes on Chapters 7 and 11 and give tours of the Edward R. Roybal Federal Courthouse.

Cal was the game-changer. When his first two albums went platinum, other artists jumped on the BGME bandwagon and Bobby found himself playing at the big ballers' table. He had respect, money, toys, women. He was on top of the world. But then Steve Jobs came along with his fucking iTunes that strangled the CD to death and sucked the blood out of Bobby's revenues. And pirating. A goddamn college kid would be pissed as hell if he got his iPod stolen but had no qualms about downloading Bobby's music for free. Overseas was a joke. The Chinese didn't know music was something you had to pay for. Bobby had to fire staff, tighten promotional budgets, and make fewer records. Artists left for greener pastures.

Bobby's white knight was the entertainment conglomerate Greenleaf Studios. Greenleaf wanted to acquire BGME but the key to the deal was Calvin. Big-name artists with a worldwide fan base and a proven track record were hard to come by and Greenleaf wanted Calvin to brighten up their constellation of stars. No Calvin, no deal.

Bobby's immediate problem: Greenleaf's due diligence would begin soon. Marty Greenleaf's army of lawyers and accountants would descend on BGME's Century City offices like the roaches in the Mar Vista apartment and they'd crawl over every contract, sales report, bank statement, spreadsheet, expense account, and copyright since the company's inception. And Marty would want to meet Cal. Bobby could just imagine that conversation. Cal in his bathrobe, high on weed and pills, and holding that stupid cat while he talked about Mr. Q and the giant pit bull and putting Noelle in jail and burning up his meaningless possessions in the backyard. Marty would insist on hearing the new tracks too. All two of them, the best of which was a twenty-three-second song about the fuck am I doing on this earth. The bonfire was a metaphor, thought Bobby. Everything he'd worked for was going up in flames. The house in Brentwood, dinner at Spago or Matsuhisa, drinks at Bar Marmont, on the list at the Sayers Club and Greystone Manor. He'd seen and done things he couldn't have imagined when he was promoting raves and club events back in Sactown. He was on the other side of the rope now, in a world all of young America could only dream about.

Bobby partied at Young Snap's mansion in upstate New York. The place had the same square footage as a football field and you could take a piss every day for three weeks and never be in the same bathroom. Bobby estimated a family of four could survive just eating the fish in Snap's private lake. Bobby got a backstage pass at a Layla concert and was staying in the same hotel. Aside from the usual battalion of bodyguards and makeup artists, the icon's entourage included a laundress, a food taster, a Buddhist monk, and a Botox technician. Somebody told Bobby her Labradoodle had its own suite.

Bobby was invited to the Monaco Grand Prix by one of Cal's sponsors. GKnight and his girlfriend Nia were there and Bobby spent the weekend on their luxury yacht, the *Colossus*. You didn't board the boat, you landed on it like an island. Bobby thought if you put a few cannons on the decks and loaded up some Tomahawks you could send the *Colossus* to the Persian Gulf. No way he was giving all that up and he'd commit suicide before he went back to the ramen diet. If he was anything he was a survivor.

"I am not going down," Bobby said.

"What?" Hegan said. "Who's not going down?"

"Bobby Grimes," Bobby said. "Bobby Grimes is not going down."

After dropping Dodson off, Isaiah went home. He swept the driveway, watered the front lawn, and mowed the grass in the back. He let Alejandro out of the garage, the bird pecking at insects fleeing the mower blades. After, he let the bird snoop around in the house while he made some soup and ate it standing at the counter.

He thought about Bobby Grimes. Bobby needed Cal to make an album, that was clear. He was more desperate than you'd expect but there was no question his anger and frustration were real. Charles and Bug. It was obvious they hated Cal but their livelihood depended on him. Killing Cal was killing the goose that laid the golden records. Without Cal they were back on the streets.

The question mark was Anthony. He was the only one who defended Noelle and he didn't seem to care about his job, the album, or Cal for that matter. But if that was his attitude, why didn't he leave? He could get a job somewhere else. There had to be some other reason that was keeping him around and that would explain his impatience. Anthony wasn't interested in the next thing on Cal's agenda. He was trying to finish. To be done. Anthony wanted everything to be over.

All that made sense but Isaiah was uneasy. He had a feeling he was on the wrong track but so far there weren't any other tracks to be on. And there was something else flitting around the edges of his awareness like one of those dragonflies in the backyard. There and gone, there and gone. If only it would stay still. It was the case-breaker, he could feel it.

And it was something he already knew.

CHAPTER THIRTEEN

Is That You?

September 2005

It was irritating, Isaiah making him guess what the job was. No doubt the boy was feeling foolish about the Pet City score and was trying to get some leverage back. Kinkee played that game too, knowing you were down to kibbles and bits and making you ask when the reup was happening. Then he got to tell you: "That's some classified shit, nigga, above your lowly-ass pay grade, you feel me? I'll let you know when I let you know."

Dodson tried to hold out but by the time they got on the 710 he couldn't stand it anymore. "What is it?" he said.

"A beauty shop," Isaiah said, victorious.

"How come you didn't take me with you when you cased it?"

"Didn't need to. It's perfect."

"I don't know it's perfect and what can you steal from a beauty shop?"

Isaiah told him what he'd found on the Ruby's Real Beauty website. Ruby's stocked the largest, most complete inventory of human hair extensions in the South Bay area. The most highly prized were Virgin Remy.

"Virgin because the girl still had her cherry?" Dodson said.

"No. Virgin because the hair wasn't chemically treated," Isaiah said.

"What's Remy mean?"

"It means the hair was carefully cut so the cuticles and roots stayed in the same direction. Otherwise, they mow it down like weeds and throw it in a bin."

Isaiah went on explaining like a college professor talking to a not very bright middle school student: A Brazilian-weft Virgin Remy human-hair single-drawn superior-grade twenty-eight-inch naturally curly extension from a woman in São Felipe whose hair was half the family's income retailed at Ruby's for four hundred and thirty-four dollars. A Russian Virgin Remy human-hair superior-grade double-drawn naturally straight twenty-inch extension from a teenager in Volgograd who wanted a new pair of boots was five hundred and nineteen dollars.

"So *that's* what you can steal from a beauty shop," Isaiah said. "Anything else you want to know?"

As they got out of the Explorer behind Ruby's, Dodson said, "This time try and handle your shit."

The battering ram took the door out no problem. The siren was as loud as Pet City's but the burglars wore noise-suppression head-phones like the pit crews at NASCAR. They didn't block the sound out completely but at least your head didn't explode. Isaiah was overanxious but it was an easier score. All the Virgin Remy extensions were on the same set of shelves and he'd replaced the trash bags with collapsible hampers. They were lightweight and stayed open by themselves and you could load them with two hands.

"Four minutes," Isaiah said as they drove away. "We were in and out in four minutes. What'd you think of the hampers? Made a difference, didn't it? The heat's still bothering me and the glasses keep steaming up, I've got to fix that. *Four minutes.*"

Dodson could feel the boy's head swelling, probably thinking he was a man now. That was all right, let him believe it if he wanted to. The main thing was this burglary shit was working out. If they kept it going he could quit the crack business, tell Kinkee to go fuck himself, and be a man of leisure.

A customer came in, the only one in the last couple of hours. The man had the shakes and was looking around like he'd lost a child at the county fair. He was a regular, somewhere between forty and sixty, his face sagging like Auntie May's basset hound, his eyes yellow and bloodshot from seeing too much of his own life. He was a typical customer these days, older and a longtime addict. Youngsters were staying away from crack. They'd seen too many crackheads wandering the streets all stank-ass nasty, groveling for change and trying to sell you a toaster oven with the power cord cut off. Crackheads weren't cool and if you wanted kids to stay away from something, uncoolness was all it took.

Which was a problem for Dodson. Without new people getting on the pipe he was competing with every other dealer on the block for the same dwindling pool of dope fiends. The only way to make a buck was repeat business. Fiends shopped around. To make them come back you had to have the good shit. Dodson's shit was hit or miss and today was a miss. To make the same money he'd have to stay longer, serving it up to the fiends who were too sick and desperate to walk six blocks and buy from the Locos. It was Kinkee's fault. He was Dodson's supplier and a burly surly Ice Cube clone who scowled even when he smiled and treated everybody except Michael

Stokely like an intruder. Kinkee didn't weigh the cocaine before he cooked it into crack and cut it with too much baking soda, always in his favor. To make up for it, he added what he called *flavorings:* vodka, furniture polish, bleach, laundry detergent, kitchen cleaner, whatever he had around. Dodson felt bad for the crackheads. "The fuck you put all that shit in there for?" he said. "You trying to get 'em high or kill 'em off?" Kinkee never answered.

Dodson went to 7-Eleven and bought grapefruit juice to get the crack taste out of his mouth. He dreaded going back to work but he was the sole breadwinner at the apartment now and it pissed him off. He should have been rolling in dough. In the two weeks since the Ruby's job, they'd hit the Sunglass Emporium, Tight Lines Fly Fishing, and Luogo Di Lusso, a shoe store in Studio City. The take was crazy. Three hundred pairs of Oakleys, Ray-Bans, Maui Jims, and Michael Kors, none of them under a hundred dollars, most of them closer to two. Dodson was skeptical about Tight Lines until he found out a Sage four-piece carbon-fiber trout rod weighed an ounce and a half and sold for five hundred and ninety-five dollars. Dodson said for five hundred and ninety-five dollars he could eat at the Red Lobster every day for a month and never get his feet wet. They took twenty-nine rods. The shoe store was a diamond mine. Jimmy Choos, Pradas, Valentinos, and a bunch of other designer brands at five-six-seven hundred dollars a pair. Dodson wasn't getting paid because of eBay.

"EBay?" Dodson said. "The fuck you talking about eBay?"

"Marcus had a seller's account," Isaiah said. "PayPal too, for buying his tools. I got the passwords."

"Fuck the passwords. That shit takes forever."

"You have to be patient."

"Yeah, well, come on down to the House and tell me about patience, in there all day with a bunch of messed-up niggas ought to be wearing that Frontline and where the fuck are you? Sittin' in here playing with your laptop. Let me call my boy Pook. He'll scoop up the sunglasses and pay us cash today."

"No middleman."

"Why the fuck not? EBay's a middleman."

"EBay can't roll over on us. The only ones who can do that are you and me."

Dodson stood idly by while Isaiah jumped headfirst into the eBay world, writing detailed item descriptions, checking the comps, setting the prices, keeping track of sales on a spreadsheet. He tripped out on the photography. Dodson watched him fuck around with a fly rod, standing it upright, laying it sideways, shooting close-ups.

"How many pictures you gonna take of a stick?" Dodson said.

Despite the excellent photography sales were slow. People bought things one at a time. The shoes, the sunglasses, the fly rods. Isaiah thought the dog supplies would sell fast but there was a lot of competition and the prices were really low. Made you think everybody was ripping off pet stores.

"Let me help you with the eBay stuff," Dodson said. "Make the shit go faster."

"I got it," Isaiah said.

"I know you got it, just show me what to do."

"I said I got it."

Dodson was tempted to knock Isaiah off his high side, put a knot on his head, put the boy in his place. The only reason he hadn't done it already was because Isaiah seemed breakable, like a steering wheel lock sprayed with Freon. Hit him and he'd shatter into pieces and Dodson would never see real money. Another irritation, Isaiah kept adding tweaks. Defogging pads for the sunglasses, flashlights with wider beams, and fishing clothes he'd picked up at Tight Lines. Pants and shirts in pastel colors, the kind rich guys wore bonefishing in the Bahamas. Dodson tried them on with the ski mask and sunglasses. "I ain't wearing this shit," he said. "I look like some kinda homo terrorist."

"They're lightweight, breathable, and they dry fast," Isaiah said. "You can wear your own clothes if you want to."

"I can? That's big of you."

Isaiah was reluctant to show Dodson the storage locker but he had no choice. They had to keep their growing inventory somewhere. The first time Dodson saw the locker he said: "Damn. What'd your brother do, run a hardware store?"

Marcus kept his tool collection in here. The drills, saws, grinders, impact wrenches, sanders, and nail guns were displayed on a peg board like a gun collection. Likewise for the dozens of hand tools. A table saw and a miter were on the long workbench. Storage bins on shelves held nails, nuts, screws, washers, and such. The floor-standing tools were in their own area.

"You've got to have the right tool," Marcus said, trying to make the collecting sound practical. "You don't have the right tool you'll do half the job in twice — why're you laughing, Isaiah? Something might come up when I need this."

"Need it for what?" Isaiah said. "Fixing the space shuttle?"

Isaiah saw something in Marcus's eyes when he held a new tool in his hand. Turning it over, inspecting it like there were clues on it, seeing if the heft felt right. Then he'd smile like this was the one he was looking for, the one that would complete the set and fill the empty space in his toolbox. It took a week for the tool to become just another tool and another week for Marcus to be online searching for something else.

The locker's roll-down door was halfway up, the space divided into sunlight and dark. Isaiah was on the dark side, sitting at the workbench looking at sales figures on his laptop. He liked the busywork. It kept Marcus out of his head and Marcus was close by, waiting to sneak up behind him and walk on his heels and ask him why his little brother whom God had blessed with a gift had turned into a common thief.

Dodson ducked under the door looking fed up and pissed off. He tossed a roll of cash on the workbench.

"What's this?" Isaiah said.

"Your cut for the hair extensions," Dodson said. "I sold 'em to some beauty shops. Lady said we ever get more to bring 'em on down."

"I said no middleman."

"I know what you said but who the fuck are you?"

"What if the hairdressers get busted?"

"What are they gonna say if they do? A nigga we don't know walked in, sold us some extensions, and walked on out again? I ain't no new jack at this. I was criminalizing while you was in Miss Petrie's class raising your hand every two seconds."

Isaiah was picking up in the living room, throwing Dodson's laundry into a pile, wiping off the coffee table, and taking dirty dishes back to the kitchen. Dodson had been scrupulous about keeping the place clean but lately he'd been slacking off. "Do you think you could clean up after yourself?" Isaiah said.

"I will, nigga, damn," Dodson said, coming out of the bathroom. "I just got home a minute ago." Dodson was wearing a new Clippers jersey, new Diesels, and a pair of patent leather MJs that looked like spats. "Oooh shit I'm looking good," he said. "Bitches gonna be all over me."

"You shouldn't buy all that stuff," Isaiah said. "It attracts attention."

"I'm *trying* to attract attention."

"What are you gonna say if somebody asks you where the money's coming from?"

"You need to step back on yourself, Isaiah. Stop stressin', take a day off, smoke a joint, go get some pussy 'fore you forget what it looks like. Enjoy the fruits of your labor."

Dodson brought a girl home. Deronda was thirty pounds lighter back then but still had booty that followed her around like a roll-on suitcase. When she met Isaiah she looked him up and down and said: *"So?"* Isaiah retreated to the bedroom and listened to them wear out the foldout, Deronda saying is that all you got? Is that all you got? Dodson saying oh you want some more? You want some *more?* The TV was on the whole time.

After Deronda left, Isaiah came out, wincing at the smell of sex and latex. Dodson lay facedown wearing only his socks, one arm hanging over the side. "That girl wore my ass out," he said. "That last time didn't nothing come out my dick but some mist."

"You shouldn't have brought her here."

"I live here, nigga, I'll do what the fuck I want."

"What if she tells somebody we have our own apartment?"

"Why you always worried about what somebody gonna tell somebody? That girl thinks the apartment is your brutha's and he ain't home."

"Doesn't matter, it was stupid to bring her here."

Dodson got up on one elbow. "Did you just call me stupid?" he said. Isaiah leaned his head to one side, looked bored, and went into the kitchen. "Yeah, walk away, muthafucka," Dodson said. "If I wasn't buck-ass naked I'd be kicking your ass right now. Say it one more time, Isaiah, you hear me? Say it one more time."

Deronda went out of her way to mess with Isaiah. Dropping his toothbrush in the toilet, leaving her thongs to dry on the bedroom doorknob. She liked to come out of the kitchen with a mixing bowl full of chocolate pudding and bobble it wide-eyed like she was going to spill it on him. *Uh-oh, uh-oh, look out, look out!* She'd cuddle up with Dodson on the foldout and scratch his balls, grinning at Isaiah as he went by, the two of them laughing while he was still within earshot.

They did more jobs. Electric shavers, cigars, swimming pool pumps.

Deronda stayed an entire weekend. On Sunday night she and Dodson went out for tacos before she went home. When they got back Isaiah was standing in front of the TV watching the news.

"The police are calling them the Battering Ram Bandits," the reporter said, "because they've used a battering ram to bash their way into businesses all over Southern California—Long Beach, El Segundo, Lawndale, Culver City, Lomita, Torrance, even as far as the Valley."

"Why we watching this?" Deronda said.

"Seen here on surveillance video," the reporter said, "the two suspects batter their way into Danny's Dive Shop in Long Beach. Police say the suspects are males, African-American, and in their late teens or twenties. One suspect is approximately six feet tall, the other around five-three."

"Five-four," Dodson said. Isaiah looked at him sharply and then shifted his gaze to Deronda.

"Is that you?" Deronda said.

"The police say the suspects are professionals," the reporter said. "They get in and out of the store in minutes and only take high-priced items. They're believed to be driving a dark-colored Ford Explorer."

"Y'all drive an Explorer," Deronda said. "Is that you?"

The reporter continued: "The LA Chamber of Commerce has posted a five-thousand-dollar reward for information leading to the arrest of the suspects. If you have any information about the suspects call the police hotline at the number on your screen."

"That *is* you," Deronda said.

Isaiah got the Explorer painted white and from then on Dodson rode in the backseat. A cop would only see one occupant. They did more jobs. Tankless water heaters, golf clubs, AC motors, airless paint sprayers, German kitchen faucets. The pipeline was full to overflowing, the money coming in steady now.

Dodson quit the House. He bought more clothes and another gold chain and a TV so big they had to take down Isaiah's awards. He spent a lot of time with Deronda. Shopping for clothes, getting high, playing *GTA,* going to clubs that would accept their fake IDs, and lounging on the foldout watching cooking shows and buying things from HSN. A shiatsu foot massager, a panini press, a waterproof radio, a botanical stem cell moisturizer, a juicer that could juice wood, and a bunch of other stuff that was still in their boxes. Deronda got her nails done every three or four days. New colors, new sparkly things. They ate out every meal. They drank Heineken and Hennessy. If Isaiah wouldn't give them a ride they took a cab. They went to bed at three in the morning and got up at three in the afternoon. It was like being a celebrity, living your life instead of chasing it.

"Fuck tomorrow," Deronda said. "Fuck it to death."

One in the morning. They were lying on the foldout eating Thai food. Isaiah came in and went into the bedroom without saying anything.

"Well?" Deronda said, looking at Dodson.

"Let me finish my noodles," Dodson said.

"I'll hold 'em for you 'til you get back."

Isaiah had night-walked for hours but knew he wouldn't sleep. He was hungry and smelled the Thai food but wasn't going to ask them for anything. They'd look at each other like it was a shocking request, huddle like it needed discussion, and then reluctantly give him half a spring roll or some leftover rice.

More and more, Isaiah had been thinking about how to get them out of the apartment. Deronda might as well have been on the lease; there every night, her stuff all over the place. She only went home when she had to babysit her little brother. She'd also transformed Dodson into a complete asshole and had gotten it into his head that he was in charge.

Dodson came in without knocking. "What do you want?" Isaiah said, his space invaded.

"When we doing the next job?" Dodson demanded.

Isaiah restrained the impulse to say fuck you. "What's your hurry?" he said. "You need a bigger TV?"

"I have a temporary cash flow problem."

"You do? You spent all that money?"

"I'm living large out here. When?"

"Couple of days."

Dodson left the room, an *it better be* look on his face. Isaiah thinking, *We'll see about that.*

Isaiah took a week to give the go-ahead on the next job, Dodson bugging him every time they saw each other. *Who's in charge now?* Isaiah thought. They drove in silence to Speedway Bicycles in Culver City and parked in the alley behind the store. They readied their equipment and took out the door, all routine. Now they were in the storeroom filling their hampers with Shimano Dura-Ace cranksets and Ultegra front derailleurs, Dodson throwing the boxes in like he was trying to break them.

"Five minutes," Isaiah said.

"I got a watch," Dodson said. "And I can tell time too."

Isaiah shook his head and sighed, glancing through the storeroom door at the back of the service desk. Over it, you could see the front window and the street. A patrol car had pulled up at the curb, a cop already getting out. "Cops," Isaiah said. They ran out into the showroom and headed for the back exit but the cop was almost at the window. "Down!" Isaiah said. They dived to the floor and crawled for cover but the cop was looking into the window, shining his flashlight. They froze in place, behind a row of brand-new bicycles, parked at an angle. They were shielded but not completely. Look through the spokes and there they were.

The cop's flashlight beam roved around the store, bright as the one that glared down from a police helicopter chasing a carjacker. Isaiah flattened himself out like a halibut, putting his arms straight out, his cheek on the floor. *Please don't see me please don't see me please fucking God don't see me.* Dodson was flattened out the same way; they were looking directly at each other. The flashlight beam went by quickly and didn't stop. Was the cop done? There was a moment of hope but then the beam started over, going slower this time, inspecting instead of scanning.

"Shit, man, he's gonna see us," Dodson whispered.

"Maybe not," Isaiah whispered back. "Just stay still."

"You took a week to plan this? The fuck was you doing?"

"You rushed me into this. We shouldn't even be here!"

The beam was heading their way, moving across displays of helmets and bicycle clothes. *Please don't see me please don't see me please fucking God don't see me.*

"Shit, man, I got a fuckin' record," Dodson said. "They could try me as an adult, send me to Corcoran." The beam moved closer, spotlighting a family of eyeless mannequins pedaling along in matching spandex. Light spilled over onto the row of bicycles, handlebars, and fenders gleaming. "I ain't goin' to the joint," Dodson said. "No muthafuckin' way." He squirmed and reached under his shirt.

"What are you doing?" Isaiah said. "Stay still."

Dodson had a gun.

"Are you crazy?" Isaiah said. Dodson clicked the gun's safety off with his thumb. "Don't, Dodson, for fuck sake, *don't!*" Miraculously, the beam went up to the loft, more bicycle stuff up there. "Put the gun away!"

"Fuck you, Isaiah."

"Put it away or I'm giving up."

"Bullshit."

"I swear to God I'll do it."

"Then I'll shoot you too."

The beam hovered like a vulture, the two of them lying there like they'd been shot in the back, the sides of their heads pressed to the linoleum, glistening puddles of drool under their mouths.

"You can't do this, Dodson. You can't shoot a cop." In the next instant, the beam was on them so bright it was hot. You could count the dust particles in the air and the beads of sweat on Dodson's face. He'd moved his hands in closer to his head. One held the gun, the other was flat on the floor so he could push himself off. The beam held.

"He sees us!" Dodson started to get up—

"No, Dodson, no!"

The beam vanished. There was a moment of disbelief but the cop had turned and was walking back to his patrol car. Isaiah blew out a long breath and went limp. Dodson was on his knees, head down, hands on his thighs. "Man, that was some shit right there," he said. "How'd he miss us?"

"The reflection off the bicycles," Isaiah said. "And the beam was too high. We were just on the bottom edge of it."

The cop had paused to say something into his radio. Isaiah's stomach fell into his Nikes. "He's going around the back. *The car.*"

They took off, sprinting across the showroom, bursting out of the rear exit, and jumping into the Explorer. Isaiah started the engine—and stopped with his mouth open.

"What?" Dodson said.

"The cop car was facing the same way we are," Isaiah said. "He'll come into the alley right in front of us!" He slammed the shifter into reverse and stomped on the gas. The tires chirped, the car jerking backward, accelerating, the gearbox winding up like a jet engine at takeoff. Isaiah was half turned around, stretching his neck to see into the darkness, one hand on the steering wheel. *The cop is coming.*

"Step on it!" Dodson said.

"I am!" Isaiah said.

The Explorer veered offline. Isaiah cranked the wheel but over-corrected, the back end swinging to the side and banging into a dumpster. *The cop is coming.*

"Straighten out!" Dodson said.

"Shut up!" Isaiah said. He cranked the wheel the other way, overcorrecting again and shearing the side mirror off on a telephone pole. He spun the wheel back and forth, trying to center the car, but the back end was wagging wildly, banging into walls, the glove box popping open, stuff crashing around in the back. *The cop is coming.*

"Straighten out! Straighten out!"

The car skidded completely sideways and lurched backward before Isaiah could shift out of reverse.

"The fuck you doing, Isaiah?" Dodson shouted.

Isaiah stomped on the brakes but it was too late. The car rammed into something solid, their heads thrown forward and back into the headrests. They sat there stunned. Isaiah turned the ignition off. The car was in a parking area, the alley in front of it now, the rear bumper smashed into the loading dock of a produce market. There was a building on either side. If the cop hadn't seen them already he couldn't see them now. Headlight beams crossed in front of them. The cop was in the alley.

"Did he see us?" Dodson said.

"I don't think so," Isaiah said, "but he might have heard the crash."

The beams got brighter. Would the cop stop at the bicycle shop or keep coming and find two seventeen-year-old boys in fishing clothes and ski masks hiding in a dead man's car? They waited, the windows fogging up. The beams stopped. Isaiah's chin dropped to his chest, sweat dripping into his lap. "That was close," he said.

Dodson was staring blankly, his mouth hanging open like the firing squad had emptied their rifles at him and missed. "Could we get the fuck outta here, please?"

On the trip back to Long Beach, Isaiah was as still as a person can be and still drive a car. Dodson pulled his S&W .38 Special from under his fishing shirt. It was a revolver, lighter than a Glock, the barrel two inches long. The fellas preferred semiautos but Dodson liked pulling the hammer back and hearing it click. Just the sound of it scared the shit out of people. He flipped open the gun's cylinder, pushed the ejector rod, the bullets falling into his palm. "Safety first," he said. He put the bullets in his pocket and tucked the gun away. "Whatever you got to say, say it."

"You were really going to shoot me? Shoot a cop?"

"Maybe, but I know I wasn't going to jail."

"I told you no guns."

"I know what you *told* me, nigga, but I don't give a shit. I took enough orders from my old man and I ain't taking no more from you or anybody else."

"They're not orders, they're just—you're messing everything up, you know that, don't you?"

"You the one messing shit up. I'm telling you, Isaiah, y'all better get your boot up off my neck or some shit gonna happen."

"Like what?" Isaiah said, angry now. Dodson threatening him with a gun. Threatening to take his life away the way life had taken Marcus. "What are you gonna do? What? Tell me. Because whatever it is, stop trying to intimidate me and do it."

"Don't push me. We get into it I'll fuck you up."

"And wreck the whole thing? End it? You won't, I know you won't. You need this too much."

"Yeah, but you need it worse than me."

"How do you figure that?"

"I figure it like this. I need the money. You just need it."

CHAPTER FOURTEEN
You Can Make Anything Run

July 2013

Skip parked the Speedy Appliance Repair van and put on his Kenmore cap. The kids playing football in the street were too busy arguing about the out-of-bounds line to notice him getting out of the van with a duffel bag full of tools and walking across the street to Q Fuck's house. He rang the bell even though he knew nobody was home. He took his time, ambling down the driveway toward the garage and backyard. Since when do repairmen hurry? Music was coming from the neighbor's house. A good thing. He checked the kitchen door but the locks were indestructible.

Skip found a narrow path on the other side of the house overgrown with bougainvillea. He used the thorny bushes for cover and set up at a window. He put on latex gloves, opened the duffel bag, and got out the Halligan, a titanium pry bar the fire department used for forcible entries. He wedged the adze end between the wall of the house and the frame of the burglar bars and with a padded sledgehammer drove it all the way in. He stopped a few times to listen but the music was still playing and the kids were arguing about something else. Skip yanked, pried, and wrenched the

Halligan until he'd leveraged the frame away from the wall, the anchor bolts, chicken wire, and chunks of stucco coming out with it. He broke the window and climbed in.

The bedroom smelled a little like ammonia, weird but no big deal. The bed was made and a couple of photos were on the night-stand. No empty beer bottles, no laundry, no shoes on the floor. Smart-ass was a neat freak. Skip was unloading his gear when he heard a car pull into the driveway, the rumble of the engine telling him it was the hot-rod Audi. His cell buzzed. A text said *on his way*. "Thanks for telling me, asshole," Skip said.

Hurrying now, Skip slipped on his ski mask and popped a high-capacity magazine into the Glock 17, the shorter barrel better in tight spots. The clip held thirty-three rounds and extended five inches below the grip. Skip inserted the Glock's barrel into an ordinary automobile air filter fitted with a special adapter. It looked odd, like the gun had a can of soup stuck on the end, but with the subsonic ammo the gunshot was no louder than the snap of a mousetrap. He thought about meeting smart-ass at the front door but it was risky. He might be seen or heard before he got off a shot. Better to stay here and wait. He'd come into the bedroom sooner or later.

Isaiah drove home, smelling like melted plastic and ashes, hoping it wouldn't stay in the car. Cal was truly crazy, burning up thousands of dollars' worth of his belongings, stuff people clawed and struggled for used as firewood. Put a perspective on it, though. Owning all that didn't help Cal any. He was lost before the fire and lost afterward. The common denominator was Cal.

Isaiah pulled into his driveway, on high alert now. He got out of the car quickly and stepped behind it. He was afraid of that target gun with the long barrel but there weren't any lines of sight where Skip could set up. Isaiah had driven home fast, changing lanes, making sudden turns, watching for that blue truck coming up behind him.

Isaiah scanned the street from end to end. Nothing happening except for some kids playing football. But there was an appliance repair van parked in front of Mrs. Marquez's house. If Mrs. Marquez wanted an appliance repaired she'd have called him. The tinny taste of adrenaline expanded on his tongue. He crossed the street to her house and knocked on her door but she wasn't home. He approached the kids. "Say, did you see where the repairman went?" he said.

"What repairman?" a kid said.

"I didn't see nobody," another kid said. The others shrugged or looked away.

"Did you see anybody around my house?"

"I didn't," the first kid said. The rest were already going back to their game.

Isaiah got his mail out of the box, unlocked the front door, and pushed it open with his foot. He could see through the living room and into the kitchen. The back door was intact and he relaxed a bit. There was no other way to get into the house. He went in and dropped everything on the coffee table except the Visa bill. Looking at it first made the other bills seem not so bad. He opened the envelope and went down the hall reading the charges. Flaco's extra sessions of physical therapy were killing him. There was nothing left over for the condo fund. Without Cal's bonus money the plan would fall apart.

Skip waited, the bedroom warm and humid as a laundry mat. He blinked the sweat out of his eyes, both hands leveling the Glock at the door. He liked this part. The buildup. It was almost better than offing the guy. Q Fuck was in the hall. Skip could hear his sneakers squeaking on the cement floor...getting closer...closer...and then they stopped. Long seconds went by without a sound. *What the hell is he doing? If he knew I was here he'd turn and run. Unless he has a gun.*

Isaiah looked up from the Visa bill just in time to see the green blobs of chicken shit on the floor. He'd brought Alejandro inside that morning and forgot to put him back in the garage. Hopefully, the bird was pecking around somewhere and not roosting on the closet rod and crapping all over his clothes.

"Alejandro?" he said. "Are you in there?"

Skip's eyes darted around the room. *Who the fuck is Alejandro?* Something in the closet moved and fluttered. Skip turned and fired. SNAPSNAPSNAPSNAP. There was a hellish squawk that scared the living shit out of him and he kept firing into a cloud of swirling white things. SNAPSNAPSNAPSNAP.

Isaiah ran back down the hall. A right turn to the front door was the quickest way out but there were kids playing in the street. He went left, racing through the kitchen to the back door. He saw Skip, swinging into the living room gun first. For a split second they made eye contact. Skip fired. SNAPSNAPSNAPSNAP but Isaiah was already through the door, bullets blowing up canned goods in the pantry.

Isaiah streaked across the yard toward the back fence but Skip came out of the kitchen shooting. SNAPSNAPSNAPSNAP. Isaiah cut sharply, slamming his shoulder into the side garage door and flattening himself against a wall, nothing to hide behind but Alejandro's cage and the lawn mower. SNAPSNAPSNAPSNAP. Rounds punched through the roll-down door in the front, shafts of sunlight beaming through the holes. Skip was keeping him from moving around and finding a weapon. SNAPSNAPSNAPSNAP. Isaiah thought about dying. The only way out was the way he came in and he could hear Skip going over there. His one advantage was the brilliant sunny day. The rest was up to Skip.

Skip approached the side door. "I'm coming for you, Q Fuck," he said. Wary of an ambush, he shot into either side of the door. SNAPSNAPSNAPSNAPSNAP. "Got anything to say now, smart-ass?" Skip stepped inside and was momentarily blinded while his vision adjusted from sunlight to dark. He wheeled the gun back and forth, firing randomly SNAPSNAPSNAPSNAPSNAP—and saw, through the Milky Way of his recovering eyes, Isaiah in the far corner. Skip whipped around and fired. SNAPSNAPSNAP-CLICKCLICKCLICK. Isaiah came off the floor like a stingray. No shirt, oil stains on his chest and cheek. He knocked the gun aside with an inside-out forearm and threw a straight right at Skip's face but Skip turned his head and the punch clipped him on the ear. Isaiah came back with a left that caught Skip flush on the jaw and another right that skimmed through his hair as he fell to the floor. Skip went for the Beretta but Isaiah was already gone.

"Son of a bitch!" Skip said, getting to his feet. That fucker was fast, the blows seeming to come all at once. And then Skip saw it. The bullet-riddled T-shirt fitted over the lawn mower handlebars, the Harvard cap balanced where the head should be. "You're dead," Skip said. "You are so fucking dead."

*   *   *

Isaiah ran, cutting between houses until he was sure he was in the clear. He stopped and took a blow, bent over with his hands on his knees. He was glad he'd counted right. He'd seen the high-capacity magazine extending below the gun's grip as he was going out the back door. If it held a few more rounds he'd be dead. He'd missed with a couple of punches. Damn. If he'd connected, Skip would have been out cold. And he felt foolish for provoking him in the first place. All that nonsense about shaking his tree hadn't accomplished anything except almost getting him killed. He thought about calling the police but Skip was wearing a mask and gloves and had no doubt ditched the gun and the van. The police could arrest him on a parole violation. Skip always had a gun in that back holster and there were all those shell casings on the ground at Blue Hill. But Skip was the only link to his employer. With him out of the picture there were no leads at all. It was risky leaving Skip out there waiting to kill Cal but that didn't seem too likely. All Cal had to do was stay in the house and he'd be perfectly safe.

In the evening, the bald hill turned a blue steel color like the S&W ProMag Skip used to own. The dogs were rolling over the desert like a blitzkrieg in the fading light, scaring up rats, rabbits, birds, and ground squirrels; Skip with his AK shooting anything the dogs hadn't already killed. He wanted to see blood and suffering and death. He wanted to release some of his anger so he wouldn't go back to Q Fuck's house and empty a clip into his smart-ass mouth. Skip was out of ammo when Kurt called.

"Hey, how are ya, 007?" he said. "I've got that *intel* about the rapper. Should I tell you over the phone or put it in a secret code?"

"Just give it to me," Skip said, wanting to shoot him through the phone. "Yeah, yeah," he said. "I can work with that."

*   *   *

Santa Monica Boulevard was the main thoroughfare through West Hollywood, an area where a lot of gay people lived and worked. Isaiah drove, a little embarrassed. He didn't know what he was expecting but it didn't look any different than any other retail street. Shops, stores, restaurants, bars. Maybe the men were a little tidier than most but otherwise that was it.

"Didn't I tell you Skip would come after you?" Dodson said. "I still can't believe you said that shit about the puppies."

"Shot the house to pieces, nearly got me too," Isaiah said. "It was a setup. Skip got there the same time I did or he'd have shot me coming through the door. I think the inside man was supposed to give him a heads-up after we left Cal's place but he was tardy making the call."

"Lucky for you. You know who it is yet?"

"The inside man? No. Not yet."

They met Blasé at an outdoor café. He was Isaiah's former client. He'd been a child prodigy like Stevie Wonder, singing professionally since he was twelve years old. He had a historian's knowledge of the rap and hip-hop world, knew everybody that was anybody and considered it his civic duty to dish.

"Back in the day, Black the Knife was a group," Blasé said. "Like the Wu-Tang Clan without the Wu or the Tang. Charles was the headliner, if you can believe it. I suppose he could spit some but his beats were reruns and his rhymes were tired tired tired. Calvin was the hype man, getting the crowd up and coming in on the hook. Bug didn't do anything but walk around on stage like a caveman yelling *Yeeeah, Black the Knife in da houuuse.* Poor Charles. Out there trying to flow with all the ladies looking at Calvin and throwing their thongs at him. Everybody knew who the real star was and

I'm sure Charles knew it too." Blasé paused to take a sip of his nonfat hazelnut caramel latte. "Oh this is nice," he said. "Nothing like a six-dollar cup of coffee to wake you up in the morning. We always had Maxwell House at our house, came in that big blue can? My mama used to use them as flowerpots."

Isaiah's cappuccino tasted okay but the barista had made the foam too thin. "What happened to the group?" Isaiah said. "What happened to Black the Knife?"

"Calvin threatened to leave and go solo if he wasn't the front man," Blasé said. "Charles knew he wasn't going anywhere by himself so he stepped aside and Cal took over. Must have been humiliating and Cal had no problem being in charge. He took Black the Knife as his personal name, wouldn't perform any of Charles's songs and when Bobby Grimes showed up with that first record deal he offered it to Calvin, not Charles and Bug. From then on they worked for Calvin's LLC and lived in his crib like house niggas until Noelle threw them out."

Dodson glanced at a buffed-out white man in a tank top strolling by, his tan as even as the brown Barbie doll his sister, Lavinia, used to play with.

"What's the matter, baby?" Blasé said. "Having feelings you've never felt before?"

"Oh I've had the feelings before," Dodson said, "but I was locked up in the joint."

Blasé continued: "You'd think Charles and Bug would have left by now but I guess living the high life under Calvin's thumb is better than going back to selling dope and eating pork and beans with crushed potato chips. Not me, baby. Nobody treats me like that. I would have strangled Cal with a microphone cord a long time ago."

"Heard anything about Noelle?" Isaiah said.

"My ex, Byron? He told me she sold her engagement ring and she might need money. I sold mine. You give me a ring and it's forever or never."

"Who's DStar?" Isaiah said.

"The dealer to the stars? Jimmy Bonifant. It's like everybody is something to the stars these days. I'd stay away from him if I were you. People who mess with Jimmy end up dead in a ditch somewhere—I'm sorry, Isaiah, but I have to go. It was nice seeing you both. Call me if I can do anything else." Blasé got up and slipped on a messenger bag that looked like it was made from poured honey. "And say hello to Anthony for me. That boy is cute cute cute. Bye now."

Dodson waited until Blasé was gone. *"Anthony?"* he said.

The Moody brothers lived in a white stucco cracker box with white burglar bars and an old-fashioned TV antenna on the roof. It was late, Isaiah and Dodson were sitting in the Audi waiting for Bug. Charles was still in custody. Ordinarily, he could have paid his own bail and walked but the guns in the bonfire were a probation violation and he'd have to see a judge in the morning.

"Why didn't they move back in with Cal, live in luxury?" Isaiah said. "They could have after the divorce."

"Better to be a big fish in Inglewood than a sardine swimmin' around in Cal's ego," Dodson said.

"Good point."

Bug came out of the house and got in his Escalade. The engine roared to life, the trick exhaust burbling like it was underwater. He backed out of the driveway and drove off.

"He's wearing Cal's cologne," Isaiah said. "That stuff is like tear gas."

They went around to the back of the house and Isaiah bump-keyed the door open in thirty seconds.

"We could have done it faster with the battering ram," Dodson said. "Whatever happened to that thing?"

"It's still in the locker," Isaiah said.

Isaiah thought Bug and Charles's parents must have died or remarried and moved out. The living room was all dark wood and plush fabrics, family photos on every surface, and plastic covers on the lampshades. The brothers had made a couple of decorating changes. A sixty-five-inch 3-D HD TV hung over the fireplace and a stripper pole was planted in the middle of the room.

Charles gave everything in his pockets to Bug before the cops took him away. Car keys, cherry suckers, loose change, lighter, and his phone. Isaiah found the stuff in a candy bowl on the coffee table. He removed the SIM and SD cards from the phone and replaced them with new ones, leaving the phone completely blank. Charles would blame Bug. The phone was working until Bug had it, who else could it be?

Isaiah heard Dodson say: "Isaiah, come and see this."

Cal's recording equipment that was supposed to be thrown in the ocean was crowded into a bedroom. Mikes, studio desk, monitors, Mac Pro, sampling station, mixing console. A stack of CDs were on the desk. The hand-printed labels said: GRANDYOSE IS TAKING OVER.

"Grandyose is Charles?" Isaiah said.

"I imagine so," Dodson said. "And guess who he's taking over for."

Isaiah lifted his head. "Somebody's here."

They stepped behind the door as a sleepy-eyed buck-naked white girl clumped past in the hall, her booty like a backpack that had slipped down too low. "Bug?" she said. They left while she was in the bathroom.

Back at the house Isaiah sat at the kitchen counter and used a transfer program to move the data on Charles's memory cards to the MacBook. Charles's *Takin' Over* tracks were on the stereo sounding like the same old same old.

"Noelle's on his contact list," Isaiah said, "but it could have been there for years." Dodson was at the stove, cooking. Isaiah thought about telling him not to but didn't. "The phone stores a hundred calls," Isaiah said. "Most of them are to the fellas. Some to Bobby but they weren't returned. A few to DStar. None to Noelle and I don't see an area code from anywhere around Fergus but Skip probably used a burner. The rest are to girls."

"Maybe they're fake names," Dodson said.

"I'd have to call every one of them to find out," Isaiah said, "and I don't see any clusters of calls on the day we were hired or went to Blue Hill or when Skip was in my house." Isaiah did a quick scroll through the texts. There were the usual suspects and more girls. A few to DStar about when he was coming over. No Noelle, no area codes, no clusters.

"Well, I'll tell you this," Dodson said. "Charles ain't making no comeback with these tracks. He copied every MC out there."

Charles didn't use email much and there were none that caught Isaiah's eye. He'd have to go through them again with a search app but this wasn't a good sign. If there was no connection between Charles and Noelle they were still at square zero.

"Are you listening to this?" Dodson said. "Charles did a diss track."

Black the Knife, down without a fight
A termite, a flea bite,
Got stage fright, no right to life
Boy's an absentee, a detainee, no number on his caller ID
Nobody home at the addressee
His time is passed, miscast, outta gas, second class
In foreclosure, never sober, I'm in clover, I'm taking over.

"Makes no sense," Dodson said. "Cal ever hears this Charles and Bug are out of a job."

"Maybe they don't think they'll need one," Isaiah said. "Listen to the background vocals."

Charles had done his own background vocals, overdubbing himself to get a thicker sound; a woman's voice was weaving in and out, roller-coastering up and down three octaves and yeah-ee-yeah-a-ing.

"Hear the woman?" Isaiah said.

"Yeah, what about her?"

"Before Noelle was Cal's wife she was a singer."

"I *knew* that," Dodson said. If he wasn't frying okra he would have snapped his fingers.

They sat at the counter eating gumbo over rice and fried okra.

"This is good," Isaiah said.

"Good?" Dodson said. "That's all you got to say?"

The gumbo was different than the version Dodson made back in the apartment. Isaiah tasted traces of honey and white vinegar and some kind of herb that tasted a little like root beer. "The okra's good too," he said. They'd downloaded one of Noelle's songs from iTunes and her voice matched the woman on Charles's track. It didn't prove anything but at least there was a connection.

"Noelle needs the life insurance money," Isaiah said, "and if Charles is going solo he'd need money too. They both hate Cal so they partner up. They lived together, might even have had a thing. The question is, who's going to take out Cal? They could use Charles's Inglewood boys but it's too obvious. They need somebody that can't be traced back to them. They need a hit man."

Dodson was disappointed Isaiah didn't remember about the gumbo but what really pissed him off was not catching the thing about Noelle and what pissed him off even more was that he hadn't made Isaiah stumble once. "So how do Noelle and Charles hook up with somebody like Skip?" Dodson said. "They sit next to each other at the BET Awards?"

"Through DStar," Isaiah said. "He delivers to Cal's house twenty-four seven. He had to know both of them."

"That doesn't mean DStar knew Skip."

"DStar's real name is Jimmy Bonifant and Skip was talking to somebody named Bonnie when we were at Blue Hill."

"Who made the deal?" Dodson said, not giving up. "Noelle went out to the desert in her Jimmy Choos, sat down at the picnic table Skip don't have, and worked out the details with all them dogs barking? I ain't seeing it."

Isaiah hesitated. Dodson thought *Oh shit*.

"She had a go-between," Isaiah said.

"Go-between like who—Charles?" Dodson said. "Skip sat down with Grandyose at Starbucks and them two unstable mutha-fuckas worked out a deal? You know that didn't happen."

"So it was somebody else," Isaiah said, softer than before.

Dodson thought, *I landed one. He's hurt*. "Maybe it was Bug got together with Skip," he said. "Skip talked about being in the

Olympics and Bug told him how he might be something in Fergus but he wasn't shit up in here. Be serious, Isaiah. Noelle wouldn't trust either of them fools to go to the store and buy a soda, now would she?"

Isaiah looked at his gumbo.

"Well?" Dodson said. *He's down for the count.*

Isaiah put his spoon down and wiped his lips with a napkin and in those few moments Dodson knew he'd been sandbagged. "No, Noelle wouldn't trust them," Isaiah said, "but she might trust her bodyguard."

"I'm sorry to bother you, honey," Blasé said, "but I've got a little problem. A stalker's been following me around, popping up everywhere I go. You know the kind, looks at you like he wants to see you in his basement chained to the water heater?"

"I've been in that situation myself," Noelle said. "Had some silverback on my trail. I think Cal sent him to scare me and it worked too. Did you get a restraining order?"

"Not yet. We don't even know his name."

"Anything I can do?"

"I don't know how to say this but—I'd like to borrow your bodyguard."

"Rodion?"

"Is that his name? Rodion?"

"That's what we call him."

"Does he have a last name?"

"If he does he hasn't told anybody. Why him?"

"You know that club on Melrose, Nirvana? It's always so crowded you can't even raise your arms? Byron said he saw Rodion at the bar and it was like he'd just come back from Liberia with a runny nose. Nobody was within ten feet of him."

"Yes, he is a frightening individual. Consuelo calls him *el monstruo feo,* which I believe means tell me when he's gone so I can clean the damn house."

"Can you spare him, honey?"

"I would if I could but he's on vacation."

"Where does somebody like that go on vacation?"

"I don't know. Maybe he went to Comic-Con. He'd fit right in and wouldn't have to wear a costume."

After the gumbo, Dodson went home and Isaiah mulled over his Noelle-Charles-Rodion theory. It sounded good in an argument but he had the feeling that's all it was, a way to win an argument.

Once, Marcus and Isaiah spent the afternoon at Mount Baldy having snowball fights and sliding down the icy slopes on a cardboard sled. They were having so much fun they lost track of time and got a late start heading home. The two-lane road was pitch dark and windy, clumps of snow on the roadside. Isaiah was eleven years old and a city boy. It made him nervous being out here, driving an old clunker with a broken muffler and a knocking engine. When they got off the mountain and into the high desert, the road straightened out but Isaiah didn't feel any better about it. Billboards for strip clubs and bail bondsmen going by. The houses isolated, junk in the yards. Marcus said he could hear the domestic abuse. They were coming down a long grade when something in the drive train thumped.

"What was that?" Isaiah said.

"Damn, the car's stuck in second," Marcus said. He pulled the car over to the shoulder and messed with the clutch and gearshift. "I've got to get underneath."

"Underneath *the car*?" Isaiah said.

"There's no room to work down there," Marcus said. He thought a moment, then drove the car over a drainage ditch and stopped, the wheels straddling the ditch. "Okay, let's take a look," he said. He got his toolbox out of the trunk, put a flashlight in his mouth, and slid into the drainage ditch and under the car.

Isaiah waited in the cold, stamping his feet, and wondering what was taking so long. He could hear Marcus squirming around, grunting, the tools clanking. "Everything okay?" he said.

Marcus crawled out from under the car, filthy with grease and mud. "It's the pin that holds the shifter to the fork in the transaxle," he said. "It's broken."

"Can we get another pin?" Isaiah said, looking around at the dark.

Marcus rummaged around in the trunk and found a road flare. He cut off the wire stand with a wire cutter and slid under the car again. More tool noises and grunting.

"What are you doing?" Isaiah said.

"Replacing the pin," Marcus said, "but I've got to bend the wire to fit."

Isaiah waited another year.

"Got it," Marcus said.

Isaiah smiled like he'd known it all along.

As they drove over the ditch and back onto the road, Marcus said: "Let that be a lesson to you. You can make *anything* run."

And the car *did* run until the improvised pin broke, the yoke bent, and the trans froze up completely. Isaiah worried about his theory for the same reason. Had he *made* it run? Had he cobbled parts together that would freeze up and leave him stranded? And then there was the case-breaker. That dragonfly flitting around his cortex faster than a synapse. If he ever caught a glimpse of the thing would it help him or put him back to square zero? He was afraid he already knew.

Noelle had only just ended the call with Blasé when the number she was waiting for popped up on the caller ID. "Well, don't keep me in suspense," she said, "what's happening? Damn, he just won't cooperate, will he? As if I didn't have enough pressure already. Yes, I know it's hard but we talked about this. We *talked* about this and you said you'd—okay, that's better. Now you stay with it, don't let me down now. It's going to happen, I promise you."

CHAPTER FIFTEEN

When We Ride on Our Enemies

March 2006

Isaiah was in the storage locker brooding about what happened in the bicycle shop and trying to write item descriptions. What if Dodson had shot the cop or got shot himself? Isaiah thought. They'd be in jail right now. He considered walking away from everything but Dodson was right. He couldn't, and even if he did, Dodson would still be in the apartment and there was no way to get him out.

Earlier in the day they'd had another argument. Dodson needed money and wanted to lower the prices on the paint sprayers from thirty percent to fifty percent off but Isaiah held firm. People were paying the prices. Why take less just because Dodson couldn't handle his money? They'd almost come to blows.

Isaiah stopped writing. Tonight they were doing another job. He knew he should cancel, let things cool off, but Dodson might think he was intimidated. No. The job was on. Fuck Dodson.

Eleven-thirty. The Explorer pulled up and parked behind La Cucina Felice, a kitchen store in Torrance. Isaiah and Dodson hadn't spoken the whole way over, the tension like a stranger in the car. They got out the equipment and set up at the rear entrance as if the other wasn't there.

The door was reinforced. There was no exterior lock and there was a security bar on the inside. Battering the door took some time and the alarm went off before they got in, this one like a giant sparrow on steroids chirping in your ear.

"Stick to the clock," Isaiah said as they entered the storeroom. "We'll have to take less stuff." Dodson didn't answer and went his own way.

At the six-minute mark, Isaiah was loading Wüsthof knife sets into the car. He glanced back, thinking Dodson was right behind him, but he wasn't. Go after him and he'd think it was condescending and start something. Isaiah got into the car, his eyes on the rearview mirror. He felt his watch ticking. Seven minutes...eight minutes. Where was Dodson? Isaiah felt the tingle of new sweat on his scalp. He jogged back inside and into the storeroom, dancing along the front of the room, looking in the aisles. No Dodson. His hamper was against the wall like he'd walked away. Or been led away. Isaiah's heart was revving to the red line. He checked the restrooms and the office, calling Dodson, Dodson, the giant sparrow screeching like a snake was in the nest. *Where did he go? Why would he leave?*

Dodson was in the showroom carrying a shopping basket and looking at a display of copper cookware. He wondered what a roasting pan could do to make it worth three hundred and thirty-nine dollars. For that money it should come with HoneyBaked Ham and somebody to baste it.

Isaiah ran up to him with his palms up. He had to shout over the giant sparrow. "WHERE WERE YOU? LET'S GO!" Dodson walked past him and stopped at a table of ceramic jars, kitchen utensils sticking out of them. "DODSON, WE'RE AT NINE MINUTES. WHAT'S WRONG WITH YOU?" Dodson selected a stainless steel whisk and shook it like a maraca. He didn't seem to know Isaiah was there. "CAN'T YOU HEAR ME? WE HAVE TO GO!" Dodson put the whisk in his basket and continued shopping, Isaiah backing up in front of him. "DODSON, ARE YOU CRAZY? WHAT ARE YOU DOING? LET'S GO!" Dodson stopped at a revolving stand of gizmos and gadgets. He took a tomato stemmer off its peg and began reading the blurb. "TEN MINUTES, DODSON, TEN MINUTES! WHAT'S THE MATTER WITH YOU?" Dodson looked up as if he'd heard something far away and wondered what it was. Isaiah grabbed his arm. "DODSON, WE HAVE TO GO! CAN'T YOU HEAR ME? WE HAVE TO GO! DODSON, PLEASE! WE HAVE TO GO NOW!" The ski mask hid Dodson's face but his eyes were lazy and merciless. Isaiah couldn't yell anymore. "I don't know what you want," he said. "I don't know what you want." Dodson sighed like he was letting Deronda hold the remote. Then he dropped the tomato stemmer into his basket and strolled away, a hitch in his stride.

Dodson had a key card to the front gate at the storage place and a key to the padlock on the locker door. He borrowed Deronda's brother's Tacoma, backed it up to the locker, and took out three loads of merchandise he thought would move fast while Deronda sat on a box of books poking at her phone.

"This shit is for you too," Dodson said. "Get your ass up and help me."

"I just got my nails done," Deronda said. "Can I do something with my elbows?"

Dodson had rechecked the prices on the paint sprayers. Isaiah had *raised* them and on everything else too. "Fuck your nails," Dodson said. "Help me with these tools."

They held a garage sale. Nona volunteered her backyard in exchange for two pairs of shoes. Word spread there were bargains to be had and the yard got busier than Walmart on Black Friday. Didn't matter what the deal was as long as it was cash. The tools went fast, people knowing they were valuable even if they couldn't use them. They were sold out of everything by suppertime.

Dodson lay on the foldout smoking a joint, cash scattered around him like leaves off a dead tree. Deronda was dancing to Tupac, holding a bottle of Dom by the neck that fizzled when she twerked. *When we ride on our enemies I bet you motherfuckers die. When we ride on our enemies bet all you motherfuckers die.* She eased up some, afraid her skintight jeans might bust a seam even though they were new.

Isaiah came in, his jaw so tight he looked like his teeth might explode. "What did you do?" he said.

"I moved the merchandise," Dodson said. "What do you think I did?"

"Those tools are mine. I want them back."

"You don't use none of 'em. What are you gonna do, build a house?" Dodson nodded at a loose wad of cash on the coffee table. "That's your cut less my ten percent sales commission."

"The tools weren't yours to sell. Go get them."

"Fuck you, Isaiah. Go get 'em yourself."

Deronda had never seen anybody this pissed off. If Isaiah's eyes were butcher knives they'd be chopped to shit by now.

"Go get my tools."

"Don't do that. Don't give me orders."

"Go get them now."

Dodson got up slowly, dusted off the weed ashes, and handed the joint to Deronda. She could smell his anger, feel him like a fever. He went over to Isaiah and stood in front of him.

"Gimme one more order," Dodson said. *"One more."*

Deronda wanted to see some shit happen. Dodson was all grumpy and irritated at the garage sale, not even enjoying the action. Maybe a fight would snap him out of it. He was chest to chest with Isaiah now, sparks from an arc welder where their eyes met. She thought Tupac was getting louder. *When we ride on our enemies I bet you motherfuckers die. When we ride on our enemies bet all you motherfuckers die.* Deronda saw something change in Isaiah's expression. Not like he was scared, like he was thinking. For some reason that made her afraid. Isaiah turned around, scooped up his money, and went into the bedroom.

"You was a pussy when I met you and you'll be a pussy all your life," Dodson said.

"Punk-ass Einstein muthafucka," Deronda said.

Isaiah crept out of the apartment while they were sleeping, taking only a suitcase of necessities and his laptop. He used Marcus's ID, checked into the Wayside Motel, and got a room around back. It smelled like Pine-Sol and dust and a fly was tapping against the window. It was a relief to be here. No TV, music, or weed. The quiet was soothing and lonely.

Isaiah changed the padlock on the storage locker to an Abus Extreme Security steel padlock. A core-hardened lock body, seven-disk cylinder, and twenty-five thousand pounds of tensile strength. You'd need dynamite to bust it open. A week went by. Isaiah passed the time working on the merchandise still in the pipeline. His hatred for Dodson was searing his stomach lining, but the longer he waited the more Dodson would sweat. Once Dodson was out he'd cut him off completely.

Dodson and Deronda were watching TV from the foldout, surrounded by a landfill of empty liquor bottles, Heineken cans, fast-food wrappers, magazines, dirty dishes, shopping bags, shoes, and pizza crusts. Piles of laundry were everywhere like somebody was separating clothes at the Goodwill. It was Isaiah's apartment so who gave a shit? *Iron Chef* was on. Dodson's favorite show.

"Will you look at that?" Dodson said. "Got a football player out there trying be a judge. Unless the secret ingredient is Gatorade what the fuck does he know?"

"We almost out of money," Deronda said, "and the rent's coming due."

"Oh shit, it's that chick who always says it needs more crunch. That's all the fuck she knows about—crunch. Wait, see what she says—see? What'd I tell you? Look at Morimoto. If he wasn't on TV he'd be slappin' the crunch off that bitch right now."

"Dodson."

"I hear you, damn."

"Well, what are you gonna do?"

"I don't know."

"Yes you do."

"No I don't."

"Yes you do."

"Girl, I said I don't."

"But you do."

Isaiah got texts. *Where u at? Call me. Holla back. You go someplace? We got business.* Now what, Dodson? Isaiah thought. What are you gonna do without your punk-ass Einstein? *You being disrespectful. Call me. You better answer this. Last chance or we got a problem.* Fuck you, Dodson. Fuck you.

Isaiah was at Vons pushing his cart down the water aisle when he ran into Deronda.

"Where you been, Isaiah?" Deronda said.

"Around."

"You moving out?"

"Why would I? It's my apartment."

"How come you ain't called Dodson back?"

"Got nothing to say."

"He wants to know when the next job is."

"Don't know."

"What do you mean you don't know?"

"I mean I don't know."

"Swear to God," Deronda said, "Dodson ain't gonna mess around no more. He's gonna play it straight, no bullshit. He told me he's sorry about the tools and everything. He's trying to get 'em back right now."

"Don't lie."

"I'm not lying. It's a hundred percent true."

"Now you're lying about lying."

Isaiah stopped and put a twelve-pack of water into his cart. Deronda stood close and pressed herself into him. Her breath smelled like Hennessy and Juicy Fruit. "I ain't gonna mess with you no more, I promise," she said. "You gonna be the boss like you was before. I'll be good, you won't even know I'm there."

"Do what you want," Isaiah said, moving on.

Deronda followed him, whining like a five-year-old denied her

Froot Loops. "I cleaned up the apartment," she said. "I put your awards back up on the wall and everything. Dodson said let bygones be bygones."

"Dodson would never say that or anything like it."

Deronda stopped and stamped her foot. "Dang, Isaiah, help us out. You know we broke."

"Not my problem," he said. He walked away. Let them twist in the wind a little while longer, get really desperate. And then make them an offer they can't refuse.

Another two days and five more texts went by. Isaiah went to the storage locker to wrap some packages. Dodson was waiting for him. "Who the fuck put this lock on here?" Dodson said. "I can't get in."

"You're not supposed to get in," Isaiah said. "It's not your locker."

"There's all kinds of shit still in there and half of it's mine."

"It's paying me back for the tools."

Dodson walked away three steps, spun around, and came back to where he started. "I could drop a dime on you and wouldn't think nothing of it," he said.

"Drop a dime on me and you'll be dropping one on yourself," Isaiah said. "Don't you want to do more jobs?"

For a moment it looked like Dodson was stumped. But only for a moment. "Oh it's gonna be like that?" he said. "Well, go on and put your shit on the table and quit fuckin' around like a bitch."

"I want you out of the apartment," Isaiah said.

Dodson smiled like he admired the move. "I'm gonna be in that apartment 'til the day *you* die."

"Then I'm not doing any more jobs."

Dodson walked away three steps, spun around, and came back with the revolver pointed at Isaiah's head. "You think you can do me like that? Starve me out, make me beg? You fuckin' with the wrong nigga."

Isaiah glanced up and nodded at a security camera bracketed to a light pole. "They're all over the place," he said. "The one at the front gate takes your picture." He turned his back and went toward the Explorer. "Let me know what you want to do."

Dodson's gun hand was shaking. He wanted to cap this condescending disrespectful muthafucka more than he'd ever wanted anything in his life. He took a hop-step, swung the gun like he was throwing a fastball, and brought the barrel down on Isaiah's head. Isaiah crumpled forward, fell into the Explorer, and slid to the ground. He curled up, groaning, holding his head, blood coming through his fingers. Dodson stood over him. "You think you out of this? You think you can walk away from me and take my manhood with you? I shoot myself 'fore I let that happen. You in, nigga, and you ain't out 'til I say you out."

Dusk. Wavering flames of light were coming through the ragged curtains. Isaiah lay on the bed with a bag of ice on his head. The bleeding had stopped. There was an ugly gash above his right ear, the pain throbbing like a hot electrode.

It was time to end it. Just end it.

He rested a day, put a new dressing on the gash, dropped a handful of Tylenol, and went to the locker. Dodson hadn't touched the box of books, twenty-one thousand dollars of burglary money hidden in a carved-out copy of *Manchild in the Promised Land*. Isaiah called the landlord, gave him notice, and told him to keep the security deposit. Leaving would be painful. He'd fought hard to keep the apartment but he had to separate from Dodson before something really disastrous happened. Even if he somehow got Dodson out of there he'd be under siege and the war of wills would never end. He had to make a clean break. Besides, the apartment wasn't home anymore and whatever was left of Marcus's spirit had left in disgust. He wouldn't have gone back there at all but he'd left Marcus's ashes on the top shelf of the closet.

When he came into the apartment Deronda was on the balcony, her back against the railing, her arms folded across her chest, for once not talking or texting or bobbing her head to her earbuds and Crip-walking. She came in sniffling, her mascara smeared, cheeks wet with tears.

"What's the matter with you?" Isaiah said.

"Dodson can't do no jobs by himself," Deronda said. "I knew it but I said it anyway. He's going to get himself killed."

"What job? Who's going to kill him?"

It was the day after Dodson hit Isaiah with the gun outside the storage locker. Dodson and Deronda were on the foldout staring at the TV. They'd been there for a couple of hours, didn't matter what was on.

"We need a way to get some money," Deronda said.

"Like what?" Dodson said.

"I don't know."

"The fuck you say anything for?"

Deronda needed him relaxed and open-minded. She reached for his package. "Come here, baby," she said. "Let me release your tension." After they had sex and Dodson was almost asleep, Deronda made her move. "Where does Kinkee get his dope from?" she said, trying to sound casual.

"Junior," Dodson said. "He got a cartel connection."

"How much do he pay for like a kilo?"

"Fifteen, twenty thousand, around in there."

"How many kilos do he get?"

"I don't know. More than one."

"Reup day he must be carrying some real money."

Dodson dozed off for a moment and then his eyes popped open. "You better blank that outta your mind, girl. We could get shot just sitting here thinking about it."

"I'm not saying we do anything."

Dodson's voice went falsetto: "Do anything like what?"

"Dang, baby, I'm just curious, that's all." She nuzzled his neck and walked her fingers over his groin. "I mean like, how's it go down, reup day?"

"We run out of stones, Junior goes to Boyle Heights with a bag full of money and comes back with a bag full of cocaine."

"He don't worry about gettin' robbed?"

Dodson told her Junior was no fool. If you wanted to rob him your first problem was the building he lived in. The Sea Crest over in Bluff Park where people drove hybrid cars and had names like Jason and Laura and Chin Ho. Not the kind of people who'd be eager to buzz your gangsta ass in and even if you managed to catch the door when the FedEx man came out you'd still have to get Junior to open his door and not shoot you with his pistol or his AK.

"Does Junior got security?" Deronda said.

Dodson shook his head like he was looking at tornado damage. "Booze Lewis, he said."

Booze Lewis, known on the street as Peen, was sixteen years old when he was tried as an adult for attempted kidnapping, mayhem, and aggravated assault. When he went into Corcoran he weighed a hundred and sixty-one pounds. When he got out thirty-nine months later he was a hundred and ninety-five pounds of prison yard muscle and any fat you found on him was on his plate.

"Why do they call him Peen?" Deronda said.

"'Cause he killed Cole Campbell with a ball-peen hammer and he ain't but the half of it."

"What's the other half?"

"Michael Stokely. If you on his hit list and still alive it's because he's busy shooting somebody else. Carries that sawed-off Mossberg. Aim that bitch up in the air and you'll hit four or five niggas — and why we even talking about this? Ain't no way to rip off Junior."

"I think you downgradin' yourself."

"I have never in my whole life downgraded myself."

"How many jobs you pulled off? A bunch, right? You got some experience, you got some knowledge. You a professional you ask me."

Dodson nodded. That was true. "Yeah, but robbing a pet store ain't nothing like trying to jack Junior."

"I'm not saying they the same. I'm saying you could work it out in your mind, ask yourself how the shit could go down."

"Ask myself how the — I *am* myself. Why would I ask somebody who don't know?"

"You *could* know. I got faith you in, baby. You could pull this off, I know you could . . . if you asked yourself the right question."

"What right question?"

"I'm gonna say something now, don't get mad, aight?"

"Just say what you say, girl, damn."

"What you need to ask yourself is . . . what would Isaiah do?"

Dodson told her shut the fuck up and sent her out for Thai food. Then he watched a rerun of *Chopped*. Then he smoked a joint. Then he went out on the balcony and walked back and forth for a while until he finally got down to it.

What *would* Isaiah do?

He'd check everything out, do his research, and Kinkee had done most of that already. On the last run to Boyle Heights, Booze was in the hospital and Kinkee took his place. He talked about it every chance he got like it was some kind of honor risking his life for free. Dodson and Sedrick had heard the story twice already but had to hear it again because Kinkee hadn't doled out the new product yet.

"So like me and Stokely go to Junior's crib, right?" Kinkee said. "And it's like ten in the morning, people gone to work. That way ain't no cars around, you could see what's comin' both ways, can't nobody drive up on us—that's sharp, ain't it? So then like I get buzzed in and I'm thinkin' Junior's in the penthouse, you know how he be luxuriatin' but check dis. His crib is on the first floor. Wanna know why?"

"So he can't get trapped in the elevator," Sedrick said.

"So he can't get trapped in the—who's telling this story, nigga? Shit. See what kind of rocks you get this time—where was I? Oh yeah, so I get buzzed in, right? And I goes to the apartment, knock on the door. Junior checks me in the peephole, comes out with a shopping bag full of paper and that gun he likes, what's it called?"

"Sig Sauer forty-cal," Sedrick said.

"Who gives a shit, Sedrick? Okay, so now we go back to the lobby and it's like glass across the front and we could see Stokely waitin' in his car. So if he like nods in a certain way the coast is clear. If he nods another way we sit tight. That's thinkin' in the forefront, you feel me? So then Junior gets in my car and Stokely follows us in his car with that damn Mossberg because—"

"The Locos like to drive up on you and shoot you at a stoplight," Sedrick said. "Can I get some stones now?"

Dodson went to the Sea Crest, found a side door the janitor used, and bump-keyed his way in. He walked Kinkee's route to Junior's apartment. It was in the middle of the hall. No way to sneak up behind him. If you came through the fire exit at the far end he'd see you coming. Dodson made a list and drew a couple of diagrams. It felt good working something out in advance, visualizing what would happen. It was like controlling the future, having that airtight plan.

Next day he went back to work at the House, which had moved to another fucked-up apartment on Seminole. He told the fellas he went to see his people in Oakland. With his last money he bought some product and served it up to the fiends just like before. For some reason he thought things would be different but they were exactly the same. The fucked-up atmosphere, the fellas talking shit and doing nothing, the dope fiends killing themselves one rock at a time. He served it up for a week and a day until everybody was down to two-dollar chips and the crackheads were buying from the Locos.

It was Sedrick that asked Kinkee, "When's the reup happening?"

"That's some classified shit, nigga," Kinkee said. "Above your lowly-ass pay grade, you feel me? I'll let you know when I let you know."

Dodson was outside wondering why the air smelled like dirt, weeds, and dogshit no matter where the House was. Kinkee was there, pacing back and forth and talking on his cell.

"Come on, Stokely," he said, "we down to kibbles and bits out here. Tell Junior we need some product. When? *Now,* shit, why you think I'm callin'? Well, can you tell me like in a general way—above my pay grade? See, you fuckin' with me now. Wednesday? You couldn't say that at the start? Damn, man, why you always got to grind on people? That shit ain't funny. What? No-no-no-no, I ain't disrespecting nobody, Stoke, don't take that shit personal."

Deronda sat on the edge of the foldout, wiping her nose with one of Dodson's T-shirts, Isaiah leaning back against the bookshelf with his hands in his front pockets. "It's like crazy dangerous," she said. "But it seemed like a movie, you know? Like it was a game or somethin', but when Dodson left it got real to me. There's a million ways he could get himself killed."

"Wait a minute," Isaiah said. "He *left?*"

"I texted him four five times but he don't answer."

Massive hands wrung Isaiah's chest like a dishrag. If there was gunplay the police would get into it and if Dodson got arrested it was over. Dodson's phone had Isaiah's number in it. The key card to the locker was in his wallet and Dodson would rat him out before he got to the police station.

"Where does Junior live?" Isaiah said.

CHAPTER SIXTEEN

I'm Not Doing It

July 2013

Cal said who gives a shit at least a dozen times a day. About Bobby Grimes, the crew, the album, his career, the phone calls from his business manager telling him the IRS had a tax lien on the house. He was just too tired, too drugged, and too confused to do anything about it except take more drugs. He was sunk in a hopelessness so deep he'd forgotten what he was hoping for. Cal heard voices coming from outside, Bobby's the loudest. He was always the loudest. Throwing his weight around, cutting everybody off at the knees. Cal thought about going down there and putting him in his place. Tell him to shut up and send him out for Krispy Kremes but then he'd have to listen to the man talk and if there was ever a reason to stay in the bed it was Bobby talking. Besides, who gives a shit?

Anthony didn't know how he was going to get through another meeting, if that's what you could call it. Standing out in the driveway like a bunch of valets after the dinner rush, Bobby talking in his usual pompous, pretentious, bullying way. You'd think at some point he'd get tired of himself but that hadn't happened since Anthony had known him. He'd interned with Bobby while he was in business school and after graduation he was kept on as Bobby's executive assistant. At the time it seemed like a good idea. Learn the music business, network, find a career path. But Cal needed someone to keep him organized and Bobby said take Anthony, he could organize a room full of naked babies. Anthony thought it would be temporary but other opportunities for a glorified flunky were other glorified flunky jobs and none had the perks of working for a rap star.

"Anthony, are you listening?" Bobby said. "This is about your future too."

"Yes, Bobby, I'm listening."

Hegan was watching from the BMW. Charles was muttering at Bug, something about fucking up his phone. Isaiah and Dodson were leaning against the Audi, Bobby in front of them, pacing back and forth, nodding sagely, hands clasped behind his back. "Calvin wants evidence that Noelle was behind the plot to kill him," Bobby said, "and if he doesn't get that evidence he will stay locked up in the house, causing untold damage to his career as well as serious problems for his colleagues and his record company. We can agree on that, can't we, Mr. Quintabe?"

Isaiah had complicated things tenfold but Anthony admired him. Calm, watchful, not giving anything away, and how he looked at Bobby like he was a desk or a lamp.

"Now what I'm going to suggest here may seem extreme," Bobby said, "but I believe at this point, extreme is our only recourse. As I said before, Calvin wants evidence that Noelle is behind the plot to kill him and what I'm proposing is that we manufacture that evidence."

"You mean run a game on him," Isaiah said.

"Please let me finish before you make a judgment," Bobby said. "Now let's say you were to tell Calvin you have a recording of Noelle and Skip making a deal. A bad example but you understand what I'm getting at. Of course, Calvin would want to hear that recording but you would tell him the police have seized it as evidence and Noelle will be arrested shortly. Therefore, you have accomplished your mission and Calvin is perfectly safe to go about his business without further worry." Bobby put his palms out, cutting off Isaiah's reply. "Yes, I understand, you're a man of scruples," he said. "I applaud you for that but this impasse must be broken for all our sakes."

Anthony knew what was coming next. True to form, Bobby plopped down a thick envelope on the hood of the Audi. Some bills fanned out, all hundreds.

"If you could see your way clear to helping us resolve our problem," Bobby said, "I'm prepared to give you twenty thousand dollars in cash."

For once Anthony hoped Bobby's shady tactics would work but Isaiah was still unreadable. The entire Las Vegas Strip was flashing in Dodson's eyes.

"Thank you, Bobby," Dodson said. "That's a very generous offer. Don't you think so, Isaiah?"

"Bear in mind," Bobby said, "Calvin will still be obliged to pay you the fifty-thousand-dollar bonus and you'll already have twenty thousand from me. What do you think, Mr. Quintabe? It's a win-win for everybody concerned."

"Can't do it," Isaiah said.

"Why not?" Bobby said.

"Why not?" Dodson said.

"Take it, fool," Charles said, "you know you want the money."

"I said why not," Isaiah said. "I'm not running a game on Cal."

Anthony was enjoying the back-and-forth but this *had* to end. "Look, you're not being fair or realistic," he said. "You haven't made any progress on the case and there's no reason to believe you will. You're stuck, admit it. Come on, Isaiah, it's time for everyone to move on."

"I've got a new lead," Isaiah said, shooting a quick glance at Dodson.

"A new lead?" Bobby said. "What new lead?"

"He's bullshitting," Charles said.

"Shut up, Charles. What new lead, Mr. Quintabe?"

"There's a man who knows Skip," Isaiah said. "I'm meeting him tonight at JC's, a bar in Long Beach. Around eleven."

"Well, what does this new lead have to say?" Bobby said.

"I'll tell you if it pans out. I don't want to jump the gun and piss somebody off."

"Piss somebody off like who? You're not making any sense, Mr. Quintabe. Can we get back to reality, please? Now will you or won't you go along with the program?"

"No. I won't."

Bobby put his hands on his hips, looked down at the ground, and took a deep breath, Anthony thinking *Uh-oh*. When Bobby looked up again, his eyes were frozen solid, an ice pick in his voice. "I happen to be a very influential man, Mr. Quintabe," he said, "and I know a lot of influential people. It would be a shame if something were to diminish your stature in the music community. You know how people talk."

"There are a lot of communities out there besides music," Isaiah said, "and none of them give a damn about your influence and I'll tell you something else, *Mr. Grimes*. I can't be diminished by people talking no matter who they are but I will be if I take that money."

Anthony felt a surge of pride and wished it was for himself.

They were driving down Pacific to Dodson's place, Dodson staring out the window at his bank statement. "Turn down twenty thousand dollars," he said, disgusted. "Even for you that was off the rocker."

"I had to," Isaiah said.

"No, you didn't. You got pissed off and lost your common sense just like you did with Skip and fucked up my situation in the process. I got a nut to crack. Turn down twenty thousand dollars. You took the case to make some money and here you are walking away from it? What kind of bullshit is that? And don't tell me you gonna solve the case. Ain't nothin' to solve. We got nothing to go on and nowhere to go, do we? *Do we?* Shit. You pay your mortgage with your scruples? Buy your damn groceries with it? I tried to spend mine at the supermarket and they told me they only accept money. And what was all that shit about meeting somebody at JC's? If you making a play the least you could do is tell me about it."

"Skip is the only lead we have," Isaiah said. "We have to *make* him talk."

"Make him talk how? Waterboard him? My old man showed me how to do it and damn near drowned me. Oh I know. Let's kidnap Skip's mama and cut her toes off 'til he talks. Shit. That crazy muthafucka might not even *have* a mama."

"It's not his mama."

Dodson thought a moment—and then his face exploded into abject terror. "No, unh-uh, forget it. Get that out of your mind, you hear me? I ain't doing that shit no matter what you say."

"It's that or give up the fifty grand."

"What am I gonna spend it on, my tombstone? I don't want no part of it and you know why. Let me out of the car. I gotta pick up some ice cream for Cherise." Isaiah stopped and Dodson got out of the car. "I'm not playing, Isaiah."

"I know you're not playing."

"I'm not doing it."

"I heard you."

"No, I don't think you did. *I'm not doing it.*"

"Okay, you're not doing it."

"Well, all right then."

The Drop In Diner was open twenty-four hours, the animal control truck parked in the lot. From there you could see the dirt road leading to and from Skip's place. The truck was on loan from Harry along with a tranquilizer gun and a special gurney for transporting unconscious animals. The gun came with darts loaded with Sucostrin, a muscle relaxant, the dose calculated by species and weight.

"Why do you need me?" Dodson said. "Can't you shoot the dog by yourself?"

"I told you ten times already," Isaiah said. "I need you to help me get the dog on the gurney. That's a hundred and thirty pounds of deadweight."

"What if he gets loose? What if *all* them dogs get loose? Shit. You don't even know if that dart gun's gonna work. They don't use 'em on dogs."

"No, just bears and mountain lions. Will you please relax? All you have to do is bring the gurney and you'll only be in there for a minute."

They saw headlights. Skip's truck was coming up the road. It turned onto the pavement and drove away.

"Ready?" Isaiah said.

"No," Dodson said. "And I never will be."

They drove the two miles to Skip's place, the moonlit desert like the desert on the moon. The house looked more isolated than it did in the daytime.

"Every scary movie I ever seen happened in a house just like that," Dodson said.

The animal control truck was too wide to make it around the fence posts and the exercise yard, so they parked it alongside the house with the archery target and the mountain bike with the bent fork. Dodson waited on the back patio with the gurney. He'd come when he was called. Isaiah walked off toward the barn wearing a backpack and carrying a ladder.

"Hurry up, you hear me?" Dodson said. "Don't leave me out here forever."

Skip was on Highway 58 heading into Barstow and he was already low on gas. He should have filled up in Fergus but he was distracted, thinking about Q Fuck meeting someone that knew him. He couldn't figure out who that could be. Having no friends made the list of suspects really short. He called Bonnie.

"Let me get this straight," Bonnie said. "This IQ guy is going to meet somebody who's got info on you?"

"Basically, yeah."

"Like who? You don't have any friends."

"That's why I'm calling, Bonnie, I want to know who it is."

"Didn't I tell you not to call me Bonnie?"

"Okay, *Jimmy,* what do you think's going on?"

"Well, it's not any of the people you worked for. They'd give you up to the police, not some ghetto detective. What about a house-keeper or a gardener?"

"You've been to my place, haven't you?"

"One of your dog breeding people?"

"None of them know what I do for a living."

"Then it's a setup."

"Setup how? I go to this bar and that asshole puts a gun to my head and forces me to talk? He couldn't do that if he wanted to."

Jimmy was quiet a moment and then he laughed.

"What's so funny?" Skip said.

"This guy is pretty smart. No wonder they call him IQ."

"Quit fucking around, Jimmy. *What?*"

"He's not trying to get you to some bar. He's trying to get you out of your house."

Skip's heart shot up to his throat. He yanked the wheel, the tires screeching, the suspension bucking as he drove over the median and made a U-turn across all four lanes of Highway 58.

Isaiah was eager to get this done, telling himself it was all about the case. He didn't like thinking he wanted to hurt Skip. Take something from him. Make him feel the pain of losing a loved one. When he got to the barn, the dogs were barking and yowling and banging against their kennels. Attila was loose, his wet nose snuffling on the other side of the door. No way to shoot him without opening it and Harry had warned him the dog might not go down right away. Fifteen feet overhead was the bay door to the hayloft. On his last visit here, Isaiah had seen a big sliding bolt on the inside. Getting in that way meant removing the track that held up the door. Take out a bunch of heavy bolts and move the ladder from side to side. The easiest access was through one of the two skylights but the roof was steeply pitched. He'd have to wield the circular saw while he stood on what amounted to the side of a pyramid.

Isaiah went around to the long side of the barn and set the ladder against the wall. He already had on the climbing harness. It fit him like a diaper made of nylon straps. He climbed the ladder to the drip edge of the roof, set the backpack down in front of him, and took out a three-pronged grappling hook and a coil of climbing rope. With practiced ease, he lofted the hook over the top of the roof. He yanked, setting the hook against the roof cap. Then he tied the tail end of the rope to a metal loop on the climbing harness, put the backpack on, and rappelled up the roof to the skylight, holding himself there with an ascender clamp. He got out the circular saw and began cutting through the plexiglass, the sound huge in the desert quiet. He knew this was a desperate move, maybe a stupid move, but it was a stupid case. He never would have considered it if it wasn't for Flaco—and now Bobby Grimes.

Skip had given a lot of thought to protecting his place. Dog theft was not uncommon, especially pit bulls. Some gangbangers had actually tried to rob him, driving up in a Honda Civic with blacked-out windows and blue kerchiefs over their faces. They were approaching the house and drawing their guns when Skip came out firing a fully automatic assault rifle with a North Korean helical magazine that held a hundred and fifty rounds. A water show of bullets sent the gangbangers running for their car and sent the car hobbling back down the road with three flat tires and smoke billowing out of the engine. What really worried Skip was being at a strip club or on a job somewhere, the dogs and his property left unprotected.

He could leave Attila loose in the barn but what about the rest of the place? Skip was limping back to the house with the mountain bike when he had a flash of brilliance. *Let Goliath roam free.*

Goliath had tracked a coyote all the way to the bald hill when he sensed the intruders. He lifted his sledgehammer head and let the air collect in the chambers of his nose; holding it there, sorting through hundreds of different scents, his olfactory memory recognizing ones he'd smelled before. If someone had been there to see him they'd have sworn he was grinning as he turned and ran off toward the house.

Dodson was sitting on the gurney, taking deep breaths and fidgeting. The barking was relentless, the sound of the circular saw cutting off his nerve endings. He was about to smoke a joint when he saw a dark shape bounding over the moonscape. The big black pit bull was barreling toward him like a four-legged linebacker, snarling and slobbering, fangs glowing in the dark. "Ohhh SHIT!" Dodson said. Instinctively, he ran for the house and thank you Jesus the back door was open. He got inside and slammed it shut. He waited but didn't hear the dog. "Where'd he go?" Dodson said. He went into the living room and looked out the different windows. The dog was nowhere in sight. "The fuck happened?" he said.

The fuck happened was Skip planning for this scenario, some asshole in the house with the doors closed thinking he was safe, not knowing Goliath was trained to jump through the window in the den that was always left open. Dodson turned just in time to see two yellow eyes and a mouth full of fangs leaping for his throat. He reacted like a boxer, jerking his head aside and leaning away, the dog bumping his shoulder and tumbling to the floor. Knowing he wouldn't get far, Dodson ran to the hallway entry, pulling over Elsa Gunderson's grandfather clock and arming himself with a chair. The dog came at him but couldn't get around the clock, Dodson sticking the chair in its face so it couldn't jump over. "Get back, get back, goddammit!" Dodson yelled. "Isaiah, where the fuck are you?"

Suddenly, the dog ran off. Dodson stood still, puzzled. He could hear the dog moving, scrambling on the Mexican pavers, getting louder now. A jolt of terror hit Dodson like a stun gun. The beast was circling through the house and would come into the hallway from the other end. Dodson ran into a bedroom and reached for the door but there was no door. Skip had apparently removed them all. Dodson heard the dog coming. There was nowhere to go, the window painted shut. "Oh Lord have mercy," he said.

Isaiah lowered himself into the hayloft on the climbing rope, the disassembled dart gun in the backpack. He looked over the edge of the loft and saw Attila at the bottom of the ladder, snarling, the laser-green eyes glaring up at him, the other dogs in a frenzy. It was like looking down on a dog insane asylum. Isaiah's first move was to put a dart in Attila, then he'd go down there and put another one in the big dog. Isaiah's eyes honed in on the oversize kennel and then pinballed around the barn. *The big dog wasn't there.*

The truck vacuumed up the desert highway, the speedometer touching ninety, Fergus still a few miles away, Skip's fury like a burning comet. "IF HE TOUCHED MY DOGS I'LL KILL HIM I'LL KILL HIM I'LL FUCKING KILL HIM."

There were louvered doors on the bedroom closet, Dodson getting just enough grip to pull them shut from the inside. The big dog charged into the room, gluey slobber dripping off its fangs. Growling, it pawed at the doors and sniffed like it was trying to inhale Dodson through the wood. "NO!" Dodson screamed. "GET AWAY! GET AWAY! SIT! LIE DOWN! FETCH! ISAIAHHH!" The dog was getting frustrated, barking and whimpering, trying to claw its way in. Dodson saw a movie where the character gave commands to his attack dog in a foreign language. *"¡VÁMONOS! ¡HASTA LUEGO! ¡VAYA CON DIOS!"* The dog bit into the louvers, rattling the doors, Dodson keeping them closed with his fingertips. "ISAIAHHHH! WHERE THE FUCK ARE YOU?" The dog kept biting and gnawing, hooking a louver in its teeth and tearing it off. The dog got more excited, savaging the louvers, chomping and ripping, drool coming through the spaces where the louvers were missing. *"SAYONARA! ACHTUNG! SIEG HEIL!* GO THE FUCK AWAY! ISAIAHHH!" More louvers were torn off, the dog sticking its massive head into the closet, lips pulled back over its teeth like the alien in *Alien,* amber eyes fierce and murderous. "DON'T KILL ME DON'T KILL ME LET ME ALONE!" The dog pushed its whole body in, splintering louvers and roaring like a werewolf. Dodson fell to the floor, screaming, not believing it was Auntie May's yard all over again—and now the dog was on top of him, its searing breath in his ear. He couldn't die like this, he couldn't—

Isaiah swung the door open and shot the dog with the dart gun at point-blank range. "Get off him," he said. The dog bawled, snarled, and lunged at him, Isaiah stumbling backward into the hall, the dog leaping at him, knocking him down, its jaws at his throat, thick spittle dripping on his face—and then it collapsed, its weight like a building on his chest. Isaiah heaved the dog off and stood up.

Dodson came out of the bedroom. "Where were you?" he sobbed. "That muthafucka was about to eat my ass alive! Goddammit, Isaiah, I told you I didn't want to come here! I told you, I fuckin' told you!"

"Go get the gurney," Isaiah said.

"That's all you got to say? Go get the gurney?"

"Go get the gurney."

Muttering and blubbering, Dodson staggered away. The dog was paralyzed but conscious, panting heavily with its eyes open. It looked like a dog now instead of a killing machine. Isaiah wanted to comfort it.

Dodson ran back in. "Skip's coming," he said.

Skip swung the truck into the yard, slid to a stop, a storm cloud of dirt and gravel peppering the house. "I'LL KILL HIM I'LL KILL HIM I'LL FUCKING KILL HIM." He ran inside and a moment later the animal control truck came around the side of the house and sped off toward the happy lights of the Drop In Diner.

Skip would have gone after the truck but he saw Goliath collapsed in the hallway. He rushed him to a twenty-four-hour vet in Victorville who thought the dog was a Great Dane. The vet gave him oxygen and fluids and said he should stay overnight as a precaution but Skip took him home.

Skip's new mission in life: Kill Q Fuck. He could go into witness protection and hide in the fucking jungle but Skip would find him and shoot him and let Goliath go at him until there was nothing left but guts in a puddle of blood.

CHAPTER SEVENTEEN
Die, Bitch

April 2006

At ten o'clock in the morning, when most of the residents of the Sea Crest were at work, a Navigator and a Cadillac CTS rolled up in front of the building. Booze Lewis emerged from the CTS, got buzzed in, and crossed the lobby, wincing with every step. His foot was heavily bandaged and he was wearing a slipper with Velcro straps. He should have been on crutches but he didn't want Kinkee taking his place again.

Booze limped down the hall toward Junior's apartment, nobody behind him or coming out of the fire exit, everything like it always was. He was halfway there when some little midget muthafucka stepped out of the electrical room aiming a gun. He was completely covered up. Ski mask, shades, turtleneck, long-sleeve gangsta flannel, gardening gloves, and a red flag in his pocket.

"Don't move, pendejo," the midget said.

"You must be blazed on lean," Booze said. "Do you know who you fuckin' with?" The midget got behind him, reached under his shirt, and took the .357 Magnum out of his shoulder holster like he knew it was there. Booze felt the midget struggling to get the five-pound gun under his shirt, fumbling around, getting frustrated. He didn't want this muthafuckin' dwarf to accidentally pull the trigger. "Y'all be cool now," he said, "I ain't going nowhere." Booze was scared of accidents. He'd modified the trigger bar on the gun, bringing the pull down from the standard six pounds to two. A hair trigger. He was trying it out and accidentally shot his little toe off.

"Fuck it," the midget said, dropping the big gun on the carpeted floor. "Don't try nothing, pendejo," he said, "or I swear to fucking God I'll pop you."

Dodson had gone out with Lupita Tello for three months, long enough to pick up the accent and learn some vocabulary. Mostly things she called him. *Pendejo, puto, pinche, cabron,* and a few others. At the moment the only thing he could remember was *pendejo.*

"Put your hands behind you, pendejo," he said. Booze obeyed, not unfamiliar with the procedure. Dodson looped a zip tie around his wrists and yanked it tight. "Let's go, pendejo." Dodson frog-marched Booze down the hall, raising his chin to see over the gangsta's mountainous shoulder, his view partially blocked by the back of Booze's head, the tiny knots of cornrows perfectly tied, shiny scalp between them, wet heat coming off him that smelled like almonds and coconut.

Booze limped like a man with one leg shorter than the other. "Hey, come on, dog," he said. "Take it easy."

"Shut the fuck up, pendejo," Dodson said. By the time they reached Junior's door, Booze was whimpering, his face squashed with pain. "Get me in, pendejo," Dodson said. "Be a fucking hero and you're fucking dead."

"It's me," Booze said, knocking on the door. Dodson could

barely hear over his thundering heartbeat, his hands dripping wet inside the gloves. Another flash of panic. Nobody else in the gang had a revolver. What if Junior recognized it? The chain was rattling. Do or die.

Junior opened the door carrying an Adidas bag, the Sig Sauer in his belt. Dodson pressed the barrel of his gun into Booze's temple. "Drop the bag and put your gun on the floor or I'll blow his fucking head off."

Junior looked like he'd been asked to do something so ridiculous it was insulting. "Is this a jest or are you an ignoramus?" he said. "Your mind has depreciated extensively if you think your objectives will be finalized with this kind of activity. I think you need to reconsider yourself."

"I *said* drop the bag and put your gun on the floor," Dodson said, pushing the gun in harder.

"Hey man," Booze said, "y'all take it easy with that thing."

"Look here, brutha," Junior said. "Let me try and clarify your perilous circumstances. You are in danger of lifelong extermination if you proceed with this foolishness."

According to Dodson's airtight plan, Junior was supposed to be scared and cooperating, not scolding him like Auntie May with a bigger vocabulary. "Do what I told you, pendejo," Dodson said, "or I'll shoot this motherfucker. I swear to God I will."

"I don't think that's prudency on your part," Junior said. "Repercussions will manifest beyond your ability to cope. Now I suggest you evacuate while you still have the mobility to maneuver your ass on outta here."

"The fuck you doin', Junior?" Booze said. "Don't you see this nigga got a gun to my head?"

"You think I'm playing, pendejo?" Dodson said. "You want your homie to die?"

"No he don't, he definitely don't," Booze said. "Tell 'em, Junior!"

"Why do I have to justify my postulations to this farmworker?" Junior said. "If he was credible he would have proceeded with your death by now."

"Oh I see what you doin'," Booze said. "You *want* this nigga to shoot me so you can shoot *him*."

"Give up the bag and drop the gun or I'll pop him right fucking now!" Dodson said, the plan turning to shit. He thought about turning the gun on Junior but that would leave Booze unguarded.

"Give it up, Junior, damn!" Booze said.

"This is what happens when you don't consummate your duties properly," Junior said. "You have formulated a problem of your own causality."

"I'm gonna get you for this, Junior, I swear to God."

Dodson knew he couldn't shoot Booze in the head, not at this range. "This is your last chance, motherfucker," he said, knowing it was his own. "Give it up or he's dead."

"Becalm yourselves," Junior said, talking to the both of them now.

"Junior, did you just hear the man say this is my last chance?" Booze said.

"This man is lying mendaciously, Booze. Can't you ascertain a falsehood from a factuality?"

Cock the gun, Dodson thought, but before he could put his thumb on the hammer, Junior had darted back into the apartment and Booze was pushing off with his good foot, backpedaling into him, the big shoulder forcing his gun hand up, the momentum knocking him backward and to the floor. Booze fell on top of him, his rock-solid butt cheeks landing on Dodson's midsection. Dodson felt an explosion of pain, every molecule of oxygen leaving his body in one breath. He doubled up and let go of the revolver.

Booze rolled off him and got to his feet. "What you got to say now, pen-day-ho? It better be your muthafuckin' prayers."

Junior came out of the apartment, the Sig in one hand, a folding knife in the other. He cut the zip tie off Booze and then kicked Dodson hard. "Prepare yourself for complete denigration, muthafucka," he said. Dodson was curled up in a ball, trying to suck in air through a throat the size of a nail hole. He had one arm over his head, the other across his gut, Junior kicking him again and again saying: "You—will—now—cease—to—res—pirate—un—til—you—are—de—ceased—for—life."

Through his half-closed eyes, Dodson could see Booze limping back and forth, vibrating with homicidal energy, the revolver in his hand. "Try to rob *me?*" he said. "Put a gun to *my* head? You done, nigga, you finished. It's lights-out, you feel me?"

"Advance your agenda, Booze," Junior said. "Terminate this peon with prejudice."

Dodson couldn't believe he was helpless and about to die. He tried to speak, plead for his life, or say *it's me* but he couldn't get a word out. Booze was standing over him, the revolver aimed at his head.

"Die, bitch," Booze said. He cocked the gun, the sound like a skull cracking. The gunshot was loud as a thunderclap, the shock wave jarring the air, two more shots right after it and then... silence.

As far as Dodson could tell he was still alive. Was Booze fucking with him? Dodson waited, the stillness amazing. Slowly, he unfurled himself, gasping, the pain clouding his vision, the cordite smell strong as crack fumes. Booze had his head on the floor, his ass up in the air like a stinkbug. Junior was in the fetal position, blood leaking out of him, a rust-colored stain expanding on the carpet. Isaiah was standing ten feet away with his mouth open and Booze's .357 dangling by his side, one finger through the trigger guard. Dodson struggled to his feet, staggered into the apartment, and came out with the Adidas bag. He picked up his gun, grabbed Isaiah's sleeve, and yanked him down the hall. "Let's go," he croaked. They ran to the end of the hall, crashed through the fire exit, and took off in different directions, neither of them looking back.

The news was on. Police were milling around the Sea Crest, yellow tape closing off the building. A middle-aged reporter was doing a standup, his suit sagging in the heat, his comb-over like a beach ball covered with a handful of straw. "Around ten o'clock this morning," the reporter said, "police say a resident of the Sea Crest apartments in Bluff Park and another man were shot outside the resident's door. Both victims were transported to Long Beach Memorial, where the resident was described as critical, the other man in stable condition. Police have no motive for the shooting but believe it may have been gang-related."

Isaiah stood with his forehead against the apartment wall, a slide show blinking behind his eyes. *Blink.* Running into the hallway. *Blink.* Two men standing over Dodson screaming and kicking him. *Blink.* A gun lying on the carpet. *Blink.* Picking it up, running toward the men. *Blink.* One of them saying *Die, bitch* and cocking his gun. *Blink.* Shooting him. *Blink.* The other man shooting back. *Blink.* Shooting him. *Blink.* Bodies on the floor.

"I had to do it," Isaiah said. "I *had* to."

The clothes he was wearing were in a gutter, the gun at the

bottom of the LA River, the Explorer parked in the Vons lot. He'd taken a twenty-minute shower and used a pumice stone to get off the gun residue. He hadn't seen any cameras or witnesses but that didn't mean there weren't any. And Dodson. Did he tell anybody about the robbery besides Deronda? Did Deronda tell anybody? What if Dodson got busted and gave him up? He knew he should get out of Long Beach but he was too terrified to leave the room.

Eighty-five thousand dollars of Junior's money was on the coffee table. Banded tens, twenties, and hundreds stacked in separate piles. Dodson would have been celebrating if he wasn't nauseous, deaf from the gunshots, and bruised all over his body. In a way, the injuries were a good thing. They distracted him from being scared out of his mind. Did Booze and Junior buy the accent? Did they see he wasn't a Mexican? Did they recognize the gun? Did they recognize *him?*

Dodson's phone buzzed. Deronda picked it up. "Says nine-one-one-star-sd-star-eleven," she said. "What that's supposed to mean?"

"Nine-one-one means an emergency meeting," Dodson said. "You gotta come or get a beatdown. Sd means Sedrick's crib. Eleven is eleven o'clock." Dodson closed his eyes. If he didn't go it might be suspicious but if he went he might be killed. The obvious thing was to book but where would he book to? Take the Greyhound to Oakland and start all over again? And what if he was free and clear? He'd have left his hood for nothing.

"What are you gonna do?" Deronda said.

A corroded spotlight put a feeble yellow circle on the patchy grass, Michael Stokely in the middle of it holding the sawed-off Mossberg like a tomahawk. "Junior's in the ICU," he said, "but I talked to

Booze. He took one in the hip, went right through him. His people was there, all crying and carrying on. His mama was yelling at me like I'm the one that shot his ass."

The Crip Violators were gathered in Sedrick's backyard, the membership scattered around where the light faded to shadow. The OGs were sitting together on the picnic table. Others were on the rusty swing set and on the stoop and leaning against the beat-up van with one headlight. A few were in that pose you see in every group gangsta photo ever taken. Hunched down with a forearm on a knee. Dodson was standing near the gate. A sheen of sweat on his face, wet rings under his arms, his body a solid block of pain.

"I feel like I'm responsible for this shit," Stokely said. "I was Junior's security, you feel me? I'm supposed to keep shit from happening but it didn't come down like that. Booze say it was two of 'em that did it. He didn't see the shooter, just the muthafucka who did the stickup part."

"Did he say who it was?" Sedrick said.

"I'm getting to it, nigga," Stokely said. "Interrupt me one more time and see if I don't put the Mossy up your ass and blow your muthafuckin' brains out." Sedrick seemed to become part of the lemon tree he was standing under, brothers laughing at him. "Booze say the muthafucka had himself all covered up," Stokely said. "Had on a mask and shit but he was short like Dodson. A li'l midget muthafucka."

There was some chuckling. Dodson almost bolted but he heard something in Stokely's voice that made him stay.

"Now you niggas listen up," Stokely said. "This here's the key part to the whole episode. Booze say the stickup man was a Mexican. Said he had a red flag on him. Said he was muthafuckin' Loco."

A tsunami of testosterone engulfed the backyard, the entire membership in gangsta mode. On their feet, waving their straps, throwing up signs, tick tocking their heads. *Muthafuckas is going down. Let's go pop them niggas right now. The fuck we sittin' here for? It's game on now, niggas, you feel me? Let's go smoke some Mexicans, y'all. It's time to get active, put a burner on them niggas, make they mamas cry.* Dodson joined in, thinking, *Thank you, Jesus. Thank you with all my heart.*

Stokely held the shotgun high. "It's payback time, you feel me?" he said. "We hittin 'em hard, scorchin' the earth. It's total annihilation by any means necessary. It's war, muthafuckas. It's a muthafuckin' war."

Amelio, Jorge, and Lil Genius came out of the Big Meaty Burger like they were in ankle chains. An XXL Everest Burger with bacon and a fried egg plus a large order of chili cheese fries tends to slow you down. They walked up the street to Jorge's whip parked around the corner. They didn't see the beat-up van with one headlight rolling up behind them until it was too late. The side door slammed open and two homies with blue flags over their faces and Tec-9 machine pistols emptied their clips, the sound like a couple of speed freaks pounding nails. Amelio took three in the back. Jorge caught one in the throat. Genius was hit in the forehead and died before he hit the ground. As the van sped off, a shooter yelled: "Yeah, muthafuckas, how you feelin' now?"

The reporter with the comb-over was doing a standup in front of the Big Meaty Burger, his manner so detached he might have been thinking, *Another* shooting? Gimme a break. "The Hurston area of East Long Beach was the scene of a deadly drive-by," he said. "Amelio Aguilar, Jorge Ochoa, and a third victim, a minor, had just finished eating at the Big Meaty Burger on Pacific Avenue when a van drove past them and an unknown number of suspects allegedly shot them with semiautomatic weapons. All were pronounced dead at the scene. Police suspect the drive-by was related to another shooting last Wednesday in Bluff Park. A police spokesperson said the situation had all the signs of a gang war and warned residents in the area to be extra cautious."

More press arrived, some of them national; making their reports with the You Know You Want Some posters in the background. The two girls who worked at the restaurant were suspected of tipping off the Locos and wouldn't go on camera for fear of reprisals. People who lived in the area were interviewed. They said the gangs were really bad, there's too much violence, somebody should do something, and the neighborhood didn't used to be like this.

Kaylin Kennedy had come in second in the LA's Hottest Weathergirl rankings. Kaylin didn't know what she hated more, coming in second or being called a weathergirl. She told Doug she wanted to be a reporter or she was leaving and he started her off doing features. A man with the world's largest collection of Flintstone memorabilia. A kid that carved whistles for the troops overseas. A potbellied pig that could say I love you.

Kaylin was thrilled when Doug said she could cover real stories but this was her first week and she was already having second thoughts. Yesterday, she and her cameraman Roddy covered a brush fire off the 210 Freeway. It was ninety-seven degrees, the wind blew her hair to shit, and the smoke aggravated her asthma. Then she broke a heel and had to interview the fire captain barefoot and stepped on an anthill.

Now she was in Hurston about to interview a gangster involved in the gang war. It seemed hotter here than at the brush fire and the air had some kind of grit in it. The backdrop for the interview was a stucco wall crawling with indecipherable gang graffiti that made it seem like a foreign country. The gangster towered over her. He had on a black cap with a C on it and a blue kerchief over his face. A sawed-off shotgun was nestled under his arm like he was about to go duck hunting.

"Let's talk about your weapon, sir," Kaylin said. "Do you have it with you all the time?"

"Hell yeah," Stokely said. "This shit ain't no game. It's a muthafuckin' kill zone out here, you feel me? I ain't strappin' I ain't surviving. Niggas could roll up on us right now."

"So you believe your life is in danger standing here talking with me?"

"Uh-huh, and I believe *your* life is in danger standing here talkin' with *me*."

"Let's talk about the war itself. Could you tell me what's behind it? The reasons the war started?"

"This shit is ongoin', you know what I'm sayin'? The latest flare-up ain't no muthafuckin' surprise. This shit is business as usual."

"Could I ask you to tone down the language? This is for broadcast."

"I don't give a shit what it's for and I ain't tonin' down nothin'. You don't like how I'm dropping it get the fuck up outta my hood."

Kaylin's armpits were dripping and she was losing her patience. She remembered being in the cool studio bantering with Ted and Patricia and pointing at imaginary clouds on the green screen for ninety seconds. Roddy was nodding at her to keep going.

"You were saying the violence is business as usual?" Kaylin said.

"This is the hood," Stokely said. "It's live out here. You don't get a nigga 'fore he gets you your shit is over."

"Is this war about drugs?"

"In an offshoot kinda way but that ain't the heart of it. This shit is about respect, you feel me?"

"That's a term I hear a lot, respect. What does it mean to you?"

"It means it don't matter who the fuck you are or what you got to say. If I feel like you defyin' my will? I'll put your ass down on the spot."

"Let me see if I understand. You're saying that respect is not challenging you in any way about anything by anyone. Is that the idea?"

"That's it in a muthafuckin' nutshell."

"Can you tell me if there's a racial component to the war? African-Americans versus Latinos?"

"I ain't got nothin' against Latinos per se. I'll shoot a nigga no matter who he is."

"Do you have any idea when the war will be over and the people of Hurston will be safe again?"

"Niggas wasn't safe *before* the war. Why they gonna be safe after it's done?"

Kaylin signed off. Stokely pulled his flag down and lit up a joint. "Want some?" he said.

"No, thank you," Kaylin said. The weed smelled like somebody pissing on a pile of burning leaves. Stokely offered a hit to Roddy, who shook his head but smiled as he did it. "Can I ask you something?" Kaylin said. "There's a question I hear all the time but I've never heard a satisfactory answer."

Stokely took a hit and held it in. "Yeah, what?" he said, squeezing out the words, his eyes watering.

"How come it's okay for you to use the N-word but it's not okay for someone like me?"

"Let me make it real for you," Stokely said. "If a nigga calls me a nigga I know what he means. But if *you* call me a nigga you might mean *nigga*."

The gangster left and Roddy packed up while Kaylin stood in the shade of the news van and smoked a Marlboro Light. She'd asked the gangster the right questions but after editing bleeped out all the profanity there'd be nothing left but adverbs and pronouns. Maybe the job would get better, she thought. She'd get used to it, toughen up, get hard-nosed and courageous. Be one of those women reporters wearing a flak jacket and crouching behind a mud wall because the rebels were shooting and talking to Anderson Cooper via satellite. Yeah, she could see herself doing that.

Frankie La Piedra Montañez was the Locos' shot caller. His shaved head was all angles like a Stone Age cutting tool, his mouth the same shape as his drooping mustache. He was shirtless, a thicket of tattoos on his chest and arms. A grinning skull in the middle of a spiderweb. A cholo and a hot chica wearing sombreros and ammunition belts. The letter M on a palm print with the caption in Spanish: *When the hand touches you you go to work,* and the Aztec war glyph to show pride in his heritage.

Frankie was a carnale, a high-ranking member of the Mexican Mafia, the prison gang also known as La Eme. The Locos bought their drugs from La Eme distributors and kicked back a percentage of the profits. They did this voluntarily because every homie knew that someday he'd go to prison and if La Eme had a beef with you you might as well stab yourself twenty times with a sharpened spoon handle and save them the trouble.

Frankie called an emergency meeting and the Locos gathered in the amphitheater in McClarin Park where people played chess and ate their lunches around the dried-up fountain. They fled when the gang showed up. "Those fucking Violators came up from behind like the fucking cowards they are," Frankie said. "Supposedly we had something to do with robbing Junior but that's like bullshit, that's like an excuse so they could attack us. It's like they're throwing down the gauntlet, like they can intimidate us, like we're going to back down." The gang yelled their defiance; tick tocking their heads, waving their straps, and talking shit. Frankie raised his arms for quiet. "It's war," he said. "No mercy, no quarter, shoot on sight. Somebody looks wrong to you take 'em out first and ask questions later." Frankie looked solemnly from face to face. "The Violators have to pay in blood for what they did to us," he said. "This is our mission and we gotta take it all the way. We can't let our fallen brothers die in vain. They were Locos, nuestra familia, and they will live in our hearts forever."

Expecting retaliation, the Violators traveled in packs now, nobody walking around solo or sitting on their front porch smoking a joint. Kinkee, Sedrick, Hassan, Omari, and Dodson were eating chili dogs on a cement picnic table behind Hot Dog Heaven, a spot you couldn't see from the street. A building had been demolished on one side of the restaurant. Nothing left but piles of old lumber, broken concrete, and rusted rebar. On the other side, European Auto Mart, Trone over there checking out the rides.

"Look at him," Kinkee said, nodding at Trone. "Nigga ain't got the money for a muthafuckin' hot dog over there like he's gonna buy a car."

Dodson was still in pain from the beating. His ribs were taped up, painkillers were part of his diet now, and he was smoking a lot of weed. He thought about calling Isaiah and thanking him for saving his life but all he'd do was give him shit. Fuck Isaiah.

"Booze is coming home soon," Kinkee said. "Junior's still in there, need another surgery but he ain't gonna die. His mama said she taking him to Stockton, get him off the street. Shit. They got streets up there too."

Trone had his hands cupped over his eyes and was trying to see into a Benz 500SL. A white salesman in a blue dress shirt with the sleeves rolled up was talking to him and smiling with just his mouth.

"Salesman don't know what to do," Kinkee said. "Trone might be a rapper, buy the car for cash."

"Or he might be what he looks like," Dodson said, "a thug with no money."

"What I want to know," Sedrick said, "is how the Locos knew about the reup? Like what day, what time."

"That ain't no damn mystery," Dodson said. "The Locos was tracking Junior the whole time, sneaky muthafuckas. If you can sneak over that wall and get past the border patrol with all them cameras and night vision you can sneak up on anything."

Kinkee was looking at the car lot. "Oh shit," he said.

The salesman was hauling ass for the office. Trone was running toward the group, hurdling the chain that bordered the car lot. "They comin'," Trone said.

Dodson saw a group of Locos sneaking between the rows of cars, red kerchiefs over their faces. They stood up and started shooting. "Kill 'em, kill those fuckers," a Loco said. Dodson sprinted for the empty lot, Sedrick and Omari right behind him. Trone raced to the dumpster and dove in headfirst, rounds punching holes in the green metal. Hassan couldn't get his legs out from under the table, took two in the chest, and died with his mouth full of onion rings.

A Loco shouted: "I got him, I got him."

Dodson, Sedrick, and Omari crouched behind the demolition rubble and returned fire, bullets exploding off the concrete, whanging off the rebar, and ripping into the old lumber. Kinkee was on the side of the restaurant sticking his gun around the corner and blasting away. It was shock and awe, a full-on gunfight: .9s, .38s, .45s, and .357s going off in salvos, both sides emptying clips through a haze of smoke.

A Loco was hit. "They got me," he said, "they fucking got me."

A round smashed into Omari's temple, his brains spraying out the other side.

"Oh shit," Sedrick said, "Omari's fucked up."

"Enough of this shit," Kinkee said. He stepped out from behind the building and did his Denzel impression, walking toward the Locos holding two guns sideways and firing them at the same time. He looked cool until he caught one in the thigh and had to hop back to safety.

Another Loco went down. "They got Frankie," a Loco said. "Somebody help him."

Dodson was behind a chunk of foundation firing a Saturday-night special he'd bought after ditching the revolver. He was missing on purpose. If a Loco got killed the spent rounds couldn't be matched to his gun unless the police dug them out of the Porsche Panamera he was aiming at.

The Locos were advancing, ducking and dodging and shooting as they came over the chain. Kinkee had run out of ammo and hobbled away. Dodson and Sedrick got up and ran.

"They're running!" a Loco shouted. "Get those fucking cowards."

Dodson raced around the restaurant and took off down the street, relieved he wasn't hit. Gunshots popped behind him, the windshield of a car in front of him shattered. *The Locos were chasing him.* Dodson sprinted for the end of the block. Get around the corner and he could wait, shoot them if they followed. But the pain and weed were slowing him down. His lungs were scorched, a stitch stabbing him in the kidney. The Locos were getting closer, their gunshots getting louder. Dodson was about to stop and go down fighting when he saw an OPEN sign hanging in the window of a taquería. He burst through the door, streaked through the dining room and out the back, gunshots and breaking glass behind him.

Only the lamp was on, the 25-watt bulb like a single candle, darkness all around. Isaiah was sitting on the floor with his back against the bed. The news was on.

"Two rival gangs shot it out behind the Hot Dog Heaven in Hurston today," the anchorman said. "Police say it's the latest skirmish in what they're describing as an all-out war. As many as fifteen gang members exchanged dozens of rounds. Four of the combatants were killed. One suspect was found dead in a dumpster. He hadn't fired a shot, and another victim was only fourteen years old. Three others were wounded and transported to local hospitals. But the story doesn't end there, I'm afraid. Police say a gang member who was involved in the shootout was escaping from rival gang members and ran through the Los Amigos Taquería. The first gang member got away but the owners of the restaurant, Selena and Héctor Ruiz, were killed in the crossfire and pronounced dead at the scene. Equally, if not more tragic, their ten-year-old son was struck once in the head. The boy was taken to Hurston Community

Hospital and is listed in critical condition. The boy's surgeon, Dr. Amelia Lopez, told reporters the boy suffered severe brain trauma and underwent surgery. His chances of surviving are unknown, but if he does make it, he'll be facing the awful news that his parents are dead."

Isaiah got up, walked in a circle, and stood with his forehead against a wall. *How could this happen? Those people were killed? Killed? The boy has brain trauma? This is insane. The war did this. The war Dodson started. Dodson. Fucking Dodson.*

He couldn't stay in the room anymore and walked aimlessly. *This mess is all his fault, the idiot. How fucking stupid do you have to be to try something like that? Now where am I? What am I going to do? Fucking Dodson. I never should have let him in the apartment.*

The apartment. Thinking about it filled him with longing and pain. "I want my life back," he said. "I want Marcus back." It was saying his name that did it. Isaiah's conscience came busting through the wall of his denial like the battering ram, Marcus storming through the gap. Isaiah knew exactly what his brother would say and how he'd say it. His voice raw like he'd been screaming, one hand judo-chopping the other like he was trying to cut it in half.

What have you done? What have you done? This is your fault. Yours. *Don't shake your head.* You *made the war happen. You tipped the first domino the minute you decided to be a criminal and one after the other the whole chain fell and now here we are. Those innocent people dead and their son without a mother or a father. Yes, I know you were grieving but you couldn't deal with it any better than this? The only choice you could make was to be a thief? What happened to your sense of decency? What happened to your morals? Wasting my time on you all those years and for what? So you could use your gift to be a leech, a parasite, a scum-of-the-earth lowlife criminal?*

Isaiah walked faster, almost running, but he couldn't get away from Marcus's voice, his presence so real it was breathing down his neck and stepping on his heels, making him stumble.

Where're you going, Isaiah? Think you can walk away from this? You can walk all the way to Timbuktu but those folks will still be dead and that boy will still be an orphan. What are you going to do about him, Isaiah? Haven't given that a thought, have you? Well, you better start thinking about it and figure out how to make this right or I will be in your face and in your dreams every day and every night for the rest of your miserable life.

CHAPTER EIGHTEEN

The Inside Man

July 2013

Cal's second cell phone was buzzing for the fourth time in twenty minutes and nobody had the number except DStar, the crew, Bobby Grimes, and his mother. It pissed him off. Everybody had been told not to call, text, or even knock on the door unless the house was burning down. Maybe that was what he should do, thought Cal. Burn up the biggest meaningless possession he had. How 'bout that, Dr. Freeman? How 'bout if I set my house on fire? The phone kept buzzing. Cal only got up to answer it because it might be DStar and the Klonopin supply was running low.

"Is this Mr. Wright? Mr. Calvin Wright?" A white boy's voice.

"Yeah, this is Mr. Calvin Wright. Who the fuck are you and how'd you get this number?"

"My name is Brian Sterling, sir. I'm Dr. Freeman's executive assistant."

"'Scuse me?"

"I work for Dr. Freeman. Dr. Russell Freeman?"

"The Dr. Freeman I heard on the radio? The Dr. Freeman that wrote that book?"

"Yes sir, and let me tell you why I'm calling. Your internist, Dr. Macklin, spoke with Dr. Freeman and gave him a detailed report about how you were experiencing severe burnout symptoms. Dr. Freeman was concerned and asked me to call you."

"Dr. Freeman knows about me?"

"Like I said, sir, Dr. Macklin gave him a full report."

Cal couldn't remember giving Dr. Macklin permission to give full reports to anybody, let alone Dr. Freeman, but his memory was shot to shit.

"We understand there's been a problem utilizing Dr. Freeman's book."

"I can't seem to get the full effect."

"Sometimes that happens when the case is as complex and critical as yours."

Calvin was relieved to hear his case was complex and critical. Everybody else thought he was crazy.

"Fortunately, Dr. Freeman had a cancellation," Brian said, "and there's an opening in his schedule tomorrow at eleven. Would you be able to come in?"

Cal hesitated. He wanted to see Dr. Freeman but he didn't get up until two or three in the afternoon and he needed time to prepare himself, get his mind right, get some more Klonopin from DStar. "You got anything next week?" he said.

"I'm afraid not, sir. Dr. Freeman is leaving town on his book tour. Europe, Asia, Germany. He won't be back until January."

"That's my choice, tomorrow or next year?"

"Basically, yes."

Brian told Cal not to discuss the appointment with anyone, not even his friends. A famous rapper seeing Dr. Freeman would be a headline in the tabloids. Brian also explained that special accommodations had been made for celebrities so they could visit the office unseen, and he went over them twice.

"Aight then," Cal said, "I'll see y'all tomorrow."

"Very good, Mr. Wright," Brian said. "Dr. Freeman is looking forward to meeting you. He's a big fan of your music."

After Skip got off the phone he took the dogshit rake out of the trash can and walked north toward the hill. He turned left at the boulder shaped like a turtle and hopped from one flat rock to another until he reached a pile of boulders no different than hundreds of others. On one side of the pile was a tangle of whitethorn acacia branches, the thorns a half inch long and needle-sharp. Skip raked the branches away, revealing a deep hollow between two boulders. He poked the rake in there to check for snakes and dragged out a waterproof camper trunk. The trunk held guns. They were new and wrapped in plastic. Skip had paid straw buyers to buy them at gun shows in Utah and Arizona where there weren't any background checks.

There were two assault rifles, a tactical shotgun, a Remington 700 sniper rifle, and a half dozen handguns. Skip chose the Glock 18c. A special gun he'd bought from an associate of Bonnie's. The 18c was a fully automatic machine pistol and the so-called plastic gun. It was made from a polymer and light as a feather. The Glock's rate of fire was twelve hundred rounds per minute and it would empty the thirty-three-round clip of multiple-impact bullets in 1.65 seconds. It would be like shooting thirty-three fishing nets and every knot was lethal. Whatever happened, he wasn't going to miss and when it was over he'd go after the smart-ass and shoot that fucking Kurt too.

Skip thought he'd get in a little practice. Take Goliath out to the scrub, see if the dog could scare up something to shoot. To make it fair he'd use regular ammo and put the gun on semiauto. Drawing a bead on a zigzagging rabbit got his adrenaline going and shook the rust off his reflexes. When he hit one it twisted and tumbled before crashing into the dirt, Goliath on it in a heartbeat, snarling and shredding, little tufts of fur floating in the desert air.

They were in Dodson's apartment waiting for *The Shonda Simmons Show* to come on. It was a nice place, Isaiah thought. Muted creams and beiges, Berber carpet, gentle art on the walls. Cherise must have put it together.

Dodson came out of the kitchen with two espressos and a plate of warm Danish. "You see what I'm doing here?" he said. "It's called hospitality."

Shonda Simmons was interviewing Noelle, the promos had been on all week. Isaiah didn't know why he'd agreed to watch it here or watch it at all. The case was over and done. The failed dognapping was his last option. Maybe he should have swallowed his pride and accepted Bobby's twenty grand. That was a whole lot better than no grand at all and he would have been that much closer to Flaco's condo. Now it was out of reach forever. Then there was Skip to deal with. Crazy as he was, he might try to kill Isaiah again but he'd deal with that when the time came.

"Here it is," Dodson said.

Voluptuous didn't quite capture Shonda Simmons's figure. It was more like the number 8 in extra-extra-large. She had an attractive face but her makeup had been applied like mochaccino icing on a chocolate cake, her eyelashes long enough to sweep the floor, her earrings like the chandeliers at Cal's house.

"Thank you, Shonda," Noelle said. "I try to keep myself together."

"That dress may help. I haven't seen anything that tight since I took the shrink-wrap off my new vibrator."

Noelle laughed. "I must admit, I had some trouble getting into it."

Noelle was naturally alluring, no need to hype her sexuality but she had anyway. Her skirt might as well have been a pair of men's boxer shorts, the blouse scoop-necked and glittery. Her gold-tinted hair looked windblown, her smile, wily and entitled.

"Damn, Noelle's hot," Dodson said. "But you know what they say. No matter how fine a woman is, somebody somewhere kicked her ass out."

"Why are we watching this?" Isaiah said.

"You said you never seen Noelle before. Well, here's your chance."

"So tell me, how's your ex?" Shonda said.

"I have no idea. It's not like I talk to him," Noelle said.

"Yes, I suppose conversation would be difficult after you hit the man with Don Juan's pimp cup."

"Allegedly," Noelle said.

"Now I know you had a lot of reasons for divorcing Calvin," Shonda said. "That's Black the Knife's real name, for those of you who didn't know—but was there something in particular that drove you two apart?"

"Yes. Calvin's DNA," Noelle said. "He's part megalomaniac and part pervert. If he's not telling you how great he is he's trying to get you to do something nasty."

"Ooh, we're taking off the gloves now."

"They've been off for quite some time. You hit Calvin with anything other than your bare knuckles he wouldn't know you were in the room."

A wave of snickering and light applause rippled through the mostly female audience.

"Now I've heard from several sources that Cal is having serious problems, which I'm guessing means drugs," Shonda said.

"Calvin's always had a drug problem but now he's crazy too," Noelle said.

"Crazy? Crazy how?"

"Let me put it this way. Wake up tomorrow morning and begin your day the way Calvin does. Start with a handful of Focalin, Fentanyl, Klonopin, and Wellbutrin and a dozen Krispy Kreme Originals and wash it all down with Spicy V8 and vodka and if you weren't crazy before you'll be crazy later that day."

"I guess you would be," Shonda said. The audience laughed and clapped. "Now a little birdie told me you have a new project in the works," she said.

"How do you know about that?" Noelle said.

"It's my job to know."

"Well, it's still in the planning stages but when it comes to fruition, you'll be the first to know."

"Is that a promise?"

"Of course it is. You know you're my girl. Can we talk about my handbags now?"

The interview ended. Isaiah stood up. "I'm going," he said.

"You're not gonna eat the Danish?" Dodson said.

"I don't like Danish."

"You don't like espresso neither?"

"I already had mine."

"Well, go on and get the fuck outta here then. I guess your brutha taught you everything but manners."

"Don't talk about my brother." Isaiah stood there like he had in the bedroom at the old apartment. Angry beyond words, fists clenched at his sides with nothing to punch. He knew now why he'd come.

"What's your problem?" Dodson said. "You pissed off about the case? You should be. You know I had a nightmare last night? I was stuck in a bowl of dog food and guess who was coming to dinner?"

"Flaco Ruiz," Isaiah said. "Do you know who he is?"

"Yes, I know who he is," Dodson said. "He was that boy who got shot when them two Locos was chasing me through the taquería. They killed his parents and he caught one in the head. Is that what you been grindin' on all this time?"

"Wait. They were chasing *you?* That's unbelievable."

Dodson didn't look remorseful or even embarrassed. He looked like Dodson. Unfazed, unworried, ready to go if you were.

"Do you know what happened to Flaco?" Isaiah said. "Do you care?"

"What I care about is my business," Dodson said.

"Flaco has brain damage and he'll be disabled for the rest of his life."

"Yeah, what about it?"

"What *about* it?"

"I didn't shoot the boy or his parents."

"You started the war. You started the war when you robbed Junior."

"I played my part. So did you. So did a lot of people."

"Doesn't your conscience bother you, or do you even have one?"

Dodson finally reacted, raising his chin, the too-cool expression hardening into belligerence. "You better check yourself, son. You ain't no angel sitting on my shoulder. I got one up there already and what he says to me ain't none of your concern."

Dodson took the dishes into the kitchen. Isaiah stared at the TV. He'd waited a long time to confront Dodson. Unload some of the guilt, make him feel like a scum-of-the-earth lowlife criminal.

Dodson was supposed to confess, ask for forgiveness, and offer to make amends but instead he was offended like Isaiah was an asshole for bringing it up. Isaiah was angry but mostly what he felt was an overwhelming sadness. This was what Dodson was like. This was what people were like. So what if you fucked up and ruined someone's life? You came through without a scratch. Isn't that all that matters?

A commercial for Tylenol was on. A grandfather was holding his grandchild up in the air and was whirling him around, the voice-over saying how Tylenol was the number one doctor-recommended pain reliever for everything you do. Isaiah had taken a lot of Tylenol in his time until he found out the generic was a fraction of the cost.

Isaiah went still. A realization was surging into his bloodstream. He went through the logic again and almost allowed himself a smile.

Dodson came out of the kitchen drying his hands with a towel. "I thought you was leaving," he said.

"I know," Isaiah said.

"You know what? That you're leaving?"

"The inside man. I know who he is."

Brian Sterling's instructions went like this: Cal was to go to the Amos Center building at 453 Capital Way, a half block south of Ventura Boulevard. The tenants were lawyers and financial consultants. Anyone who saw him go in would think he was there on business. Once inside, Cal was to cross the lobby and go past the elevator to the hallway on the left. At the very end, there was an emergency exit. Cal should proceed through the exit and walk straight across the alley to the parking garage of Dr. Freeman's building. Brian would be waiting there to escort him up the back stairs to the side entrance of the office.

Except Dr. Freeman's office was in Beverly Hills and the second building was under construction. Nothing in the parking garage but empty space. Skip was parked in the alley between the two buildings in an ancient, nondescript Corolla. The rapper would pass right in front of him. The plan was to drive in after him, shoot him, and drive out the far exit. It had taken a long time to find exactly the right setup.

The car radio was on, the Dodgers game. Skip was wearing brown corduroy pants and a gray hoodie he'd bought at the Goodwill, the bill of his cap tilted down to put his face in shadow. He'd been wearing latex gloves since he'd stolen the Corolla. The Glock 18c and a ski mask were under the seat, the Beretta in an ankle holster. His phone was mounted on the dash, the Uber app on the screen, leftovers of a McNuggets meal on the seat beside him. He'd leaned the seat back to lower his profile but still had a clear view over the dashboard, and his mirrors were adjusted so he could see behind him. He pretended to doze, his arms crossed and resting on his chest, gloved hands hidden in his armpits. If someone happened by he was just your average Uber driver, taking a break and listening to the ball game.

He was ready.

Cal was in his walk-in closet, which was only slightly smaller than the racquetball court. He was checking himself out in the three-sided tailor's mirrors. Fortunately, he'd only burned up a fraction of his meaningless wardrobe. For his meeting with Dr. Freeman he'd chosen Dolce & Gabbana five-pocket walking shorts, an Alexander McQueen piqué logo polo shirt, and Jimmy Choo Sloane paisley jacquard slippers. Casual but letting Dr. Freeman know he had money and was no ordinary patient. If he drove there himself he was almost sure to get lost so his plan was to tell Bug he had a toothache and needed to go to the dentist—*now,* nigga. No, not in five minutes and no, he didn't need to tell the fellas, just get in the fucking car. Do it like that. By the time anybody knew he was gone he'd be gone.

All things considered, Cal was feeling good. Drugged and not too sharp but pretty good. He was tired of being crazy and confused and staying in his room. It was time to put this shit behind him.

He was ready.

Isaiah, Anthony, and Dodson were downstairs in the kitchen, standing around the center island where Cal ate the barbecued tempeh and saw the giant pit bull come through the doggie door.

Isaiah was uncomfortable. He felt like he was jumping the gun. The case-breaker was visible now. Something shiny under rippling water.

"Okay, what's this about?" Anthony said.

"How long have you been seeing Noelle?" Isaiah said.

"I'm not. Where'd you get that idea?"

"You've been seeing her all along, maybe while she was still living here. Makes sense. You make a nice couple."

"Well, thanks, but you're mistaken and I asked you where you got the idea of us being together."

"Noelle was on *The Shonda Simmons Show.*"

"Yes, I saw that. She didn't say anything about me."

"Noelle knew the brand names of Cal's medications and how would she know that unless you told her? Bug and Charles wouldn't know and Bobby doesn't care. You told her, Anthony. Can't be anybody else."

"What can I say? You're wrong."

Isaiah looked at him, Anthony meeting his gaze for a moment before wilting into weary relief. "Okay, yes, I'm seeing Noelle," he said. "We're serious and we plan to get married. What's wrong with that?"

"So why tell her the names of the drugs?"

"I just told her, okay?" Anthony said. "Maybe I was just showing off."

"*That's* how you show off?" Dodson said. "It's a wonder you even *got* a girlfriend."

Out in the driveway an engine roared to life, the trick exhaust burbling at idle.

"Where's Bug going?" Isaiah said.

"I don't know and I don't care," Anthony said. "I'll say it one more time. What's this *about,* Isaiah?"

Isaiah was feeling worse and worse. Something was wrong. He could hear Mrs. Washington's stern voice: *But here's where inductive reasoning can lead you astray. You might not* have *all the facts.* Dodson was fidgeting, nodding, itching to get into it. "Go ahead," Isaiah said.

"You been keeping track of Cal for Noelle," Dodson said.

"Yeah, I tell her what's happening," Anthony said, shrugging both shoulders. "She enjoys it, thinks it's funny. You can hardly blame her."

"Give it up, cuz, we onto you. You and Noelle been trying to get Cal out the house so Skip can put a bullet in him."

"You guys think it's a conspiracy? Oh my God, that's insane."

"What else you been telling Noelle?" Dodson said. "When Cal goes outside? When he's standing by a window? When he's by himself?"

"Look, you don't understand—" Anthony looked like he was stuck in traffic and had to take a piss. "Okay, I'm not going to talk about this anymore," he said. "Now if you don't mind, I have other things to do."

Charles came in. "Where'd Cal go?" he said.

"What do you mean?" Anthony said. "Isn't he up in his room?"

"Bug took him somewhere, they just left. I called Bug but he got his phone turned off. Cal hung up on me."

As Isaiah ran out of the kitchen he thought he saw Anthony smile.

Isaiah raced down the hill from Cal's place at twice the speed limit. He felt in charge when he was driving, slick as K-Y with the six-speed, eyes focused, not even blinking, seeing the turn-in and the line like they were painted on the road.

"Damn," Dodson said as they slid around a hard left-hander, the tail end of the Audi drifting out wide. "Who taught you how to drive?"

Isaiah called Cal and put him on speaker. "Cal, it's Isaiah."

"Whassup, Mr. Q?" Cal said. "You got something on that evil bitch yet?"

"Where are you?"

"On my way to my appointment."

"With who?"

"Why is that your business? I want to go see Dr. Freeman, that's what I'll do."

Isaiah heard the wheeze of a bus. They were on the streets and Dr. Freeman's office was in Beverly Hills. Bug would take the freeway to Beverly Hills. "Listen to me, Cal," Isaiah said. "Don't go to the appointment. It's a setup."

"A setup? Why would Dr. Freeman set me up? Bug, we got time to stop for a dozen? What? I do if I want to be late? How 'bout you gonna be late to keep your job? How 'bout that, Bug?"

"Where's the appointment, Cal? Cal?"

"Damn, Bug, look what you did—yeah, it's your fault. I wouldn't have spilled it on you if you hadn't been going so fast, you nondriving clumsy muthafucka."

"Cal, pull over and wait for me."

"Will you look at this muthafucka? Hey, hey! You see who's riding in this car? I know I can roll my window up, Bug, you don't think I can work a goddamn window? Which button is it? What? Look at the numbers? *You* look at the goddamn numbers."

"Cal, can you hear me? Cal?"

"There it is, Bug. What's all that bullshit? Look, Bug, a parking spot, go on and take it. What do you mean you can't? Did you forget how to park?"

"Listen to your phone, Cal, can you hear me?"

"Damn, Bug, we passed it now. I swear to God, you ain't good for shit. I should replace your ass with one of them butlers. Diddy had one held an umbrella over his head to keep the sun off."

"Don't go, Cal. Don't go!"

"I should have drove here myself. Least I know a parking space when I see one. Well, go around the muthafuckin' block and drop me off. You think you can do that, Bug? Go around the block and drop me off or is that too much for you? What? Did you just say shut the fuck up? You must not know who you talking to. What do you mean this is the day? What day? What are you doing, Bug? Why you stopping here?"

You could hear Bug get out of the car and a moment later Cal's door opening. "What?" Cal said. "Get out of the car? Why should I get out of the car? Don't put your hands on me, Bug, you fuckin' up my—I don't want to get out of the—okay, okay, I'm gettin' out, you don't have to—I'm choking on the seat belt, Bug." The phone clattered to the pavement and the call went dead.

Isaiah downshifted, blasted off the hill, and swung into traffic.

"Where are we going? They could be anywhere," Dodson said.

"Cal said he wanted a dozen," Isaiah said. "He was talking about Krispy Kremes."

Skip waited in the Corolla. The appointment was for eleven and it was eleven-fifteen. The rapper was late, big surprise. Skip slipped on the ski mask and racked the slide on the Glock. "Come on, asshole," he said. "Where are you?"

Cal entered the lobby of the Amos Center. His throat hurt where the seat belt had cut into him and he was dripping wet. After Bug yanked him out of the car he'd thrown him in the fountain in front of the Fidelity building. Cal hesitated. Brian Sterling's instructions were a little waterlogged now. Brian said something about a hallway but there were three of them branching off the lobby. Cal said: "Eenie meenie miney."

The Audi was on Ventura Boulevard, weaving through traffic, slowing as it passed the Krispy Kreme. "So?" Dodson said. "There's Krispy Kreme. Now what?"

"Cal spilled his drink on Bug," Isaiah said. "If you make a right turn, the passenger leans left." Isaiah made a right.

"How do you know he turned here?" Dodson said. "Maybe he turned into that alley we just passed."

Isaiah didn't answer, looking ahead, worried. "Cal was yelling at somebody and he wanted to close the window—why? Why did he—up there, they're fixing the street. The guy's got a jackhammer. Cal wanted to shut out the noise. This is the right street."

Dodson was getting aggravated. It was as if his job was to lob softballs so Isaiah could knock them out of the park. "Okay," Dodson said. "But we still don't know where we going."

The eenie hallway opened onto a courtyard. The meenie was like a maze, Cal turning corner after corner until he was back in the lobby. The miney went straight but there was supposed to be an exit sign. Was that it? The red blur way at the end or was that one of those floaty things he saw when he drank and took too much Ativan?

Skip heard something coming up behind him. He looked in the rearview mirror and saw five skateboarders. Caps, no helmets, T-shirts with logos on them, and black or blue Vans. Probably seniors in high school. They went past the Corolla, Skip's jaw dropping as the whole pack of them careened into the parking garage. "I'm fucking cursed," he said. He listened to them figure-eighting between the pillars and scraping their wheels on the parking blocks. He could go in there and tell them to leave but what if they didn't? He'd have to shoot them. "This can't be happening," he said. The rapper came out of the Amos Center's emergency exit just like he was supposed to. He looked woozy, pausing in the vestibule to get his bearings. Then he crossed in front of Skip and went into the parking garage. Skip heard the skateboards scritch and clatter to a stop.

A skateboarder said, "Dude, are you serious?"

Dodson had forgotten about Cal. All he wanted was for Isaiah to say I don't know. "What are we doing now?" he said.

Isaiah slowed the car to a crawl, horns honking behind him. "Cal said, 'There it is, Bug.' Had to be the address."

"Every building on the block got an address," Dodson said.

"Right after that Cal saw a parking space but Bug said he couldn't park there. Why?" Isaiah's eyes zeroed in on a fire hydrant. "*That's* why!"

Shit, Dodson thought. *Almost had him.*

Isaiah pulled over and they got out of the car. There were office buildings on either side of the street. A clock on the Fidelity building said 11:17. The appointment was probably for eleven. After the morning rush but before lunch.

"Which building?" Dodson said. "They all look alike."

"Cal said, 'What's all that bullshit?' " Isaiah said, turning in a circle. "What bullshit?" He stopped. A tar carrier and a truck were parked in front of the Amos Center, a crane extending from the truck to the roof, scaffolding over the entrance. "That one," Isaiah said. He took off, Dodson trailing behind. *Son of a bitch.*

Skip had his forehead on his forearm and his forearm on the steering wheel. The kids and the rapper were rapping.

I'm announcin' my bouncin', got her face in my fountain
I'm all up in her plumbin', my second comin' and comin'
I'm cocainin' and drainin' and runnin' a trainin'
My Genghis is Khannin', I'm spawnin' and yawnin'
the new day is dawnin' and I still got that longin'
Bonin', bonin', bonin' 'til the break of dawn
Bonin' 'til my trumpet swans
Bonin' 'til my seed is gone.
Bonin', bonin', bonin' 'til the break of dawn.

"Seriously?" Skip said.

*   *   *

Isaiah and Dodson entered the lobby of the Amos Center and crossed to the elevators. "Skip needs isolation to kill Cal," Isaiah said. "The roof." The elevator doors opened. They got on and Isaiah immediately got off. "Go on up," he said.

"Where're you going?" Dodson said.

"I want to see what offices are vacant. Skip might be using one. Just go." The doors closed.

Isaiah knew Cal wasn't on the roof because he never got on the elevator. There was no cologne smell in there but there was in the lobby so he *was* here and he wouldn't have taken the stairs in his condition. Skip could have lured Cal into an office on the first floor or into the parking garage but that made no sense. There were cameras and people going in and out. In fact, it made no sense killing Cal anywhere in the building. Isaiah had that prickly feeling on his scalp. He was the one who put Cal at risk and if Cal got killed it was his fault. Marcus would haunt him for all eternity. *Why here?* Isaiah thought. *Why in the Amos Center?* There had to be a reason...unless there was no reason...unless this wasn't Cal's final destination.

Dodson rode the elevator up, the car stopping at every floor, people getting on and off. He had the sneaking suspicion Isaiah had gotten rid of him, thought he'd be in the way, disrespecting him once again. And what if Skip *was* on the roof with Cal? What was he going to do without a strap? He could not go up there but if Cal got shot Isaiah would blame him and if he did go up there he might get killed. Was twenty-five percent of fifty thousand dollars worth risking his life? He knew what Cherise would say. *Dead people don't need money, Dodson. Don't be a fool.* Cherise was hard on him but she'd brought him to his senses any number of times. Yeah, he'd get off on the next floor and tell Isaiah to go fuck himself.

At long last the rapping stopped. Skip could hear the kids laughing and congratulating themselves, probably doing that stupid hand-shake and bumping shoulders, their voices loud off the cement walls. A few moments later the pack of them came skating out of the garage. The rapper was in there alone. Skip wanted to go in and get him before anything else happened but the kids were rolling right at the Corolla, filling up the alley. Skip honked the horn and lunged the car at them but they kept coming. *Fuck you, dude, yeah, come on and run over us. Yeah, bitch, run us over.* They banged their fists on the hood. *What are you doing in there, jerking off, you fucking loser?* A kid in a hoodie and a cap that said PLAN B hawked a loogie on the windshield. Skip could hardly keep from shooting him.

Finally, the kids moved on. Skip stepped on the gas and the car rattled and died. "I don't fucking believe this," he said. He got out of the car and walked quickly toward the garage entrance, the Glock at his side. He could hear the rapper right around the corner.

"I have been misled," the rapper said. "Brian has misled me."

Isaiah came running out of the Amos Center. He tried to turn back for the door but it had already closed. He was trapped in the vestibule.

"This must be my lucky day," Skip said. He grinned, the twink-ling eyes like death stars. He walked toward the smart-ass, aiming the gun at his face. He'd planned to use the multi-impact rounds on the rapper but this would be better. Splatter this prick all over the alley, nothing left for his family to see, pieces of him in the coffin. Shoot the rapper with the Beretta.

"What have you got to say now, asshole?" he said, cupping his ear. "What's that? I can't hear you. What did you say? Please don't shoot me and I won't be a smart-ass anymore?" Skip wished he would beg or cry or piss himself, anything besides stand there and look at him. "I knew I'd get you," Skip said. "I knew I would."

Isaiah was more furious than scared. This piece-of-shit killer about to put a bullet in his heart. His life didn't flash before his eyes but Flaco did. The boy's face lighting up when he saw Margaret. And Marcus, coming out of the bathroom with that big sunny smile singing "The Way You Do the Things You Do."

"Ready to die?" Skip said.

"Ready as I'll ever be," Isaiah said.

Skip never saw the eighty-pound roll of roofing paper falling out of the sky. He crumpled like a Red Bull can stomped into the pavement. The Glock went off. Thirty-three multi-impact rounds hitting the Corolla in 1.65 seconds.

Isaiah looked up at Dodson peering down from the roof. "I got tar all over my Pumas," he said. "That muthafucka owes me for a new pair of shoes."

Cal came out of the parking garage and blinked a few times, not sure his eyes were working right. What was Mr. Q doing here? Weren't they just talking on the phone? Did he have something to do with Brian Sterling? Why was that car all shot to shit and who was that white boy lying on the ground with a gun and a big roll of black paper? Was that Brian Sterling? Was Brian Sterling dead? "I don't understand," Cal said. He put the back of his wrist over his eyes and started to cry. "I don't understand."

CHAPTER NINETEEN
One Damn Bullet

April 2006

The day after the shooting at the taquería, Isaiah went to the hospital, Marcus's voice resounding in his head. He asked to see the boy that was on TV but the nurse told him he couldn't visit because he was a minor and not a blood relative. She wouldn't tell him anything, not even the boy's name. If he wanted to speak to Dr. Lopez he'd have to call her office and make an appointment.

Isaiah went to the cafeteria and stationed himself near the cash registers. Hundreds of people streamed past carrying their trays. Around two o'clock, when the flow had slowed to a trickle, he saw a Latina woman in green scrubs and running shoes. Her name tag said AMELIA LOPEZ MD. She was bony but fit. Long arms and sharp elbows, deep tan, hair in a tight bun. Marathons, Isaiah thought. He waited until she was eating a Yoplait and then sat down in front of her. "That boy," he said, "the one with brain trauma. I'm the one that got him shot. I'm the one that got his parents killed."

Isaiah told the doctor his story beginning to end, leaving out nothing.

"I don't know what to say," Dr. Lopez said.

"It's my fault," Isaiah said. "It's all my fault." He was crying now, his head bowed, tears falling into his lap.

"I think you're being hard on yourself. You didn't know that would happen."

"I have to make it right."

"How?"

"My brother Marcus was my only family and he was taken away from me. I want to be the family I took away from the boy."

She looked at him. "I think you have a good heart, Isaiah. I really mean that and I think your intentions are admirable, but I can't give you permission to see him. Only the family can do that."

"What should I do?"

"If it were me? I'd pray for forgiveness."

Weeks went by. Flaco's only visitor was a caseworker from a state program for the medically indigent. Flaco had fallen into a deep depression, groaning something that sounded like *mommy* over and over again. Dr. Lopez prescribed an antidepressant but it didn't help.

She was relieved when the boy's uncle showed up. He was antsy in his maroon shirt, maroon tie, and pleated gray slacks, his hair slicked back over his ears. He asked about the taquería and if the Ruizes owned the building and if they had life insurance and was there a case to be made against the city. Flaco? Oh yeah, how's he doing? The uncle left without seeing him.

The grandparents visited. They lived in a retirement village in Colton, one of the staff brought them in. The grandfather had milky eyes and could hardly see. The grandmother walked with a walker and could hardly hear. Dr. Lopez asked if there were any other family members who could help out. No, there was only their son, who sold annuities and wasn't reliable. There were other relatives in Mexico but they had their own problems.

Dr. Lopez had seen this before. A kid alone and bereft, longing for his parents and sinking into despair. It was a psychological problem but there were medical consequences too. Increase in blood pressure, stress, cortisol levels. She hated to see the little boy suffer, a little boy not unlike her own. She remembered Isaiah. His earnest sincerity. His need to be the family he'd taken away from Flaco.

Isaiah met Dr. Lopez in her office. "I'm going to put you on the visitors' list," she said. "But if you cause a disturbance or upset Flaco in any way you're out." She showed him Flaco's MRI, pointing with her pen at the spot where the nine-millimeter bullet smashed into his skull and ripped through the left side of his brain, annihilating millions of brain cells before exiting near his left eye.

"The trauma caused his brain to swell," she said. "It could have killed him. I had to cut a hole through his skull to release the pressure."

"Cut a hole through his *skull?*" Isaiah said. "How?"

"The scalp is peeled back, a bur hole is drilled through the bone, and a section is cut out with an electric saw. It's not pretty. Then we put him on a ventilator and medically induced a coma."

Isaiah had never been seriously ill or injured and had never been in a hospital before. Getting an A in biology didn't prepare you for this. "Wait. You *put* him in a coma?"

"Reduces blood flow, lets the brain rest. Then his breathing tube was replaced with a tracheotomy tube. You'll see it sticking out of his throat."

"How does he eat?" Isaiah said, horrified. Did they actually cut a hole in his neck?

"Nasal feeding tube. Then there was another surgery to remove the bone fragments from his fractured left eye socket and there's more surgery to come. We've got to repair the damage to his cranium and replace the skull section with a ceramic plate."

It took a moment for Isaiah to take all that in. "But he's doing okay?"

"I'd say he's doing as well as can be expected," Dr. Lopez said.

"How long before he gets back to normal?"

"He won't," she said. "His right side is paralyzed, he'll be in a wheelchair for the rest of his life. His cognitive functions are impaired. He'll have to learn how to speak again, read and write, move his arms, use his hands. And the names of things. He'll have to relearn those too. Chair. House. Car. The psychological damage remains to be seen." She tapped her pen on the MRI. "All that from one damn bullet."

Isaiah stood at Flaco's bedside. The boy was small and pale as wax paper. Bruises around his eyes, Frankenstein stitches on his shaved head, tubes coming out of everywhere, monitors flashing numbers. "Hey, Flaco," he said. "My name is Isaiah. I'm gonna hang around if you don't mind." Flaco was sedated and didn't react. Isaiah sat down and read about brain injuries on his laptop. He stayed for two hours, said he'd be back the next day, and left.

He came every day and did the same thing. Said hey Flaco and sat down with his laptop. He resisted the urge to say I know how you feel or I've been there myself. Nobody knew what it was like to lose Marcus and nobody knew what Flaco was feeling now except in words that had no meaning. Scared, abandoned, angry, confused. For now, it was enough to be there, not making it better but not making it worse.

Dr. Lopez looked in on them from time to time. She saw Isaiah reading aloud from *Harry Potter* and Flaco listening to music on Isaiah's earbuds and Isaiah juggling tennis balls and doing magic tricks. She left without saying anything.

Isaiah rented a one-room apartment near the hospital. The tan shag carpet had holes in it and there was a sewage smell in the bathroom. He visited Flaco twice a day. When he wasn't there he went to the library and looked for books to read aloud and learned how to juggle and do magic tricks. Flaco enjoyed them.

Isaiah got his meals at the hospital cafeteria or got plastic-wrapped sandwiches from Vons and ate them on the curb like a bum. He still had a lot of time on his hands. He took lessons in Krav Maga because the gym was near the hospital. Krav Maga was a martial arts system developed by the Israeli military. The guiding principle: Defend and attack in the same move. He got pretty good but had no interest in belts or tournaments.

Flaco started rehab. Motor therapy, cognitive therapy, aphasia therapy, speech therapy. Slowly, he made progress.

Marcus's voice was never far away. He sounded so real and close it was like he was there, with Isaiah in the hospital room, sitting on the curb while he ate his sandwiches; standing over him while he was trying to fall asleep.

If you think reading Harry Potter *to that boy gets you off the hook, you are sadly mistaken. Flaco is only the start of it. The war caused death and destruction and made innocent people worry for their lives and their children's lives and made them feel ashamed of where they lived. You were supposed to raise people up, ease their suffering, bring them justice, do some good out there—Oh, I'm sorry, are you crying again? Well, I hope it's not for yourself because I don't feel sorry for you and neither should you. What? What was that? You can't pay back everybody for everything that's happened? Is that your excuse? You can't pay back everybody so you're gonna pay back nobody?*

Isaiah stopped spending the burglary money and set aside what was left for Flaco. He didn't know what else he could do. Broke now, he got a job at the Hurston Animal Shelter. He liked the animals and he liked Harry but the city cut the budget and Harry had to let him go.

Isaiah worked as a night janitor at Hopkins Machining and Welding. He learned how to use the machines by watching videos and practiced on them at night. Mr. Hopkins caught him working on a canopy for a client's vintage Spitfire airplane. He was impressed but couldn't hire Isaiah because it was a union shop.

Hopkins referred Isaiah to Garrison Robles, a gunsmith who made custom firearms and ammo. Garrison was looking for a machinist who would work cheap in exchange for learning the trade. Isaiah had reservations about taking the job. Since the shootings he was gun-shy and Dr. Lopez and her one damn bullet had made him almost phobic.

Isaiah was eleven years old and afraid of spiders. He refused to take a bath because a daddy longlegs was in the tub.

"That little thing?" Marcus had said. "It can't hurt you."

"I don't care," Isaiah said. "I'm not going in there."

"I was scared of snakes. Couldn't even look at a picture of one. So I studied up on them, learned what made them tick, got them down to their nuts and bolts. Made them a thing instead of a boogieman."

"Are you still afraid of them?"

"Oh yeah, I'm terrified — but I know what I'm dealing with."

Isaiah learned a lot about guns and ammo working for Garrison. He was still afraid of them but he knew what he was dealing with.

Other jobs came and went. He worked as a barista at the Coffee Cup, making espressos, lattes, and mocha frappuccinos. He learned about coffee and its smells. Separating the aroma into notes of charcoal, chocolate, red fruits, caramel, and a dozen others. He began paying attention to smells in general. Walking into a room, meeting someone, opening a package. He worked for a law practice as a process server. He liked finding people who didn't want to be found and he liked reading the documents he was serving. Divorces, summonses, lawsuits, subpoenas, cease-and-desist orders. A mini-course in the law. He worked at a sporting goods store. It had a rock-climbing wall and he got into it, the guy there taking him on climbs to Eagle Peak, Stoney Point, Joshua Tree.

His best job was at TK's Wrecking Yard. Twelve desolate acres near the Dominguez Channel. TK was a skinny old man who smelled like motor oil and sweat, enough room in his overalls for two more TKs, his cap so filthy you could barely make out the STP.

"What's your name, son?" TK said, wiping his hands with a rag that was dirtier than his hands.

"Isaiah Quintabe," Isaiah said.

"You ever work on cars before, Isaiah Quintabe?"

"No sir, but I know my tools and I learn fast."

"Must be six hundred vehicles out here plus all the parts. You can't tell one from another you're of no use to me."

"I can tell one from another," Isaiah said. He'd seen every make and model ever made come off the Anaheim off-ramp. After he'd named all the cars within a forty-yard radius TK said: "Say, have you heard this one? These two old peoples was at the church service and during the prayer the old man leans over to the old lady and says, 'I just cut a silent fart. Should I say something?' And the old lady says, 'No, but you better put a new battery in your hearing aid.'" Isaiah laughed for the first time in a long time. TK lit a Pall Mall, his eyes narrowing as he inhaled. "Well, I guess you got the job, boy," he said.

As a young man, TK raced a Turbo Eclipse on the wide streets near the Ontario airport and ran super go-karts at CalSpeed and drove a highly modified CRX in SCCA races until he couldn't afford it anymore. Isaiah found boxes of dinged-up trophies in the warehouse. TK taught Isaiah how to drive. Really drive. How to heel-and-toe, rev match, drift with the hand brake. They set up their own race course. S-turns through the rows of crushed cars, a straightaway along the perimeter fence, then a sweeping right-hander around the mountain of tires and back through the S-turns to the finish line in front of the warehouse, where you had to brake hard or run into the crane.

TK would get a car up and running, put Isaiah behind the wheel in a scratched-up motorcycle helmet, and class was in session. TK knew his stuff but patience was not a virtue he cultivated. He'd bounce around in the shotgun seat, pointing at things Isaiah couldn't see and rounding the curves with his hand.

"Get wide, wider, goddammit — okay okay, here comes your turn-in, brake to the threshold, pick your line — no, not *that* line, you're early, steer, steer, come off it now — too much, too much — shit, boy, if they gave points for sliding off the road you'd be a goddamn champion."

*   *   *

It was late afternoon. Oil and rust were cooking in the heat, the glare off the windshields like six hundred suns. Isaiah and TK were dismantling an Audi that had rear-ended an eighteen-wheeler. Isaiah had always liked Audis and this one was an S4. A pocket rocket in sheep's clothing.

"You heard this one?" TK said. "Good-lookin' woman's walking down the street and her blouse is all open in the front and one of her titties is hanging out. Well, a cop comes along and says, 'Lady, did you know your titty is hanging out? I could arrest you for indecent exposure.' And the lady says, 'Shit, I musta left my baby on the bus.'"

Isaiah laughed and got inside the Audi to remove the seats. They were undamaged and so was the rest of the interior except for the dash. It occurred to him: If he could take a car apart why couldn't he put one back together?

"I want to buy this car," Isaiah said.

"*This* car?" TK said. "This car needs a bumper assembly, radiator, wheels, struts, shocks, front cross-member, the engine's messed up, and who knows what else."

"The engine can be repaired and the drive train is okay. The back of the car is like new."

"The parts for this thing cost an arm and two legs and we don't get a lot of Audis coming through here, you know."

"This one did."

"This ain't some old Chevy. These German cars are a nightmare to fix."

"Then you'll help me."

*   *   *

Isaiah was nineteen years old and adrift. He worked at the wrecking yard, visited Flaco, and occasionally hung out with the guys at the gym. The few girls he'd slept with were only around for a week or two. They thought he was strange, this quiet insomniac who was really smart but had a menial job, never did anything fun, and spent all his free time with a crippled boy.

Other than Flaco and Marcus's constant rebukes, what concerned Isaiah most was the state of his brain. He could feel it getting rusty, the neurons granulating and hardening into a crust. He thought about going back to school but he was a high school dropout. He'd have to get his GED and slog through years of undergrad courses before it got interesting. There were other jobs to be had but they'd be entry-level and climbing the corporate ladder had no appeal. He might have gone on that way indefinitely if he hadn't caught that first case.

It was laundry day. Isaiah gathered up his dirty clothes and took them down to the laundry room. An elderly woman was there, her face creased and dark as a dug-up baseball mitt from the forties. She was wearing a flowered muumuu, her copper-colored wig styled in an unlikely pageboy. She looked frustrated and in pain, one hand on the small of her back.

"Excuse me, young man," she said, "but would you mind helping me get my clothes out of the dryer? My lumbago is giving me fits."

Isaiah piled her still-warm clothes on the table. Her entire wardrobe seemed to consist of muumuus, gym socks, and white panties big as parachutes. Isaiah folded the towels.

"I'm Myra Jenkins," she said, "but everybody calls me Miss Myra. You're Isaiah, aren't you? I've seen you around. You're a very nice young man, always neat and polite, none of that rough talk. You're a little young for my Brenda but I wish she'd met you before she got involved with Bernard. I knew that man was a no-good bum the moment I laid eyes on him but Brenda married him anyway, not that she had a lot of choices, being on the homely side. They got married over the weekend and Brenda was as beautiful as she was ever going to be. The ceremony went fine and the reception did too except they delivered the wrong cake. A sorry little coconut thing that said 'Happy Birthday Sheldon' on it."

"That's too bad," Isaiah said. He wanted to get out of there and do his laundry later but it was too late now.

"Of course, Brenda being Brenda there had to be a major tragedy," Miss Myra said. "The wedding presents were stolen. Must have been thirty or forty of them, all wrapped nice and everything. Poor Brenda. She cried her eyes out."

Isaiah stopped folding. "What happened?" he said.

"Oh, the hotel didn't have the reception room ready and we didn't want folks with presents in their laps while Bernard was fumbling with his vows so we put them in a room we rented. You know, for Brenda to get made up and such. Well, after the ceremony we came up to get them and they were gone. It was such a shame. Poor Brenda. I say that every day."

"What did the hotel security people say?"

"The security man said the hotel wasn't liable. What else would he say?"

Isaiah thought for a moment and said, "What's the name of the hotel?"

The Blue Waves Resort and Spa had seen better days. A plastic sailfish hung crookedly over a table full of brochures. The blue carpet with gold crests on it was worn in places, the blond wood furniture spotted with watermarks and cigarette burns. Isaiah smelled lemon Pledge, vacuum exhaust, coffee, and mop water.

Isaiah and Miss Myra took the squeaking, clanking elevator up to the sixth floor. "That's our room, 604," Miss Myra said, nodding at the door and sounding puzzled. "Is this what you wanted to see?"

When they got back to the lobby they were met by a young Asian woman in brown slacks and a bright yellow blazer. She had a wide face and small eyes, her limp hair parted in the middle, her complexion as pebbly as the surface of a basketball. She looked at them like they were the line in front of her at the DMV. "Can I help you?" she said.

"We'd like to see the security supervisor," Isaiah said.

"You mean Ed?" she said, as if they were making a silly mistake.

"If that's his name."

"What do you guys think of the blazer? The color is really in for spring."

"It's not that bad," Miss Myra said.

"You're being nice. I look like a jar of Chinese mustard."

She said her name was Karen Mochizuki. She led them to the basement and down a long harshly lit hallway that smelled heavily of bleach, industrial washing machines groaning through the walls. "You're getting a rare behind-the-scenes look at hotel security," she said. "It's not all glitz and glamour, you know. Gotta stay sharp around here. You never know when Al Qaeda might try to blow up the gift shop."

Miss Myra thought the supervisor must be low man on the hotel totem pole. His office was cramped and painted a high-gloss beige like a restroom, the ceiling crowded with ductwork and electrical cables. The man himself was seated at a gray metal desk, leaning back with his hands behind his head.

"Come on in," he said without getting up. "I'm Ed Blevins. Please, sit-sit, we're not formal around here. Let me guess. You're here about the stolen presents. It's Mrs. Jenkins, isn't it? And you are—"

"A friend," Isaiah said.

Miss Myra wondered if Ed was auditioning for a part in a movie about rednecks with his Hitler haircut and Mr. Potato Head ears. His short-sleeve white shirt was straight out of the hamper, his cheap striped tie stiff as the dorsal fin on that sailfish.

Ed sat up, smiled sympathetically, and put his hairy knuckles around his coffee cup. "Ma'am, like I told you before, I'd compensate you for every last one of those presents but hotel policy is hotel policy. I must have said it a thousand times to a thousand different guests. The hotel is not responsible for stolen items. It was right there on the rental agreement and there's a sign in every room too. I mean, what else can we do? Right, Karen?"

Karen was standing with her back to the door, her arms folded across her chest. "If you say so, Ed," she said.

"These kinds of thefts are common as bums at a soup kitchen," Ed said, yawning. "Even happens at the Marriott and the Hilton. Karen, could you sit down, please? You look like a Secret Service agent."

A duffel bag that said HUMMER on it was on the Fanta-orange couch. Karen picked it up, held it like a dead rat by the tail, and dropped it straight to the floor. She sat down and said: "This okay, Ed?"

Ed paused, inhaled deeply, and exhaled through his nose. Miss

Myra thought she could hear him counting to ten in his head. She was annoyed with Isaiah. He'd brought her here and hadn't said a word.

"Ma'am, it's like I told you before," Ed said, "this guy had you in his sights the minute you walked in, probably dressed up like a tourist, maybe even said hello to you. These guys are slick, let me tell you. Then he waits until you're at the wedding, gets in your room, gets what he wants, and is in the wind before you or anybody else knew what happened. You almost have to admire the guy. He was a real pro."

"How did he get out?" Isaiah said.

"How did who get out?" Ed said.

"The pro. How did he get thirty or forty presents out of the room and out of the hotel without being seen?"

"Good question," Ed said, like he was responding to a kid on Career Day. "But try to understand, this hotel has a hundred and eighty rooms, twelve ground-level exits, and four more to the garage. No way two people can cover all that. Right, Karen?"

"If you say so, Ed," she said.

"Was there anything on the surveillance cameras?" Isaiah said.

"No, I'm afraid not," Ed said. "The system was down for the whole weekend. Damn computers. What can you do?"

"There was more than one thief," Isaiah said, "and they were amateurs."

Karen cleared her throat.

"I'm not following," Ed said.

"One person couldn't get thirty or forty presents out of there, not without being seen. There were other guests and housekeepers around. There had to be two of them and they weren't professionals. A pro wouldn't have taken *all* the presents, especially the big ones.

They're hard to carry and there's no point stealing a punch bowl unless it's Waterford crystal and this isn't Beverly Hills. A pro would have gone for the smaller ones that might have had jewelry or electronics in them. No, these were amateurs." Isaiah looked directly at Ed. "And they were employees."

The washing machines were still groaning but the room seemed to go quiet. This was too much tension for Miss Myra. She wanted to go home and watch *Shonda Simmons* and where was Isaiah getting all this? Was he making it up?

Ed had his lips pursed like he was kissing his mom. "Now that's a very serious charge you're making," he said. "I hope for your sake you can back that up."

"The employees knew which room had the presents in it and when it would be empty," Isaiah said. "They'd have access to key cards so getting in was no problem. They got the presents out of the room by stashing them in another room and then they took them out of the hotel a few at a time in something like that Hummer bag."

"*Well,*" Ed said, standing up, "that's a very interesting theory but unfortunately it's pure speculation and if I were you I'd leave the detective work to me. Now I've got a really busy schedule today and—"

"Room 605," Isaiah said.

"605?" Ed said.

"That's the room you hid the presents in and why nobody saw you. It's right across the hall from Brenda's room and it's always vacant because it's next to that noisy elevator. You used it again today, didn't you? Want some advice? Take a shower when you're done. Both of you smell like the lubricant on a condom."

"Oh my God," Karen said, sniffing her hands.

Ed did the gorilla pose. Leaning forward, arms straight down, palms flat on the desk. "You can spin all the theories you want but you've got no proof, no witnesses, no nothing."

"Good, Ed," Karen said. "Way to not give it away."

"I talked to a housekeeper," Isaiah said. "She said everybody knows about the stealing and she said you've done it before."

Miss Myra looked at him. What housekeeper?

"That's a bald-faced lie," Ed said, "and I know who told you that. That bitch Esmeralda. Woman's got it in for me but I couldn't tell you why."

"You call her Chiquita Banana," Karen said. "Maybe that's why."

"Only once or twice and if she thinks management's gonna take her word over mine—"

"*I'd* take her word over yours," Karen said. "God, you're an idiot. How I let you talk me into something like this I'll never know."

"Karen, I'm handling this."

"Shut up, Ed, for God's sake shut up." Ed started to reply but Karen looked at him hard enough to break his jaw. She pushed the hair out of her eyes, her face shinier and redder than before. "I'm really really sorry," she said. "Is there any possible chance we could make this go away? We'll do anything you say."

"What do you think, Miss Myra?" Isaiah said. Miss Myra looked at Isaiah like he'd sprouted wings.

"I suppose that would be all right," she said.

"I only slept with Ed because I was bored," Karen said. "You believe me, don't you?"

Brenda was thrilled. She got almost all her presents back and three hundred dollars for the ones that were missing. As a thank-you, she baked Isaiah some chocolate chip cookies that Miss Myra warned him not to eat.

"This young man is special," Miss Myra told her best friend, Elaine. "This young man has a gift."

Elaine and Arthur Steadman were in debt and too proud to ask their grown children for help. They turned to Don Wheeler, a debt resolution specialist who advertised on bus benches and the radio. He said they needed to sign some documents giving him authorization to act on their behalf but the documents turned out to be a grant deed transferring ownership of their house to Wheeler.

"I feel like a damn fool," Arthur said. "Had the papers notarized and everything. We've been in this house for forty-two years."

"When did you sign them?" Isaiah said.

"Sign the papers? On Friday, around seven or so. Why?"

Isaiah knew Wheeler couldn't file the documents at the county recorder until Monday. It took him six minutes on the nose to break into Wheeler's house, take the documents, destroy his computers, and leave the door open so the neighborhood kids could scavenge the place. Arthur cried when he got the documents back. He told Burton Stanley about Isaiah and Burton told his sister Anita and Anita told her fiancé, Tudor.

Isaiah met Tudor at the Coffee Cup. He was in his fifties, immaculate, precise pencil mustache, manicured nails, and gold Rolex thick as a hockey puck. Before he sat down he dusted the seat off with a napkin.

"Anita's daughter got involved with a drug dealer and she's run off with him," Tudor said. "Anita's very upset. She called the police but they said they don't go looking for runaways, they usually come home on their own."

"Why'd she run off?" Isaiah said.

"Darcy and I had an argument so naturally it's my fault. Girl's completely out of control and spoiled rotten and I told her so. Then she starts talking back to me, calling me names, calling her mother names, and I slapped her. A good one too. She deserved it. Any grown man would have done the same thing."

"How long has she been gone?"

"Four, five days, something like that."

"Got a picture?"

"I can get you one."

"The dealer, what does he look like?"

"What does he look like? He's young, bald, wears a big white T-shirt and a do-rag. That narrow it down for you?"

"Do you know his name?"

"Shake. Do you believe that? His name is Shake. Oh here's something for you. Shake is not really a drug dealer even though he deals drugs. He's got a few videos on YouTube so of course that qualifies him as a rap artist. How's that for originality? And you know what I said to him? Oh you're an artist? An artist like who? Billie Holiday? Wynton Marsalis? John Lee Hooker? Art lasts through the ages and a hundred years from now folks will have forgotten all about you and your Simple Simon rhymes but they'll still be grooving on Billie and John Lee. What we were talking about?"

"Shake. How to identify him."

"Well, let me see. He's got a tattoo on his forearm, I saw it when he was drinking my orange juice straight out of the box. It was a crown, like a king's crown and some letters, CRR or CMM, something like that. And what else? Some numbers. Nineteen hundred?"

"The crown is for Prince Street," Isaiah said, "and it's seventeen hundred. That's the block number. The letters are CHH. For Crip Headhunters."

"I just remembered," Tudor said. "There were some initials too. BK. Yes, I'm sure about that. BK. That should narrow it down some, don't you think?"

"BK means Blood killer," Isaiah said. "Crips and Bloods are enemies."

"Good Lord, what's this world coming to?" Tudor said. "I grew up the hard way myself but youngsters these days are another breed altogether. Blood killer. When I was a kid we didn't have to kill somebody to settle a score. We did it one on one, man to man, fist to fist. Any fool can pull a trigger. And there was none of this beatdown nonsense. Most cowardly thing I ever heard of. Five or six guys beating up on one. Is that what passes for badass these days? That's punk behavior if you ask me. You can't take care of your business by yourself, you shouldn't be on the street in the first place."

They heard a horn honk. They could see Anita sitting in Tudor's snow-white Range Rover tapping her snow-white nails on the windowsill. She held her head high like an Egyptian queen if Egyptian queens chewed gum, wore sunglasses with rhinestones on them, and styled their hair in elaborate blond curls.

"Anita," Tudor said. "She'll be wanting to know when you're going to start, which I'm hoping is immediately."

Isaiah didn't like Tudor. He was arrogant, not asking for help, just assuming Isaiah would do his bidding, and not even polite about it. And he didn't like the man's pinkie ring or the metallic blue suit that fit him too good to be off the rack or the Rolex watch. A gold Yacht-Master, the same one Dodson had wanted. Nineteen thousand dollars and change. "I'm not doing this for free," Isaiah said.

"I guess I misunderstood," Tudor said. "I thought you did these kinds of things as a community service."

"Sometimes I do."

"But not with me, is that it?" Tudor said, flicking some imaginary lint off his lapel. "All right, young man, what do you intend to charge me for your services?"

"A thousand dollars," Isaiah said, picking a number out of the air.

"A thousand — you must be joking," Tudor said. "I'm not paying you a thousand dollars or anything like it. You think I just fell off the turnip truck? Who do you think you're dealing with? I was hustling for my daily bread while you were still in — where're you going?"

Tudor caught up with Isaiah in the parking lot. "My offer is two hundred dollars and that's overly generous if you ask me."

"No thank you."

"No thank you? You've never made two hundred dollars for a day's work in your entire life."

"Yes I have."

"I'm losing my patience, young man, but I'll tell you what. For the sake of the girl's safety I'm going to let you rob me today and today only. Three hundred dollars but only when Darcy is returned unharmed to her mother. Do we have a deal?"

"No, we don't have a deal."

"Let's have a reality check here, shall we? You know as well as I do that fetching that girl is no big deal."

"If you think it's no big deal going into a Crip hood and taking a girl away from a drug dealer I'll give *you* three hundred dollars and you can go get her yourself."

"You're a tough negotiator and I can appreciate that, but you're about to negotiate yourself out of a very substantial paycheck." Tudor looked at Anita, smiled, and said: "Everything's okay, boo, we're just coming to terms." Anita popped her gum. "Now you listen to me, young man," Tudor said, "you are making me look bad in front of my fiancée, something I can assure you I will not forget."

"What happens when you remember?" Isaiah said, letting the threat pass.

"This is my last and final offer and I am not a man who bluffs. Five hundred dollars, take it or leave it."

"I'll leave it."

"Well, you have just thrown five hundred dollars out the window and you only have yourself to blame. I won't have my arm twisted, not even for Anita."

"Tudor?" Anita said. "Don't even say the word pussy 'til you get my daughter back."

Tudor smiled like he'd farted in a crowded elevator. "Will you take a check?" he said. "I don't have that kind of cash on me."

Cruising slow through a Crip hood and looking for someone was drive-by behavior and likely to get you shot. Isaiah found three girls about Darcy's age in the Baskin-Robbins eating double-scoop cones and talking loud.

"I'm looking for my sister, name is Darcy?" Isaiah said. "Mama died and I got to tell her."

"Why don't you call her?" one of the girls said.

"I don't know how she gonna take it, you feel me? For all I know she might faint or something. I need to be there with her." The girls told him a light-skinned girl named Darcy was living in a brown apartment building three blocks up on Prince.

The brown apartment building was L-shaped. All the doors were facing in, big white patches where the paint had chipped off the stucco. Laundry was draped over the second-story railing, an overflowing dumpster in the parking lot. Isaiah parked the Explorer facing the sun so you couldn't see him through the glare of the windshield. Women sat outside their doors talking. Kids ran up and down stairs, old men played dominoes.

Isaiah was eating the last of the trail mix when Darcy emerged from an upstairs apartment. She was sixteen going on thirty-five, wearing a bathrobe over a slip and fuzzy slippers. She leaned against the railing and looked down at the parking lot like she was disappointed it was still there. Somebody called her. Her shoulders sagged. She looked skyward and shuffled back inside.

Isaiah saw himself going up the stairs and knocking on that door and Shake coming out in a do-rag and no shirt and asking him what the fuck he wanted and then explaining to him that he was taking Darcy home and Shake drawing a pistol and shooting him in the head. Clearly not his best option and after thinking a bit he came up with another.

"911, what is your emergency?"

"A girl, they're holding her captive. She's only sixteen. I think they're messing with her."

"What is the location, sir?"

A few minutes later four squad cars were jammed into the parking lot. A crowd watched an officer come out of the apartment holding Darcy by the arm. "I haven't done anything," she said. "Let go of me!"

Two more cops brought Shake out in handcuffs. "You mutha-fuckas is wrong," he said. "That girl's consensual."

It was a revelation. Isaiah made a thousand dollars in one day and there were new messages on his voice mail. Word must have spread all over the neighborhood. *They're bullying my daughter. The police set me up. I want to find my birth parents. My class's computers were stolen. I can't find my husband. I can't get away from my husband. My boy did not commit suicide.*

Why not charge them for his services? Isaiah thought. Not like he charged Tudor but get paid, be worth something. He knew what Marcus would say.

Get paid? You wanna get paid? Didn't I tell you about money?

"It's not about the money," Isaiah said. "I can help people, start giving back to the community, do some good out there just like you said, remember?" Isaiah waited. He could see Marcus at the breakfast table with his Shredded Wheat and coffee, leaning back in his chair, nodding, weighing.

"We'll see, Isaiah. We'll see."

CHAPTER TWENTY

R.I.P.

August 2013

Skip was arrested and taken to the county jail hospital with a severe concussion, cervical damage, a fractured clavicle, a broken jaw, broken ribs, and a torn rotator cuff. Just before he fell into a coma he said to the doctor: *"My dogs."*

Isaiah, Harry, and some volunteers from the animal shelter went out to Blue Hill and rescued the dogs. Goliath, Attila, and some of the others were too vicious and had to be euthanized. Harry distributed the rest of the dogs and puppies to foster homes, rescue shelters, and his pit bull breeder friends. There would be more pit bulls in the world but Harry couldn't bear to put them all down. Isaiah kept a puppy for himself. With Alejandro gone he needed a warm body in the house.

Cal voluntarily checked into the Tranquility rehab facility in Malibu and saw Dr. Freeman three times a week. Somebody snapped a picture of them walking around the grounds together and sold it to the tabloids. The sales of Dr. Freeman's book went up six hundred percent.

Anthony was going to quit his job right after Cal's divorce but

Noelle was gathering material for a book about her life with a famous rapper. When Cal started losing his mind it was too juicy to pass up and she made Anthony promise he'd stay until Cal either died or got locked up somewhere. She needed a good ending. Noelle pitched *Up from Nothin' and Back Again* to a publisher that specialized in tell-alls. She told the editors about the giant pit bull, the bonfire, the hit man, and the underground detective they called IQ. The editors gave her an $850,000 advance.

Rodion, Noelle's bodyguard, was ogre-big, his eyes like a fish on ice and a Neanderthal forehead that slanted back from his one shaggy eyebrow. Rodion was a former KGB officer who specialized in enhancing the interrogations of dissidents. His favorite implements were his huge gnarly hands and long sharp fingernails. Byron said they looked more like ostrich feet than human appendages.

When Charles heard Cal's track, "The Fuck Am I Doing on This Earth?" he knew the album would be a disaster. From his point of view, the sooner Cal got to the studio the sooner he'd humiliate himself and clear the way for Grandyose. And it was Bug who asked Noelle to be on the diss track. That was why the calls weren't on Charles's phone.

Charles shopped his *Takin' Over* album to other labels but there were no takers and without paychecks the brothers were soon broke. They hung out at Cal's crib, drank his liquor, and played video games on the ninety-inch Sharp. One afternoon, Charles was on the phone trying to get back into the drug business and Bug was cleaning up the mess from the bonfire. The PAWG and her PAWG friends were coming over to swim and ashes were getting into the pool.

"Hey, Charles," Bug said, a push broom in his hand, "get off the phone and check this out." There in the charred rubble were loose diamonds and emeralds and melted gold and platinum, the remains of the Teddi the Gleam bling. The brothers sold it all and bought a tire and rim shop.

Bobby Grimes was the hardest hit. His premier artist was in rehab and Greenleaf withdrew its offer to acquire BGME. The rest of his roster was leaving the label. Shonda Simmons said she heard Bobby was going into bankruptcy.

Skip's employer was still a mystery and Isaiah couldn't get it out of his mind. He'd slouch in his armchair, mentally flipping the case over, upside down, and sideways while Ruffin, named after Marcus's favorite singer, David Ruffin, chewed on his shoes and peed everywhere but on the pee pads. There was nothing else to do but go back to work.

Mr. Everwood had Alzheimer's and couldn't remember where he'd hidden fifteen thousand dollars in Krugerrands. Susan Paul's ex was extorting her with a video they'd made in the privacy of their bedroom. Vandals vandalized the abortion clinic. They wrote BABY KILLERS and DEATH CAMP on the walls and made off with an aspirator, a suction apparatus, and a surgical chair.

Deronda's friend Nona had a husband who beat her when he was drunk, which was almost every day. Isaiah paid for a bus ticket and brought Nona's father, Earl, in from Bakersfield, where he worked for Union Pacific coupling and uncoupling freight cars and cabling them to the hoist. Earl met Nona's husband coming out of the liquor store with a half gallon of Thunderbird. Earl beat him, stomped on his hands so he couldn't hit Nona anymore, and drank the Thunderbird on the bus back to Bakersfield.

Nona, realizing her husband could still kick and bite, decided to move in with Deronda. Isaiah said he'd help. Nona was friends with Cherise and she volunteered Dodson. They used Dodson's ten-year-old two-tone Lexus RS as a moving van, filling the back-seat and trunk with Nona's belongings and strapping a mattress to the roof. The car had a hundred and ten thousand miles on the odometer, was silent as a bank vault, and rolled over potholes like they were hopscotch lines on the sidewalk. Dodson drove with his neck pulled into his shoulders and held the steering wheel with one arm stuck straight out. Tupac rapped from the stereo. Isaiah sulked.

"I need new tires," Dodson said. "You know what they cost for this car? Something to be said for public transportation. I might have to break down and buy me a bus pass. That's okay, you don't have to talk, it's not like I crave your conversation, but just out of curiosity, did you forget to send me a thank-you card?"

"A thank-you card for what?" Isaiah said.

"For saving your life."

"I don't remember getting one from *you*."

Isaiah went still. The key to the case was materializing like a Polaroid snapshot. Streaks and blurry colors forming. Tupac's rapping was distracting. "Could you play something else, please?" Isaiah said.

"I could but I won't," Dodson said.

"Don't you get tired of him?"

"No I don't. All his albums? Must be two, three hundred songs and he recorded more than that. Yeah, Tupac was a songwriting fool. Remember Suge Knight and Death Row Records? Suge robbed the boy blind. Tupac sold millions of records and when he died he was damn near broke."

"Suge got away with it?"

"He spent the money if that's what you mean," Dodson said. "But Tupac's mama, Afeni, sued Suge, got control of the leftover songs. Was a bunch of 'em. Oh, check this out."

Tupac rapped:

*My homie told me once, don't you trust them other suckers
they fought like they were your homies but they phony
motherfuckers*

"Yeah, Tupac should have took his own advice," Dodson said. "You can't trust nobody in the music biz. You don't watch them muthafuckas every damn minute they'll steal the vision right out your eyeballs."

Isaiah squirmed in his seat. Lines were connecting on the Polaroid. A string of facts. A logic. The case-breaker. It was right there. *Right fucking there.*

Dodson hit the brakes so hard the mattress slid down over the windshield and a box of stuffed animals spilled into the front of the car.

"What?" Isaiah said, tossing a one-eyed koala bear over his shoulder.

"After Tupac died, Afeni used the leftover songs and put out seven more records," Dodson said. "People called 'em R.I.P. albums, rest in peace. Made 'em seem like collectors' items. Six of the records went platinum. *Don Killuminati* sold five million copies all by itself." Dodson looked at Isaiah and said: *"Tupac sold more records dead than he did when he was alive."*

"I *knew that*," Isaiah said, snapping his fingers.

Bobby Grimes watched helplessly as Cal's mental state went swirling down the toilet. No way his star was going to make a decent album by his contractual deadline or make one at all anytime soon. Bobby could sue Cal for breach of contract but where would that get him? The lawyers would haggle for a year, Bobby would lose his premier artist, who was also the main reason Greenleaf wanted to acquire BGME.

But Cal was more of a songwriting fool than Tupac. The average album had ten tracks but he'd record fifteen or twenty, weeding out the ones that had weak beats, were lyrically flat, or were otherwise not up to his standards. Bobby wanted desperately to use the leftover songs and make more albums but Cal wouldn't have it. The albums would be second-rate, he said. They'd saturate the market and tarnish his brand. Bobby was within his rights to release the songs anyway but Cal said he'd get an injunction and publicly trash the records. Do interviews and tweet his fans, say the songs were second-rate, and let the rap world know that Bobby disrespected his artists. If that happened the albums would tank, there'd be lawsuits, Greenleaf would kill the deal, and nobody but the lawyers would get what they wanted.

On the other hand.

If Cal was to prematurely meet his maker, Bobby could release more albums the way Afeni had. Call them the basement tapes or the lost recordings or some other made-up nonsense. Greenleaf would be chomping at the bit when they found out there were over three hundred songs in the data vault. Add in remixes, tribute songs, live recordings, bonus tracks by other artists, and Bobby would have more albums than Cal could make if he was drug-free, ate barbecued tempeh at every meal, and lived to be a hundred. At that point, Bobby could either bid up the Greenleaf deal or walk away from it altogether. All he had to do was get somebody to cancel Cal's ticket. Make it look like a drive-by, let the police chase Noelle or Kwaylud and come up with nothing. They still didn't know who killed Tupac, or Biggie for that matter.

When Bobby was promoting raves back in Sacramento, Jimmy Bonifant was dealing ecstasy and what was the point of going to a rave without a double drop of vitamin X? The two hustlers shared a condo, ate breakfast at the Silver Skillet at three in the morning, and brought tweakers home and did them in the same room.

Eventually, they both moved to LA, Jimmy pushing weight by then, a lot of dangerous people in his circle of friends. Bobby asked him for a reference and Jimmy told him about a guy named Skip who raised pit bulls in the desert. He was crazy but always came through. Jimmy would hear about that. But by the time Skip came on board Cal had stopped leaving his house and Skip couldn't set up on him for a drive-by or anything else. Then that lunatic turned that damn dog loose and brought Quintabe into the picture and he fucked up everything. Skip falling into a coma was a lucky break. At least he couldn't cause trouble but the deal with Greenleaf was deader than Tupac and Bobby's creditors were calling every day. He could declare bankruptcy but Cal's leftover songs were a company asset and he'd lose them unless his lawyers could figure something out. He'd already drained the company coffers, fired most of the staff, and moved the songs to a cloud within a cloud.

Now he was going down to Belize to check on his seven-figure emergency fund stashed in the Banco Central de Belice, the money launderer's bank of choice. He planned to stay down there awhile. Lie on the beach, drink a few mojitos, sample the local talent, and think things over. He'd make a comeback, no doubt about it. Marion Barry, the former mayor of DC, was caught on tape smoking crack with a hooker. When he got out of prison he ran for mayor again and won with fifty-six percent of the vote. If he could rise from the ashes so could Bobby.

Bobby was at the office packing his carry-on when Hegan came in rubbing his crooked arm. Bobby thought the beaded dreadlocks looked ridiculous on a white guy, like a Japanese tourist wearing a cowboy hat. You'd think the man would have changed his style by now, quit clinging to the past. The days of Hegan the Hatchet Man Swaysie were over. Bobby was bringing him along to Belize. He knew too much and it was better to keep him close. Maybe he'd have an accident, get bit by a mamba, or fall into some quicksand. You never know.

"You ready to go?" Hegan said. "Traffic on the 405's a bitch."

"In a minute," Bobby said.

"We've got to get through security."

"I've been on an airplane before. Bring the car around."

Hegan held his tongue. He'd deal with Bobby soon enough. Let him tap that emergency stash and then remind him who knew what. He wasn't about to walk away from this mess with a handshake but he'd have to watch himself. Bobby ordered the hit on Cal without a second thought and he'd do the same to him if he got the chance.

"I've got to get my luggage out of my car," Hegan said.

"Who's making us late now?" Bobby said.

Bobby was looking for his passport when Hegan came backing into the room with his good arm up in the air. "What's wrong with you?" Bobby said.

Now Charles came in with a gun aimed at Hegan's head, Bug right behind them. "Whassup, Bobby?" Charles said.

"Did somebody wave a ham samitch?" Bug said. "I thought I smelled something."

"What is this?" Bobby said.

"You taking a trip?" Charles said, looking at the carry-on. "What you got in there, Cal's songs?"

Panic skittered through Bobby like a rat along a baseboard.

"Guys?" Hegan said. "Whatever you need to know I can tell you. I was the go-between, nothing else."

Bobby gave Hegan the look of death. "Look," Bobby said, "it's all a misunderstanding. How about we sit down and I'll explain everything in detail."

"What do you want to do, Bug?" Charles said. "Do you want to sit down with Bobby, let him explain everything in detail?"

"Sho' don't," Bug said. "I got too much blubber weighin' me down. I can't be listenin' to all that."

"Well, what do you feel like doing?"

"You know what? I feel like playin' ball."

In those initial moments of shock and confusion Bobby didn't notice Bug had a Louisville Slugger slung over his shoulder. It was an aluminum model with a ventilated leather grip like a tennis racket. Bug took a few practice swings, the gusts ruffling Bobby's hair and blowing papers off the desk. "Batter up," he said.

Isaiah watched the news, vaguely dissatisfied. All that commotion and running around and to what end? What was the case *about?*

"Another story in our news tonight involves record executive Bobby Grimes," the anchorwoman said. "Mr. Grimes was found crawling out of a dumpster near his office in Century City. Grimes was suffering from a concussion, contusions, and broken bones, and was bleeding internally. He was taken to Cedars-Sinai Hospital and is listed in serious condition. Curiously, when the police asked Grimes about his assailant and the circumstances surrounding the assault, he refused to answer. And there's another bizarre twist to this story. An alleged hit man who was in a coma because of injuries suffered in another incident woke up today and implicated Hegan

Swaysie, an associate of Grimes's, in a murder-for-hire scheme. The district attorney will be holding a press conference about the case tomorrow afternoon. On a more pleasant note, we turn to the weekend forecast with our veteran meteorologist, Kaylin Kennedy. So how are things shaping up for the weekend, Kaylin?"

Isaiah brooded. A rapper of dubious value to society was saved but it wasn't as if good had conquered evil. It was more like good had let a lesser evil survive. But Skip was off the streets and that was something, wasn't it? That crazy son of a bitch *was* evil. Maybe he was being too hard on himself, Isaiah thought. Maybe. The upside was definitely the bonus money, Flaco's condo a real possibility now.

Isaiah drove over to see Tudor about a second mortgage. He was parking in front of the building when Cal's business manager called. He said he had unfortunate news. The bonus check would not be forthcoming. Cal's lavish spending and tax obligations had finally caught up with him. He was filing for bankruptcy and there was a long list of creditors. Cal owed Dr. Freeman sixteen grand. Isaiah would have to get in line and could only expect a fraction of what he was owed, if anything at all. On the bright side, Isaiah's per diem check was cut before Cal's accounts were frozen and should arrive in a day or two. "God*DAMMIT!*" Isaiah said, pounding the steering wheel with both hands. All that work and worry, not to mention nearly getting killed, only to get burned for the money, the only thing that made the case worthwhile.

Isaiah took Flaco to the Hollywood Bowl to see Margaret Cho. She was pretty funny, all tatted up and a whole lot finer than that cut-out. Isaiah admired her, walking out on that big stage all alone. No props, no special effects, just her by herself facing seventeen thousand people who expected her to make them laugh. Flaco laughed his head off even during the parts that weren't funny. When the concert ended he waved both arms like he was trapped on a desert island. "Nargret! Nargret!" he said. "I love you, Nargret! I love you!"

Isaiah and Flaco went Section 8 apartment hunting. The places were shabby and depressing. Isaiah told Flaco he could move in with him and Flaco said he'd think about it. He wanted a cool place that had a lot of girls.

Dodson came over to collect his cut of the per diem money. He wanted it in cash, saying his relationship with the IRS was in transition. "Ain't this a bitch?" he said as he came in the door. "Cal's got all the money in the world right up until payday. That's bad luck right there. All you can do is hope some good luck comes along and puts you in the black and by the way, don't you think I should get a little extra for solving the case?"

"I'd have figured it out sooner or later," Isaiah said.

"Yes, I understand. Hard to accept that someone whose intellectual abilities you've disregarded and disrespected all these years came along and did your job for you. What was that you said? This is what I do?"

"Don't you have someplace to be?"

"Don't be too hard on yourself. You know what they say, what doesn't kill you might come back later and kill you for real. Here. This is yours." Dodson gave Isaiah a cashier's check.

"What's this?" Isaiah said, staring at the amount.

"Junior was carrying eighty-five thousand for the reup. I gave five thousand to Deronda right after the robbery. That's half of the rest."

"This is way more than forty thousand."

"I bought muni bonds. Seven percent coupon. You can't get that anymore. They didn't mature 'til a few days ago or you would have had your money sooner."

"You couldn't tell me this before now?"

"I wanted to surprise you. Oh, I almost forgot." Dodson tossed Isaiah a set of keys.

"What are these for?" Isaiah said.

"You catch the Lakers last night?" Dodson said. "Kobe was hurt and coasted for most of the game. Cherise said it was old age and he should retire before he made a fool of himself. I told her Kobe was saving himself up so he could score when it counted. Six minutes to go in the fourth quarter, Kobe scored twelve straight and won the game."

"What's going on, Dodson?"

"Talk to Tudor, he's got the paperwork. I made a down payment with my half. Your check should cover the balance and then some. You might want to start a college fund. That shit is expensive. Cherise got student loans won't be paid off 'til *my* children need student loans. Did I tell you Cherise is pregnant? Yeah, found out yesterday."

"Congratulations."

"Holla at Flaco for me," Dodson said, turning for the door. "Tell him I seen some fine-ass females over there."

Isaiah leaned against the doorway holding the check and watching Dodson stroll across the street to his car, a hitch in his stride.

Isaiah stood on the roof cradling the urn of Marcus's ashes like a newborn. The sun was dipping behind the skyline, amber and pink on the bellies of the gray clouds fading into darkness. Isaiah opened the urn and tossed the ashes into the air and like a frosty breath they vanished into the breeze, blessing the house and the neighborhood and the city and then on into the jet stream and out into a world that surely needed it.

Isaiah went inside, heated up some soup, and ate it standing at the counter. The house was quiet, not unusual, but something was different. An emptiness — no, that wasn't right. Something removed maybe, like when Dodson took his awards off the wall to make room for his big TV. Even if you didn't know what was there before you knew something was missing.

Isaiah was still brooding on it in the morning as he sat in the armchair drinking his espresso and reading his emails. It was only when, on impulse, he put on *The Best of the Temptations* and heard the opening bar of "My Girl" that he realized Marcus was gone. Which made sense when you thought about it. His ashes were in the wind, why wouldn't he go with them? Why hang around if his little brother with the gift from God only needed the memory of him? Which wasn't absolution but Isaiah hoped it was at least forgiveness.

Epilogue

Isaiah had scraped off the Audi's chin spoiler chasing the pedophile. He went to the wrecking yard to find a replacement. He hadn't been there in a long time and it was good to see TK, same as ever. TK told him there were two Audis over in the German section. "When you get back, I got a good one for you," he said.

There were a dozen ways to get to the German section but Isaiah chose the old race course route, remembering how he'd been late on this turn and early on that one. He was coming around the mountain of tires when he saw it lined up with a bunch of other wrecks. It had been there awhile, covered with a thick coating of dust, grass growing around the wheels sunk in the dirt. The front fenders and the hood were missing, the engine bay empty, the interior gutted and full of cobwebs. Isaiah circled the car like it might wake up and bite him. Most of the back window was blown out but there in the left-hand corner on a mosaic of shattered glass was the stem of a purple L on a quarter moon of gold.

Acknowledgments

My thanks to Craig Takahashi, Dagmara Krecioch, and Gene Ferriter, who made contributions to this book that went above and beyond friendship. And to Andy Leuchter, whose counsel and infinite patience were invaluable, and Pat Kelly, writer, friend, and spiritual adviser. A reluctant nod to my brothers, Jack, Jon, and James, for enthusiastically keeping my head from swelling no bigger than my hat size. I am also deeply indebted to my editor, Wes Miller, for making me a better writer in spite of myself; to Francis Fukuyama, whose kindness and generosity have changed my life; and to Esther Newberg and Zoe Sandler, their unwavering belief overcoming every obstacle and opening every door. And to my wife, Diane, who dreams my dreams.

blog and newsletter

For literary discussion, author insight,
book news, exclusive content,
recipes and giveaways, visit the
Weidenfeld & Nicolson blog and
sign up for the newsletter at:

www.wnblog.co.uk

For breaking news, reviews and exclusive competitions
Follow us 🐦 @wnbooks
Find us 📘 facebook.com/WNfiction